THE COME-BACK KIDS

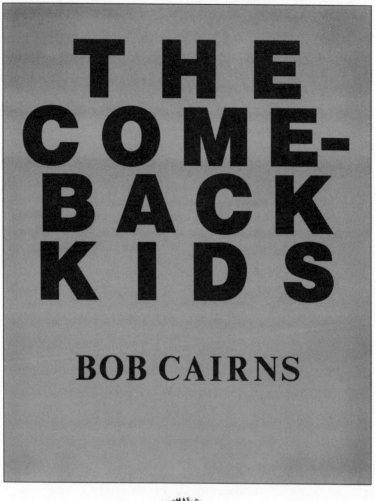

THE COME-BACK KIDS

BOB CAIRNS

A · THOMAS · DUNNE BOOK

St. MARTIN'S PRESS

NEW YORK

Design by Robert Bull Design.

Library of Congress Cataloging-in-Publication Data

Cairns, Bob.
The comeback kids / Bob Cairns.
p.   cm.
"A Thomas Dunne book."
ISBN 0-312-02929-2
I. Title.
PS3553.A3939C66   1989
813'.54—dc19   88-33070

First Edition
10 9 8 7 6 5 4 3 2 1

With love to Alyce, Matt, and Elizabeth who allowed me to close the door and dream about baseball for a year or so. To my mother (who will be allowed to read an expletive deleted version) and to my father whose love and laughter will be missed forever.

"There were perhaps two dozen of us in the stands, and what kept us there, what nailed us to our seats for a sweet, boring hour or more, was not just the whop of bats, the climbing white arcs of outfield flies, and the swift flight of the ball whipped around the infield, but something more painful and just as obvious—the knowledge that we had never made it. We would never know the rich joke that doubled over three young pitchers in front of the dugout; we would never be part of that golden company on the field, which each of us, certainly for one moment of his life, had wanted more than anything else in the world to join."

—Roger Angell, *The Summer Game*

ACKNOWLEDGMENTS

A special thanks to Guy Owen, Lee Smith, Peggy Hoffmann, Stan Grosshandler, Tony Outhwaite, and Jane (The Lady Who Never Gave Up) Wilson.
And last but not least, thanks to Ray Wilson, "Hon-Pots" Brooks, my dad, and the New Windsor Cubs, our miracle Little League team—a bunch of good ballplayers who grew up to be great guys.

TAPE 1

NOTES FOR THE ARTICLE AND A GET WELL MESSAGE/UPDATE FOR BUNNY MCKAY

Bunny, I'm cutting this tape to pull off what you might call a verbal twin killing. The stuff you're about to hear on this cassette is ideas for an article I'm going to write for Sports Illustrated, *and, of course, a "Sorry you missed it" to Bunny McKay, the infirm shortstop who failed to make his Little League team's thirtieth reunion.*

IT'S HOTTER THAN A SAUNA FULL OF SUMOS BEHIND this catcher's mask. So I could say it's sweat that's been fogging up my contacts, making me look like crap on Odie's breaking stuff. A year ago that's probably what I'd have said. But not now. It's like I told Doc Markum, the shrink I've been seeing back in North Carolina, the writing has turned out to be good therapy, it's making me be honest with myself.

I've been fighting the tears since the second inning—sitting on my haunches, batting the old orbs, trying to keep the floodgates up. Thirty years ago today the New Becton Hot Dogs, my Little League team, trounced the Penn-Mar All-Stars to put the finishing touches on what folks in this part of Maryland still refer to as the perfect season. We went 25–0 and played a spikes-high, sack-'em-up-and-take-the-cats-to-the-river kind of game that even some of the Dogs' mothers couldn't find it in their hearts to love.

Well, Elmer Thumma, our old manager, not only came up with an off-the-wall extra-base idea like a thirty-year Little League reunion, but he also tracked down the county All-Stars and told them if they'd meet us back here at Tiner Field, we'd move back the bases and fences and kick their tails again. So this isn't just a ball field full of shiny heads, gray beards, and potbellies . . . hell, it's my childhood I'm looking at.

Elmer "the Giant" is marching around in the dugout, hitching up his khakis, grazing the orange NY on his battered black Giants cap with his famous middle-fingered good-luck rub. Odie's fogging hard sliders by the hitters just like he did in 1954, and Jug Brown, the guy I was sure would grow up to be the next Willie Mays, just went in the gap in right center and plucked off a line drive that God had down for extra bases.

But superstitious old coaches, great breaking stuff, and black guys outrunning baseballs don't reduce forty-year-old catchers to tears.

Janie's gone!

Bunny, we've had our troubles over the years but never anything like this. There was a trial separation back in '82 patched up by a long series of "his" and "hers" visits to Doc Markum. Then last summer, about the time I quit my teaching job at Hargate Elementary to write sports for *The Johnstonian Advertiser,* she went to a week-long herpetology conference at Ohio State and didn't come back for a month.

So it's not like she hasn't taken a hike before, but this time she's taillights, skid marks, what my Aunt Maude calls "lost and gone forever." The last round was on Wednesday, the night before I left to come up here to Maryland for the Little League reunion. One of the snake charmers she met last summer called and offered her an assistant professorship in zoology at Ohio State. She got all hot and flashy and started playing with the cord of the phone, saying crap like "How flattering!" and "OSU is quite a jump from a little college like Wesleyan. Are you sure I can handle it?"

When she hung up and I found out who it was, I mentioned that I thought her qualifications probably were excellent. And that Ph.D.'s with big snakes sounded like something right up her alley. After she'd Frisbeed a couple of Melmacs off the kitchen wall she said, "Outgrowing someone dedicated to spending his life as a ten-year-old hasn't been hard to do."

And that's when I told her that she might just be right. The shrink and I traced it back and found out that there's a pretty damn good reason why I'm always reminiscing about 1954.

Everybody knows the Hot Dogs went 25–0, but what they tend to forget is that that's the year Dusty hit the pinch homers, Willie made the catch on Wertz, and that was the fall that Elmer and I sat there on the old freezer in his meat market and watched our beloved New York Giants shut out the Indians to win the series four in a row.

"Hell, Janie, that was the high point," I said. "My life's been going slowly down the dumper ever since." And I walked out the kitchen door.

A six-pack later I'm two-at-a-timing it up the back steps sniffing the air praying like hell Janie's come to her senses and sent out for the pizza we'd been picking toppings for.

The kitchen is as black as the inside of a bat bag. I flip on the light and there on the table where the pizza should be is this note:

Walker,
    I slept with the "Snake Charmer" for three wonderful weeks last summer.
    It's over for you and me.

Janie H.

P.S.: I put something in the oven. It's set for 350 degrees.

Now I'm numb, couldn't eat if it's a double cheese pepperoni, but I stagger over and open the oven. And sitting there on a cookie sheet staring up at me are Lockman, Dark, Westrum, Mueller, Maglie, Mays, and Leo.

The bitch baked my gum cards!

And when the draft from the kitchen window hit, I watched my Topps 1954 Giants go up in smoke.

Hell, Bunny, I'm not ashamed to admit it . . . I've been kind of screwed up ever since.

TAPE 2

MORE NOTES FOR THE *SI* ARTICLE AND A "WAIT TILL YOU HEAR WHAT HAPPENED NEXT" FOR BUN-BUN MCKAY

Bunny, I'm up here on one of the back balconies of Elmer's mansion talking into my new S911 Olympus tape recorder again. I've got a sack of ice on my head, another one on my crotch, and I'm watching the sun come up on a scene that should be tearing up a guy in my condition. If you haven't been to New Becton since Elmer struck it rich, then do yourself a favor. When you get to feeling better, pack up the wife and the kids and whisk them off to Thumma Estates—two pools, riding stables, goldfish ponds, gazebos—the fucking place looks like the "Magic Kingdom." From up here I can see our old ballpark, where little American flags are flapping over the site of yesterday's game. Behind the left-field fence a white cloud of mist is billowing up off of Tiner Lake, and if it weren't for all the fog, I could see the historic willow tree where Janie and I did it for the first time during that spring break back in 1963. Off in the distance, just this side of where the Blue Ridge Mountains butt up to the sky, are white oaks and maples and jade green hills all peppered with Elmer the Giant's black Angus cattle.

This is our childhood, Bunny, and should be nostalgic as hell, but it's hard to get into aesthetics when the scene below you looks like a Broadway and Forty-second Street gutter. Elmer's pool chairs are sagging, jammed full of what has to be the world's oldest, sickest Little League team. Bunny, it ain't the Dogs we knew!

Odie's naked, dick down in the grass by the shallow end of the Giant's swimming pool. The Bear's propped up against the bathhouse wearing nothing but a shit-eating grin and a blood-stained Little League baseball shirt. And Dr. Steven Kline, second baseman and eminent California gynecologist, is under a rhododendron, wrapped tighter than a vine around what can only be described as an elderly Little League groupie.

How's that for sick? In about an hour when this sun gets a little bit higher, your New Becton Hot Dogs are going to smell like Clydesdales pulling the beer wagon in the July Fourth parade.

So how do the returning heroes, the men a front-page story in yesterday's *New Becton Bee* called successful mid-lifers, wind up looking like centerfolds for *Shelterboy* magazine? For starters, let's take a peek at yesterday's game. Oh, I forgot. Here are your starting lineups:

Leading off and playing second base, Stevie Kline, "Gyno to the Stars." Hitting in the number two spot and playing left field, Blinker Ballard, automobile auctioneer. Batting third and pitching, former major leaguer and current baseball PR guy *par excellence,* Odie "the Enforcer" Wilt. Cleaning up, playing first base, truck driver Smokey "the Bear" Rymoff. Catching and in the fifth slot, me, Walker "Hooter" Horton, small-time sportswriter. In the sixth spot, Jug Brown, playing center field, and currently teaching phys. ed. at our old alma mater, Tiner Elementary.

Now for the bottom third. At the hot corner, Baldy Albaugh, presidential adviser and the man the *Bee* called a "high-ranking White House official." Batting eighth and subbing for Bunny "the Rabbit" McKay, the shortstop, Billy Johnson, who as near as I can tell does some kind of construction work. And last and without question least, a man who is presently unemployed but always working . . . on people's nerves, Mickey "the Mouse" Magruder, the right fielder.

Bunny, eight of your old teammates grew up and found work. Now for the bad news. Your Dogs are still 25–0. Those fortunate enough to have been there or to tune in last night in time to catch the eleven-o'clock sports on Baltimore's TV 6 know that it ended in the bottom of the fifth in what the sports guy called "the most brutal baseball brouhaha" he'd ever seen. And frankly, Bunny, if my nuts could talk they'd have to agree.

The game the WBAY-TV crew, our parents, kids, and half the town of New Becton expected to be fat guys and beer ball was anything but. I'm trying to watch my clichés here, Bunny, but both teams came to play. Joe Dougherty, a guy who had a year or two of A ball in the Carolina League, is throwing a screwgie that's tumbling in like Tylenols at us and "once upon a time Chicago Cub" Odie Wilt is boomeranging cock-high sliders around the All-Stars' asses. Nobody has a hit, and in the bottom of the fifth it's still tied at zip apiece. Odie bags their first two hitters, and Bunky Hyatt, umpire a.k.a. town drunk (Bunny, it's the guy who used to holler "ball on the corner!"), suddenly goes bat blind. A fat-assed florist, a myopic barber, and a faggy funeral director walk. This loads the bases with All-Stars. And with the tulip salesman tiptoeing off third, up steps Nehi Hibbert, a little insurance-selling shit who hasn't grown an inch in thirty years. Before Odie can toe the rubber, Hibbert crouches down and hangs his head out over the plate, pulling the same crap he used to try in Little League. Odie calls a time-out. "Hooter, tell that little fucker if he digs in like that again that the first one's up his ass!" Wilt shouts.

I didn't see the fight until last night. Channel 6 slowed it down and reran it for us from about a dozen directions. It turns out that what sounded like a breaking bat was Odie's slider sawing its way through Hibbert's ribs.

Anyway, when the sports came on, the Dogs pretty much had the Giant's mega TV to themselves. Shortly before eleven o'clock the wives decided they'd enjoyed about as much beer and Little League lore as they could stand. So they all piled into Albaugh's minivan and peeled down the Giant's macadam driveway in search of what Washington socialite Ms. Albaugh called adult conversation. As the taillights glow in the picture window we hit the tube like bugs on a light. Pretty soon the sports guy with the plastic yellow hair is stringing the *b*'s together. Brutal-brawl-brouhaha. *"A Little League reunion in New Becton that began with touching speeches and old coaches' tears ended in as brutal . . ."*

The camera's cutting back and forth trying to cover what looks like a hockey game on grass. Guys in Bermuda shorts are paired up punching the crap out of each other, and you can't see the infield because it's covered with gloves. Suddenly the camera lunges and there's Hibbert crawling up behind me while holding his rib cage in one hand and the handle of the beer keg in the other. The camera jiggles again, and now it's coming back to me, kind of slow-motion like.

Don't bend over, I think. But I do. Meanwhile, in front of the TV screen, the Dogs are about to bring new meaning to the words "rec room." They're tearing the Giant's castle down, they're laughing so hard. I'm up there on the screen, scrambling around, trying to pick up what looks like the Bear's lower plate, and WHAM! up comes Hibbert between my legs with the beer handle. I remember hearing my cup shatter and then just before the sky went black I'm thinking that Odie and Hibbert have just screwed me out of the biggest break of my writing career.

All we had to do was finish the game, play six lousy innings, and I've got my life's dream, a legitimate shot at seeing Walker Horton, my byline, in *Sports Illustrated*. I didn't tell the guys because I didn't want to make them nervous. But last week, after Janie slithered north on me, I called the magazine with my story idea. A Sue Anderson, who handles what she called "regional pieces," listened politely while I babbled away about two rival Little League teams meeting in a thirty-year-old grudge match. When I'd finished sweating all over the phone she said, "Walker, if you're willing to write it on speculation, I'd be glad to give it a read." "Walker!" "Walker!" "Glad to give it a read!" I almost loaded my laundry. Bun, I'm not looking for sympathy, but after what Janie pulled, I mean with the gum cards and packing off to Ohio, this was like a major-league shot of sunshine.

So why don't I get my aching nuts off ice and write it? Here's the part that gets a little bit tough to believe. What Elmer dumped in my lap last night is even bigger than *Sports Illustrated*. Now what I've got on my hands is a book to write.

TAPE 3

MORE BRIEFS FOR THE BOOK AND ANOTHER TAPE FOR BUN-BUN

I've moved again. For the past five minutes, I've been crawling on my hands and knees following a phone cord across the parquet floor of a rec room that dwarfs the playing surface of Boston Garden. The trip over ashtrays, across couches and chairs full of open-mouthed, snoring faces ended happily. The phone was buried in Baldy Albaugh's left armpit. I just called Sue Anderson at *Sports Illustrated* and explained why I can't write the story for *SI*. You don't want to trade off an article, even if it's for *SI*, when you've got a legitimate shot at the best-seller list, was the logic I used. She was so agreeable that while I had her ear I took the opportunity to sort of give her a thumbnail sketch of my idea for the book.

Don't worry, Bunny, I didn't blow the lid off all my characters. I just wanted to kind of test the water on somebody literary, to see if she thought readers would believe guys like Elmer Thumma and Odie Wilt. I mean, your characters have to at least *appear* to be real. I told her that the boring stat type stuff on Odie and the Giant was something she could look up in her *Baseball Encyclopedia.* So, of course, what I described was what you won't find in books, copies of old *Sporting News,* or any other baseball document.

After his playing days with the New York Giants, Elmer parlayed a one-grinder New Becton meat market into a multimillion-dollar hot dog business called Elmer's Little Giants, I said. If you haven't tried one, hustle down to your local A&P or Safeway and check between the Oscar Mayers and the Ballparks for the wieners in the orange and black wrappers. My wife says they're too spicy (Bun, for her I'd believe much too short), but anyway, Elmer makes a hell of a wiener, and they're great with beer, I says.

The Giant has been friend, father, and coach to more New Becton kids than you can shake a Louisville Slugger at. Hell, he raised me. Even Aunt Maude admits to that. For now I'll leave it like this: Most people love him, so they'll tell you the big guy's a saint. There're a few in town still holding some old grudges; ask them and they'll say he's full of crap. But here's the bottom line on Elmer: When it comes to goodness—Jesus, the Pope, and the Giant finish win, place, and show.

Of course, it doesn't hurt to watch the big guy's eyes. When he's had a beer or two and starts telling one of his "back when I was with the Giants we had a guy" stories, if his look gets kind of distant, run for your boots. But when the old orbs are that steely blue color and cutting you half in two, you can sack up what the big fellow has to say and drop it off at the New Becton Bank.

Oh, yeah, I didn't go into a lot of the gory details, but I mentioned Odie to the *SI* editor, too. I asked her if she'd ever seen him pitch when he was up with the Cubs. She hadn't had the pleasure.

What I did say was that if I didn't know his mom so well, I'd swear that Odie was Elmer's illegitimate son. They both pitched in the bigs, could pimp in a monastery, and make respectable livings, and they have been in cahoots in some kind of business venture ever since Odie and I were kids. No offense to Elmer, but when it comes to looks, the similarity ends. Odie's still got the blond surfer hair and one of those long, tanned, broad-shouldered, assless swimmer's bodies you see in TV commercials.

Hell, the only reason it's Jim Palmer and not Odie Wilt wearing the underwear in the ads is the little matter of Jim having him by 242 wins. After his playing days Odie kicked around in insurance sales for a few years, but now that he's in marketing with the Triple-A Akron Indians, he's really started to carve himself a niche. Bunny, did you happen to catch the Bob Costas spot last month on NBC's *Game of the Week?* They featured Odie! Does Chief Wahoo Look-Alike Night, Loincloth Day, or the Ladies

Take a Chance on an Indian Blanket Giveaway sound like Wilt?

Anyway, back to last night. When Channel 6 finished publicly dropping our pants, Elmer cuts off the set and goes into that famous pose of his. The one where he folds his arms across his chest and his pecs and lats start jumping around so it looks like there's a couple of small animals humping away under his T-shirt. Add an earring and you've got a sixty-eight-year-old Mr. Clean.

"Boys, I know you're disappointed about how things ended at Tiner Field today, but there's no sense in us walking around here like somebody just crapped in the pocket of our best friend's fielder's mitt," he said.

Elmer's pacing the way he used to march back and forth in front of the dugout just before he was going to do something radical like yank Odie and put Billy in to face the right-handed hitter. "Look, we're gonna have us some fun tonight, but before we get too far along, I've got a little opportunity I want to discuss with you," he says.

We're all in kind of a semicircle, filling up the couches and chairs around the Giant's mega TV. Front and center about a foot from the screen I see the Bear easing his 260-pound personality out of one of those little metal fold-up chairs, the kind you sit on at a funeral or the PTA. "Elmer, if this is Amway, I'm gonna go take myself a shit," he says and folds up his seat and lumbers off down the hall.

Until the Amway line the guys have been kind of tight-assed, drinking, making a lot of "so you're in insurance" Jaycee-type talk. We're trying to get reacquainted and forget the game, of course. Well, suddenly everybody's rolling around the floor, kicking and carrying on. I'm holding my sides, kind of shaking, trying to keep my poor nuts as still as I can. When the hoo-has finally die down, Elmer looks at Rymoff and says, "Bear, before you put your hairy tail back in that chair, reach over there on the wall and flick off them lights."

Did I mention that Elmer's rec room looks like it was designed by Captain Video? One wall is covered by this monster TV screen, and over in the opposite corner there's a console with ten smaller tubes all lined up five to a row. When the Giant gets his dishes aimed right he can watch the San Francisco Giants on one screen and scout the other National League teams on the rest. By the conversation up by the VCR, it sounds like the Giant's managed to transfer some old home movies to videotape. So it looks like we're in for a dose of Little League film, circa 1954.

Here we go, the screen's kind of grainy and brown, now we're seeing what looks like a pair of feet and the ground. It's hard to tell because the camera's jouncing all over the place. Okay, here it comes, a huge close-up of the Giant's face is filling the screen. Elmer's holding the camera at arm's length, filming himself.

"Take off your hat, Coach," Albaugh shouts, and just like the movie has ears, that old black New York cap doffs, and what's left of Elmer's flattop gets a standing ovation. Now the Giant's herding us up the steps of St. Michael's Methodist Church, and up by the screen I hear Elmer say kind of halfway to himself, "Get along, fellas, gotta get this picture took."

The camera dollies back and forth and there we are, cuter than speckled pups, the 1954 New Becton Hot Dogs. There're Odie, Jug, Ballard, and the Bear, the tall ones all picketed like a fence along the back row.

"Hey, Bear, you need to catch a shave!" Magruder shouts.

Bunched in the middle goosing around grinning like goats are Kliny, Baldy, Brownie, the Mouse, you, Bunny, and me. Elmer's walking with the camera now because we're seeing sky and the church steeple. A couple of pigeons fly by, and then BOOM! He's down front right in little Sammy Thumma's face. This is tough to take, seeing Sambo there laughing. I'm remembering the letter from Aunt Maude now like it came in yesterday's mail.

Walker,
   Your Little League coach's son Sammy, the Thumma boy, was killed in action at a place the *New Becton Bee* called near Plei Kui. I'm deeply sorry, please study hard.

Stay in School!

Sammy's still on the screen smiling up at us and Elmer's zooming the camera in and out, probably trying to get Sam to uncross the bats. Bun, remember how Elmer was always on his ass about that? I'm losing my battle with the tears again, but this time it looks like I'm not alone. The only sound we can hear is the Bear's metal funeral chair giving an occasional squeak. Now I'm thinking how ironic life is, I mean, crossed bats being Sam's specialty and how they're supposed to bring bad luck and then, of course, how we'd dedicated today's game to Sambo, a guy who was killed in action and then to have it end in such an ass-kicking fight. Hell, who knows? Maybe Sammy would have wanted it that way.

Okay, Bunny, this is just what we needed. Action shots, a little tiny guy is on the screen now. It's Baldy Albaugh. He's trying to backhand a ground ball going to his left. Elmer hits the slo-mo button, and frame by frame we stomp and cheer. Baldy's cork-screwing himself into the ground behind third base. The Giant's home movies aren't going to push *On the Waterfront* for '54's best picture, but he did a hell of a job splicing them together like this.

Kline dives behind the bag at second, flips the ball to the sack, and Bang! Out of nowhere, Bunny, here you come wheeling across the bag to complete the double play. The Giant's got long shots from the snack shack roof, and you can see us moving into position, backing up plays. We're covering the right bags and hitting the cutoff man with rope-high throws. "Cripes, Coach, we really did know how to play," Kline says. And then the show ends with a series of quick shots. Boom-Boom-Boom. Just like the Big League Fever—Catch It! promos you see on TV.

Jug runs one down in center, Billy backhands a ball at third, the Bear Bambinos one over the snow fence. And in the finale, I climb the backstop to grab a foul pop. The camera zooms in close and I hold the ball up and shake it in the batter's face. Hell, Bunny, maybe Janie's right. If being a kid is what it takes to get back that kind of confidence . . . then let me be ten again.

The screen goes black. We cheer and run to the keg for refills. Now the tube's all lit up again, and Elmer's telling us to take our seats. Huge letters on the screen say FOX MOVIETONE NEWS. You remember the music, *da da, da dun da dun, dun dun dun dun,* and the baritone voice-over guy that made everything sound bigger than war. You know, the preview reels they used to run at the Bectonian during our JuJuBe and Good and Plenty fights.

"Now I want you guys to watch this next little film clip real careful-like. It took some doing to run down this strip," the Giant says.

The Ted Baxter guy is talking in that deep voice now, "THIS IS THE WEEK THAT THOUSANDS OF BASEBALL FANS POUR INTO PENNSYLVANIA. THEY COME FROM MAINE AND CALIFORNIA, FLORIDA AND MONTANA, TO WILLIAMSPORT, PENNSYLVANIA. THEY'RE HERE FOR THE LITTLE LEAGUE WORLD SERIES TO WATCH TOMORROW'S MAJOR LEAGUERS PLAY FOR BIG-LEAGUE STAKES. YES, IT'S THE 1954 LITTLE LEAGUE WORLD SERIES. . . ."

Parents in baggy pants and boat-necked summer dresses, kids in T-shirts, dungarees, and black high-topped sneakers are trooping across the screen and through the stadium's turnstiles. Now we're inside the ballpark looking at a big, tall kid with thick glasses, sort of a Little League Ryne Duren, warming up. "Hey, that's Pazerelli, the wild man who pitched for the Twins," Wilt says.

"THE POUGHKEEPSIE PINTAILS, COACHED BY EX-NEW YORK YANKEE GREAT AND WORLD SERIES HERO BRACKEN MCKEEN, HAVE COME ALL THE WAY FROM NEW YORK FOR A SHOT AT LITTLE LEAGUE DESTINY," the Ted Baxter voice intones.

The camera moves again real smooth, not one of Elmer's herky-jerky jumps, and now we're looking at McKeen's brown, leather-like face in a real good close-up shot. His jaw's all pooched out on one side with this big tobacco knot. His nose is kind of long, like a thoroughbred collie's, and he's got his narrow-set little eyes riveted on the kid with the heavy lenses. Just as the camera starts to defocus, McKeen turns and spits something the size of a Tootsie Roll right at the lens of the camera. "Hold it right there," Elmer says. The picture freezes the dark glob in midair. "Anybody know who this guy is?"

Of course, Bun, you, Odie, and I were raised in a meat market full of old farts who lived to hear Elmer's "we had a guy" stories about ballplayers like McKeen. So I say, "Hell, Elmer, the movie guy said it, it's the guy who beat you those three games in the '37 Series."

Now the Giant's on the move again—back and forth in front of the screen he goes. "Hooter's right, he whipped me three times, 2–1, 2–0, and 4–0. But here's what none of you know: McKeen is the reason Odie's and Blinker's old men haven't said shinola to me since August 8, 1954. Hen, McKeen's the reason why the back side of the No Lead sign at Goodermuth's Amoco said The Giant's Full of Shit for nigh onto thirty years," he said.

"Damn," the Bear pipes up, "I went through my teen years wondering about that."

For the next ten minutes the Giant's at his best. I've edited gestures, cut a lot of the crap, and sort of paraphrased it to give you a clearer picture of what took place.

The '54 Hot Dogs weren't affiliated with the Williamsport National Little League, so to the chagrin of Elmer and a lot of parents, fathers like Odie Wilt's, we were an undefeated team, 25–0, all suited up with no place to play. Then, as the Giant put it, "The sun came out for a second or two." He's reading the *Baltimore American* at the meat market one morning over a cup of coffee and sees where the National Little League champions are coached by none other than Bracken McKeen. The two aren't pen pals or anything, but you can't go head to head like these guys did in the '37 without some mutual respect. Bun, here's the Giant's account:

"I get McKeen on the phone and oil him up with some congratulations and before you know it I'm telling him about this great bunch of little country pumpkins I got and how we been beating All-Star teams like they was two-bit drums," the Giant says. "He brags on his national champs, I counter, one thing leads to another and just as I'm describing the shot the Bear launched over the two-story up in Union Gap, McKeen stops me cold with a proposition.

"Air fare, expenses, and a thousand bucks up front for me, Thumma, and you've got your game," he says.

"And you guys know what comes next," Elmer says.

How about it, Bun? Remember the sleepless nights? How about the game day parade and seeing Tiner Field all freshly painted and decked out in red, white, and blue bunting? All the hoopla leading up to the biggest day of your life isn't something a kid is likely to forget! I don't know about you, but the memory of August 8, 1954, that stuck in my gut is the sick and empty feeling I carried home that day. Hell, all Elmer did was fling his black Nokona glove against the dugout wall and say, "Boys, it's off. Now beat it and take your parents with you. No game today!"

Okay, I'm not trying to jerk you along, here's what happened to our Little World Series, simplified by me editing the Giant again.

Elmer's moving again, making tight little circles in the thick shag rug. "We'd just started batting practice when Kliny's momma, Linda, leans out of the snack shack and shouts that it's the telephone for me. Of course it's McKeen.

" 'Elmer,' he says, kind of dirty-like, 'I just drove by your ballfield. It was a long flight for me and the boys yesterday, so help me here, are my eyes all right, or did I see two little nigger boys suited up in those ugly Hot Dog suits you wear?' "

The team does a knee-jerk look at Billy and Jug, then like an E. F. Hutton ad we turn back toward the Giant and cock our ears. " 'Bracken, you're going blind,' I say, 'too much jerking off. What you saw was a center fielder that runs 'um down like Willie Mays and a right-handed pitcher that brings sweat up on white batters' asses faster than the name Don Newcombe can.'

" 'Send the niggers home or I'll pack my boys back in the DC-3 and in a couple of hours we'll be waggin' our wings over a game that ain't never gonna be played,' " says McKeen.

" 'Don't let the wind sock hit you in the ass,' I said, and that, boys, was your baseball game."

Okay, Bunny, picture this: I'm just sitting there in a fucking fog, trying to figure out why the Giant dredged all this up after thirty years. I look up and what do you think I see? Elmer and Odie are working the room like candy butchers in a big league ballpark, tossing these big boxes at everybody. Flop! The Giant chucks one in my lap. "There you go, boy, now everybody's got one. Open her up, see what you think!" he says.

I lift the lid and cripes, there it is. The Giant's giving us a little bit of our childhood back. It's a pearl gray uniform with orange and black piping, the same as the Hot Dogs wore thirty years ago. No sweat, Bun, yours is in the mail.

"Keyrist! HOT DOGS!" the Bear shouts as he reads the letters on the shirt. The den goes locker room. Pants, shirts, and shoes fill the air. Suddenly the Giant's parquet floor is full of middle-aged men sucking their guts into double knits. When I finally get all suited up I kind of go into a daze. I'm standing in front of the picture window admiring my reflection when suddenly I hear the Mouse roar, "What the hell is this?" I wheel around and see my teammates digging at their backsides like they've been hit by some sort of middle-age itch.

The Mouse told the story about four different ways, but later, out by the pool, when I got him to talk into my tape recorder, it went like this: "I been gambling for as long as I can remember, and the one thing I've learned over the years is that players choke, and horses go lame, so there are no surprises in life, except, of course, until the Giant pulled this shit tonight," Magruder said. "But in my business you travel a lot more than folks would think. No matter what you know about odds, vigorish, etc., you believe you might see or hear something that's gonna give you that edge. Anyway, because of all the traveling, miles behind the wheel, I've had what you might call a mild case of hemorrhoids, nothing serious, but today during the game they were driving me crazy. So tonight when I pulled on my new uniform pants they're kinda tight and I reach back to adjust and there's this paper all folded up in the back pocket nice and neat."

Now I'm remembering how tedious the Mouse can be, so I'll take over from here.

Everybody starts pulling these envelopes out of their uniform pockets, and as we're ripping and tearing away trying to open them up, Odie jumps up on the couch and shouts, "Now before anybody says no, hear the Giant out! This is an offer we can't afford to refuse!"

Now Elmer's talking, his lips are moving, and my hearing's just great, but Bun, what he's saying just doesn't compute. He wants us to sign the papers, they're baseball contracts, he says. I'm reading along as fast as I can, the document's loaded with afore-mentioneds and party of the first parts and a lot of other legalese. But Bunny, the bottom line is this: For three weeks next summer the New Becton Hot Dogs will be paid professionals, traveling to five U.S. cities to play the 1954 Little League champions, the Poughkeepsie Pintails, in something the contract calls "The Little World Series That Shoulda Been but Never Was."

Now, after reading something like that, is it any wonder why the Dogs are sleeping in a little late? Hell, from where I'm sitting here in the Giant's rumpus room I can see Blinker Ballard's letter. It's clenched in his fist, and by the look on his snoring face it looks like he was giving it one final read when he passed out from shock.

Dear Dogs,

Thirty years ago I had the darnedest bunch of little ballplayers God ever put on one baseball team. If you recall, I opened my mouth and said that I'd get you a shot at the '54 Williamsport Little League champs. Well, unfortunately that was a promise that's taken me over thirty years to keep.

Boys, you sign the contract you found in your back pocket tonight and next summer the New Becton Hot Dogs will be motoring across the U.S. of A. playing the Little World Series That Shoulda Been but Never Was.

Ever ask yourselves what it might be like to play in the great old ballparks, places like Wrigley Field, Tiger Stadium, Municipal in Cleveland, or Fenway? Heck's becks, if a fifth game's necessary, the finale will be in Yankee Stadium, where McKeen and I locked horns for two of those three Series games in '37.

Sound like Elmer bulling you again? Read the contract. It says, "Winners, $5,000 guaranteed"!

Love,
The Giant

P.S.: This time I've got McKeen's butt bonded. He's got ten of his '54 championship ballplayers signed. It's amazing how thirty years and a few dollars can make bygones out of something as rotten as preju-dice.

Of course, when I read that last night I went cold stone fuzzy numb. I'd just read and reread something that could change my whole life. Then I look up and there's Elmer smiling down at me. And Bunny, that's a moment I'll never forget. His eyes were as blue as the tip of a freshly chalked cue. It's all on the level, I thought, 100 percent true.

For a while nobody says much of anything. We're just walking around reading the contracts, looking up long enough to high-five another player passing by. Oh, yeah, except for Mouse and the Bear. They're slow dancing over in the corner under this big Tiffany light. If it hadn't been that they were reading contracts over each other's shoulders, I'da been a bit concerned about that. Then just as I start to get kind of emotional again, a loud screeching and hissing sound from out on the patio scares me so bad that my eyes dry up.

Bells start to play, the kind on the Good Humor truck, *bing, be, bing, be, be, bing, bing.* "It's 'Take Me Out to the Ball Game'!" Kliny shouts.

Suddenly an air horn blasts and we're all at the picture window gaping at something we can't quite make out. Rolling along the Giant's bodacious flagstone patio is the biggest hot dog I've ever seen in my life. It's a bus, a forty-eight-foot-long, ten-wheeled, weenie brown luxury bus.

Elmer's flipping on the patio lights like a maniac now, and under the bus's windows, bigger than hell, painted in sort of a Gulden's mustard yellow, it says: NEW BECTON HOT DOGS— WORLD'S OLDEST LITTLE LEAGUE TEAM.

Back by the rear wheels, where the roll hangs out, painted in cursive, it says, ELMER'S LITTLE GIANTS—THE LITTLE WORLD SERIES THAT SHOULDA BEEN BUT NEVER WAS.

I don't recall who shouted what or even if anything mildly amusing was said, but I know the exact thought that jumped into my head: "Read your contract, son. This whole thing's some kinda promotional gimmick, Elmer and Odie are at it again. But the hell with it, Bunny, I couldn't care less. Because next summer we'll be New Becton Hot Dogs again, and pros this time, chasing the '54 championship, living our boyhood dream in places like Wrigley Field and Yankee Stadium.

Bunny, the way I see it, God winks at me about every thirty years. Wednesday I'm a small-time sportswriter reminiscing to his wife about Little League baseball, then poof! The gum cards and the marriage go up in smoke. But today it's 1954 again and I'm about to catch a bus back to my childhood. So Bunny, get your little ass well because next summer we'll be hitting the road, touring the country in the greatest hot dog God ever put on earth.

Now, is this going to be a book, or what?

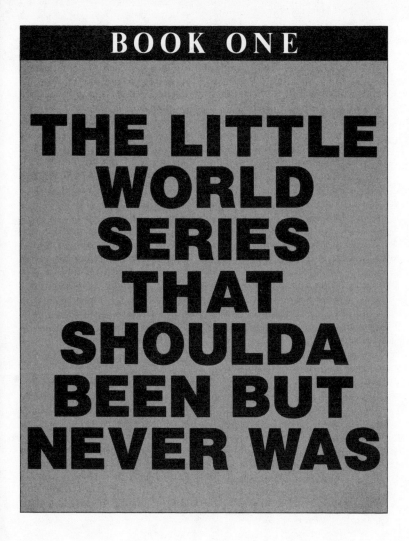

BOOK ONE

THE LITTLE WORLD SERIES THAT SHOULDA BEEN BUT NEVER WAS

•1•

THE STUB OF THE WET TOOTHPICK ROLLED ALONG
Walker Horton's freshly capped front teeth. He rocked the big
captain's chair, curled his tongue, flicked the wooden pick again,
and grinned. Horton was riding shotgun, sitting in the bus's catbird seat. Outside his window Florida flew by in waves of steamy
heat. The tinted glass darkened the greens and gave the groves,
scrub palms, and open pastureland a blueish look. Through the big
bubble windshield I-95 stretched out white and hot, basking like
a snake in the summer sun. Horton blinked, let his eyes close, then
lay back and listened to the whoosh of passing cars, campers, and
trucks. This is what Dr. Markum had in mind. His pulse had
slowed, he was beginning to unwind.

Above the dashboard framed in the rearview mirror was Horton's past. The New Becton Hot Dogs, the World's Oldest Little
League team, were together again, rolling through Florida on the
first leg of their odyssey. In less than a week they'd be suiting up
for The Little World Series That Shoulda Been but Never Was.
Chill bumps beaded up on Horton's arms like rain on the hood of
a freshly waxed car. Men like Bunny McKay, Bear Rymoff, and
Mouse Magruder pulling on their jockstraps in Wrigley Field!
Cripes, if a guy like Bill Veeck could see a promo like the Little
Series—he'd be hook-sliding into his neighbors' gravestones.

Horton rubbed his eyes, yawned, and looked up at the mirror
again. Side by side in the bus's front seats, reading over brown
half-rimmed glasses, sat Baldy Albaugh and Mouse Magruder, the
Hot Dogs' distinguished third baseman and ne'er-do-well right
fielder. Albaugh, one of President Reagan's most trusted legal

advisers, circled articles in *The Washington Post* with a red Magic Marker. Magruder, oddsmaker and tip sheet tout, read a racing form, blew cigar smoke like in *The Little Engine That Could,* and punched numbers into a tiny calculator. If hands were still a criterion for judging baseball talent, the attorney could play—the bookie a long shot at best.

Through the center of the bus stockinged feet hung over chair backs and white legs stretched out in the aisles. Jug Brown and Blinker Ballard chatted and sipped Miller Lites. Billy Johnson, a compact version of the old Giant Monte Irvin, adjusted his earplug and jived silently to music piped from a huge silver jam box. Across the aisle Bunny McKay's black high-top sneakers draped off the seat, bouncing rhythmically with the roll of the bus. Bunny always had been a sleeper, even as a kid. But the man was setting records today. Horton had been listening to the nasally snore and watching the shoes bob since that pit stop at Stuckey's north of Savannah.

In the rear of the vehicle, back past the TV, refrigerator, and built-in wet bar, the sun shone through smoked-glass windows, backlighting the participants of a raucus poker game. Horton could see Odie Wilt, the ex-Chicago Cub, in silhouette. The big blond man shrieked, flapped his long arms like an eagle, swooped down, and snatched the poker pot from the grasp of a startled Doc Kline.

Horton smiled and shook his head. Odie Wilt, what a competitor, he thought. Horton's eyes flicked back to the mirror again. He hadn't noticed it until now, but Ballard, Albaugh, and Magruder, at least a third of the team, had thinned on top. He ran his hand through his own thick black curls. He had hair to spare, enough to cover Baldy, and Ballard, maybe one or two more. But the Hot Dogs weren't headed to Florida to transplant hair. They were professional baseball players now with six days to shape up for a series of games that could change America's opinion of baseball and middle-aged men.

Horton flexed his fingers, shook his right arm, and let it swing beside the captain's chair. It wasn't a gun. Back in Little League,

Wilt claimed his rainbow pegs brought rain. He stared through the windshield as if there might be a pitcher lurking out there in the bright Florida sunshine, dipped his shoulder, and swung an imaginary bat. The left elbow flew out and his wrists broke early. Horton had never been much of a stick. He looked down at his waist and wedged his hand under the belt of his Bermuda shorts. At least his stomach was flat. There wasn't an inch of fat, nothing to pinch.

So that was the pre-series line on Hooter Horton, the Hot Dogs' catcher. Weak arm, no hit, but plenty of hair. He rolled the toothpick again. The teeth had just been capped. And he'd shucked the thick glasses for contact lenses. Hell, he'd even quit smoking. And he could jog three or four miles without throwing up, which was more than he could say for most of the men in the mirror's reflection.

The bus braked. Horton fell sideways in his seat. He grabbed the chair's armrest and watched the big vehicle fishtail into a barrage of black rubber. A rear tire on the trailer in front of them had exploded, and the big bus skidded and slalomed through the disintegrating rubber. Horton's stomach flew into his backbone, then slammed into his belt.

A picture of Janie flashed before his eyes. There was no apparent reason, no warning at all. It was so lifelike, her all naked, shivering there on the laboratory table. The ugly little scientist groped and drooled as he made his examination.

The bus straightened. Horton took a deep breath and wiped his forehead. It was soaked with sweat. Anxiety, he thought. Markum had educated him about the attacks. Any sudden shock, neurosis was like that.

"Close call, Coach," Horton said.

Elmer Thumma sat hunched on the driver's side, gripping the steering wheel between two bony knees.

"Had her all the way," the big man said.

Then the old coach shook a red bandanna the size of a picnic cloth so hard that it popped. Horton watched the hanky parachute gently down on the driver's bald, perspiring head.

"You tired?" Horton asked.

Thumma's laugh hadn't lost a decibel in thirty years. He reared back and heaved it like a good overhand fastball. The left leg kicked, then his head and shoulders flew forward, and behind the herky-jerky motion came an ear-ringing roar.

"Tired! Boy, I'ma gonna tell ya. Back when I was playin' for Macon in the Sally League, I'd drive bus all night and half a day, then walk out there and throw 'em nine shutout innings," he said.

Up ahead an eighteen-wheeler swayed out of a turn. The rig righted itself, the trailer wagged, and the truck hit the straightaway wide open, barreling into the late-afternoon sun. The driver's hand flew up; he was fighting the glare.

"Okay, Elmer, you're on again, another beer," Horton said. And before his tongue could flip the toothpick again, the sucking sound of the passing truck was lost in another of Thumma's lion-like roars.

"Six in a row! Cripes, that son of a biscuit didn't look, he gaped! 'It's a friggin' hot dog!' is what he said. I read his lips on that one as plain as day!" the big man shouted, beating a fist the size of a catcher's mitt into the steering wheel.

"Hooter, those beers are addin' up. By the time we hit West Palm, the Giant's big hot dog is gonna have paid for herself," he said.

The voice from the rear of the bus was unmistakable. "Elmer, you'd stare, too, if you'd just been passed by a fifty-foot dick!" Bear Rymoff shouted. Then lowering his voice he said, "Who's in?" and dealt another hand of gin.

The *Hot Dog,* the Giant's ten-wheeled weenie-look-alike bus, was a direct reflection of its owner. It was huge, forty-eight feet from the tip of its pinkish-red, meat-colored hood to the rounded blintzlike rear end, where the spare wheel was mounted. A bread-colored fiber fabrication covering the roof swept up from somewhere under the chassis and sandwiched the weenie in a way that Elmer said looked good enough to eat.

The interior was motor home plush, equipped with fourteen mustard-colored recliner chairs, a color TV, a forty-eight-beer refrigerator, a wet bar, and a one-man sit-down john with a bronze plaque on the door marked THE GIANT'S OFFICE—ENTER AT RISK.

The predawn New Becton send-off for Elmer's creation had been as auspicious as though they'd pulled out at noon. For the farmers, the bus's 6:45 A.M. departure proved ideal. The parade made a nice morning break, something to do between the milking and the other chores. From where Horton sat in the *Hot Dog*'s cab, the signs waving there in the gray morning light were tough to see. But the cardboard placard that Albert Baker pressed to the bus's window was clearly visible: DO-DO-DO WHAT YOU SHOULDA DONE DONE IN '54.

But a New Becton native couldn't mistake the sound of the Tiner High pep band. They played the alma mater, "The Caissons Go Rolling Along" and "Roar, Lions, Roar," a song that Elmer said they'd learned for the New Becton Lions' annual broom sale the week before. And as the big dog rolled up Quality Hill, the team waved their good-byes to an original orchestration of "Take Me Out to the Ball Game." The tune never failed to bring a tear to Walker Horton's eye. The band's off-key version only made the moment sweeter, and as they pulled past Goodermuth's Amoco, Horton reached for his handkerchief.

If the farm traffic drifting into town that morning was shocked to see the forty-eight-foot *Hot Dog* pulling up Derr's Hill, Hooter Horton didn't notice. He was as excited as a man in his mid-life can be. He'd driven three hundred miles from his home in Rocky Mount, North Carolina, just to turn around and go south again.

The sky was high, cloudless, and blue. Exceptionally clear for June and Horton was enthralled by the view. The Blue Ridge Mountains were a deep crayon purple, hay waved in the fields, and the smell of cow manure made the nostalgic picture perfect. And as they rumbled along Maryland's Route 29, Horton sat behind the bubble windshield picking out childhood landmarks like penny candy under a glass-top counter. He showed Elmer the twist in Sam's Creek where he, Bunny, and Odie had slain thousands of carp and sunnies. They passed Stairstep Hill, where New Becton kids held their annual toboggan race, and when they crossed the county line Horton dropped his voice and said, "See that old mill over there?" Thumma nodded. "That's where Bun, Wilt, and I triple-teamed the Thornton sisters the first time," he said.

South of Frederick the landscape had become an extension of Washington, D.C. Buildings and warehouses stood where Horton remembered seeing cattle graze and thick rows of green corn grow. But for Horton and Thumma, catcher and manager, the change was just another excuse for more reminiscing.

Elmer talked guardedly at first about Sammy's death and then finally about his wife's recent passing. With tears rolling down his leathery old cheeks he told Horton "how peacefully she'd gone" and how much he'd appreciated "that Hallmark you and Janie sent."

Horton wondered about his Aunt Maude and Uncle Urse, they'd looked so old standing there in the crowd this morning waving that pitiful little DOGS FOREVER sign up at the windows.

As Thumma weaved his way around 495, bypassing Washington, D.C., the horn blasts and waves from government workers baptized the Hot Dogs as national celebrities. They were like a rolling rock band and enjoying the attention. But if the men in the cab noticed, they showed no reaction. The conversation up front had turned to the hot stove league, stories about Dutch Bixler and Shad Myers, the guys who used to hang out in the Giant's meat market. By the time the blintz reached the Virginia side of I-95 the two men were shaking with laughter, like father and son again, up to their strike zones in baseball talk.

For Horton the ride through the Maryland countryside had been a major accomplishment. He hadn't mentioned Janie, or the divorce. Not even when the Giant reminded him how they used to snake gig down by Sam's Creek. The reminiscing was loud, nonstop, and approached debate. When Horton called up a game-winning hit or catch from the Dogs' championship season, Thumma would say, "Yep, that's kinda like a game we played in the Polo Grounds in '36—no, '37, 'cause Chiozza was playin' third base."

Horton would never question the Giant's "we hadda guy" stories. The man was an ex-major leaguer, a gum card, and listed in *The Baseball Encyclopedia.* The big guy was a most amazing man. Hell, the deal he'd just pulled off with major league baseball was a living see-it, touch-it testimony to that. The details, agreements, contracts, and logistics had tied up three of the Giant's attorneys for more than a year. And when Thumma and Horton finally caught up on old times, Horton looked out the window. He was back in North Carolina again. A road sign flashed by. "Cripes, Fayetteville's only forty-eight miles?" Horton said. The Giant rubbed his eyes, yawned, flipped on the bus's PA, and gave his road weary ballplayers a blow-by-blow of what would be expected of them during the next few weeks. The Little World Series That Shoulda Been would bring a sense of dignity, prestige, and honor to the grand old game. "It's just the kick in the butt that baseball needs," he said.

Horton stared through the bubble windshield, listened, and watched green banks of kudzu and PEDRO'S SOUTH OF THE BORDER signs flash by. The New Becton Hot Dogs and the Poughkeepsie Pintails had the blessings of Peter Stonesifer, the commissioner of big league baseball, Thumma said. "The guy's a promoter and fair as they come. When I told him about the screwin' McKeen gave us back in '54, he said that he'd have to be neutral in public but that he'd be rootin' for the Dogs to kick tail during the games."

Thumma explained that after the months of haggling was done, the way had been cleared for the games to be played as what the commissioner's lawyers called "pregame exhibitions" in five major league facilities. Then the Giant called the team's attention to the special orange and black schedules in their Little Series packets. And as Horton worked the toothpick back and forth across his shiny white caps, he read the names of America's great old ballparks, stadiums that he never thought he'd ever live to see, let alone play in. Then he checked his calendar watch. In a week he'd be squatting down behind home plate in Wrigley Field, looking up into those hallowed, ivy-covered walls. He reached under his seat and flipped the portable tape recorder on. If he was going to write a book about a series like this, he'd better damn sight get plenty of good dialogue from the Giant. The big guy could be pretty outrageous at times and might be beyond a writer's description.

Horton's eyes moved down the schedule. He felt goose bumps

turning to sweat. He heard the roar of the crowds, saw the ivy walls in Wrigley, the Green Monster in Fenway, and visualized the monuments in Yankee Stadium. He could barely read the first date, his hands were so out of control.

CHICAGO—WRIGLEY FIELD
JULY 4, 12:00 NOON
HOT DOGS VS. PINTAILS
PRECEDING CUBS-CARDINALS GAME

DETROIT—TIGER STADIUM
JULY 6, 4:30 P.M.
HOT DOGS VS. PINTAILS
PRECEDING TIGERS-ORIOLES GAME

CLEVELAND—MUNICIPAL STADIUM
JULY 8, 4:45 P.M.
HOT DOGS VS. PINTAILS
PRECEDING INDIANS-A'S GAME

BOSTON—FENWAY PARK
JULY 11, 7:00 P.M.
HOT DOGS VS. PINTAILS
PRECEDING RED SOX-MARINERS GAME

NEW YORK—YANKEE STADIUM
JULY 13, 12:30 P.M.
HOT DOGS VS. PINTAILS
PRECEDING YANKEES-ANGELS GAME

Horton wet his lips and whistled. The toothpick shot out of his clinched teeth like an ejected pilot. When it came to fantasies, nobody topped Elmer the Giant.

•2•

THE GIANT LIKED TO PAUSE, TAKE HIS TIME BEFORE answering a question. It was as though he were on the mound again, had the ball, and the batter could damn well wait until the big guy was ready.

Blinker Ballard's eyes batted like a hummingbird's wings. He tilted his horn-rimmed glasses, lay his schedule on the bus seat, and waited for Elmer to deliver.

"Now, boys, listen up, 'cause the Blinker's made a purdy good point. Blinks, it's yes and no. If we should be so fortunate to beat these bigots three straight, then it's over in Cleveland, and everybody gets their five thousand bucks, o'course. But no, we ain't gonna quit playin'. You got your pride and I still got restaurants to open in Boston and New York," he said.

For the next ten or fifteen miles Ballard and Kline bench-jockeyed the Giant like they were suiting up for a Harvard business professor instead of an ex-big leaguer turned hot dog salesman.

Economics were the least of Horton's interests. He closed his eyes and nodded, sort of half listening as the Giant railed on about restaurant franchises called Doggie Dugouts, free wieners for Little Leaguers, and the coupons and prizes that his company had kicked to the major league teams to use as customer come-ons.

"Then Little Giants are sold at the concession stands in all these ballparks we're playing in?" Kline asked, running his finger down the orange and black Little Series schedule.

"Youser, as of this year we're in sixteen of the major league parks, so I had a pretty good in when I pitched them the Little World Series idea," Thumma said, and reaching over, he gave

Horton a wink and a pop on the arm that spun the captain's chair halfway around.

Horton turned his seat and checked the mirror again. One, two, three, he counted silently. The bobbing heads during Elmer's talk hadn't all been nodding in agreement. Jug, Billy, and Magruder had joined Bunny. The Giant had put his team to sleep.

The jade green grew darker by the mile. And as the bus rolled along the flat highway, Florida's biggest orange disappeared behind a thick knot of groves in the western sky. It was dark in the bus now, but the mirror reflected an act that Horton had been waiting for more than a year to see. It had been slow in coming, a lot of small talk and getting reacquainted. But thanks to Magruder and Rymoff, things had taken a sudden change. At a gas station/pecan emporium back in S.C. the boys kicked the reunion off by turning a five-minute comfort stop into what Thumma called "a dodcasted pyrotechnics shoppin' spree."

And for the last four hundred miles, everything that moved along the Interstate had felt the Mouse's and the Bear's cannon fire. Cherry bombs, Roman candles, rockets, and elaborate cracker displays exploded against the hazy Georgia sky.

"Judas Priest, these Rebels are gonna think Sherman's back!" the Giant said.

On Route 295 as the tube steak circumnavigated Jacksonville, Florida, Magruder fired Roman candles across the bow of a red mustang convertible chock full of what Rymoff described as "suntans and tiny halters full of big fat titties."

And it turned out to be the shot of the trip. The women in the Mustang had been playing tag with the *Hot Dog* ever since.

FT. PIERCE 12
WEST PALM 66

The highway signs flashed by in the bluish dusk.

BOOM!-BOOM!-KA-BOOM!BOOM!

Green tracers flew over the tip of the wiener. The red convertible sped by, and a blonde in the back seat turned and blew the World's Oldest Little League team a kiss. Not Janie, Horton thought, but not bad. Bear was right about the boobs.

Behind Horton the bus was alive, cards shuffled, beer cans popped. Ballard clamped his palms together and massaged out a string of handmade farts. Kid names like Jug, Bunny, and Bear flew up and down the aisle.

It's just like the Giant promised, Horton thought. The Dogs were together again, heading to their West Palm training camp.

Horton heard Wilt's voice and turned his chair full circle. The vowels were flat, he sounded midwestern, more Chicago now than Baltimore. The Dogs' star pitcher and the ex-Chicago Cub was working the bus, seat by seat, regaling his old Little League team with big league stories.

"Wrigley Field, hell, yes, the fans are close, you could hear us fart in the dugouts from any seat in the house," he said.

Horton popped on his tape recorder. Quotes like that could make the difference in a book.

"You in shape, Mouse?" Wilt asked, settling his lean cowboy body into the empty seat next to the Dogs' right fielder. Magruder struck a match, touched it to the wick, and watched it fizzle for a second, then flicked the cherry bomb through the bus's open window.

KA-BOOM!

Horton jumped, punched the button on his tape recorder again, and said, "Mouse is still a jerk; some things never change."

"Yeah, pretty good shape for an old guy, still beatin' off twice a day, just like Little League," Magruder said.

Wilt looked up, caught Horton's eye, and winked.

"Mouse, you remember Scooter Allen, the guy that played right back when I was with the Cubs?" Wilt said, raising his voice over the hum of the *Hot Dog*'s engine. "Well, he jerked off so much that an ad agency in Chicago got him a TV spot with a razor company."

"Bullshit, Odie," Mouse said. His squeaky giggle reminded Horton of Gus-Gus in *Cinderella*. He'd have to make a note of that.

"Hell, he turned it down, said no way he'd shave his palms on national TV."

Horton spun the captain's chair toward the steering wheel. "Cripes, Coach, if Wilt can still pitch like he shoots the shit, we'll win this series in three," he said.

The water glistening and beading up on Thumma's shiny white head had Horton chewing his toothpick to stave off a laugh. It was unbelievable how little the man had changed since '54. Still built like a washing machine, Mr. Clean in a New York Giants' cap, he thought. Thumma ran his bandanna inside the white band of the old black hat he'd worn in the '37 Series, then jammed it on his wet head so hard that the connection sounded like a fire hydrant being capped.

"Come on, Giant, you've gotta be bushed—you've been driving since Maryland. Let me take a shot. Hell, I can handle this thing," Horton said.

"I'm worn a might, but it ain't by the drivin', Hooter," Thumma said. He kept his eyes fixed on the road and tugged the cap again.

Horton threw his dirty white Nikes on the dash and gave his chair a gentle rock.

"Tell old Hooter your problems. Hell, I've become a regular little shrink over the past year. I've got group on Tuesdays and then for an hour every Friday afternoon Dr. Markum uses my head as his private little playpen," he said with a laugh.

Thumma wiped his brow, then licked the middle finger on his pitching hand. Horton's neck snapped, and the pain shot through his shoulder and halfway down his throwing arm. The Giant wasn't crapping around. Cap to forehead to mouth, damn, that's his middle-finger good-luck rub, he thought.

"Elmer's Little Giants is in trouble," Thumma said. The engine purred. Beer cans popped. Bear Rymoff cut a ferocious fart.

"Church House Ripper!" Horton shouted. "Good one, Bear!"

Baldy Albaugh frowned and raised his eyebrows.

"Hey, Coach, no sweat, we'll quit crapping around, settle down, and get in shape. With Odie I figure we can win this thing in three, four tops. Hell, when we hit the Big Apple, we'll be on vacation," Horton said.

"It's business trouble."

"Bullshit, Elmer," Horton said with a laugh. "If you want to talk money problems, ask me about the Sears and Penny bills the judge awarded me custody of in the divorce."

A cherry bomb exploded. Two Roman candles arched across the weenie's hood.

BOOM! BOOM! BOOM!

The gray-black sky streaked in reds and greens. Off in the distance, Horton could see the pink taillights of the Mustang flashing. The blonde stood, waved both arms, and then she was gone, lost in the dusky night.

"That shit's getting old, Bun-Bun's trying to sleep," Horton snapped. He spun his chair and squinted, until he spotted the glow of Magruder's cigarette.

The Giant hunched his shoulders and tugged his cap.

"I'm in some deep dirt," he said. "What my accountants call a cash flow situation." Thumma's huge right paw found Horton's shoulder and delivered a squeeze. "This is just between the two of us, Hoot. Nobody, not even Odie, can know," he said.

Horton squirmed to shake the shoulder free. Thumma's face flushed and he loosened the viselike grip.

For the next fifty miles the dark ribbon of traffic and the blue-black silhouette of Florida's groves, pasture, and standing cattle was one big wet blur to Horton. The sounds of trucks, cars, and the Dogs' revelry played in the background as he listened to Thumma's tale of woe.

Elmer's Little Giants, Thumma's multimillion-dollar hot dog business, had sunk a bundle into the research and development of a new product called Baby Bunts, a bite-size nugget for little kids. To Horton it was just business, but the Giant had a way of making it sound so sad. And listening to him describe the demise of his Baby Bunts made him wonder if Ray Kroc had ever talked so lovingly when he spoke of his first McNuggets.

Test markets in Jersey and Massachusettes all ready go, it seemed, but when the product hit the meat counters in grocery stores, "Hell, we couldn't give the little dingleberries away," Thumma said.

"Hooter, the bottom line is this: The Little World Series That

Shoulda Been but Never Was ain't gonna be the lark we thought it was. The Baby Bunts I could've lived with, but I went out and trumped myself by investin' in what looks like a souring franchise deal."

"Franchises?" Horton was tired of hearing Elmer's business problems. He wished they were back watching pine trees and red Georgia clay flash by the windows, talking Giants baseball again. This was supposed to be a vacation. Why did a conversation like this have to happen now?

"I'm talkin' about the restaurants we're gonna promote. In theory the idea was sound," Thumma said, and tugged the lobe of the ear where Mr. Clean wears his ring. "Hell, when I sold it to the co-op of Baltimore pediatricians, everything was hunky-dory. We're calling them Doggie Dugouts; it's a good concept for a fast-food restaurant. Customers step down to enter, sit on long benches, and get their soft drinks from big, clear glass jugs that bubble when you tap them, just like a dugout's water cooler.

"The squeeze came in the promo angle. I timed them to open this summer in—"

"Chicago, Detroit, Cleveland, Boston, and New York. Where we're playing the Series," Horton said. He loosened his seat belt, dropped down on his haunches, and flipped his tape recorder on. Then he felt under his chair again and pulled out his Rawling's Fast-Back model catcher's mitt.

"That was the whole deal, we come rolling into town in a hot dog bus, play a game of the Little World Series, uniformed Little Leaguers get into the ballpark free, plus a couple of comp Little Giant franks.

"Hen, a big wiener bus, hot dogs, kids, baseball, old guys trying to relive their childhood! How friggin' American can you get? I figure the newspapers and TV have gotta eat something like this up."

"Sounds good to me," Horton said and jotted a line in a spiral notebook: Elmer still uses fake curse words, says things like "hen" for "hell."

"It better, my franchisers took a hike. A Judas named Gross, a guy on my own board of directors, toasted my weenie deal real good. The peckerwood stands up right in front of the pediatricians, just as they're about to sign on the dotted line, and says, 'Elmer, suppose your geriatric Little Leaguers stink it up, get their asses beat real good. I've checked out the Pintails, that team you're playing is stocked with ex-big leaguers. Biggie Ensor, Donnie Graham, and that big Italian Pazerelli all played in the majors. What you've got on your hands, Thumma, is a busful of assholes rolling into cities where our product is already well established. Forget the franchises, you wind up a joke, and you not only screw up your grand openings, you'll also make boat anchors out of this company's stock!' "

HORTON HATED BUSINESS. HE'D HAD A YEAR OF lawyers and accountants. They'd sorted out the bills, divided up the marriage spoils. All he wanted to do was forget Janie, write a lousy book, get some sun, and play ball with his Little League buddies.

"So, where are you?" Horton said and slapped the glove again.

"Well, no backers and all five restaurants timed to open with the Hot Dogs' arrival into town. The Doggie Dugouts are not only all mine, now I've got Gross hustling around buying up loose stock trying to give the old Giant the hook."

"Gross could take over? You could lose the whole thing?" Horton's voice cracked. Maybe this was more than just a business chat.

"Everything. The little jewfish is like a shark smellin' blood. If he wins, they'll come dig up my pool. My horses are glue. The board says I'm too reckless, they wanted me to give up the Little Series idea.

"Reckless! Hell!" the Giant shouted and slapped the dashboard with his racquet-size hand. "Elmer the Giant didn't build this business letting grass grow under his ass. Ask Oscar Mayer, he'll tell you that."

Horton felt cold, then hot. His pulse quickened. A familiar tightness radiated through his chest. "How about our contracts?" Horton asked.

He'd told his lawyer that he'd be getting five thousand dollars by August 1, he'd planned to pay off their fees, then get Janie's bills caught up.

Elmer's eyes were nowhere. He had that distant look a pitcher gets just before he makes his move to first. Horton leaned forward, fumbled for a second behind his back, then pulled a small brown paper bag from his right rear pocket. He unfolded the sack carefully and laid it in his lap.

The bus was drafting on a Sunkist truck, wedged in a pocket of speeding traffic.

"Hooter, don't you wanta know why I'm dumping all this garbage on you?" the Giant asked. His cap was off, and the last rays of the afternoon sun popped out from behind a low cloud, streamed through the tinted windshield, and turned his head a rosy bubble gum pink.

Horton's bag lay flat against his leg. He'd rubbed it warm. All the wrinkles were ironed flat. "I was afraid to ask," he said.

"Well, it's simple. You're the only player that can make the Hot Dogs win. Only one they respect," Thumma said. "In fact, the only one they ever did."

He tossed his antique cap over the gearshift, skimmed his perspiring head, and flicked a wave of sweat against the *Hot Dog*'s windshield.

Horton saw a flash of green sign fly by.

WEST PALM 35

The last road sign seemed two days back. One minute he was cocked back talking about how Preacher Roe used to load his spitter, reading a sign saying West Palm and the time of your life only sixty-six miles away. And now this, sweating like an overweight Class D catcher, scratching his arms, setting up fire lines trying to head off a rash. The Giant had screwed up a year's worth of psychiatry in less than thirty miles.

The chest pains, racing heart, and dizziness were back. Another surprise attack. The same symptoms he'd delivered to Dr. Markum the week after Janie left.

"Why me?" Horton managed. His breath was short. The symptoms broke against his brain like hard foul tips.

"Hoot, you did it in '54, and you can darn sight do it again, I'm convinced of that," the Giant said.

"Get Odie up here—you need a ballplayer, you don't need me," he said, and forcing air through his mouth, he made a wheezing sound.

The Giant looked straight ahead, didn't make a move. Horton spun the chair; Wilt was near the back, sitting in with Kline and Albaugh, playing a hand of gin.

"I know you guys like to talk about being 25–0, undefeated and all, but the fact is we won only three games in 1954. Hell, the rest weren't even baseball. It was worse than what our Giants did to Chuck Dressen's Reds back in '37. Men against boys we were," Thumma said, and reaching into his khaki pants pocket, he pinched himself some snuff.

"Yep, you beat Mount Shannon in a practice game, 3–2, Union Gap, 6–5, that was the night Wilt's old man ran out and sat on home plate over the ump's missed third strike," Thumma said. "And, of course, there was that friggin' All-Star game."

"You won't find it in any of those old newspapers Odie drug out at the reunion, but Hooter Horton, our butterball catcher, won all three of those games. And that's a fact," he said and dug into his pouch for another helping of snuff.

Horton cradled his wrist. His pulse was wild, racing too fast to count.

"You laid down a perfect bunt to beat the Mount, told that a-hole Odie, Sr., if he didn't get off your plate you were gonna have his son stick the next one in his ear, and in the All-Star game. . . ." Thumma adjusted the rearview mirror and looked back into the depths of the bus.

The Russian Bear was butt up in the backseat, nose to the glass, gyrating his hand up and down, communicating some kind of sexual message to the convertible women.

"In the All-Star game that big jerk back there struck out twice trying to launch one on the roof of Tiner Elementary." The Giant's face relaxed, wrinkles fell, and he pushed back a smile by pressing more snuff under his upper lip.

"It's his last time up, bottom of the sixth, two men on, and we're down by one. You stalk in to the on-deck circle, grab the big bugger by the only tuft of chest hair I ever saw on a Little Leaguer, and you tell him if he doesn't take a strike that you'll pull out every follicle one by one.

"The rest the newspapers had right. The Bear waits for his pitch, drills one the other way, into the hole in left center she goes, and thanks to you we win by one."

"Bullshit, Elmer, we had an ex-New York Giant coaching us, a future Chicago Cub pitching, and the Bear woulda made it, too, if he hadn't had half his toes blown off in Vietnam. What I did didn't amount to a good healthy—"

"You think I'm conning you?" the Giant said. Horton hung his head for a second, then looked up. It was dark in the bus, but he could see the Giant's eyes. They were midnight blue, the color of an umpire's suit.

"I can handle guys like Mouse, Blinker, and the Bear, but the Wilts, the Klines, and the Albaughs, hell, they're big time now, in another league," Horton said. "Come on, Elmer, you think an ex-major leaguer, one of Reagan's top attorneys, and a millionaire Beverly Hills doctor are gonna take orders from a little hack like me?" he said. He blinked his eyes and tried to focus on a yellow U-Rent-It passing the *Hot Dog*'s hood. The tailgate appeared warped. His eyes weren't right. The truck was deformed, out of sync. He zeroed in on the silhouette of a distant palm. It waved, then appeared to shrink. He was seeing things in a fun house mirror.

"They'll think I'm a real prick," he said.

"Nope, a leader; nobody said 'prick' in '54," Thumma said.

"Gross is trying to take my company, McKeen is playing us to show me up and make himself a buck. Now, when the final lineup is penciled in, those are the guys that are gonna be the Man Upstairs' designated pricks."

"I thought the whole thing was so we would all be kids again, go play ball, beat McKeen—hell, that's what you said."

Thumma's foot flew at the floor mashing the *Hot Dog*'s brakes halfway through the transmission. The wheel whipped, Horton lunged sideways, and his head banged hard against the side window of the bus. The screeching of tires and the fishtailing had the bus on a collision course with the back of an old flatbed spilling grassy rolls of Florida sod.

"No friggin' taillights," the Giant said. The brakes grabbed, and the bus righted itself and continued on course. His eyes were large and wet. If it hadn't been the Giant, Horton could have sworn he'd seen a tear or two there in the blue.

"Yeah, I did, the trouble is we're not kids anymore, never will be. I guess I'm a little disappointed, though—see, I was thinking that you'd be bustin' your tail to run this team again."

Horton gave the paper bag another rub.

"It's not that. I—hell, it's hard to explain, let's just say I've had a pretty screwed-up year," he said, giving the Giant a forgive-me look.

"Christ, Elmer, get Kliny or Wilt, they're the ones that can help you now," he said.

The Giant raised his hand and dropped his voice. Billy had unplugged his box, and "Lean on Me" blared in the background. Horton bent toward Elmer and turned his head to hear.

"Horton, Kline's on vacation. And Odie, well, you know him, love him like a brother or son. But we've seen the temper . . ."

"Yeah, but he doesn't mean it. He's just—"

"Look, Hoot, how many times has George hired Billy?"

Horton tapped his glove. "Five times!" he said.

"How many times did he fire him?"

"Five!"

"I rest my case. Good men with terminal tempers, they're great baseball guys but two of a kind. And you know I'm right," Thumma said.

Horton's stare went to the window. Thumma drummed the wheel then raised his hand and dropped his voice.

"Look, I didn't want to get into this, never thought I'd have to." Thumma's voice was almost mournful. "This ain't the way it was supposed to be. When I kicked off I wanted it to be a great big bad news-good news thing. A sad occasion, of course, but a nice surprise for my Little League team."

"You're not—"

"Hen, no, I'm gonna be running the bases for a long, long time, but when the Big Guy puts the tag on me"—Thumma leaned forward and peered up into the brackish sky, then glanced up at the mirror—"whatever I've got goes to those a-holes back there."

"You're leaving everything—"

"To the New Becton Hot Dogs," he whispered, "so beating McKeen and getting the Doggie Dugouts off to a nice, healthy start isn't just about an old guy trying to save his butt in business. When I hit the showers I want you guys to pick up something besides a cake of soap."

While Horton fought the incoming waves of shock, Thumma popped on the PA, cleared his throat, and amended an earlier message:

"Something I meant to tell you back there when I was giving you the breakdown on the Little Series," he said. "When you're on the field, Hooter's the boss, like an Al Dark or a Pee Wee Reese, he'll be your captain. Haven't asked you yet, Odie, but I want you to be my front man, be an extra dollar or two in it for you. This thing's gonna need one hell of a promoter."

The mike went dead. The Giant rocked in his seat and cracked his walnut-size knuckles joint by joint, one bone at a time.

"Now, when you're running the ball club, whipping those mothers into shape, I'm gonna take Odie's pleasing personality and send him ahead, to help me sell these dodcasted Doggie Dugouts."

The bus had fallen silent. Horton nodded with Elmer, but his attention had gone to the mirror again. The team was moving, falling into groups of twos and threes. Someone mumbled his name in a questioning way.

"Wilt's gonna be really pissed," Horton said. "You know he wants to run this club."

He watched Kline and Albaugh amble back toward where Odie and Ballard had dropped their cards and set up court.

Horton wasn't much at math, but as a kid he'd been a loyal reader of Scrooge McDuck, so the picture of a roomful of money sacks was a pretty easy fantasy to conjure up.

"In case you're wondering, you'll get three shares," Thumma said.

"I wasn't," Horton snapped.

"Well, that's what you're gettin', it's already written in the will. You're special, Hooter, like a son, and I'm leaving a double helping to Bun-Bun's widow. Everybody else gets one."

"Bun-Bun's what?" Horton said.

The Giant lowered his voice to a whisper again. "I thought you knew. He's got MS. It's in remission, but Hooter, this is Bunny's last series, the little feller's roundin' third."

The paper bag was there. Thank God for the bag. Back at the Stuckey's just before he'd fallen asleep, Horton had been talking to the Rabbit about his health. The Rabbit lied, said how much better he'd been feeling lately, claimed the reason he'd missed last year's reunion was a viral attack and that all he needed now was plenty of sunshine and a little rest.

"Be back, gotta take a leak," Horton said, and standing on legs that felt like they'd just caught an August doubleheader, he staggered toward the bus's toilet.

"HOOT! HOOT! HOOT!"

The Dogs' chant rolled over Horton like a wave of desert heat. He bumped into seats, banged into Jug's leg. He was seeing "fun house" again. Albaugh sat back in his chair, the half glasses perched on his nose, reading by an amber magazine light. Horton saw the writing board on his lap. The bus swayed, and he fell sideways. Baldy's pen scratched across the page. "That's a federal offense, Horton, I was writing the president," he said in a condescending way.

Bun-Bun dying. Why hadn't he thought of it? And what a great little athlete he'd been. Pound for pound better than Odie Wilt, Elmer had said earlier that day. McKay looked so different now, stretched out there across the seat of the bus. Horton could see it in his face. Damn, the Giant was right. This wasn't just a little loss of weight.

Horton's breath was short. It hurt to take in air. A couple more feet and he'd be in the privacy of the can. Two more steps. He sidestepped Wilt's gin rummy game, ducked a flying Nerf ball, the bus swayed again, and he banged into the bathroom door. He'd made it. Home at last.

He dropped the inside latch, crouched on the seat, and blew air into the open bag. One-two, one-two, in and out the bag billowed with the bump of the bus.

"Fucking anxiety attack," he said with a gasp. It was the first big one since Janie's Christmas phone call. A major setback. Why did the Giant have to dump all this crap on him now? He knew he needed to relax. All he wanted to do was play ball, write a book. What was so wrong with that? So what if he was a little prick in '54? These guys weren't kids anymore, and Hooter Horton wasn't the man he used to be. He held the bag one-handed and thumbed his neck. It was impossible to keep up with the machine gunlike pulse. He closed his eyes. Bunny was lying on the bus seat. Now Horton saw the coffin. He couldn't shake the notion. Black sneakers hung over white satin lining. He blew into the sack. His mind flipped again.

Now he was in Wrigley Field, pacing the Hot Dogs' dugout, sweating over a lineup card. Kliny leading off, Albaugh second. He dropped the bag and shot up off the seat. "Christ, I can't let Bun-Bun play, we'll never beat McKeen," he said and sank back on the oval lid.

The door lock jiggled, then lifted slowly off the latch. Horton didn't notice. His head was down, breathing rhythmically into the sack. He mumbled an impromptu prayer of forgiveness. How could he have considered denying a dying ballplayer his final wish?

BOOM! BOOM! BOOM!

The water closet blew red, then flashed in hot, white incandescence. Horton squalled, dropped his bag, and threw a death grip on his heart.

KA-BOOM! BOOM! BOOM! BOOM!

Another volley followed. This was it, the big one. He'd passed Bun-Bun at third, he would beat the Rabbit home.

WORLD'S OLDEST LITTLE LEAGUE CATCHER DEAD AT 40.

A newspaper headline flashed before his eyes. Horton gatored across the floor; one hand gripped his heart, the other groped wildly, searching for his missing sack.

"HOOT! HOOT! HOOT!"

Mouse and the Bear shouted, beating their fists on the WC door. From his prone position Horton managed a weak kick. The door swung closed. He panted into the bag and crawled up on the john again.

"Assholes," he said with a wheez into the bottom of the sack. "One-two, one-two. All assholes."

The New Becton Hot Dogs had just cherry-bombed the only player they'd ever respected right off his toilet seat.

WALKER HORTON BENT OVER IN THE BOX SEAT AND pressed his aching temple to the cool metal railing. West Palm's Grove Stadium was church quiet, an empty sanctuary on a weekday morning. The vacant ballpark was just what Horton needed. He had a head to clear. No more Valium hangovers! From now on it's back to beer, he thought.

The early morning check-in had been a nightmare. Horton rubbed his head. He recalled sitting on his suitcase in the Ramada's lobby watching the TV credits roll over David Letterman's gap-toothed grin. Then flags waved, the national anthem played, and Elmer lifted his voice over the roar of the Flying Tiger jets. "Bun-Bun McKay and Hooter Horton, room 1644!" he shouted. Horton walked to the lobby's water fountain and popped his first pill. How could the Giant screw him like that? You tell him you're feeling anxious and depressed, so he bunks you in with a guy who looks like he might not live through the night.

When the unpacking was done and Bun-Bun had drifted to sleep, Horton tossed and turned on the Ramada's starched sheets, wondering what he'd do if the Rabbit's high, whining snore should suddenly stop. When he couldn't stand the wheezing, he stalked into the bathroom and swallowed another pill.

Horton shielded his eyes from the sun, tipped the Guzzler cup, and spat. The round chunks of ice squirted through the backstop screen, tumbled to the ground, and disappeared into the fine gray mat of the warning track. Had guys like Mays, Dark, and Westrum ever played with heads like this?

The sun fired down over the old scoreboard in right-center field and lit the freshly watered outfield grass in a shiny, iridescent green. A motor coughed. Horton looked and saw a huge black man in a white Panama steering a red tractor his way. The man's backside overlapped the seat in a way that reminded him of his favorite doodle, King Farouk on a barstool. The guy's a dead ringer for the drawing, he thought.

The black hands whipped the wheel, and as the tractor's canvas drag swerved across the third-base line, a fine red cloud of diamond dust kicked up over the infield grass.

Horton closed his eyes, turned his face to the morning sun, and tried to concentrate. He had a team to run, talent to assess. Good pitching would beat good hitting, but Odie Wilt couldn't win a five-game series, not all by himself. Maybe Billy would get the knuckler perfected. And he'd have to make a move on Bun-Bun right away. No way the Rabbit would ever play short again. His mind wheeled and spun. Kliny could play anywhere. Jug could still go get them. But the Bear was way too heavy, and he had the missing toes now, so he'd have to stay at first.

The metal railing had warmed. He crooked his arms on the pipe, making a pillow for his head. The sounds of the Florida ballpark were foreign to Horton's ears. Powerboats slapped the water in West Palm Beach Bay, gulls squawked over stale popcorn in the right-field stands, and out on the boulevard, traffic moved politely along without the aid of horns. Horton's arm slipped; he jerked forward, then lay his head back down to sleep.

The hammers rang gently at first, then built to a deafening crescendo of booming-banging heavy equipment. An army of workers marched across the center-field lawn. Ladders went up. They were scaffolding the walls. Fences fell. First left went, then center. The ground crew was moving the earth. Horton hung suspended in his dream, looking down from high above home plate. The palm trees that canopied the stadium were gone. Dingy red brick buildings had taken their place. Behind the scoreboard in center, where the trendy glass high-rises stood, factory chimneys cluttered the skyline, assaulting the blue horizon with plumes of thick black soot.

The field was trapped in a monstrous green horseshoe made of iron and wood. Horton smelled stale beer, cotton candy, and cigarette smoke. Down the right-field line, where the sea gulls had roosted, hundreds of pigeons lifted from the stands in a billowing cloud of grayish smoke. The maze of beating wings shadowed the field for a second, then disappeared over the big clock and Chesterfield scoreboard that loomed high above center field.

The clapping wings woke Horton. He sat up, rubbed his eyes, and stared out at the empty field. The hangover was gone. The dream had left him warm inside. He closed his eyes, saw the scoreboard clock again, and for the next few minutes stood still in time. He was back in the Polo Grounds, with the old Olympic portable on his lap, listening to the voice of Russ Hodges describe

Mays digging in at the plate. "Two out, bottom of the ninth, Labine looks into Campy, gets the sign . . ."

He learned the Hodges trick in 1952, the summer he turned nine. The events that preceded the announcer's debut into his psyche would forever be etched there in his mind. Manhattan's P.S. 756 had closed its doors for summer recess. He and Izzy Silva raced down Edgecomb Avenue singing their year's end song. "No more teachers, no more books, no more of Miss Rizinsky's ugly looks." They would drop their reports off, catch the train at Fifty-seventh, and be in the Polo Grounds before Dark and Irvin had finished batting practice.

Then Horton rounded the corner and saw his summer fall apart. The old black bathtub Mercury parked in front of his mother's brownstone handed down his sentence. He could forget Giant baseball, Aunt Maude had arrived. She was serious about her threat.

"Janet, face facts. You haven't been feeling well, you need time to yourself. The summer in New Becton would be better for that boy than an Adirondack fresh air camp."

Hooter had found the letter on his mother's nightstand the week before. "He could work the garden with his Uncle Urse, make new friends—why, New Becton is even going to field its very first Little League team."

His memory of the trip to Maryland wasn't quite so clear. He recalled a blur of heat, the smell of Urse's cigar smoke, and the steaming car hood spewing water under a sign that said, ELKTON MARYLAND—POPULATION 3,984—BABE RUTH MARRIED HERE.

And that night, before New Becton had a chance to roll up its streets and go to sleep, Horton had locked his mind and thrown away the key. He hated the place "worse than Brooklyn," he told his uncle. The kids talked funny, the buses and cabs were crap spreaders and pickup trucks, and a three-sewer stickball shot would land in cow manure. The only similarity to his Manhattan home had been the couple of acres of dirt and grass he'd spotted when they drove into town.

The following morning Horton's impression was confirmed. The sun that skyscrapers and smoking chimneys blocked and blotted so a city kid could get some sleep popped up over Urse's cow barn and blazed through his aunt's guest bedroom window like a headlight on a subway train. Horton pulled his catcher's mitt from under his pillow, grabbed his baseball, and headed off in search of the grass and dirt.

The ramshackle grandstands felt warm in the morning sun. Horton crawled to the top row and sat in front of the old wooden one-man press box. The view wasn't much, a rocky dirt infield skun back to some fescue and crabgrass. A pinkish, weather-worn snow fence dipped and curled like an ocean wave. He felt sick inside, as though he might throw up. Then he closed his eyes and prayed out loud, "Let this summer end, make Momma well, and give da Giants a break."

Three decades had passed since Horton first visited Tiner, but the memory was as clear as the cloudless West Palm sky. He'd prayed, blinked his eyes, and presto chango! The scruffy Maryland ballyard became Coogan's Bluff. And as he dreamed of Mays running down balls in center and watched Maglie move imaginary hitters off the plate, the voice of Russ Hodges, the Giants' old play-by-play man, flowed through the warm morning air, and Horton's mood began to lift.

"It's a breezy one here in the Bluff this afternoon. The wind's swirling in the old horseshoe, and the Wilhelm knuckler's giving the Reds fits. Heck, it's not just the Reds, it's got Westrum bouncing around back there like a busy fishing bobber.

"Leo has to be happy, the club's been on a real tear of late. We've won eight out of the last ten and got the last-place Pirates coming in for four. Hoyt's working that tobacco chaw pretty good. He looks in to Westrum, gets the sign. Now Kluszewski's holding up his hand, he wants time out. Speaking of time, this might not be a bad time to light up a Chesterfield, it's a real smooth smoke.

"The big guy flexes those bulging biceps and tugs at the sleeve of his muscle shirt. Now he's back in again—ready to go. Hoyt rocks, and it's another butterfly for a swinging strike three," Hodges intoned.

It sounded crazy, but from that day on, if the setting was right and he needed a lift, Horton could somehow always manage to conjure up Hodges' soothing voice. When he was in college it had calmed him while taking tests. He'd even used it when making love to Janie—it prolonged ejaculation. And it wasn't always just a way to kick his mind out of gear. It was Hodges' habit to counsel Horton when things got out of hand.

And so it was today. As Horton sweated out a hangover and wrestled with his responsibilities, Hodges was in his ear again, warming to his task.

"Well, the New Becton Hot Dogs have certainly taken the country by storm. It's a real little piece of Americana, all right. A bunch of middle-aged Little Leaguers touring the country in a forty-eight-foot weenie bus, trying to pull their old coach's business out of the fire. And Ernie, for my money, the man who will make it happen for New Becton is Hooter Horton. He was the trigger spring for that club when they made that twenty-five-game run back in '54."

"Bullshit!" Horton spat ice and pounded his catcher's mitt, making the pocket pop. Watching imaginary ballplayers and listening to a man who had been dead for more than a decade. Cripes, no wonder he hadn't sprung the Hodges thing on Doc Markum. Shrinks wouldn't commit you for hearing an occasional voice from the past, but this was the kind of thing that would have the little guys in the white coats revving their meat wagons up.

Horton's head was bowed as if in prayer. He stared blankly into the cup of ice. His heart had slowed, he was coming around. Hell, Hodges wouldn't be agreeing with Elmer if he didn't think he could run the club. Maybe I'll be like Reggie Jackson—Hooter Horton—the straw that stirs the drink, he thought.

Whop!

The ball slapped the metal backstop piping inches in front of Horton's face. His arms flew up; he kicked the Guzzler cup, sending a spray of Pepsi and ice into the seats behind home plate.

"Whaddya say, fuckstick?"

Horton looked up and shook the ice water out of his catcher's mitt. A sudden grin broke across his face. "Here we go again, déjà fucking vu," he thought. The man on the mound toeing the rubber looked like a Marlboro commercial. Wilt had a cowboy hat slouched down over one eye. A cigarette hung from his bottom lip. He glared in at the imaginary hitter with a look that would back Clint Eastwood off the plate. Wilt rocked, kicked his leg, and fired. The ball shot toward Horton's box seat. The catcher turned, backhanded the ball, and raced down the steps of the stadium, whooping and laughing.

On Odie Wilt, the hat, the Levi's, and the white flannel Cub uniform shirt looked like something thrown together by Ralph Lauren. His eyes were puffy and pink and his beard was at gameday length. But clothes, women, life, somehow everything came together on Wilt.

The grin took Horton back to New Becton again. It was his first week in town. He'd been in the stands at Tiner listening to Hodges describe a screaming match between Durocher and Jackie Robinson when the orange-and-black Schwinn slid broadside into the pitcher's mound. When the dust settled, a tall, blond kid stood on the hill flipping a baseball off his bicep and catching it behind his back.

The mound, the grin were both still there; only the Schwinn was missing today. Horton vaulted the red metal railing and hit the field running.

"You remember that fight we had that day at Tiner?" Horton asked, puffing. "I saw the orange-and-black bike and thought I'd found me another Giant fan. Cripes, how did I know I was going to grow up catching a Chicago Cub?"

Wilt's grin could be misleading. Horton had seen it flash, and seconds later a batter would be down in the dirt, shaking his head. Wilt opened his smile a bit, cocked his head, shrugged his shoulders, and flipped Horton a big, high roundhouse curve.

"Where the hell were you last night? We beat on your door but Elmer ran us off, said Bun-Bun was trying to sleep. What's the fucking deal with him? He queer, anemic, or what?" Wilt asked.

Horton backpedaled, reached out, and picked off another one of Odie's big, soft, spinning hooks. He cocked the wrist behind his ear, snapped the throw, and hit the pocket of Wilt's huge pitcher's glove.

"I don't know, Odie. He's been sick, that's all, still just a little weak, I guess," he said.

"Mouse thought you might still be ripped about that terrorist attack when we blew you off the bus's shitter." Wilt laughed and fired another pitch. This one cracked in Horton's mitt. He flexed the glove to chase the sting. "Hell, that kinda crap goes on all the time in the bigs," Wilt said.

"The Rodent never could play, but when it comes to drinking, hustling women, and making book, I've gotta give it to the boy, he's big league all the way."

"You guys get in any trouble last night?"

"Naw, don't worry, Captain. We just hit an all-night place called Benny's. Mouse, Steve, and Bear had the convertible girls. They're all still in the rack, so I guess they're doing all right."

"They nurses?" Horton asked.

"Better yet, schoolteachers," Wilt said, and came down over the top with a three-quarter–speed fastball that Horton short-hopped off the soft green grass.

Horton backed slowly toward home plate. Wilt had fallen into a rhythm now; it was no longer a simple game of pitch and catch. The right leg kicked high, the back bowed, and his left arm windmilled toward the plate. He released the ball at the height of the arm's extension. The form was still there. He'd be tough to beat.

As Horton bent to scoop up a tight-spinning curve, a flash of white behind third base stopped him dead like a bunt in thick wet grass. A blonde had thrown long, tanned legs up on the box seat railing. Horton stared at Wilt, then back at the stands. This wasn't one of Mouse's grade schoolteachers. Under the big floppy hat and behind the Candy sunglasses, Horton could detect a touch of class. The white halter top gave the tan contrast. The lady had a golden look. The woman twisted in her seat, adjusted her legs again, flipped open what looked like a spiral notebook, and began to write.

"Cripes, how long has she been out there? Is she with you?" Horton's questions ran together.

Wilt did one of his grins and fired another fastball. It dipped and tailed, then busted a bull's-eye in Horton's mitt.

"Reporter. Might as well get used to them hanging around. I've gotta feeling that one way or another we'll be making news before this thing is over," he said, and broke off a hard slider that brought a grin to his catcher's face.

WILT WORKED EASILY, KICKING THE LONG RIGHT leg up at the empty grandstand and driving hard off the rubber in a way that made his motion smooth and effortless. Tight-spinning curves and three-quarter fastballs slammed into the pocket of Horton's new glove. The soft meat of his hand had numbed. Horton reached into his back pocket, produced a thick orange sponge, slipped the rubber pad into his palm, squatted down, and waved one finger in front of his cup. The paper bag was there in his pocket, safe and sound. But he wouldn't need any anxiety helpers, not today.

Horton's head had cleared, the sun was shining, and he had a leggy blonde in the stands watching the action. In Horton's mind he was a big league receiver today, catching the old Cub Odie "the Enforcer" Wilt.

Elmer was right: The dream was there for the taking. The balls cracked and popped around the strike zone. One for fastball, two for curve, three for slider, they dipped and hooked as his fingers flashed the signs.

"Hey, you ever develop a change-up?" Horton asked, puffing. The sponge wasn't enough; his hand had swollen. He was desperate for relief. Wilt rocked, kicked, and flew forward in a wheeling motion. Horton lost the action of the delivery against the high blue sky. When he picked up the pitch it was halfway home. He lunged forward and stabbed at the air like a boy with a butterfly net. The ball continued its flight, bobbing and floating along.

Horton corkscrewed to his left and batted awkwardly at the pitch. The butterfly dipped, eluded the net, and caught the catcher high on the shoulder where his Adam's apple joined his neck.

"Yes!" he whooped, crabbing along on his knees to retrieve the ball. "A change-up—when in the hell'd you get that?"

Horton's eyes patrolled the third-base boxes. He flexed the shoulder, rubbed the soreness, then stopped and stared up into the seats again. If the visitor had seen his error, she wasn't letting on. He stooped over, picked up the ball, and looked up into a pouty smile. The smile opened into a grin, then she crossed her legs and made another note in the green spiral pad.

"I didn't know you had a change like that. You're making my day, my man, with that kinda stuff. If we get any kinda hitting at all, I think we'll give that fucking McKeen a pretty good run," Horton said.

They stood in front of the mound and jawed like a stalling battery, waiting for the short reliever to finish heating up in the pen. Wilt gazed off toward left field, nodding in silent response. Horton beat the red infield from his white baseball jersey and chattered maniacally about the Dogs. "Elmer get around to talking to you?" He coughed and waved his hand to fan the dust. The blonde was clearly in his line of sight. Why wouldn't she look up? What the hell could she be writing so furiously about? Certainly not a game of pitch and catch!

"Yeah, promoting the *Hot Dog* bus full of ex-Little Leaguers should be a real piece of cake. Hell, you and Elmer are sucking the fuzzy end of this lollipop on this one," he said.

"How come?" Horton said, his jaw tightening up.

"Well, I saw 'em play at the reunion, and last night I watched 'em swing from the chandeliers. Before you get a bunch of assholes like this ready to play a team like McKeen's, the Senators will be back in D.C. with a couple of fucking pennants under their belts," Wilt said.

"You don't think we—"

"Hell, Hooter, look at the Pintails! I played against Ensor and Graham. And Pazerelli pitched three years with Minnesota, and all I ever heard about him was that he was half blind, in the low nineties, and had more mean than speed.

"Look, Hoot, no offense. I mean, you can still catch the ball. But when it comes to running the ball club, Elmer's fucking up. It should be either me or Kline. Christ, you know that yourself!"

Horton reached into his rear pocket and felt the rough brown paper sack. It was folded neatly and ready to go. Why did people set him up with chest-high fastballs, then come in with junk like this?

He'd warned Elmer! He couldn't blame the team. The Hot Dogs would rather answer to an ex-big league ballplayer or a millionaire gynecologist. Who wouldn't be impressed by a guy who struck Mays out three times in one game and a doctor who had given half the *Dynasty* cast Pap smears at one time or another?

"You tell Elmer how you felt?" Horton asked.

Wilt had crossed the foul line and was ambling slowly toward the first-base dugout. Horton stayed with him stride for stride, banging the ball in the pocket of his glove. Sweat poured down his face.

"Yeah, he said, 'You can't train the animals when you're fronting the circus.' I've got the contacts and still have a name in some of these cities, so he wants me out in front glad-handing, kissing asses, trying to get someone to take a flier on these Doggie Dugouts of his," he said.

"You think Kliny knows the game better than me?"

"Hell, Hooter, who gives a shit? He played college ball, he's a big-time doctor, these jerks respect him, that's all I'm saying. They're convinced that ex-players and doctors are big fucking deals. And since winning means five thousand bucks, I'd like to see one of us calling the shots."

Horton's thoughts went to Bun-Bun's widow, then to Elmer's

will. He dropped down on the dugout's long, cold metal bench and said, "It might surprise you, but I told the Giant the same thing. I didn't play a day after high school, so I mean you, Kliny, the Bear—"

"The Bear's too flaky, and I didn't throw me and Kline up at you to piss you off. We're gonna need every break we can get. Hell, Elmer's got franchises to sell and he's not talking, but it sounds to me like he's in some kind of deep corporate shit."

"Like what?" Horton asked.

"Don't know. I saw him at the motel pool a while ago. He was swimming laps like a tuna in heat. All he'd say was that a couple of guys from his board of directors are flying in here to see him today. I thought you'd know. Hell, you two talked all the way from Maryland."

Horton shook his head and looked out on the field. The legs were dangling again. She took the white hat off, lay back, and stared up at the sky. The honey-colored hair flashed white, then gray as clouds passed over the infield.

"Look, the big fucker isn't gonna change his mind, nobody's blaming you."

"I guess you guys kicked it around pretty good last night?"

"It probably isn't gonna matter who's running the show, anyhow. McKeen's got the horses, and the way I see it, we've got a five-game series and our only hope is me. If I'm right, I can win you two."

"Okay, say you pitch in Chicago, win, come back on three days' rest and go in Cleveland and win again. Hell, then all we'll need—"

"That's my point: All you need is what you haven't got. Who the hell else is gonna get guys like Ensor and Graham out?"

A bank of black clouds ganged the sun. Where's Russ Hodges when you need him? Horton thought. The field turned cold, the grass looked blue, and the red infield faded into a brackish brown.

"No talent. One ex-big leaguer can't beat three. Is that what you're saying?" Horton said. He stepped out of the dugout and kicked the stones on the warning track.

Wilt lay supine on the dugout bench, his arms wrapped behind him like a garden hose. He propped up his head and continued to talk.

"Look, Horton, I don't know if you were taking any major newspapers during the late sixties, but I had three mediocre years with the Cubs. I won a few in Wrigley during the hurricane season when the wind was blowing in. The Bear's best year he hit about .240, and got what? About ten, maybe twelve dingers, that was Savannah, Double-A, twenty years ago. Then before he knows it, he's in Vietnam getting his fucking toes blown across a rice paddy. Kline got some offers to sign out of college, but the man was smart, he stayed in school.

"Jughead can still run, catch, and throw some. You've got a good little pair of hands, and an arm like my first wife, and like me, you can't hit your way out of a fucking paper sack."

Horton touched his back pocket and continued to listen.

"Now, that's the talent on this team," Wilt said. "I'm going on what I saw last year at the reunion. But the rest of these jackoffs can't hit their asses with either hand."

"Billy's working on the knuckleball," Horton said, coming to the team's defense.

"Could be," Wilt said, stretching his legs, and rolling up, he folded into a sitting position. "But on the bus coming down what Billy was working on was a line of coke."

"So what am I supposed to do? Elmer says whip them in shape, and if we want a shot at the five thousand bucks, I've gotta figure out how to get it done."

"Hoot, opinions are like Fords and assholes: Everybody's got one. But if I were you, the first thing I'd do is admit that this chasing-the-boyhood-dream business is pure, unadulterated Elmer Thumma bullshit."

Horton wheeled and looked down at Wilt like he didn't hear what was said. The blond hair lay wet across the big left-hander's tanned face. His jaw was angular and set. The cowboy hat hung on his knee. Was this the kid with the orange-and-black Schwinn, the guy who grew up to be the big league ballplayer, the Odie Wilt whom Horton had been bragging about for the past twenty years?

"Hooter, while you and Elmer sat up there shooting the shit about who lit the best farts in the Giants' bullpen in '37, I talked to everybody on the team. I thought I might be asked for an opinion, so I jotted down some thoughts," he said and reached into his back pocket and produced a stack of white three-by-five index cards.

"It's just gut reactions, but they might be helpful. You're gonna need everything you can get to make this crew win," he said.

Wilt fanned the notes like a deck of playing cards, grinned, and lay them face down on the metal bench. Horton reached in his pocket, thumbed past the paper bag, and felt the Leatherette cover of his memo pad.

"Here, while you and Mouse were throwing firecrackers at each other, I made a few notes myself. Remember, Odie, I'm supposed to be a writer now."

Horton glanced over Odie's three-by-fives. Wilt held Horton's pad like it was something he'd just scooped up from under his dog.

Horton checked the stands: The blonde was in place. His eyes dropped back down, and he turned the first card over like he expected an ace.

THIRD BASE—BALDY ALBAUGH

Hates baseball, Reagan read about the reunion and the Little World Series in *The Washington Post.* Remembered the '37 Series, the Giant, and McKeen. Made Baldy go, said it's American and Republican as hell, if we win he'll give us a call.
Ability: Zip.
Motivation: Politics.

CENTER FIELD—JUG BROWN

Good guy, believes Elmer's bullshit about chasing the dream. I never could communicate too well with black guys, so it's hard to say about Jug.

Ability: Phys. ed. coach, looks like he can still run, catch, and throw.
Motivation: He likes to play, but he's probably here for the dough. $5,000 is a pretty good summer when you're feeding three kids on a teacher's salary.

RIGHT FIELD—MOUSE MAGRUDER

A never was and never will be. Bullshit specialist with a gambler's head.
Ability: Strong on pussy stories, and as oddsmaker and bullshit artist, he's the best.
Will cost us at least one game if we let him live that long.
Motivation: Three weeks with ten guys he hasn't bummed anything from in almost thirty years. If it's between a bet, a beer, a broad, baseball, and the $5,000, look for baseball to finish a distant last.

LEFT FIELD—BLINKER BALLARD

A piece of work. Party animal, a gamer, give you the shirt off his back.
Ability: Great Little Leaguer, then his hormones kicked in and by comparison baseball became a pretty dull sport. Makes funny farting sounds with his hands, calls himself a massagionist.
Motivation: Three weeks away from Gladys and the kids.

SHORTSTOP—BUNNY MCKAY

??? Something's wrong here. He looks too weak to swing a bat. Says this is the biggest thrill of his life. If that's a fact, here's a man who needs to get out more. Says that if I'd been an accountant for fifteen years that I'd know what he meant.
Ability: Can't even breathe right. Does it through his mouth.
Motivation: Nerds are hard to tell about.

SECOND BASE—DOC KLINE

Slick "Gyno to the Stars." Seven-figure income,
Gucci-Gucci guy. Says he gave Joan Collins a pelvic once.
Ability: Looks good, runs five miles a day, I think he's
gonna be able to play.
Motivation: Wants to hit against Pazerelli, looks at movie
stars' twats all day, now he wants to find out if he can hit
an ex-major leaguer's fastball. Next year he'll probably be
climbing the Matterhorn. The guy's got an ego bigger
than mine.

FIRST BASE—BEAR RYMOFF

An eight-toed infielder. Looks like he's been on the
LaSorda pasta and beer diet.
Ability: A picture swing, could hit it out, no glove and no
toes, but the man used to be a player, so let's don't count
him out.
Motivation: Says he lives for four things. He likes to eat,
fuck, and drive truck, and would give up any of the three
to hear that crunching sound a baseball makes when you
get your ass into one real good, it's better'n sex, he says.

PITCHER—BILLY JOHNSON

One of Vietnam's living casualties.
Ability: Too small to have played in the bigs but had
some talent once. If he can stay straight he might be able
to throw some strikes, something for Ensor and Graham
to hit at us.
Motivation: $5,000 will buy three grams of toot.

CATCHER—HOOTER HORTON

Loves the game. Believes he's still a kid. Buys the bull
about the boyhood dream.
Ability: Good hands, can't hit, throws to second, puts
dings in low-flying planes.

Motivation: It isn't just baseball for Horton, either. The
catcher thinks he's an author now and plans to write a
book.

Horton watched his contacts fog, his neck went hot, and he held
his hand up to shade the sun. He couldn't read Wilt's last assessment; the page was shaking in his hand. Where did Wilt get off
writing crap like this?

PITCHER—ODIE WILT
Good for two games, and if the rest of them can
somehow pick up the third, we'll win Elmer his friggin'
series and pick up $5,000 instead of $3,000.
Ability: Enough to win two.
Motivation: I'm gonna show the baseball world and some
lucky future boss of mine that even with a horseshit
product like this that Odie Wilt's the best promoter in the
game.

"Asshole," "bastard," Horton couldn't find the words he
wanted. So he tapped his foot and waited. Wilt flipped the cover
closed on Horton's book and flashed the grin.
"Christ, I didn't know you were planning to write fiction. It's
damned entertaining. Reminds me of John R. Tunis," he said.
"What's that supposed to mean?"
"Bear a potential big leaguer, and me an outstanding major
leaguer," Wilt said with a laugh, pushing hair from in front of his
eyes, "and Jug will have everybody talking about how much he
reminds them of Willie Mays. If that's not fiction—"
Horton snatched the book and jammed it back in his pocket.
"So, whaddya think of my report?" Wilt asked. He flipped
sideways, stretched out, and scrunching his knees up under his
chin, he looked Horton right in the eye.
"How 'bout it sucks?" he asked.
"Then we disagree?"
"You're fucking a-right!"

The red moved quickly, passed Horton's upper lip, and stormed his face. He turned on Wilt again, and his orange-and-black Hot Dog cap fell to the dugout floor. He kicked the hat and watched it fly into the water cooler. "I came to play ball, and the rest of them did, too. We may not be major leaguers, but that doesn't mean we're losers."

"I just don't see any drive. There's no fight. They're a fat friendly bunch of—"

"No fight! Who were the fat guys that covered your ass last year when you busted Hibbert in the ribs?" he asked, then wheeled and walked out on the field.

"Hey, Hoot, no offense. Like I told you, Fords and assholes. . . . Hey, I call 'em as I see 'em, but I still love the old man too."

A gate banged. Horton looked down the left-field line. Here they came. Parading onto the field were the New Becton Hot Dogs. Sunglasses, coolers, Bermuda shorts. Billy led the way. He wore a huge straw hat and toted the big box blaring soul funk so loud it hurt Horton's ears. Ballard carried an aluminum lawn chair, Mouse a large red-and-white Playmate cooler. Baldy's cap went sideways, like a middle-aged Rudy Kazootie. This isn't a ball club, it's a fucking Mummers' parade, Horton thought.

Behind the entourage the tip of the Weenie's big brown bullet-shaped hood rolled onto the field. The door slammed, and down the steps came a grinning Elmer Thumma. On his heels was McKay. The Rabbit wiggled his nose and blinked up at the bright morning sun.

"Hey, Hooter, here comes your table of contents!" Wilt shouted from under the cowboy hat. "You get 'em to play, and I'll sell it. I can guarantee you that!"

Bags and coolers emptied, beer cans popped, Kline dumped a sack of baseballs, and players paired up for games of catch. The woman behind the dugout stood and stretched. Her hands were on her hips, and Horton could see the long, flat, brown stomach shining in the sun. "Okay, guys, who's running this bunch of kangaroos?" she shouted.

"Hoot! Hoot! Hoot!" Mouse started the chant. Horton went

red-faced again as the jeer bounched back and forth between the rows of players. "Hooter! Hooter! Hooter!"

"Mr. Horton, need to see you for a few," the woman called. Leaning over the dugout, her low-cut blouse fell in a way that afforded Horton a view of the high-water mark where her breasts stopped and the tan began.

"You have quite a cheering section," she said.

Horton dropped his eyes and said, "Right, but you need to talk to guys like Odie Wilt, he used to pitch for the Chicago Cubs, and that's our manager, Elmer Thumma, the old Giant, coming down the third-base line."

The Giant wrestled an orange Gatorade cooler one-armed while balancing a long black bat bag with the other.

"No interviews," Thumma said with a laugh. "Naw, I got some people waitin' to yap a little business at me now, so I've gotta run on back to the motel. You'll do us proud, Hooter, tell the lady all about it. How Bracken McKeen screwed us out of our game in '54," he said, and hefting the keg of water up on the third-base bench, he turned and gave Horton a good-bye slap across the rump. Then he stepped out of the dugout, stopped, leaned down, and said, "By the way, the lady you're going to be talking to is Larry Barnes of *The Baltimore Sun.*"

Horton's head did a 360-degree, Jerry Mahoney spin. "The syndicated columnist? I thought she was a—"

"Man!" Barnes purred.

Wilt stuck his head above the dugout and hit the woman with a knockdown grin. "Be gentle, Larry, it's the kid's first day on the job," he said.

Larry Barnes! The man who wrote "Barnstorming," the weekly syndicated column, was a cover girl. A hair-tossing, wet-lipped blonde. Larry Barnes, hell, he/she was the inspiration for "Hooter's Hot Korner," the weekly column he wrote for *The Johnstonian Advertiser.* Barnes wrote about the backside of the big leagues. Locker rooms, player hangouts, bars, and big-city restaurants were her haunts. The anecdotes Horton picked up from Little League parents and coaches and church softball leagues didn't measure up. And that wasn't all: "Hooter's Hot Korner" lacked the Barnes wit and punch.

"Sorry, Ms. Barnes, you're one of my favorites, I mean, I really get a kick out of your column. That thing you wrote last week about Reggie setting an all-time-stay-naked-interview record blew me away.

"The dugout okay, or would you rather me come up there in the stands?"

Janie had legs. Eyes, legs, and ass, she always said. But Larry Barnes had all the parts. She vaulted the railing, and before Horton could compose himself, she had leaned back on the dugout wall, flipped the big dark glasses back on her head, and was tossing the honey hair in the Hot Dogs' captain's face.

"You and the left-hander looked pretty good out there, at least you two can play." Horton felt a warm sensation, a gentle movement under his cup. "Yeah, well, I think we're gonna be okay."

"Look, I know you have to work out now. All I want is some background on this menagerie. Looks like you guys are going to be news now that the majors have opted to strike."

Horton's jaw went slack. Why hadn't he anticipated something as obvious as a strike? They'd been hinting about a player walkout since spring training. No wonder Wilt was so damn cocky about getting the team publicity. And why else would a writer of Barnes' caliber be following a bunch of misfits like this? Tomorrow morning there would be thousands of newspapers and radio and TV stations with nothing to tape, write, or talk about.

Now the interview had been reversed. Horton asked the questions, and Barnes fielded the inquiries one at a time, answering each with patience and authority.

Barnes saw the strike as owner-orchestrated, a bluff that the players had to call. Horton gazed up at the writer, listening to her strike explanation like the white boat neck blouse had melted away. Were her eyes green or aqua blue? Her complexion was perfect, like one of those Charlie girls in the TV perfume commercial.

A baseball skipped off the step and smacked Horton hard on the shin. Why did Wilt have to hold the pepper game right in front of the dugout? Ballard and Albaugh were fielding like croquet wickets. The Rabbit and Mouse hadn't made a play yet. While Barnes looked on and made an occasional note, the Dogs panted, spat, swore, and chased their mistakes.

"Two questions!"

"Shoot," Horton said.

"Since you're the captain, the guy Thumma says knows more about this team that anyone else, how about dinner? I'll pick you up at the Ramada, about seven o'clock."

The cup made another subtle move in Horton's jock. His arm fell across his lap. He hiked up and reached behind him. The paper bag was still all right.

"You sure? There are other guys who know as much—"

"Positive. Now, number two, this Poughkeepsie Pintails team you're playing, the guys who supposedly won the Little League championship in 1954, are they going to be like Red Klotz and those old guys who used to lay down for the Harlem Globetrotters? You know, the Washington Generals."

"What?"

"Hell, Horton, is this fucking thing on the level, or is that geezer Thumma just trying to peddle hot dogs?"

THE SHOWER BEAT A RAIN DANCE AT WALKER HORTON's feet. He cupped his hand and let the spray bang against his newly capped front teeth. The water tasted cool. He turned, drank his fill, then spat against the aqua-colored tile. It would take more than a Ramada shower to wash today's practice from Horton's mouth. Wilt was right: They were the fat, friendly bunch he'd described on the three-by-fives.

"Sure we're on the level, it's our dream, one shot at the big time, it's like spring training, we're here to get in shape like any other big league team." The recollection of the brag brought a flush to Horton's cheeks.

He moved the soap slowly, in circular motions, rubbing the soreness high on his thigh where a carelessly thrown bat had left an ugly purple bruise. Horton tossed his head back again and looked up into the surging spray. He'd just have to be more optimistic. Elmer had him by the short hairs now—Bun-Bun, the team, it was an offer he couldn't refuse.

At least Jug had made a couple of catches today. Kline and the Bear still had the good level swings, and he had to be pleased with himself. The ball he'd hit in the gap to right had rolled almost to the warning track.

But Mouse sitting on the outfield grass, fielding Miller Lites from a Playmate cooler! Baldy at third poured into those godawful hugnut swimming trunks and all lathered up with coconut oil. And Billy jiving around with that frigging ghetto blaster like he was Kool and the Gang cutting a malt liquor commercial. Nice copy for a woman like Larry Barnes. Hell, if she didn't find the geeklike behavior of interest, there was always the final play of the day to write about.

Horton closed his eyes, dropped his head, and let the water beat into the soreness of his back. He was crouched behind the plate now, watching the Bear's Ruthian swing sky an Elmer Thumma fastball into a sheet of clouds above second base. Under the ball the Hot Dogs spun like spaniels, turning, preparing to lie down for a nap. First Bunny, then Blinker, now Mouse came wheeling into the play. Horton stood helplessly looking up through the shower's spray and listened to the voice of Hodges recall the play.

"High fly ball, McKay, the Dogs' little shortstop, drifts under it, no, now Blinker Ballard's waving his arms, calling the Rabbit off. Whoa, here comes Mouse Magruder, he's got the beer can balanced in one hand and the glove stretched out, look out, Ernie . . . it's the old I-got-it-you-take-it play. A horrendous collision. Let's just pray that no one was hurt!"

Horton reached up, grabbed the bottle of Prell, and shook a glob of green soap on his head. Hodges was silent now, but the pile of infielders pretzeled around in Horton's head. From the depths of the quagmire he could hear Mouse squeaking out "cocksuckers" and "motherfuckers" like mortars launched from a two-inch gun. Just the kind of quotes that would kick a writer like Barnes into second gear, he thought.

The water surged again, and Horton shook his head. Nothing like a good fantasy to make a man forget. He closed his eyes and felt the warmth of company as Larry Barnes joined him in the shower stall. She shook the blond hair and looked up into the waterfall. Her nakedness shone in contrasting shades of brown and white and glistened like gold under the water's cascade. She was tall and tanned and Horton stared at the sun lines where his wife had been so milky white. Her breasts rose gently with the water, and he watched her push the long, wet hair back and tie it loosely in a knot. Her nipples were responding now, enjoying the shower's pulse. Horton looked down and massaged himself with the soap. Barnes would have her way with him now. There was no cup to hold him back.

If Larry Barnes got with it, old Hooter might be tempted to roll off the wagon tonight, he thought. He hadn't had a beer in more than a year, not since the Little League reunion and the first round of anxiety attacks. Hell, Markum seemed intent on forcing his hand. He'd cut his Valium off, saying this was the perfect time to go cold turkey, that he'd have to do it sooner or later.

He reached up, snatched the Prell from the soap tray, and shook the bottle like a hand-held microphone.

"Start spreadin the news, I'm leavin' today, Gonna make a brand-new start of it, be a part of it in old New York, If I can make it there, I'll make it anywhere, it's up to you . . ."

Frank Sinatra gargled better. But for the moment Hooter Horton was king. In two weeks he'd be playing baseball in Yankee Stadium. If it weren't for that friggin' Horace Stoneham, it would have been the Polo Grounds, he thought.

"These little-town blues are melting away, Gonna make a brand-new start of it in old New York . . ."

Horton stood in front of the steamy mirror. He shook the can of Gillette Foamy, pushed the soft soap across his cheeks, and took aim with his razor at a target he couldn't quite see.

Feeling the sharp metal blade on his face reminded Horton of Janie. She loved to kibitz his shaves, pointing out nose hairs and rough spots his razor had missed. Maybe the West Palm restaurant would be one of those clubby spots, the kind where long legs in short black dresses pop up and snap photos of lovers in back-corner booths. Now, that was a picture he'd gladly pay for, him curled up in a restaurant with a blonde like Barnes.

The mirror remained blurred. Horton shaved with unusual care. His cheeks had browned, and he had the base of his tan to protect.

"Damn," he said. The razor jerked and nicked his tender skin.

"Bunny! You scared my ass. How long have you been stand-ing—"

"Just a second or two. Couldn't sleep, so I thought I'd catch a shower. You wanta get a bite to eat?" McKay said. The reflection of his roommate in the steamy glass was gaunt and pale. He had a hollow look and short, ice-white hair. Horton felt the chill bumps stand again. The face was one he'd seen before. It was the *Life* magazine photo that had haunted him as a kid. A boy behind barbed wire stared with dying eyes.

"Jewish Child, Dachau, 1944," the caption said.

"Nah, can't tonight, gotta date, but get yourself a shower, it'll make you feel like a million," Horton said, and dropping his eyes, he began to calculate.

Was the Giant that rich? Would he and Bun-Bun's widow be millionaires someday?

Horton went about the job of cleaning his razor. McKay didn't move. The Rabbit had frozen there and stared at his misty reflec-tion like he'd been blinded by the headlights of an oncoming car.

"Hooter, we gotta talk."

"Sure thing, Bun, I've gotta run now, but tonight we'll do it. I shouldn't be too late."

Horton turned the hot-water faucet. A pipe banged under the

sink. He dashed water across his face and wiped a puff of shaving cream away. Where was the sting? The razor burn was supposed to hurt.

"I've got six months, a year tops," McKay blurted the message in short bursts, like an unexpected telegram. "I know you know. The Giant told me that the two of you went over it on—"

"Christ, Bunny!" The tears were instant. Horton made no move to stop the flood. They ran freely down his face, across the razor cut, offering the sting he'd been looking for.

"I wanted to say something, but—"

McKay smiled. His nose twitched, and Horton watched his reading glasses move up and down. How could the man die? He had the face of a twelve-year-old.

McKay's hand went to Horton's shoulder. He shrugged it away and stepped off the cold tile floor onto the thick shag of the motel room.

"Look, Hoot, we've gotta get something straight, I've known all about this for more than a year. So it isn't news to me. Hell, yeah, I'm scared. The wheezing that kept you up last night was a forty-two-year-old man crying himself to sleep. I still indulge myself with emotional crap like that from time to time.

"But you can't start looking at me like I'm six feet under. I'm the shortstop on this team, and I've given up three weeks of whatever's left to prove I can still play a game that's been an important part of my life. It means a lot to me and a lot to my kids."

"Two boys?" Horton said.

"Mike and Danny. Bonnie's bringing them in from Indiana to watch us play in Cleveland."

Horton recalled his uncharitable thoughts, the ones he'd had in the bus's lavatory. Wilt and Kline would never put up with Bunny, not at short. "Well, we've got a lot of work to do, and—"

"Look, Hooter, MS can bring on double vision from time to time, but we don't go blind. I was dog dirt out there today. I saw Kline and Wilt swapping looks, but if those bastards had been flat in a hospital bed two weeks ago, I wonder how good they'd look?

"It's a funny disease, I'm in remission for now. That doesn't mean it won't be back, a little double vision now and then, but chances are I'll be getting stronger as we go along. I'm gonna help you guys win this thing. All I need is a shot. Is that too much to ask?"

"This isn't pity anymore, Bun, I'm just mad as hell," Horton said and wiped his face again.

"Anybody but me and Elmer know?"

The Rabbit shook his head and twitched his nose. "Just you two, but sooner or later Kline's going to figure it out."

"Okay, for now it stays with me and Elmer. We'll deal with Kline later. Gynecologists are good at secrets," he said.

"So, am I gonna get a fair shake, no special favors, just a chance to help?"

"You bet your skinny little ass," Horton said. "Now get the hell out of my way. I've gotta go talk Larry Barnes outa telling the free world about that I-got-it-you-take-it play you assholes closed practice with today."

•7•

THE WHITE CORDOVA SMACKED THE SPEED BUMP like a hydroplane, caromed off the curbing, and rocked to a stop in front of the attendant's scrambling Michael Jordan high-top sneakers. Horton watched the would-be hood ornament change colors—from dead white to Flamingo pink, then settle on a red that matched his shoes.

"Long time, no see, Miss Barnes. How you been hittin' 'em?" the attendant grinned and opened the car door. "What's the word on the baseball strike?" he said.

She shrugged, shook the hair, turned to her slightly carsick passenger, and said, "Here we go, Horton, best scallops, sea trout, and martinis in Florida. It's where the Braves hang during spring."

Above the restaurant's entrance a blue-and-red neon sign swung in the warm Florida breeze.

LANNY'S HIDEAWAY.

It wasn't the Copa, but if it was good enough for the Atlanta Braves and Larry Barnes, it was okay with Walker Horton. As he wrestled his seat belt he watched the long brown legs and pretty derriere of one of America's finest sportswriters disappear under the restaurant's green canvas archway.

The heavy door clicked behind Horton. It was a solid sound, probably oak, he thought. He blinked and squinted. Was the place even open? At the end of a long wooden ramp he could make out what looked like a wall. The shadowy outline of a fishnet and seashells slowly came into focus.

A tinny piano played off in the distance, trays banged, and he heard soft-soled shoes scurrying about. It's open, he thought and took a deep breath. The smell of Old Bay seasoning and hot pasta sauce. Interesting combination, an Italian fish house. His eyes were back now, and grabbing the ramp's rail, he headed toward a sign that said CAPTAIN'S QUARTERS.

A large red-lipped woman toting an armful of oversize menus popped up from behind a potted palm. He retreated two steps up the ramp.

"I'm looking for a Larry—"

"Barnes. Down there by the piano bar, the blonde with the old fool drooling all over her. You a ballplayer or something? Thought you guys were on—"

"No, just a friend of Larry's," Horton said. The woman shoved the menus in his face. Horton took a handful in self-defense.

Slaloming through the maze of red-and-white-checkered-clothed tables reminded him of his busboy days in Ocean City, Maryland. Friday crowds were always the best. A lot of drinking to celebrate the weekend. Big tips. Restaurants were all the same— Ocean City, West Palm, wherever you went.

A couple sitting in candlelight, toasted and kissed. A fat man at the neighboring table wiped pasta from his face, shouted, "Tight, isn't it!" then screamed with laughter at the joke's punch line.

The lovers broke their embrace and called for the check.

A parade of trays snaked toward Horton. He darted out of the traffic and ducked a passing platter stacked high with steamed shrimp and Oysters Rockefeller. Suddenly he was facing the wall, staring at a photograph of Bracken McKeen.

The Pintails' coach was forty years younger, decked out in Yankee pinstripes. The old collie face looked almost handsome smiling up at the camera. Perhaps it was the contrast. A rather strange-looking man next to the Yankee great captured Horton's attention. McKeen's photomate was dressed in a long-sleeved white shirt and a leather string tie, and by the look of the men's expressions, it appeared that money had just changed hands. Horton followed the music, stopping to peruse the wall's picture gallery.

Little man in string tie links arms with athlete appeared to be the theme of the photo exhibition.

Horton studied the framed display and continued to walk. The man in the funny tie and Ted Williams smiled at Horton and held up two record-size sea trout. In another the old codger poured Joe DiMaggio a cup of java from a plastic pot marked "Mr. Coffee." Horton stopped and shook his head. Jim Rice and the tie man were faking an arm-wrestling match.

"If you ever make the wall with Lanny, you can bronze your jock and pack it off to Cooperstown!" Barnes shouted above the piano's song.

A man at a nearby table rose and looked at Horton. Disappointment crossed his face, and he sat suddenly and whacked his lobster with a wooden mallet.

Horton watched the couple shimmy out of a gray cloud of cigarette smoke. The leggy blonde embraced the little man suggestively, swinging him in rhythm to the bossa nova beat of "Smooth Operator."

Lanny Celebreze appeared set for his next photo opportunity.

He was dressed out in a rawhide string tie with a bright turquoise lanyard. All he needed was another unsuspecting ballplayer, Horton thought. Dresswise, Barnes was something else again. She wore a tight yellow cotton knit sweater, khaki shorts, and beige sandals a shade lighter than her golden tan.

"Lanny Celebreze, this is Hooter Horton," she said, dipping low to end the dance. The white teeth flashed and the woman at the piano bar looked up from the keyboard and gave Horton a knowing wink.

"How you doin', Horton?"

"Good," he said.

The string tie swung. The host took Barnes by the arm as though he intended to finish the dance, then turned on his heel and headed off toward the front door. Horton followed, retracing his steps through the noisy configuration of tables, past tray stands, bypassing snatches of conversation. A woman said, "I love you" and touched her date's hand. A waiter turned to the hostess and mumbled, "The lousy fucks stiffed me on a ninety-buck check."

The restaurateur led them up the ramp and turned left down a long, dark hallway.

"Thanks for callin', babe. Two minutes later and the Hideaway woulda been booked. There's this guy. Not Mafia or anything but not exactly what you'd call straight, either. Anyhow, he's got this girlfriend he's seeing on the side.

"Flies in from Maryland for long weekends, man, he loves the Hideaway, you'da thought it was the bastard's private bedroom when I told him it was booked tonight." Celebreze laughed and poked Horton in the ribs with a sharp-cornered menu.

A match flickered, and Lanny leaned across a table and lit a red wax candle. The orange flame flashed, lighting the table's wrap-around love seat in a way that made the leather a deep, rich brown. Barnes slid in first. The leather greeted her bare legs with a squeak. Horton followed her into the horseshoe seat. Their legs touched, and Horton felt himself recoil.

"No footsie now," Barnes said with a laugh.

"Sorry, I was just trying to see—"

Barnes' giggle sounded almost girlish. She leaned on his shoulder, reached up, and tugged a curtain string.

The wall opened to an ocean sunset. Lanny had nestled his hideaway in a three-sided bay window surrounded by water.

"Wow! When did we turn toward the ocean? I thought we were farther inland," Horton managed.

"We've been running parallel to the beach since we left the motel. Nice view, don't you think? Lanny built this little addition all by himself," she said.

The ocean breeze had blackened the evening sky. Heavy blue-gray clouds rolled inland, and the water swelled with the evening tide. On the horizon Horton could see a line of pink, the last piece of daylight, sandwiched between sky and waves.

"Those lights cutting across the horizon are shrimpers working ahead of the storm," Barnes said. She took Horton's hand. His fingers were warm and wet, and he wiped a drop of sweat from the lobe of his ear. Inside his body, things were worse. Vital organs clanged like loose change in a Laundromat dryer.

"Come on, relax, no sweat, think of this as a date, forget the interview," she said. Horton caught a whiff of her perfume. Shalimar. Would he ever stop comparing other women to Janie?

The wick flared. Horton flinched. Lanny leaned across the table and dropped a new candle where the stub and wax drippings had been.

"Well, I see we've got the tape recorder out. I shoulda known. Always business. And I told the wife that I thought that my girlfriend here had finally fallen." Celebreze chuckled and gave her a pinch on the arm.

"Don't tell me, let me guess: The ballplayers go on strike," he stepped back and sized up Horton like he would a catch of fish.

"Nope, a little old and a bit small to be a jockstrap. Wait a sec—Kaze Lambert, the Players' Association's hotshot attorney. You're the guy we've been seeing on TV. Larry, what the hell's he doin' here? You're supposed to be in California settlin' this friggin' strike."

Lanny wet his hand and pushed a lick of white hair in place. Then he slid the turquoise tie holder up a notch, wheeled toward the hallway's darkness, and shouted.

"Donna, bring the Instamatic, we got us another celebrity to shoot! Barnsie's interviewin' the big-deal lawyer who's gonna settle the players' strike!"

"Hey, slow down, Lanny," Barnes took Horton's hand and held it above his head like he'd just won a prizefight.

"In this corner, Hooter Horton, catcher, New Becton Hot Dogs."

Lanny's brow tightened until it had ringed like grooves on a jar. Then he raised his hand and waved toward the hall to call off the camera.

"False alarm!" he said to the dark and tossed two menus in front of his customers.

"With the sea trout you get two vegetables and a choice of soup. The flounder's fresh, but expensive as hell. For some reason they've been running scarce. Anything in the pasta line is great, Donna makes it all herself," he said.

Then bouncing up on his toes, he leaned forward and stretched himself until the string tie touched Barnes' tight yellow sweater.

"Larry, there ain't no such team as the Hot Dogs, and Hooter Horton's a big league name that don't exist."

Valium and beer, never fear. Drugs and whiskey, mighty risky. No great rhyme but sound reasoning. A man being interviewed by Larry Barnes couldn't stop suddenly and start sucking for his life from the bottom of a brown paper bag. The two yellow pills he'd popped following the session with Bunny were doing the job. And it wouldn't hurt to chase them along with a cold beer or two, not the way he felt tonight.

"Martini dry, okay?"

Lanny was back again working the turquoise bolla. Up and down it went on the leather string. He tapped his pencil on the back of a green order pad and stared through the picture window.

"Make it a double, Lan. I've been sitting in ninety-degree heat all day witnessing a major league crime."

"And your little catcher?" he said. Celebreze was proving to be a sore loser. The man thought he had another celeb picture for his wall, Horton thought.

"Oh, maybe a beer, Miller Lite, I guess," Horton said. There, he was off the wagon. The candle flickered. Barnes smiled and nodded and they watched their host shuffle into the hall's darkness again.

"A Barnes and a near beer," the order filtered down the hall.

Horton turned his attention to the window. The line of pink had been squashed by the clouds. Yellow lights twinkling from the masts of the shrimpers were all he could see. The ocean had gone black for the night.

Barnes cocked her head like a cocker spaniel. "Oh, the crime remark. Loosen up, Hooter, I've got nothing against your Little World Series."

She pushed the tape recorder under the light of the candle, reached over, and touched Horton's arm.

"Here, let me push some buttons so we can talk. Now for God's sake, this whole thing is going to be fun, but if something is off the record, just say the word and it's erased. Okay, love?"

The Valium had eased him. He felt good, kind of snug in their privacy. Hell, he was looking forward to filling Barnes in on the world's oldest Little League team.

"Double dry with two twists of lime and one near." The frosted schooner looked more like a pitcher than the mug he'd ordered.

The candle slid to Horton. Lanny nodded his satisfaction with the light. Then eyeballing his customer, he muttered something under his breath and shuffled off again, shaking his head.

"Cheer up, Lanny. When I'm through with him, he'll be a celebrity, I promise!" Barnes said.

"That's what I'm afraid of," Horton said.

"The New Becton Hot Dogs," she said, raising her glass to Horton's.

"I'll drink to that," he said. He lifted his beer. Their glasses clinked. Barnes slipped her arm around his neck and kissed his sunburned cheek.

Horton felt the rush of blood. It raced up from his toes, flowed down from his head, and gushed to a throbbing stop under his linen napkin. He chugged in short, quick swallows and spat his words like a tobacco auctioneer.

"We were undefeated in '54.

"Beat everybody we played.

"Twenty-one to three, fourteen to zip.

"Hell, they were almost all football scores," Horton said.

The flash was over now, the fire under the table out. He was talking baseball, no time for the old libido tonight. He turned the icy schooner. The beer tasted great.

"So anyway, the Giant lines up a game with his old World Series adversary, Bracken McKeen."

"They pitched against each other in the '38 Series?" Barnes questioned, checking her notes. The lips were full, the teeth perfect. The kind that kiss the screen in TV commercials.

"No, it was '37, cause the Giant only pitched, let's see"— Horton ticked them off on his fingers—" '36, '37, '38, '39, and '40. Five years before he went overseas."

The glass turned up again, Barnes waved, and a busboy stepped out of the shadows. "Refills, dear," she said.

"So anyhow, McKeen ends up coaching the Williamsport Little League champs in '54, the same year our Dogs are so hot."

"You weren't in the Williamsport tournament?"

"Naw, we were independent, we had blacks on the team, and I think Elmer didn't wanta get them into anything that might cause embarrassment."

The drinks hit the table. Horton stopped and took another healthy gulp.

"So anyway, when the Giant reads in a Baltimore paper that McKeen's the coach of the Williamsport national champs, he phones him up, tells him about us, and they come to terms. He agrees to play the Dogs in New Becton, an exhibition game."

"Playing you on your own field, that's interesting. How much did that cost Thumma?" Barnes said and scratched shorthand on the notepad.

Horton skimmed ice down the side of his schooner, lifted the big glass, and drank again. Valium and beer, quite a nice team. He couldn't remember when he'd felt so relaxed.

"Hell, Larry, I was only eleven. You'd have to ask the Giant about that."

Barnes had an infectious giggle. It wasn't like Janie's at all, it was loud and full, something she'd learned from hanging out with ballplayers, no doubt.

"Come on, a couple of beers among friends, Hooter. This is Larry Barnes, sportswriter, remember? It's not like Mike Wallace and the boys were setting up on your front lawn."

"Hell, he probably had to offer him something," Horton remembered the Giant's speech at the reunion, "expenses and a thousand bucks." "But it didn't matter because we never played the game. That's what this grudge match is all about."

"So why didn't you play? the reporter asks," she said, fighting the urge to laugh.

"We were on the field, all suited up. Why don't you ask McKeen? Hell, the Pintails are down here sharing Grove Park with us, they'll be practicing every night."

"Someone said it was because of the blacks?"

"You talk to Elmer about that. Heck, don't try to make this a racial thing. 'The Series That Shoulda Been' is Elmer's idea. It's just a great old guy's dream coming true, making good on a promise to his Little League team. For three weeks we find out what it's like to be pros, play in America's great old ballyards. Why can't we leave it at that?"

"And the Doggie Dugouts Elmer's opening?"

"Well, that, too."

Horton reached over and fumbled with the tape recorder. Barnes' hand covered his, "Here, if you want to punch it off, just hit this," she said, touching a flat black button.

"Thanks. Yeah, you can say what you want about the Doggie Dugouts, that's really Wilt's side of things. But don't quote me on

Elmer being a great old guy. 'Old' isn't in the Giant's vocabulary."
Horton looked at the ocean and continued his thought: "The big
guy would kill me for that!"

Barnes laughed again, stuck two fingers to her lips, and cut
loose a long, shrill whistle. Another waiter appoached the table.
He placed a fresh pitcher of martinis in front of Barnes and pushed
a monster beer toward Horton.

"Lanny says this round's on the house"—the boy's voice
dropped to a whisper—"but unless you wanta see them on your
check, you better tell him who this guy Horton is. He's back there
in the kitchen going through his *Baseball Encyclopedias.* It's really
driving him nuts."

Horton had conducted his share of interviews, dealt with plenty
of local councilmen and shifty, small-town politicians. If Barnes
tried to get cute, slip him any trick questions, he'd just reach over
and cut the recorder off again.

The conversation flew back and forth with the rhythm of a
pregame warm-up. And the more they talked and drank, the less
the occasion seemed like an interview. Horton was out on a date.
He might as well face the facts, the lady saw something she liked.
There! That proved it, she was touching his hand again.

He rambled on and pictured Janie flipping through tomorrow's
newspaper. She stopped at a headline, coughed, and spit her eggs
in the snake charmer's face. The large black print above the "Barnstorming" column read:

HORTON PULLS MIDDLE-AGED MIRACLE
COLUMNIST CAN'T WIPE SMILE OFF FACE

Over a heaping plate of steamed cherrystone clams Horton remi-
nisced about the Dogs' big season, offering up vivid accounts of the
Bear's tape measure shots, Jug's circus catch against Westmore-
land Kiwanis, and praising Odie's slider as the only one he'd ever
even heard of in Little League baseball. He drank more, then told
Barnes about his idea for the book. He'd passed up a deal with
Sports Illustrated and would spend each night talking into his tape
recorder, chronicling the progress of the team as they moved

through training and into the Little Series. When the thing was over and the Hot Dogs had won, he'd have the inside story of what it was like to live a big league fantasy. Hell, he wouldn't be surprised if *Sports Illustrated* came back and picked up the condensation.

When the clams had vanished and they'd put away another round of drinks, Donna, the red-lipped hostess, arrived with a tray full to the gills with mounds of hot pink shrimp.

Horton's fingers worked away, ripping open the shells.

"One more beer. How about you, Larry?" She held her hand up like a stop sign and smiled.

"Okay, Donna, great food," Horton said. "One more beer for the catcher. Damn, I didn't realize how dry I was."

"So what's the deal on the upcoming series? I mean, it's a neat enough idea, and all of you were good friends as kids, I think we've established that. But suppose you hate each other as grown-ups. Ever think of that?

"And if this strike ends as quickly as I think it will, you and your buddies are in for some pressure, playing in front of packed houses! Did it occur to you that you just might make major league assholes of yourselves?"

Horton pushed the shells, probing for another shrimp. "Larry, you're a big-time sportswriter. You're right where I'd like to be in life. Me, I'm a hack, I guess. Hell, *The Johnstonian Advertiser* is a freebie. Christ, I get up twice a week and help deliver the rag myself.

"But I know this much," he said. The words were slurred. Horton stopped in midsentence, looked down into the recorder, and spoke again. "I do know this: Baseball's 90 percent pitching, and if Odie Wilt can give us two games, throw the kinda stuff I saw out there this morning, we're gonna be choking on Pintail feathers long before we hit New York. You can quote me," he said, and covered his mouth to muffle a shrimp burp.

"If Odie can win two, old Hooter will figure a way to get us the other win. Hell, I did it all the time when I was a kid."

Barnes smiled, licked the tip of her lead pencil, and recorded another note.

"Crap sake, if Billy gets his knuckler working," he said, then stopped and stared at the recorder. "Whoa, Larry, that one's off the record. They don't need to know we've got us a knuckler. Element of surprise," he said and took another drink.

Barnes turned her head to the ocean and bit her lip, detouring the urge to laugh again. They sat in silence. Horton probed the mound of shells like a ragpicker on a city dump. Barnes looked wistfully at the rolling black water. The boats had moved out into the night, and the ocean and sky were one. Horton listened to the clank of ice cubes chasing a lime around Larry Barnes' glass.

"So, what else can I say? Pretty boring stuff for a big league writer, I guess," he said.

Barnes flipped her notepad open, pulled the candle close, and slashed a dark line across the top of the page.

"Let me see if I've got this right." She was doing the cocked-head, cute-pup shtick again. "I'm going to repeat some of your statements, what I think I heard. So you tell me if I'm wrong."

"Heck, you've got it all there on tape." Horton nodded to the machine.

"This is just for me, it'll help me later tonight. I've got to go back to my room, write the column, and call it in before twelve o'clock.

"Heck, we never got a chance to talk about you," Horton said. Barnes tapped her pencil on the pad and checked her watch.

"Okay, shoot," Horton said. His head was splitting. No more Valium hangovers! Tonight was the last. He'd managed to tie on a real bell ringer. Maybe the beer wasn't such a good idea. He didn't want to hear himself quoted. According to his shrink, his mouth tended to run at 78 rpm's and his brain at 33. What the hell, he hadn't said anything out of line, he'd be glad to stand behind his quotes.

"Elmer's like a father to you?"

Horton nodded.

"Wilt's still your hero."

"That was a joke."

"Was it?"

"Hell, yes!"

"Okay, don't get defensive. I'm not going to write it, I just thought it was kind of cute."

"The Dogs were an outstanding Little League team?"

"The best!"

"The series isn't just an ex-jock's way of getting a bunch of weenie franchises off the ground. It's a thirty-year-old grudge match between two teams that can make a tremendous statement to Little Leaguers and big leaguers as well?"

Horton downed the last swallow of beer from his schooner. "Well, what I meant was—"

"Let me finish. You said if a kid learns the game right when he's little, develops the winning attitude, he'll have it the rest of his life."

"Yeah, well—"

"And that's what you're going to show America, this winning attitude that you guys have taken into adult life?"

Barnes' demeanor had changed. Where was the cover girl who had been touching his hand, kissing his cheek? Some date, Horton thought. She held her hand up and continued to talk.

"You said we may be in our forties and most of us never played pro ball, but we don't think baseball is something that should ever be stopped just because a bunch of overpaid prima donnas decide to strike. What the hell does that mean?" she said.

"Well—"

Barnes glanced at the pad and continued. "Okay, how about this one? In the next two weeks, if America's interested, tell them to tune into The Little World Series That Shoulda Been but Never Was and they'll not only see some pretty good baseball, they'll also see a pleasant reminder of why it was once our national pastime."

Barnes stopped to take a final sip from the martini glass. "Very quotable, good stuff, Horton," she said.

"Well, okay, it sounds kinda hokey hearing it read back that way. But I guess I can live with it." Horton felt like a human Yardbird, a one-man watering system. Perspiration streamed from every pore.

He couldn't remember any of it. They were all his thoughts, but when had he said them? Was he that screwed up? How could he forget a conversation he'd had less than fifteen minutes before?

"One more thing. You're a reporter, so you know I'm going to have to check with Wilt about his appraisal of the team, the things you said he wrote on those cards," she said.

Horton felt for his bag. He was too weak to pull it out. If he started to hyperventilate, so be it, he'd die there face down in the plate of shrimp shells. Screw it—Odie was going to kill him, anyway. When Barnes wrote her story she might as well go ahead and make it his obit.

His greatest fear had just been documented, it was there on the table, recorded on a reel of magnetic tape. Hooter Horton was insane, just like his mother. If Wilt didn't get him, they'd come and take him away. He and his mother could be roommates, spend the rest of their lives climbing the same walls of their padded room at that hospital in upstate New York.

"Just one more thing. In all fairness, we know what Wilt thinks of the players. But how about you? Just give me quick impressions, one-liners," she said, and reached over and pushed the tape recorder on again.

"Wilt!" Barnes said.

"Fast."

"Rymoff?"

"Power!"

"Magruder?"

"Uh, Mouse is Mouse."

"What's that supposed to mean?"

"How about 'No comment'? And do me a fucking favor: Don't print that!"

"Bunny McKay?"

"Will get better every day."

"Albaugh?"

"A sleeper."

"And Kline?"

"A player."

"Jug?"

"Willie Mays."

"Billy?"

"Monte Irvin."

"Gross?"

"Trying to take over Elmer's company. The fucking guy's an asshole!" he said. "Hey, what the hell are you tryin to do, set me . . ." Horton shouted and pushed the recorder in Barnes' lap.

"Don't get so excited. I'm just trying to find out what he's got against the series. I cornered him today at the ballpark. I know he's a big stockholder in Elmer's Little Giants, Inc., so if you think the question was unfair, you must have a different definition of journalism than we use at the *Sun*.

She clicked the recorder off, folded her notebook, smiled at Horton, and shouted down the dark hallway toward the sound of the approaching footsteps.

"Hey, Lanny, just in time! The catcher and I need a check!" she said.

The shower fantasy had come to life. Barnes was great at screwing ballplayers. She'd proved that tonight!

HORTON WINCED AND GRABBED HIS FOOT.

"Sorry, we didn't see you there," the woman said, and yanking the baby stroller, she backed the buggy over his shoe again.

"Been looking for Gate 6A for the past half hour," she said. "We're a little nervous—first time the little one and I have flown alone. This single parenting is really the pits."

The woman tipped the stroller, eyed Horton's ring hand, and gave the carriage another rock.

That someone had cruised the entire airport and then chosen his foot to land on didn't surprise Horton at all; people had been coming down on him since ten o'clock that morning. Newspapers, TV, teammates. Now a tubby divorcée with thick, brown-rimmed glasses, jockeying a buggy back and forth across his feet. And this was just the prelim. In twenty minutes, when flight 710 from O'Hare arrived, Odie Wilt would dance down the ramp, filling the air with lefts and rights.

"This is where the flight to D.C. boards, isn't it?" she said. The mound of blankets squalled. The mother dipped; her blouse opened and presented Horton with a view that said "dinner for two."

He looked off toward the check-in desk and pointed to a huge flight chart behind the woman's head.

"Yeah, this is 6A, I've got a friend coming in; 710's due in, let's see"—he perused the schedule—"about eighteen minutes, I guess," he said.

"Oh, I was hoping you'd be flying with us. You could have sat with me and Lanie. We wuv company, don't we, Wane-Wane?" she said and fluffed the little lump of blankets. The baby coughed and spat up something white.

Horton stood and wiggled the tip of his injured toe. The numbness had become a dull, throbbing pain.

"Here, take this seat. You can keep an eye on the schedule, in case there're any last-minute changes," he said, and giving the buggy a fatherly push, he walked off in search of a safer, quieter place to sit.

West Palm Municipal had a Florida look tonight. Suntans and suitcases flowed down the concourse. Two Delta stewardesses swayed by with a silver-haired pilot in tow. Stews, all leggy blondes! Why couldn't Larry Barnes have chosen the occupation that God had intended?

"FLIGHT 678 TO KENNEDY NOW BOARDING AT GATE 5C, EASTERN 678 . . ." the public-address system boomed.

Down the concourse, under a blue fluorescent cocktail sign, a line of businessmen spun off their barstools as though they'd been choreographed. The crowds thickened into a knot of motion. The cluster racing at Horton was Florida casual in dress, tan business suits with flowered silk shirts open at the neck. The women wore light cotton skirts and see-through blouses.

A man in a white Panama and a woman in lacy white stockings trailed the group looking like a *Playboy* advertisement come to life. A West Palm to New York run, nobody flying tourist tonight, Horton thought. The stampede of wealth permeated the air with the smell of perfume and fresh cigar smoke. Past the cocktail lounge, gift shops, and airport eateries Horton could see Mutt and Jeff in silhouette. Bun-Bun and the Giant stood in the doorway of a television lounge, staring blankly at the bright screen of a color TV.

From Horton's seat at Delta's Gate 6A the distant picture tube looked like a colorful little marble. He loosened his grip on *The Miami Herald* and lay it on an adjoining seat. Numbers flashed on the big arrival board. Piedmont's flight 227 out of L.A. was changing, but 710 held tight. In thirteen minutes those lucky enough to be seated in the Delta lounge might see one hell of a fight. Horton glanced down the corridor again. Elmer and Bunny were still locked into the TV screen.

An alarm went off in Horton's head. The sprinklers cut on. Suddenly he was soaked with sweat. He felt for the *Herald,* picked it up, and rolled the paper tight in a knot. Then his eyes riveted on the distant TV. Another station must be carrying the story. The Giant and the Rabbit were shaking their heads.

The newspaper quivered in his hand. He opened it and slowly turned the pages. He'd read it dozens of times, searching for libel. One more read, then he'd throw it away. A man has a couple of beers over dinner, some conversation with a reporter about something as innocent as Little League baseball, and the next day it's lights, cameras, action! Horton and his team were national news.

Scenes from the afternoon practice jumped through his head like poorly edited film. The stadium had been a media nightmare. Cameras, cables, capped teeth, and freshly sprayed hair. The thought of Mouse's slide into second base brought another wave of sweat. When the dust had cleared, the rodent lay laughing in the dirt a good ten feet shy of the bag. The little bastard shrugged, trotted off the field, and opened a beer with his teeth. Nice example for America's Little Leaguers, he thought.

Channel 9 out of Orlando opened their six-o'clock sports with the slide-in slow motion and closed with a close-up of the ratlike teeth gnawing the cap off a long-neck Budweiser bottle. When the cameraman moved in for a close-up, Magruder looked up into the lens and belched. And at least a dozen TV, radio, and print reporters were within earshot for the Bear's historic quote. Rymoff threw a huge paw around the Channel 11 newswoman and said, "Hon, until I got laid in the cab of my first eighteen-wheeler, Little League baseball was the biggest thrill of my life."

Horton stared blankly at the twisted newspaper. He read past the "Barnstorming" headline, past the Larry Barnes byline, and settled on the first few words of print. He could feel the lights, and for a second or two he was back on the field, trying to fend off notebooks and camera lenses.

"Yes, we're serious." "No, I don't think it's just a publicity stunt." "Yes, I've been eating Little Giants since I was a kid." "Ask Elmer that one." "No, I don't know anything about Thumma's and Gross's difficulties. That's their business."

"Odie Wilt? A good friend, yes, we're still going to be able to play on the same team!" "The quotes about Wilt were out of context." And so it went. "No, I don't think he'll fly back from Chicago and punch me out." "Yes, baseball's on strike, but don't you think what you're making out of one newspaper interview is a little bit ridiculous?" "All we want to do is play. If the strike ends next week and we play a pregame exhibition in front of a full house at Wrigley, that's great. If not, we'll play it for the bricks and ivy."

His hands had steadied. He lay the paper on his lap and flattened it with the same care he used to smooth his anxiety sack. One final read; maybe it wouldn't sound so bad this time. When Wilt stepped off the plane he'd be ready, he'd apologize, and if that wasn't good enough, well, then hurrah for the folks in the Delta waiting room. They'd have front-row seats.

BARNSTORMING
By Larry Barnes

Baseball went on strike today, and before the game's billionaire owners and millionaire players could pick a posh resort to hold the haggling, scabs crossed the white lines in West Palm Beach, Florida.

If the second walkout in as many years puts major league baseball one step closer to the grave, then the exhibition I witnessed in Grove Stadium today is the game's banana peel.

A traveling circus of middle-aged Little Leaguers billing themselves as the New Becton Hot Dogs, will be, excuse the term, barnstorming America in a (have I ever lied to you?) forty-eight-foot hot dog bus!

WARNING! WARNING! WARNING! This sideshow can be seen in (perish the thought) Wrigley Field on July 4, Tiger Stadium on July 6, Cleveland's Municipal Stadium on July 8, and, God forbid, in Fenway Park on July 11 and Yankee Stadium on July 13.

The Hot Dogs are playing what former New York Giant pitcher and current hot dog mogul Elmer Thumma is calling The Little World Series That Shoulda Been but Never Was!

Here's how Thumma described it yesterday while sucking on a suds in the Hot Dogs' dugout: "Back in '54 my New Becton [Maryland] Hot Dogs were an undefeated Little League team, and through my association with Bracken McKeen, I put together an opportunity for them to play the Poughkeepsie Pintails, the outfit that won the Little League World Series in Williamsport that year."

It seems that McKeen coached the champions in '54 and yes, I looked it up, he is the Yankees' McKeen, the left-hander who made Thumma a trivia question by beating him and the Giants three times in the '37 World Series. So if you're one of those SABR (Society for American Baseball Research) nuts who like to write me, you can take a break. The scores were 2–1, 2–0, and 4–0.

So, why didn't these teams play their Little League game back when they could still do things like bend over, catch, and throw? Well, according to Elmer "the Giant" Thumma, McKeen's team came to New Becton, saw two black kids suited up, and refused to play. I reached McKeen in his West Palm motel by phone (the Pintails are down here at Thumma's expense training for the Series as well), and his comment was, "Well, let's just say that times was different then and we reneged a little bit."

Now, what we have here are two slightly overstuffed teams working out in West Palm getting in shape to play The Little Series That Shoulda Been.

Of course, if you haven't guessed it, this really doesn't have much to do with baseball. Thumma's business, Elmer's Little Giants, Inc., just happens to supply weenies to sixteen of the major league ballparks, so look for free hot dogs, giveaways, and, yes, pon my soul, a midget dressed in a blintz costume, are you ready? Named FRANKIE!

It's all a massive promotional gimmick devised by Thumma to kick off the grand openings of his Doggie Dugouts, a Little Giant's fast-food venture, with starter units set to open in, yes, Chicago, Detroit, Cleveland, Boston, and New York.

Now, to my Chicago readers, since Ebert and Siskel weren't in the stands in West Palm today, I feel obligated to warn you about the show that's headed your way. Feature the Weight Watchers' picnic and you've got the picture.

I laughed, I cried, I belched, Okay!

Then last evening Hooter (a family name) Horton, the Weenies' captain-catcher, and I went out for drinks and a meal on *The Baltimore Sun.* And as it turns out, Horton and three or four pitchers of Miller Lite made a rather charming couple.

He loves Elmer "the Giant," his old manager, thinks Odie Wilt (yes, SABRs, he's the left-hander who had the cup of java with the Cubs) is as good as ever. He's aware that Pazerelli, Ensor, and Graham, the Pintails' three ex-pros, are suiting up for the series but confident that Wilt's slider will "pin their tail feathers back." He sees the series as the greatest thing that ever happened to baseball and called the trip an odyssey back to his boyhood.

Did I mention that he intends to write a book? "I'm really optimistic about the boys getting into shape," Horton said, somewhere between pitcher three and his second pound of steamed shrimp. He went on to say how sorry he was that Wilt had called them "a fat, friendly bunch of insurance salesmen who couldn't hit their tails with either hand."

And to tell the story of the Little Series, I think I owe it to you to let you know that Horton let something else sort of slip. It looks like a real tong fight's under way within the corporate structure of Elmer's Little Giants, Inc. A member of the board named Daniel Gross is fighting the series and trying to give the old Giant/CEO what's known as the corporate hook. So look for more on this.

Now, fans, Larry Barnes is no betting lady, and this column isn't a tip sheet, but if Vegas should decide to make book on something as bizarre as the Little Series, you take Odie Wilt's wisdom and run right to the nearest ten-dollar window. According to my editors (I'll get you for this one, guys), I'll be following the big weenie bus until the major league strike is settled, so this is a personal statement I'm about to make.

For God's sake, Stonesifer, kick your fat owners out of their lounge chairs, whistle the players out of the pool, and get this thing settled.

And Elmer Thumma, you're a lovable old coot, but for the sake of Little League, the majors, the national pastime, and those of us who make our livings writing about the grand old game—CALL OFF YOUR DOGS! The pack I watched today ain't gonna learn any new tricks!

"Oof!" Horton sucked the words and grabbed his stomach. The rolled-up newspaper had been delivered to his soft spot, just below the rib cage. The pain shot to his heart. He looked up into the tight-lipped grin of Odie Wilt. The left-hander fired at point-blank range.

"At least you and your girlfriend managed to spell my name right," Wilt said.

"Hey, I can explain, I said some stuff that—"

"Sorry! Sorry! Shit, you're my hero, you asshole." Wilt's grin straightened, then bent upward, opening into uncontrolled laughter. This was Odie Wilt; the good guy was back. Wilt lunged. Horton's hands flew up. The pitcher was too quick; he'd broken through the defenses and ruffled the catcher's black curly hair.

"Do you know what you've done? Do you? You asshole!"

Horton's hand fought Wilt away. He rolled out of his assailant's reach and pulled the plastic chair between them.

"Made a dork of myself in the newspapers and on TV, showed you up, fucked up Elmer with his board of directors. Help me here: Am I missing anything?"

The two men circled the Delta chair, Horton backpedaling like a weary prizefighter, Wilt a tiger smelling blood.

"You are an asshole. Christ, all you've done is made the fucking series national news. I thought the strike would kill us, but not so, thanks to my fuzzy-headed little friend, Mr. Bottom's Up 'Larry, Let Me Tell You More' Horton," Wilt said and threw the right hand out and noogied Horton on the head again.

"Hell, I'm sitting in the dining room of the Lake Front Sheraton eating breakfast this morning, sweating my eggs off wondering who the hell's going to buy into a weenie franchise promoted by a bunch of forty-year-old farts playing to echoes and empty seats in Wrigley Field, when I start reading Larry's column," Wilt said with a chuckle.

Horton stopped circling long enough to catch his breath.

"So you weren't pissed about—"

"Pissed! I've been running around with a foot-long on ever since. It's a promoter's dream. I've got an appointment on the East Side at Funfood, Inc., at ten o'clock this morning, and I'm passing out Xerox copies of the article, telling every wimp who will listen it's the best promo to hit baseball since Veeck suited up the midget.

"This afternoon I'm West Side with a group called Quickchow, convincing them that if they buy into Doggie Dugouts they'll open their little beaneries with the hottest promotion since that time the House of David shaved their beards."

Horton felt a rush of relief. "So they bought the Dugouts, Elmer's off the hook?" he said.

"Hell, no, they're not brain-damaged, but I got a 'yes if' from both groups that won't quit. Funfood wants the East Side operation in Chicago and an option on Iowa, Nebraska, and Indiana. Quickchow opted for the West Side franchise and is talking about building six more in the South. They wanta go the Florida-to-Maryland route."

"Cripes, that's great!" Horton said and removed his hand from his rear pocket and unhanded his paper sack.

Wilt's grin closed, the lips pulled tight. Horton's hand dove back in the pocket and rubbed the bag again.

"It's real simple, Hoot. We're in the spotlight. Now all we gotta do is win!"

"That's the deal? Win and they buy in? Great! What if we get blown out?"

"Christ Almighty, Horton, use your curly fucking head. I'm Ray Kroc out selling McDonald's back when people still think Big Macs are overalls. Ronald's still a twinkle in Ray's eye, okay?

"We lose and look bad doing it, and the dugouts go down the dumper. Funfood and Quickchow sell somebody else's cholesterol."

The plastic felt cold and hard as Horton slumped down in his seat. His eyes fell, then fixed on the tip of his dirty white Nikes.

He held the stare and wiggled his toes slowly up and down. It wasn't just his foot. He was numb all over now. Wilt dropped down beside him. Horton looked up and managed another question.

"So if the strike continues, you're saying that these people think we'll still get fans in the stands and press coverage, too? Just because I made an ass of myself, Barnes printed some crap out of context, and the local TV stations picked it up?"

"Hooter, Hooter, my boy, if the strike holds, Barnes will follow us. Trust me, she loves it, it's just the kind of crapola she likes to write. And TV is going nuts over it. They need pictures to show, and a bunch of old men trying to play baseball is just the kind of stuff they're looking for," Wilt said with a laugh.

And without missing a beat, he turned the conversation by dropping his voice an octave.

"You ever hear of a Joby Suehowicz?" he asked.

Horton shrugged.

The pitcher continued. "Me neither, but I checked him out: He's for real, and he's the reason why we're gonna get people into the parks, strike or no strike." Wilt walked over, eyed the big airline schedule, then turned back to Horton.

"Our friend Joby's reading 'Barnstorming' this morning about the same time I am. They had this little sidebar kind of a blurb, like in *USA Today,* in the *Trib* about me, saying how I'm already in town trying to peddle the Dugouts. So anyway, when I get back to my room after breakfast, I'm sitting on the john and the phone rings.

"Quit fucking with me, Odie. Who the hell's Suehowicz?" Horton said.

"He's the guy who cut that big stink a couple of years ago when the players walked. He's a fucking fan activist, one of those little red-assed liberals who think owners and players are gang-banging the fans."

"Oh, that guy. Yeah, I remember—"

"So anyway our man Joby is connected with fan groups all over the country and claims that we're just what his people need to give major league baseball the punt in the nuts it's been asking for."

"What group?"

"Well, he just came up with the idea, so he said it's still like a working title, but it's a spin-off of the original group and he wants to call it something like . . ."

Wilt paused, and jamming a handful of fingers in Horton's face, began to count.

"It's the FLLSFYTBLB—yeah, that's it for now, the FLLSFYTBLB, Former Little Leaguers Say 'Fuck You' to Big League Baseball," Wilt said. "FBLB for short!"

"Sounds like bullshit, and how the hell's Elmer gonna take all this? He's got a deal with big league baseball and—"

"If the strike's on, it's his only hope to get people in the park. If it ends—well, hell, we'll deal with that then. Crap, we can't stop this guy anyway. I mean, he saw your interview and now he's going for it, big-time wide open."

"He's for real?"

"According to some friends of mine on the sports desk at the *Tribune,* he's a real little ass-kicker. He's going to try to buy up every seat he can in Wrigley for our debut, and fill the place with as many ex-Little Leaguers cheering their butts off as money and free hot dogs will buy. If the strike should be over by then, when the Cards and Cubbies take the field, if Joby has his way, the place will empty out like a steel mill at five o'clock on payday. Of course, they'll be marching and picketing before the game, trying to convince everybody who goes in that day to follow them out and show the big leaguers up."

"You think it'll work?"

"He says the bleacher bums are already behind him, and he got that taken care of with one phone call."

"So we're going to be part of some sort of big-assed protest now?"

"Who knows? But I'll tell you how serious he is: he's flying down here to talk to us after our last practice, and when he gets here, he'll have his shit together, the FBLB will be buying up tickets and painting signs for our arrival in Detroit and the other major league cities, too."

"You tell your Doggie Dugout prospects about all this?"

"Absolutely, and they love it. A guy at Quickchow said he might just paint a sign up himself. He's tired of paying to see Double-A pitchers play hopscotch in major league bullpens for six figures a year."

"I don't like it. Two days ago we're off on a vacation—I mean, I can't believe it, all the shit that's coming down, it's not real . . ." Horton said, wiping an icy sweat drop from his chin.

"Welcome to the big leagues, Horton, that's what you wanted. Now you've got the big league fantasy, so you're gonna have to live with it. Hey, cheer up, win or lose you've got something now that's shaping into something pretty exciting. Who knows? I might even break down and buy your book," Wilt said.

Horton looked over Wilt's shoulder. Thumma and McKay marched along the corridor, headed their way. He shrugged and forced a smile. "Better get your bags. Elmer's got another bug up his ass," he said.

"What now?"

"We're sneaking into the press box at Grove Stadium tonight, gonna check out the Pintails, see what they've got."

"The fucking Hardy Boys! I love it—give me ten minutes, I need to make a quick phone call," Wilt said and walked off just in time to miss seeing the puffy little woman with the baby stop halfway through the metal detector, turn, and blow Horton a good-bye kiss.

THE BRIGHT LIGHTS LOOMED ABOVE THE OLD BALL-park, picketing the macadam lot in long, thin, black shadows. The Giant's scouts crept like commandos, moving quietly across the strips of darkness. Gate 16 was the target. Elmer had the key and the plan. Once inside, they would slip along under the first-base grandstands. When the press box elevator had been located, Horton, Wilt, and Thumma would ride quietly to the second level, leaving Bun-Bun behind to train his radar gun on the arms of the Pintail pitchers.

One surprise after another. Horton was on an elevator of another kind. Barnes screws him in print, Wilt is elated instead of pissed, and now the Giant's spy mission. A fitting way to end the day—grown men in sneakers creeping across an empty parking lot under the cover of a black Florida sky.

But Horton sensed something positive in the air. A day that started as badly as this one couldn't end that way. This just might be the night he'd look on as the turning point. He checked his pocket. The bag was there, folded flat between the pages of his reporter's spiral notebook. He was prepared to make a full scouting report on McKeen's team. Hell, a clandestine operation like this might even be worth a chapter in his book.

The shadows played tricks on Horton's eyes. His comrades were behind him, lost in the darkness of the old macadam lot. Horton broke into a trot. The Pintails were on his mind again. Who was this team that Wilt called "too big league for the Hot Dogs to beat"? How fast would Pazerelli be? Would Graham and Ensor still hit with big league power?

The adrenaline kicked through Horton's veins, and his mood lifted. He felt himself pumping up, preparing for the challenge that lay ahead. Above the stadium's oval rim, high-intensity lights glowed a brilliant white. Flags flapped gently like tiny boat sails in silhouette.

Horton stopped suddenly. The Nikes screeched, making a bird-like sound. He popped a fresh toothpick between his teeth. He would follow Markum's advice: "Don't let your feelings take control. If things seem out of sync, stop and think—you'll take charge of your own life."

The slap of the Giant's size thirteen Chuck Taylors cut across the quiet night. The Hardy Boys were on his heels. Horton broke into the trot again.

Was it the lights? Had he run to lights like this before? Brooklyn! It was Brooklyn, 1952—no, 1951!

Horton let his mind go back in time. The evening had been warm and sticky, a front stoop kind of night. And if it hadn't been for the tickets forced on his mother, that's where they'd have been, perched on the front steps of the old brownstone, listening to Russ Hodges make Giant baseball come to life.

Horton felt his heart accelerate. He could feel his mother's hand in his. That was it—they'd raced down Franklin Avenue looking up into a yellow glow high above another enemy camp.

Cutting through the mob, he'd felt a strange sensation. Pushed into a revolving red turnstile, they'd squirted out on the other side like immigrants passing into a foreign country. The crowd's momentum moved the little black Giant cap along in the flow of Dodger blue. He hated Ebbets Field, the Dodgers, and Walter O'Malley. His mother's boss had given them the tickets. He'd be offended if they didn't go, she said.

The crowd propelled them up a ramp in a way that reminded Horton of the newfangled escalator he'd ridden at Macy's the week before. The aromas of fresh popcorn, beer, and stale cigar smoke filled his senses. Then above the roar of the raucous crowd, Horton heard the crack of a bat. The mob froze on the runway and listened for clues to the hit. A second passed. The sound of a distant thunk drifted across the third-base stands.

"Come on, Mom, Lockman just creamed one!" he shouted and led the charge to the top of the ramp. At the incline's end, above bobbing heads and craning necks, Horton caught his first glimpse of major league baseball—a sliver of green—a snatch of a yellow-and-red GEM razor sign. Then a mountain of a man in a rainbow-colored Arthur Godfrey shirt leaped to his feet and blocked the view.

"Catch the ball, dago! Dat was a lousy pop fly!" he shouted. "Ya bum, ya!"

When the color wheel slammed his program down and fell back in his seat, Horton was striken dumb, paralyzed by the sight. Nothing in his eight-year life had ever looked so big, so green. He stood in reverence on the walkway and painted a picture he'd never forget.

Dust settled around the bag at second base. Lockman leaped to his feet, tugged the black cap down over a white mop of hair, and beat a brown cloud from the Giants' pearl gray road uniform. The old scoreboard jutting out over the right-center field fence was a mass of angles, sharp right- and left-hand turns. And high above the Shaefer beer sign, the outline of monstrous apartment buildings looked like mammoth red brick dinosaurs lumbering across the Brooklyn sky.

A brilliant moon sat on the highest chimney looking down on Ebbets' yellow lights. Horton watched the scoreboard. The first "e" in Shaefer flashed. Below the blinking letter, Carl Furillo stalked the carpet like an angry panther. He stopped and gave the WIN A SUIT sign a ferocious kick.

The Florida ballpark that triggered Horton's memory was empty this evening. No Giant-Dodger game would be played under this park's lights. But Horton had been in touch with some very special feelings. Markum would have been proud of him tonight.

The bowels of the stadium were cool and damp. In the distance a soft red light spilled across the tunnel. Horton's eyes were acting up again, having trouble adjusting to the lack of light. He took a mincing little step, tripped, and grabbed the the wall.

"Hey, that was my foot!" McKay said, wheezing. Horton's contact lenses were clearing now, and he blinked and nodded to the shadowy figure he'd trod upon. He could see the tunnel clearly now. It swept down the first-base line, then horseshoed right toward home plate and the glow of the red exit light.

"Elmer, I hope you've got your shit together on this elevator deal," Wilt whispered.

"Watch your eyes," the Giant said, and on the tail of the warning came a stream of fresh tobacco juice. The party halted, listened for the splat, and then moved out again. Slowly this time, and with more deliberate steps.

"Wilt, all you gotta do is march past that red light, waltz into the first door you see, and push the button. If you feel yourself goin' up, then the Giant's got his crap together!" Thumma said. "Now get your butts down, 'cause I gotta let one fly again."

The scouting party groped past huge shadows reminiscent of a time warp machine Horton had seen in a sci-fi movie on cable the week before. "Blacker than the inside of Billy Johnson's jock," Wilt said. A cool, musty smell confirmed his suspicions. Ground crew tractors! The place reeked of limestone, gasoline, and pesticides. The slap of their shoes echoed off the walls. Horton stopped and listened to what sounded like distant games of pitch and catch. He held his hand to his ear again. No bats cracking, just leather popping leather.

"They're still warming up," he said. Bun-Bun shook his head. Horton smiled. The hunters would be socked back in their press box blind in plenty of time. McKeen and his Pintails were sitting ducks.

"Christ, Bunny, pick the fuckin' broom up, will ya? You can't carry a sweeper, how you gonna get a bat around?" Wilt said.

The little man swung the big push broom up on his shoulder. Horton ducked, dropped back a step, and followed along behind the Rabbit, watching the stick bob up and down. Bunny's outfit—the broom, the Beetle Bailey fatigue cap, and the blue overalls—was authored by the man who gave America Baby Bunts and Doggie Dugouts. Whether the ensemble would serve its purpose was still too close to call. But Bun sure as hell looked more like a janitor than a baseball scout. Nobody would argue the Giant on that. How long he'd be able to sweep around in the stands with a radar gun hidden under his arm was the question Horton had. McKeen might be a lot of things, but blind and stupid weren't on the list. At the red exit light, McKay's broomstick turned right, bobbed up the ramp, and disappeared into the dark stadium seats. Seconds later Horton, Wilt, and the Giant stood in an old wooden elevator cage, bumping up to the second level.

"Looks like the old man can still get it together every now and again," the Giant said. Then he spit through the rod iron bars and watched the brown projectile twist and fall down the elevator shaft.

The cage jerked to a stop. The Giant pulled the metal door, and the men moved quietly out—Wilt, Horton, and then the Giant. Through cobwebbed glass Horton saw a dim light bulb swinging from a chain. The Giant opened another door, stepped down, and ducked his head. Wilt and Horton did the same.

The press box reminded Horton of his tree house. The one that Urse wedged between the two thick oak limbs above his aunt's grape arbor. The misshaped wooden room looked like a drunken fan clinging to the side of the stadium's upper deck. The floor trembled under their feet, and the place smelled of cigarette smoke just like the clubhouse after one of their Secret Order of the Beaver meetings. Furnishings were sparse: folding chairs; a couple of three-pronged electrical sockets; and a long, Formica-topped table. But an ideal place for writers to crank out their copy.

Horton lay the high-powered Otasha binoculars on the table and eased into a seat. From where he sat it looked like a turnkey operation. Bun-Bun down in the boxes, Jug's gun trained on the Pintail pitchers, relaying speeds with prearranged hand signals. A brain trust in the booth eyeballing the athletes, noting strengths and weaknesses. When it was all compiled, he'd have a nifty scouting report, something to study on that long trip from Florida to Chicago. By the time Odie toed the rubber for game one in Wrigley, his catcher would know every feather on the Pintails' backs.

Sitting in the press box gave Horton a different perspective. The lights that beamed him into the park didn't appear to be nearly as bright. Only half the lamps were lit, and center field, out where all the glove popping was taking place, was shrouded behind a curtain of black. Horton pressed the binoculars tight to his face; the rubber eye cushions felt warm and moist in the hot summer night. He pushed the dial, left to right. It was hard to focus on the ghostly figures. He could see movement but nothing clearly. The slapping and popping of the mitts continued. They were out there, all right, floating around like some kind of apparitions. It was like trying to focus on fog in a swamp.

"There're eight, maybe nine of them, hell, I can't tell. You take a look," Horton said, passing the binoculars to Wilt.

"Come on, McKeen, hit the lights," Wilt said between clenched teeth. "I got an appointment to get myself laid tonight!"

"Here we go," the Giant said. "The son of a biscuit's finally turning them on. Here we go, come on, McKeen, let's see what you got. I'm paying the electric bill, not you, you little piker." A huge paw shot the length of the table and snatched the lenses from Wilt.

Above the booth, lights flashed and popped like press conference cameras. Left field turned a brilliant green. The bank of lights behind third base clicked on, home plate lit up, and the infield took on a big league look. The bright glow flowed over into the press box. Three chairs slid back in search of the shadows. Horton had the binoculars aimed dead ahead, zeroed into the bank of lights behind the left-field bullpen. Another light display arched above the scoreboard; he turned and was blinded by the brightness. Horton squinted, spun the focus wheel, and watched the picture sharpen.

His reaction ran an emotional gamut from surprise to disappointment to a sudden urge to laugh out loud.

"Christ Almighty, they're wearing Bill Veeck's black Bermuda shorts!" Wilt said, and he punched Horton on the arm. "Quick, the binocs! I gotta see this shit!"

No wonder they'd been so transparent in the dark. Black caps; black shorts; and long, dark stockings; hell, if the devil had a softball team, that's the way he'd suit them up.

Horton watched the parade marching to the infield. The players had fallen into ranks of twos and threes. The light was perfect now. High noon without the glare. He framed the binoculars tight on the men's faces and tried to look inside them, see right through to their psyches.

The Pintails were more fat than thin, taller than short, but somehow, even in those god-awful uniforms, still managed to look like a baseball team. Ensor and Graham were disappointments. He'd thought that the years would have had their way with them. But they looked just like gum cards, strolling along the outfield grass. The men were tall, with long, sloping shoulders. Graham cut a better figure than he had when he wore the Cardinal uniform.

Ensor was still brick hard, built like a Coke machine. Horton glanced at the catcher's backside and jotted a note on his pad: "Big through the butt, legs, and ass, that's where he gets his power." Ensor stooped over to pick up a baseball, and Horton took a second look. Not an ounce of fat on the man. Double knits didn't lie about things like that.

"Where's Pazerelli?" Horton asked.

The tight smile crossed Wilt's face. "The big boy in the dark shades, the one with the escort," he said.

Horton trained the binoculars on a clot of players crossing second base. If Ensor and Graham are the Pintails' Twin Towers, here comes their Sears Tower, he thought. The big man loped in arm and arm between two potbellied stoves in baseball caps. Horton glaced at his poop sheet: Alderman and Smith. The pitcher's portly stablemates looked like forty-year-old men are supposed to, not some bronze steroid gobbling mesomorphs.

Pazerelli pushed the dark green glasses back on his nose, turned, and lofted a glob of tobacco over the shorter men's shoulders. Horton noted a black gap in his mouth. Half of the pitcher's bottom teeth were out. He remembered the headlines from a decade ago. He'd read it out loud to Janie at the breakfast table:

PAZERELLI LOSES TEETH IN BEANBALL BOUT

The Giant's massive fingers rolled like drumsticks on the Formica tabletop. The rhythmic beat appeared to be moving the feet, playing the parade across the grass.

"Anybody seen that weasel McKeen?" he said.

Horton shrugged. Wilt shook his head. The Giant leaned over the railing and spat again.

"Here he comes, thar she blows," the Giant said. His voice rose, and he licked his finger and touched his cap. Up on his elbows now, the Giant spun the focus on the binoculars like a Vegas wheel and dialed his old adversary in.

The manager of the Poughkeepsie Pintails was smaller than Horton imagined, more stooped, and the long, collielike snout had taken on a few new lines. The old man had fleshed out since the

MovieTone News and his pose for the photo on the restaurant wall. McKeen yanked off his black cap and jammed it into the pocket of his Bermuda shorts. Where the Giant was bald, McKeen boasted a bumper crop of carrot-colored hair.

"No wonder the beggar chose the Gay Nineties uniforms and caps. He's grown him one of those queer little wax mustaches," the Giant said. Then he turned and arched a stream of juice that twisted and turned all the way to the backstop net. "Bull's-eye!" he said, watching it splash in the path of Bun-Bun's sweeping.

"Infield, let's go!" McKeen shouted. "Shake it!" The clipped orders sent nine black uniforms in motion.

McKeen banged slashing line drives and ground-ball bullets to his infielders. Silence blanketed the booth like carnations covering a funeral casket. A shot richocheted off the sack at third. A long, limber, lantern-jawed man backhanded the ball and fired a bullet to first.

"Elmer, these boys are gonna go through us like a coat hanger into a camp fire weenie," Wilt said.

And Horton knew he was right. If the Pintails had a weakness, it would have to be pitching or at the plate. Their glove play had Horton touching his anxiety sack and Elmer licking his good luck finger.

"Fat up the middle," Horton wrote, and before he could close his book on the critique, Smith, the cookstove shortstop, smothered a line drive and flipped it to Alderman, who pirouetted over the bag and tossed a rope to first.

When a McKeen fungo fell beyond the outstretched glove of a bespectacled fielder, Horton scribbled, "no speed in right." Suddenly the ball shot out of the darkness. This time Alderman plucked it off. And bang! Another gun went off. The throw rifled past the mound, skipped once, and slapped waist high into Ensor's outstretched mitt.

Batting practice spread gloom on Horton's despair. And while cannon shots exploded in the batting cage and baseballs arched high into night, Odie and Elmer fouled the air further by whispering business back and forth.

"Funfood and Quickchow like the Dugouts, but we've gotta win this series if they're gonna kick off their promotion with the games. They see us as being kinda like the Miller Lite guys, and wanta shoot some TV ads featuring the World's Oldest Team, that kinda crap.

"Agency guys from both outfits were there. They don't expect us to be world-beaters, but we can't play like crap, either. Nobody's gonna buy hot dogs out of pity, and I'm quoting Harry Zingraff, the CEO at Quickchow on that," Wilt said.

Thumma nodded; his eyes were fixed on the field.

"I like the Miller Lite concept; you guys could make a real nice ad program, heh, heh, an aging Little League team.

"Hooter, that guy's stepping in the bucket on batting practice fastballs, make a note of that," he said.

Horton nodded and added a line to the Giant's assessment. "For an old man, McKeen can throw. He's got excellent control and great breaking stuff."

"Another thing." Wilt's voice lowered an octave. Horton and the Giant looked up from the practice.

"What's the story on this guy Gross? Thanks to silver tongue here, Barnes has him in this morning's paper. I go to Chicago and find out that he's already been there ahead of me, bad-mouthing our hot dog deal, and I've never even heard of the fucking guy," Wilt said, slapping the table.

Horton shifted in his chair and jotted another entry in his book. "Graham pulls everything, even the outside breaking stuff."

They were here to scout the Pintails. Why couldn't Wilt and Thumma leave the business back at the motel? It was tough enough to concentrate, watching players, keeping an eye on Bun-Bun, without Wilt and the Giant doing their Lee Iacocca, Ross Perot act.

"Gross is a pirate," the Giant said. "It's as simple as that. He comes alongside a good company real friendly-like, then when he's aboard, he turns the tables on you. Hell, he's worse than a pirate, he's a friggin' mutineer," the Giant said and slammed his fist so hard that Horton's notebook jumped. The Giant wasn't thinking baseball; Horton had seen the look before. The man's mind was in a corporate conference room. He was miles away, back in Baltimore.

"I got a position where I felt it would be to our advantage to take in some outside investors on special deals. I wanted to get some spin-off ventures off the ground and—"

"You in trouble?" Wilt spun, tipping the metal folding chair up on two legs.

Don't answer, Horton thought.

"Nah, just got a bad egg in my basket. The guy came highly recommended, but we're gonna win us this Little Series, get the Dugouts sold, and then I'm gonna shell him good. Yep, he's a rotten little egg, all right."

"Ensor's up," Horton said. Wilt and Thumma snapped to attention. The business meeting closed. Horton brought the binoculars to his eyes a split second late. The bat exploded. For a second he thought a kid had snuck in the booth and stomped a paper cup.

Horton swung the glasses; the ball was gone. All that remained was a smacking sound in the grove of palms behind the right-field fence. A coconut splatted as it hit the ground. The Giant made a funny sound down deep in his throat. Then he covered it with a cough and said, "Boys, we've got our work cut out. They got 'em a few that can play."

Wilt did the lopsided grin. "Mouse says he's a gambler," he said.

"Ensor?" Horton asked.

"No, Gross! Mouse says he started out in Govens making book years ago, had a tax consulting business as a front," he said.

"So you and Mouse checked him out, did you?" the Giant said and spit in a paper cup.

"Well, I'm supposed to be selling our franchises, I thought it might be nice to know who's out there trying to screw me out of my commission," he said.

Horton was slow off the mark again. The Giant's thermometer had already topped out. His baldness was a brilliant red. The cool-down was under way now, and Horton watched his face go from pink back to its natural shade of white.

"Wilt, what're you gonna do with yourself when you grow up?" the Giant asked.

"Move up to the majors, do what I did for the Akron Indians for the past couple of years, except up there they'll pay me what my ideas are worth," he said.

"Yeah, you might hook on with a club and make a pretty good dollar, but don't take what we're doing now too lightly. I make no promises, but I've thought of you and Horton as like sons to me, even more so since Sammy's been gone.

"So let's all just bust our humps, do the best we can on the Little Series thing. If it goes well, then who knows? Maybe we'll all go uptown together."

Horton stared at his brown book and read a recent entry. Wilt leaped off his feet and pointed down at the box seats.

"Here we go, check the screen, Bunny's got the gun on Pazerelli," he said.

In the Rabbit's nest, six rows deep behind the screen, blue coveralls blended with dark blue seats. The tip of the radar gun popped up like a submarine periscope above a choppy sea. Bun-Bun swung the gun slowly toward the mound and Pazerelli. From the booth, weight and height were hard to judge.

"He's an aircraft carrier, all right," the Giant said. "A good six-four, maybe -five."

The thick prescription sunglasses and the unshaven blue-black beard jogged Horton's memory. Was this the gangly kid Horton had watched warm up in that MovieTone News film clip from Williamsport? If so, the years had been unkind to the pitcher; ugly had run amok.

Along the sidelines, knots of black-suited players bent and dipped in their games of pepper and flip. Bellies bulged over San-sabelts, and knobby knees topped long black stockings. Horton spotted the glasses back and forth, watching the men laugh, curse, and retrieve their errors. Horton turned his attention back to the battery soft-tossing on the grass between the mound and home plate. Ensor flipped the ball to Pazerelli; it ticked his glove and rolled until it banged into the left-field boxes.

"Damn," he said, giving the binoculars a twist.

The lights caught the blond hair just right. The sparkle of gold gave Horton a jolt below his waist. Barnes curled her legs, rolled up on her buttock, and turned sideways in the seat. The white jogging suit, the lights on the platinum hair, she looked like a white Persian cat curling up for a nap.

He turned the glasses back to the mound. Quite a contrast, Barnes and Pazerelli. Maybe not, he thought. One's as dangerous as the other, just different deliveries, coming at the Hot Dogs with different kinds of stuff.

Ensor pulled his mask over a beakless black batting helmet, squatted, and spat. A white stream splattered dead in the center of home plate. He pounded the glove three times and shouted, "Yo, Pazzie, let's see dat old knockdown pitch!"

Horton's adrenaline blew in like an unexpected storm. He yawned, flexed his shoulder, and shook his hands. A spray of sweat splattered the Formica table. Pazerelli rocked into his motion, then hitched. The windup ground to a sudden, unexpected halt. Was Pazerelli disoriented, a little tipsy? It looked like he'd had a few too many to drink. He'd been having trouble catching Ensor's throws. Pazerelli shouted at Ensor, something that Horton missed. The absence of teeth blurred his speech. "Cligger me in." It made no sense.

Pazerelli pawed the rubber, cocked his head, and aimed the dark green lenses at Ensor's target. The sideline games stopped dead. Twelve black hats turned toward the mound. Over by the first-base dugout, McKeen spun sideways on his three-legged stool.

Ensor looked like a black bank vault squatting behind home plate, a Vic Wertz look-alike wearing the tools of ignorance, Horton thought. He spat again and slapped the mitt. Horton panned the field. Barnes wet-lipped her pencil tip. McKeen rubbed his carrot-colored hair, and Bun-Bun eased the Jug's gun up.

CLICKET! CLICKET! CLICKET!

The summer sounds cut through the Florida night. Horton looked at the Giant. "Crickets in Florida?" he said. The Giant nodded yes.

The windup was a blur of motion. Horton missed the kick and release. Ensor spun sideways. They heard metal rip and tear like snapping tendons.

"The friggin' ball broke through the home plate screen," the Giant said, snatching the glasses from Horton's trembling hand.

"That sucker busted clean through the screen. Now the Rabbit's got both hands up. What the hen's that supposed to mean?" Thumma said and passed the binoculars back to Horton.

"Counting the thumbs?" Horton asked, bringing the Rabbit's message into focus. "Yep, ten fingers, thumbs and all. He clocked him at a hundred, maybe more, he said." He reached back and pulled the brown bag out of his pocket, smoothed out the wrinkles, and slid the sack under his notebook.

Wilt's smile was back. "Look at the bright side: The count's ball one. The cocksucker never could throw strikes."

The shelling was the Vietnam that Horton missed.

Pazerelli's pitches pounded the metal piping; gravel flew from the warning track and kicked gray clouds of dust that plumed and floated like napalm into the press box.

Strike one exploded into the pocket of Ensor's mitt at precisely 9:06 P.M. Horton noted it in his book. The preceding seventeen offerings had been everywhere, one so wild that it separated McKeen from his milking stool. Horton checked the glasses and counted: Bunny had nine fingers up.

"Another nine?" the Giant asked, and unrolling an aluminum pouch he exchanged his chewing tobacco for a pinch of snuff.

Ensor's home plate dance continued. He dove up the line to spear a pitch. "A left-handed hitter like the Bear takes that one in the ear," Wilt said.

The next offering sent the square-shouldered catcher pancaking to his left. He crabbed counterclockwise in time to short-hop it off the wooden backstop screen. Pazerelli's teammates had gone back to their sideline games of flip. And as the ball flew up and down the line without a miss, he made another notation: "If flip and pepper is any indication, our ass is grass! McKeen's loaded with lawn mowers!"

He didn't like what the binoculars did for Pazerelli. They enlarged a man who was already bigger than life. The pitcher had settled down considerably. The hitch was gone. His last two wind-ups had been as smooth as ice. His arms swung like twin pendulums, the knee dipped, and he exploded off the mound like a bull out of a rodeo shoot.

Something troubled Horton, the way the pitcher cocked his neck. Maybe it reminded him of Hoyt Wilhelm, the Giants' old knuckleballer.

"Hoddarn, he's got her going now, those last three Bunny had as nines and two of 'em was strikes," the Giant whispered. Horton nodded and made the toothpick dance across his mouth. He had Larry Barnes in his sights again. She was on the steps of the dugout, laughing at something McKeen had said.

"Here we go," Thumma said. "I've got a buck that says he's in the strike zone and in the nineties again."

"You're on," Wilt snapped. "This prick never threw three straight strikes in his life."

"Anybody seen Bun-Bun?" Horton asked as he leaned over the railing and peered down into the rows of empty seats. Larry Barnes laughed her ballplayer guffaw. Horton pulled the glasses back in time to see McKeen turn and glare into the seats toward Bunny's nest. Only the broom was in evidence; it lay across a folded chairback.

The press box door swung open, and three men fired out of the metal chairs like heat-seeking missiles. Bunny stumbled in, dropped the gun, and said, panting, "They spotted me! Let's get the hell out of here!"

Two mammoth hands shoveled the tabletop. Notebooks, binoculars, and Jug's gun dangled from the Giant's fingers like prizes from a claw machine.

"Clicker," Bun-Bun said with a wheeze. "He's using a clicker."

"You all right?" Horton asked. Bunny nodded. "Let's hit it," he said.

Wilt popped the elevator button. The door opened, and the Giant pulled the cage in place. Horton looked at Bunny's eyes. It was the "rabbit-in-headlights" look again.

"He's blind. Pazerelli's blind," the Rabbit said.

"No shit, Sherlock, as a fucking bat," Wilt said and pushed the button marked DOWN again.

"No, I mean literally, legally blind. Didn't you hear that clicking before each pitch?" Horton nodded. He felt the sweat break across his neck and pulled his collar back. Why wasn't the elevator moving? Wilt mashed the button again.

"Ensor's got one of those little metal clicking gadgets. Pazerelli can't see three feet in front of the mound." Horton heard the elevator groan. It bumped, dropped, and jerked slowly toward the ground. An instant replay flashed before his eyes. McKeen's players, the hefty infielders, had Paz between them, walking him in to the mound like Seeing Eye dogs. The bastards were leading the blind.

Horton couldn't see the Giant. The light was too dim and yellow. But he'd heard the tone before. The Giant's eyes were definitely blue. "Boys, that cocknocker's gonna turn a fastballer loose on us that aims with his friggin' ears," he said.

The elevator smelled sweet, like ballpark concessions, cotton candy, and caramel corn. Horton recalled a grade school trip to Hershey Park, cotton candy, caramel corn, and a ride called the Dippsie Doodle. He'd lost his lunch on about six unfortunate classmates. And if the doors to the elevator didn't open soon, history would repeat itself.

The car bumped. The number two lit. He felt the car jerk. It was moving again, bucking down the shaft. The heat was overwhelming. One more floor and fresh air. He touched his bag and said a silent prayer. Horton wanted out. He could hear his heart slapping blood around. The car slammed hard. "Here we go, ground floor, let's move it now," the Giant said.

The car pitched Horton forward. Wilt mumbled and elbowed him in the ribs. Horton felt a wild sensation. His testicles were flying, they were rocketing up again.

"Wait a minute, we're going up . . ." Bunny said.

The car climbed, lights flashed above the doorway. They were headed for the top.

"What's the fucking deal?" Wilt said and banged the button with his fist.

Horton blurred. The scene went hazy. He heard the elevator PA box squawk and broken laughter. A cackling sound faded in and out. Wilt said, "fucking stuck." The static from the box snapped and popped again and he heard Bun-Bun say, "We'll just have to call for help."

A man laughed, a deep guttural growl. Then a woman's voice cut in, "Just a few questions, boys, and we'll bring you down, safe and sound."

"McKeen and Barnes," the Giant said, and kicked the door with his big black Chuck Taylor shoe.

Horton reeled in the darkness. Above him the elevator numbers spun like digits on a Vegas wheel. And when his lights had dimmed to darkness, he saw the shadowy outline of the Giant waving in front of the PA box. I'm dreaming he thought, the Giant doesn't talk like that.

"McKeen, you balloon-balling little asshole!" the big voice boomed. Then the tone softened to syrup.

"Larry, hon, don't quote me on that. Now . . . if you're the little reporter I think you are, you're gonna wanta let us down. Because when I step outta this car you're gonna get one hen of a story. The Giant's gonna go for a Guinness record, Larry. I'm gonna sweep up a stadium with the ugliest red mop in the state of Florida."

•10•

WALKER HORTON LAY BACK IN THE CHAISE lounge, looked up at the blue-black sky, and recalled the airline ad he'd read while waiting for Wilt. Delta had it right: Florida had its star-splashed nights, all right. Above the Ramada's kidney-shaped swimming pool, long-leafed palms fanned a silver moon.

At Horton's feet, water flashed black, then shimmered like a mirror in the moon's white light. He wiggled his toes, popped a beer, and drank. The breeze kicked the palms and blew the scent of jasmine across his poolside station. The fresh air felt cool. He rolled his head, adjusted the pillow, and wiped sweat from the nape of his neck.

The Florida night was just as advertised. A man could walk the beaches, catch a swim, make love, then get a good night's sleep. But for Hooter Horton it would be none of the above, not tonight. The Hot Dogs' captain-catcher had blacked out for the second time in a week. And before the palms had fanned the morning moon away, the newspaper account of his latest attack would be rolled up, rubber-banded, and on front porches and in driveways across America.

No, save for the three-minute anxiety nap in the corner of a ballpark elevator, Horton would get no sleep this evening. If hotel security questioned his all-night poolside vigil, he had his answer ready: He was waiting for the morning paper. His teammates didn't need Barnes' yellow journalism to spur them on. Wilt would fill them in on all the gory details this afternoon at practice.

Above the pool, windows blinked and curtains closed. Horton lay back again and watched the big hotel bed down for the night. The elevator memory made him sick inside. It was the same gut wrench he'd taken to Dr. Markum a year and a half ago.

A woman in a hot pink halter on a tenth-floor balcony looked down through the palms at the pool's blue water. Janie with boobs, he thought. Horton's eyes patrolled the building. He counted. Floors twelve and thirteen were dark. But above the blackened strip, seven rooms were brightly lit. Albaugh would be writing briefs, calling the White House, making national policy, doing whatever a presidential adviser does. If Baldy could handle a bat and glove the way he did a telephone, I wouldn't be passing out in elevators, Horton thought. Magruder's light went out. He'd finished calling in bets on the West Coast games for the night. The greyhounds were running at Leland Park. The rest of the Hot Dogs' rooms were brightly lit. Night-lights! Horton wondered why. By the time they staggered in, they'd be able to undress by the sun. A room went black. Horton counted, three from the end. It was Bun-Bun; his little roommate had nested in again.

His eyes clipped along, dropped six floors, and targeted on a lighted window. A man and woman embraced, then pulled their curtain shut. On a balcony two floors higher, a boy swung his arms and tossed something overboard. Horton heard a splat in the parking lot. A water balloon, no doubt.

There was action up on fourteen again. The Giant's room was lighting up. He'd be burning the midnight oil, cooling down from his round with McKeen. Horton could see his shadow now as he paced in front of the balcony curtains. The Giant would have made good on his promise to Larry Barnes if Wilt hadn't stepped between the men. Horton pieced the scene together from scraps of conversation he'd picked up on the ride back to the motel. "If you hadn't pulled me off him, I'da handed the man his tail," he'd heard the Giant say.

Horton continued his motel bed check. The Giant's light dimmed. The pacing shadow disappeared. Later, when things got really slow, he'd play a game. The Bear and Mouse were odds-on favorites, but it might be kind of fun to see who'd be the last Dog to hit the sack.

Horton dropped his foot in the pool and watched the water ripple. The rings circled and broke against the tiles below the diving board. Suddenly he was gasping for air. Anxiety! Waves of a different kind. Here they were again, out of nowhere.

It was crazy. A man's staring up at hotel windows trying to figure out who's getting laid; seconds later he's drenched with sweat, wondering if he might hurl himself off a balcony the way the kid had tossed the water balloon.

"You feeling any better?" The Giant's voice surprised Horton. It was soft, almost unrecognizable. Thumma had cut through the poolside garden.

Horton straightened and forced a smile. The Giant paying a visit, typical of the big guy, he thought.

"Yeah, better, much better, more embarrassed than anything else," he said.

Thumma wore a gray athletic T-shirt with a big black bull's-eye laundry mark. His baggy blue swim trunks were apparel from the past, the kind of clothes he'd seen old men wear at Jones Beach and Coney Island. The black cap sat back on his head. The Giant smiled. Horton wondered how a man his age could look so young, so at peace with himself.

"Well, we ain't played a lot of ball yet, but you can't say it isn't getting off to a rousing start," Thumma said.

Horton nodded. The woman on the balcony leaned over and craned her neck. The big guy was back in voice again. She couldn't see them. The waving palm fronds blocked her view.

"What do you think?" Horton said.

The Giant walked on his toes, measuring his steps. He pounced on the diving board, fashioned a little half skip, sprung, and jack-knived cleanly into the pool.

No splash. A perfect circle. Thumma's long shadow snaked under the bright blue water. The surface exploded at the shallow end, and Horton watched the big white torso climb the metal ladder. The Giant shook his shiny head.

"Think about the team, you mean?" Thumma said.

Horton nodded.

"Well, I'd like to know what you think, you're the captain. That's the way it works, you know. The field general goes to the old man with an opine; at least that's how it was with Bill Terry back when I was with the Giants," he said.

Horton's eyes were on the darkened rooms again. He wanted to be careful with his words, to think before he spoke.

"I always thought people like us, you know, guys who wanted to be big leaguers, would act differently if we got the chance. Hell, these aren't the New Becton Hot Dogs, they're worse than the guys Jim Bouton wrote about," Horton said.

"And on the field?" the Giant asked.

"If their attitudes don't change, they're the team Larry Barnes described in this morning's paper," he said.

"And if they do change, then what?" the Giant asked, toweling himself off with his gray T-shirt.

"Well, we've still got one hell of a team to beat."

"And?" the Giant snapped the shirt like a locker room towel clipping the end off a potted frond.

"Well, I was just sitting here thinking, the Indians won 111 in '54, and coming into the Series, nobody gave our Giants a prayer."

The Giant flopped in a cushioned chair and unfolded an aluminum pouch he'd stashed in the grass. He rolled himself a wad of Levi Garrett.

"Here's something you can stick in your locker, Hooter. We ain't gonna let this bunch of middle-aged crazies embarrass themselves," he said, and pushing the wad with his tongue, he fired a shot across his captain's lap.

Horton held his hand up as if to block the missile. The Giant continued his thought. "First thing, you gotta quit worrying so much. You been doing just fine, trying your best. I got no complaints with what you been attempting to do; we're still in the early stages, but it's time we made some moves."

"How about my Rip Van Winkle act in the elevator tonight? That oughta instill pride in our players when they read Barnes' column tomorrow!" Horton said.

"Right now I'd say Larry's editors are flipping a coin on the angle they'll take. I came outta that gondola and made a pretty good front-page play myself, you know. Grabbing McKeen and holding him aloft by the seat of his little black shorts like that wasn't exactly a gentlemanly thing to do.

"Hellfire, boy, you slept through the best part," the Giant said with a laugh.

The woman on the balcony leaned over the rail and looked again.

Thumma was up now, pacing figure eights around the kidney of water. Two laps later he stopped in front of Horton's chair, slapped his flat white belly, and deposited his plan in his captain's lap. The address was orated as though his entire team were poolside, hanging on every word.

"Boys, I hope you've enjoyed your nights on the town," he said. "Because curfew starts tomorrow night at eleven. In by eleven, up by six. We'll eat breakfast after our morning run."

The Giant paused for a second, then fell in the chair so hard that the cushion coughed. "Hooter, back when I was a Marine crawling across Pacific Ocean beaches capturing and shooting Japs for a living, we had a guy, a captain, a real little hard tail.

Horton kicked the water. Another we-had-a-guy story, he thought.

"Funny-talking little guy that routed all his words outta the right side of his mouth. We'd be slapping along in the landin' craft so dadburned scared that we couldn't suck a prayer's worth of air and out would come Captain Troxel, talkin' sideways like Georgie Jessel. 'Girls, he'd say, see that friggin' beach in there sparklin' in the moonlight? Well, I want you, Maxine, and you, LaVerne—he'd be patting us on the helmets as he talked—I want you ladies to hustle on in there and sweep the sand clean of Japs because the colonel and I plan to be sittin' under an umbrella drinkin' rums and Cokes by, shall we say, oh, fourteen hundred.' "

"Piss you off," Horton said. Another light flipped on, and he watched a couple throw clothes across the bed. Give me a break, he thought, let's see some action, the big guy's at war again.

"Hah, talk about a guy who knew how to make a Marine's tail turn a darker shade of red. Took me to Corregidor to figure out that it was nothing but a hoddarned act," the Giant said and pounded a dent in the arm rail of his aluminum chair.

"He turned out to be okay?"

"Nah, he got himself killed by sniper fire trying to cut a parachuter out of a tree when we was taking that beach.

"That night there was some discussion as to whether we'd miss old Troxel, and that's when Sergeant Edwards straightened us out.

"Hen, Hooter, Troxel was a good man, it was all just an act. He was, as you kids say these days, just psyching us up to go kill Japs. He'd move through the ranks callin us Jap-lovers, pussies, whatever it took to get us riled. Then Edwards would come along behind him patting heads and asses, saying crap like 'Boys, don't let that bastard git ya down, we're gonna get us that sand, all right, but it's 'cause we're Marines that love the U.S. of A., not 'cause some dickhead officer is lookin' for an oak leaf.' "

The light on the tenth floor went out. Horton kicked the water again. He'd heard the war stories a million times. Wake, New Britain, Midway, Guam, and now Corregidor again.

The blonde on eleven opened her curtains, stepped out on the balcony, and hung the pink halter across the railing. Was that a see-through gown? The palm waved across his field of vision. It was tough to fantasize with the Giant in your ear telling John Wayne stories.

"So anyhow, Horton, you and me are gonna Troxel and Edwards the Hot Dogs until they're pantin' and lookin' for shade," Thumma said.

"Huh?" Horton said. It wasn't a see-through at all; the woman had on her bathing suit. If Elmer ever shut up, maybe she'd come down and take a dip. He could pass out, she'd give him mouth-to-mouth. Barnes jumps out from behind a palm and has herself another headline:

WOMAN SAVES WIMP

"Youser, we'll double-team them," the Giant said with a chuckle. "You know, like they work 'em for confessions in those TV police shows. It's just like Troxel and Edwards, 'cept they call it good cop-bad cop, something like that."

"Hell, coach, they're liable to turn on you and walk right outta here," Horton said.

"Nah, I'm gonna be Edwards, the ass-pattin', head-rub guy. They're gonna love my tail to death," he said. The Giant spat again. Two red gardenias parted in the flower bed.

"Hoot, you'll be Troxel. Now, they're gonna hate you at first. I'm not denying that. But when we win that series, and then later, when they read my will, they're gonna be thanking Hooter Horton for the rest of their happy lives."

Horton felt as though he might be just seconds from vomit. He stood and looked down at the Giant in a way that made the old man choke on his tobacco plug.

"What do I have to do to get through to you? Can't you see that this shit's killing me, driving me crazy? Christ, I'm so fucked up now I carry a bag to breathe in and I'm still passing out every day or two," Horton said.

The Giant coughed, recovered his chaw, and stood. He and Horton were nose to nose. Neither man looked good.

"Hooter, I don't claim to know much about psychology. I'm not up on this kinda hocus pocus, but I'll tell you what I do know. There's things I can't make happen in this life, and some I believe that I can.

"Now, I can't bring Sammy back, or Marie, or do a damn thing 'cept love Bun-Bun till he's gone. And I can't guarantee that good cop-bad cop will make us beat the Poughkeepsie Pintails. And I don't know for a fact that Gross won't end up sitting in my chair at Elmer's Little Giants.

"But since you brought it up, I'll tell you what I do know. This is a golden opportunity for you and Odie Wilt to grow up and become adults. And I'll tell ya something else, Walker: You're both way overdue."

Horton dropped his eyes and scuffed his toes on the rough apron of the pool. He heard the splash. The water broke across him like an ocean wave. Cannonballed, he thought. Thumma kicked toward the shallow end, and the water exploded again. The Giant climbed the ladder and disappeared into the thicket of palms.

The Giant had done it again. Just when the shit was about to hit the fan, the big guy was always there turning the speed up a notch.

Tires squealed and a spray of gray stones dinged the pool like machine-gun shrapnel. Horton covered his head, then checked his watch: 4:46 A.M. Above the hedgerow, headlights panned the sky. The cars were making a second pass. Horton crouched behind the boxwoods and watched double lights fly up the hotel drive. The bumpers banged. The cars twisted sideways. They'd locked themselves together.

The yellow cab ground into its running mate, broke free, and spun a perfect circle, 360 degrees. Then both cars screeched to a rocking stop. A wheel of the yellow cab balanced on the edge of the Ramada's circular fountain, the bumper of the other vehicle wedged between two potted palms.

Bear Rymoff leaped from the yellow cab and threw his hands in the air. Mouse sprung out of the hack, waving and squeaking like he'd just won the Indy 500.

"Winner, Lucky Teeter!" the rodent shouted.

"Bullshit, I got you by a bumper!" Rymoff screamed. And leaping on the car, he did a victory dance on the Call 829-8976 phone number stenciled on the hood.

The team tumbled out of the cars like circus clowns. Ballard, Billy, Jug, an unshaven old man in a leather cap that Horton didn't recognize. Ballard and Kline staggered off to some potted plants, fumbled with their flies, then gave the flora a drink. Billy marched purposely over to Horton's hedge and heaved a night of drinking inches from his captain's Nikes.

At 4:59 A.M., the last light went out. The Ramada was black, its guests were tucked in safe and sound. Except for Wilt, of course. An away game for the old Cub, Horton surmised. He closed his eyes and began to coast. Conversations he wished he'd had, women he'd wanted but couldn't ask, doubts, misjudgments, a past of indecision drifted across his psyche.

Janie and the Giant had him pegged: sexually, mentally—nothing about him was mature; Hooter—he didn't even have a grown-up name.

Headlights shone across the pool. A dark green cab pulled slowly under the hotel overhang. If Wilt hadn't been among the missing, he'd have never bothered to look.

Horton cut along the hedgerow, dodged Billy's deposit; then, standing on tiptoes, he peeked up over the top.

Odie leaned over and paid the cabbie. A woman laughed. The engine roared. The vehicle slowly passed. One head, just the man behind the wheel. Horton looked back at the entrance. Late again, Wilt and the woman had disappeared.

The pool chair was turned like an arrow, aimed at Odie's window. A light blinked on the second floor. Someone taking a leak, no doubt. Wilt's light flashed on, then off again. A crack in the curtain showed the room's salad green walls. Maybe they were scrubbing up!

He remembered the path Wilt had cut through New Becton High School. And to think that they'd started dead even atop the Thornton sisters. His eyes were out of focus, looking at the window but seeing nothing. The light seemed brighter now; maybe Odie had one of those let's-look-in-the-mirror girls.

The movement on the balcony wasn't registering. Three men, fourteen stories up, perched on the landing adjacent to Wilt's. Horton bit his lip. Mouse grabbed the railing, swung, scissor-kicked and lit softly on his neighbor's landing. Drink made the degree of difficulty downright dangerous. Kliny was over before Horton noticed; he'd been preoccupied watching the Bear limber up with toe touches and deep knee bends. The Bear's jump dissolved into a forward roll. His body hit Wilt's railing. The doctor grabbed him in mid tumble and pulled the big man in.

Horton felt a pang of jealousy. They were going to watch Wilt screw. The curtains flashed the perverts. They jumped back and pressed their backs to the railing. The drapes were moving now, closing slowly. They stopped short and afforded the visitors a narrow gap of light. Now the men were fighting for position. The Bear and Mouse he could understand. But Kliny, a gynecologist, the guy really had to love his work.

His mind whirred away as he watched them fight for position. He'd call security, report three guys breaking into a fourteenth-story room. Maybe he'd buzz Wilt and ask him what he was charging, tell him it looks like a pretty good crowd for a week-night. Suggest that it might be one of his famous come-ons, another Ladies Take a Chance on an Indian Blanket give-away in room 1453.

The human totem pole stood stacked still for twenty-six minutes. Then Mouse skinned down from Bear's broad shoulders, and Kline crawled backward from between Rymoff's hairy knees. The smaller men vaulted the rail, braced themselves, and broke the Bear's arrival.

The moon had swung behind the hotel. Birds chirped, and the sky had turned a gunmetal gray: 5:29 A.M. The red numbers on the digital watch looked misty in the morning light. The air had chilled during the night. Horton wiped water off the chair's plastic cushion. Maybe he'd winked off a time or two; he couldn't be sure. His stomach growled, a door slammed. Something thudded on the sidewalk.

The papers! Now he could read about himself, then try to get some sleep.

He passed the lobby entrance, scooped up the stacks by their ropes, and took them for a walk. At the dumpster he pulled a *Miami Herald,* a *Palm Beach Tribune,* and a *Tampa Times,* one from each stack. The remainder of the load he lowered quietly into the mounds of hotel trash.

The side entrance was an excellent choice. No reason to give the front desk any clues to their missing papers. Horton swung the door, opened the *Herald,* and flipped the pages as he climbed.

By the thirteenth landing he'd paged to Larry Barnes' column. It was in a color box, on the sports page upper right, page one.

OLDSTERS LITTLE LEAGUE SERIES KIN TO PRO WRESTLING
TEAM CAPTAIN PASSES OUT ON EMOTIONAL ELEVATOR RIDE

He turned the corner and walked into a trench coat full of something soft. The woman screamed. Horton slipped back a step and looked up into the jade green eyes. Larry Barnes! Horton's favorite writer had come to life, jumped right out of the *Herald*'s freshly set type. Her face went red, then white and settled on a chalk gray somewhere between clay and death.

"Well, shying away from elevators, I see," Barnes managed.

Horton stopped and caught his breath.

"Yeah, different strokes for for different folks. Speaking of rides, how's Odie doing? Still going up and down, I bet!" he said.

•11•

THE CEMENT FLOOR CRINKLED LIKE GLASS UNDER
the spiked shoes. The man stopped, flipped a cigarette butt in the
urinal, and walked down the row of dented lockers.

BALLARD, KLINE, ALBAUGH, MAGRUDER, BROWN, WILT,
RYMOFF. Name signs marked the dressing cubicles. A valve shut
off, and water hissed. He looked back toward the row of toilets.
The vacant room smelled of Ben Gay, wet clothes, stale beer, and
cigarette smoke.

HORTON

The man read the sign across the aisle and stepped over the gray
wooden bench. Horton's black microrecorder sat on a stack of
freshly laundered towels. Nice item for a visiting scavenger. Too
fucking bad, he thought. He wouldn't touch it. The little prick
would just have to take his chances. An empty aisle, nothing but
benches, dented green lockers, and that god-awful Ben Gay beery
smell. He grinned and punched the rewind button. Might as well
leave the novelist a quote or two.

He hit the button again. The tape hissed. He heard the voice of
Hooter Horton.

". . . been acting like a bunch of assholes . . ."

He slapped the button again. The tape rewound. He pressed the
switch marked "Play."

"This is Hooter Horton, tape number nine, notes for the novel,
June 27, West Palm Beach, Florida. Things have been really going
down the dumper since Elmer put this good cop-bad cop crap into
play. Most of them just don't give a damn about the game. Billy's
probably hooked on cocaine. His eyes look funny, and he's sniffing

and wiping his nose all the time. As of this morning's run Kline, Ballard, Magruder, Albaugh, and Wilt still aren't speaking. Rymoff does from time to time, but it's always something like 'get fucked' or 'up yours.'

"Elmer's got practice closed to the press, and that's pissing everybody off. Larry Barnes I haven't seen since the stairwell after her all-night deal with Odie Wilt. I can't even ask any of the balcony guys what they saw. None of them is speaking. My guess is that Wilt's been screwing her all along. Bunny thinks that's why she came down here in the first place. I wouldn't be surprised.

"Hell, I can take the silent treatment. The thing that pisses me off is I'm convinced that we might still have something special on this team, something we're never going to see again. Crap like I saw today. Odie can really bring it when he wants to. Great speed, great quickness. If it weren't for his temper he might still be in the bigs. Bear hit two balls into the big palms behind the right-field fence, the trees I described in yesterday's tape. Kline made a play at second that was—let me see if I can reconstruct it. I called for a breaking ball on the fists to Rymoff. So, of course, Wilt decides to blow one by him about belt high on the inside corner of the plate. The Bear nails it in the hole between second and first. Steve goes flat, spears the thing, and rolls almost into the first-base dugout. Now, that's the kinda play that makes me kinda sick. I mean, it shows me just how good we can be—not great, maybe, we've got our weaknesses here and there—but good enough to win three games.

"Hell, I've said it before and I'll say it again: The problem is attitude. They've been acting like a bunch of assholes all week . . ."

The tape stopped. He backed it up and listened again.

". . . been acting like bunch of assholes all week, undermining everything I've tried to do. I knew Elmer's good cop-bad cop wasn't going to win me any popularity contests, but . . ."

Holding the recorder at arm's length, he relaxed his grip, and watched the plastic case bounce on the concrete floor.

A locker slammed, a wooden bench banged to the floor, and a white medicine cabinet tipped sideways, spilling bottles of alcohol and rolls of white athletic tape. The door to the dugout tunnel slammed.

". . . so anyhow, if we can get any help from guys like Ballard and Albaugh, Bunny comes through, and just doesn't hurt us, then we've got a shot. I know it sounds crazy, but I was telling the Giant the other night, if Billy throws the knuckler for strikes, if we get in some kind of shape, if we get any hitting from . . ."

The recorder droned on to the empty room.

The door clicked open. The spikes creaked past the lockers again. The man dodged the overturned cabinet, reached under the bench, scooped up the plastic panel, and clicked it in place where the recorder's batteries were exposed.

"I've been meeting the ball pretty good, still no real power, just punching it, trying to go with the pitch. I . . ."

Handy little items, the microrecorders. He slipped it into his uniform pocket and clacked out of the room again.

Horton read the newspaper headline, leaned back on the bench, and spit his toothpick at the water cooler.

OBEDIENCE SCHOOL ENDS TOMORROW
HOOTER HORTON STILL IN DOGHOUSE

Barnes had nailed him again. Let the bitch blast away. He'd keep making his notes, recording the diary. In a year or so she'd be browsing around some Baltimore bookstore and there he'd be, grinning up at her from an autograph table. Horton closed his eyes and smiled. Barnes had the book under her arm and had lined up in front of the big handpainted sign:

MEET HOOTER HORTON
THE COMEBACK KIDS
NEW YORK TIMES BEST SELLER
TENTH WEEK

Albaugh ducked into the dugout and smiled at Mouse Magruder. "What's happening?" he said. He drew a cone of water from the cooler and flopped down on the bench.

"Hey, don't ask me, the what's-happening man is over there. How 'bout it, Horton, you're our little fact-gatherer, right?" Mouse said.

Horton saw the grin. His eyes dropped back to the newspaper again.

Good idea, Elmer, Horton thought, get old friends together for a major league fantasy, be something they'd remember for the rest of their lives.

Magruder laughed, patted Albaugh on the back, and walked out on the field. Albaugh swirled a long, wet piece of hair in a way that wound around and covered half his head. Horton popped another toothpick in his mouth.

Bats cracked, gloves pocked. The Giant kicked and threw. Kline hit a climber into the gap in right. Jug Brown turned, took two steps, leaped, and grabbed the ball in front of the 340-foot sign. Albaugh pulled a short-stemmed pipe from his hip pocket and struck a match on the metal bench.

"She knows just how far to go. Nothing's libelous. Snide but damn good. At least she's not writing politics, thank God for that," Albaugh said, and blew a smoke ring toward a rack of long metal bats.

"I don't know what you did to get her started, but I'd go to her, try to talk. Horton, politically speaking, this series is killing me. Every Democrat in the country is reading this crap. We're embarrassing the president. I hope you know that!"

Horton nodded, picked up the *Palm Beach Tribune,* and folded the paper in half. At least Baldy's silent treatment had ended. It was the first time the attorney had spoken since Elmer's good cop-bad cop plan went into effect.

"Thanks, I'll keep that in mind," Horton said, and closed his eyes. The bench squeaked, cleats scraped. When Horton looked up, all that remained was a lingering ring of smoke. It drifted for a second, then broke in the catcher's face. He coughed, spat another toothpick, and opened the *Tribune.*

BARNSTORMING
By Larry Barnes

There's trouble in Fantasyland. Cheer up, Mickey. It's not Orlando. The New Becton Hot Dogs are at it again.

If you'll recall Monday's column, we left Hooter Horton, the team's appointed captain, sending his pets to obedience school. Now, if my sources are correct, the fetching, sitting up, and heeling has been going rather slowly. You might even say that Horton's Dogs have been rolling over and playing dead. A few have lost their manners completely. Albaugh, Wilt, Magruder, and Kline have forgotten how to speak.

Oh, here's another, by the way: That wasn't really a freak snowstorm that hit West Palm Beach. Horton closed practices to the press last Monday, and we've been throwing confetti all week. But when the Dogs come out of hiding, they're in for a spanking, I fear. Horton's discipline hasn't exactly been following them off the field. Here's the latest West Palm scuttlebutt on our Dogs, sort of a day-by-day tally sheet on rugs chewed, piddled carpets, etc., etc., etc.

Monday, June 27—Five players are seen heaving their Cheerios after a three-mile morning run.

That afternoon Odie Wilt is stricken with a viral attack and misses practice. As it turns out, he's so ill that he falters on the backside at Lagoon Lake Country Club and closes bogey, bogey, bogey. The poor pitcher just isn't up to par.

Horton is in trouble. It's like he's had a personality change. The Hyde side of the persona is in camp, driving the Dogs insane. An unnamed source on the roster calls the captain "a loser who's trying to turn something fun into a @#&*ing marine boot camp."

Tuesday, June 28—Daniel Gross, board member of Elmer's Little Giants, Inc., rumored to be attempting a company coup, is seen at Marietta's Bar and Grill drinking it up with two Hot Dog players and a couple of Poughkeepsie Pintails. Hearsay on this one, but the word on the street is that Elmer the Giant has declared Gross off-limits. This is beginning to sound a little like professional wrestling—good guys, bad guys, a couple of filthy McNastys as managers. Help me on this one, readers. Is Larry getting sucked in? Is this Little Series becoming some kind of glitzy Wrestle Mania-type deal?

Wednesday, June 29—Around the Ramada pool today the postpractice talk doesn't sound much like Horton's big league fantasy. The little boys are growing up before our very eyes. A few beers after practice, a cannonball here, a can opener there, and pretty soon we're talking contracts and endorsements. Here's what one sunning Dog suggested.

Get ready: If Elmer's Little Giants, Inc., sells the Dugout deal, then they all should renegotiate. The $5,000 is peanuts, he said. With the right agent, hell, who knows? We might find ourselves doing afterdinner stuff—we'd be perfect for a Miller Lite commercial.

I'm sure the Ramada's poolboy isn't keeping score on our training athletes, but if anyone is interested, here's how the empties counted out: beer cans 47, rum bottles 3, wine bottles 4. I cleaned up after the pups myself.

Thursday, June 30—I've got to give it to the old coot. Elmer Thumma knows his way to the tiny, tight hearts of America's sporting press. An all-you-can-eat-and-drink press conference today in the Grove Stadium parking lot. Plenty of food, lots of booze, and more quotes than you can shake a pencil or a microphone at.

Oh, the real reason for this little get-together? Elmer thought it might be a good way to introduce America to Joby Suehowicz, a fan activist who believes the Little Series will bring a sense of consciousness to the major league players. Suehowicz is the guy from Chicago who led several aborted fan walkouts during last summer's strike. Long hair, wide mustache, short legs, tall poles, large signs, a guy you might have stepped over on Stanyan Street if you toured Haight Ashbury in the summer of '68. Joby plans to launch a "peaceful protest" in conjunction with the Little Series.

And the Giant appears to be dancing on this one. He needs to bring all the attention he can to the Series with an anti-big league guy like Joby, the commissioner's liable to (1) squelch the series before it gets going and (2) start tossing Elmer's Little Giants, Inc., out of major league ball parks like it was a fan who'd just touched a fair-ball double. And as if that weren't enough to make our spinners tingle, the big guy leaked us a telegram from the board of Elmer's Little Giants, Inc., saying that if he goes ahead with the series, the next time he tries to sit in the ELG, Inc., president's chair, not to be surprised if he lands in this guy Gross's lap.

Great, Larry, you say, you've given us the *National Enquirer* angle—Dogs hates Hooter, Daniel hates Elmer, Elmer hates McKeen—but how's the team shaping up?

Tomorrow, okay! Elmer's opening up the pups' final practice for one last look-see. The man is precious. Here's how he closed his press conference today: "I know everybody's going to be packing for Chicago, but if you'll just drop by our last practice tomorrow, I think it will be worth your while. You know, it's amazing what a bunch of 'talented' ballplayers can do in a week's time. We just ain't the Dogs we used to be!"

Let's have a show of hands from the fans! Are we holding our breaths? Is anybody turning blue? Tomorrow, okay! Now for the Lord's sake, even if you have to take something, try to get some sleep.

The shrieks of Mouse Magruder's daily five/ten/fifteen-dollar pepper game drowned out the ring of the dugout phone.

"Mouse, how about clearing away from the steps, somebody's gonna back down here and bust their ass," Horton said and tossed the newspaper on the floor.

"How about getting bent! And while you're up, answer the fucking phone," Magruder said. He pounded a ball between Ballard's legs and screamed with laughter again. Horton's players were coming around. Now if Wilt would only speak.

Horton stopped at the cooler, filled a paper cone, and drank. "Cripes, hold your water, I'm coming," he said and picked up the telephone. "Yo," he said. He frowned, then smiled in a curious way. "You're kidding! Hell, yes, I'm glad. Well, Larry, I'm sure you'll write it how you damn well please. No, the New Becton Hot Dogs are delighted. So try to work that somewhere into my quote," he said, and dropped the receiver on the floor.

Horton walked to the top step of the dugout, cupped his hands, and shouted, "Now, hear this! The New Becton Hot Dogs will play to a capacity crowd in Wrigley on Sunday! I repeat, a capacity crowd!"

Thumma balked midmotion and stared in from the mound. Kline dropped his bat and walked out of the cage. Magruder slapped another ground ball at Wilt's feet. "Says fucking who?" Mouse said.

"Says Larry Barnes. They just settled the strike," Horton said.

•12•

HORTON GRABBED THE METAL BAR AND YANKED
the mask from his sweat-soaked face. The water sprayed the batter's box, dust puffed, and the powder turned a coffee brown.
Above the left-field stands the hot Florida sun enriched the diamond, making the grass a dark jade color.

Horton adjusted his chest protector, pulled up the mask, and let
his eyes rove freely through the park. A volley of cups popped in
the right-field bleachers. A squadron of Little Leaguers recruited
by Thumma for "photo opportunities" patrolled the empty seats.

But inside the box-seat railing, the old ballpark was alive and
well. The strike had ended. The press had been reprieved. They
were like ants on a wine bottle, crawling in circles, celebrating
baseball's good news. One last pre-series story about Elmer's Little
League circus, fly to Chicago, and watch the old man's hot dog
promo shrivel up and die, write the "I told you so" piece, and
they'd be home free, back covering major league baseball again.

Horton heard Wilt tell a reporter, "I haven't seen you guys this
high since the day Bowie suspended George."

In by the dugouts, cameras jockeyed for position and photographers leapfrogged tripods and cables searcing for angles and van-
tage points. In front of the third-base box seats, McKeen's pros
held bats, posed for still pictures, and conducted TV interviews.
One setup had Pazerelli linked arm and arm with Ensor and
Graham. A fat man with an old four-by-four Kodak was straight-
ening the black caps and positioning players. No need to turn
Pazerelli away from the sun, he won't squint, Horton thought.

Horton felt a hand on the shoulder of his chest protector.

"Would you mind, just the two of us over by the dugout?" The
voice had a familiar raspy sound.

He turned into a sheepish smile.

"Lanny Celebreze," the man said. The right hand went out. Then he pushed the ruby bolla on the string tie up a notch.

"Hey, Mr. Celebreze. How's it going? Does this mean I'm gonna make the wall?"

"Yep, I got your spot marked off. I just got one taken with Thumma and one with Wilt. I'm startin' a whole new wall, down that hall to the Hideaway, back there where you and Barnsie sat."

The little man pranced back and forth in the grass as he talked. "I guess I was a little impolite last week. Hell, I didn't know who the hell the Hot Dogs were, and you know with Larry how she's always yanking everybody's chain.

"Over here, Donna."

The Instamatic flew up in front of the bright red lips, an arm wrapped around Horton's shoulder, and both men looked at the camera and grinned.

"There, painless, now you're famous," Celebreze said. "It's crazy. I mean, I still can't figure out why, but you guys are the hottest thing to hit this beach in a long, long time."

A bell rang and a squad of groundskeepers rolled the cage away. "Let's shake it up!" Horton shouted and the New Becton Hot Dogs straggled out on the field. Elmer took the mound in long-legged stretching steps. He tossed a resin bag on the grass, cleared his throat, and addressed his guests. "We hope you'll enjoy the action. We're gonna play a little something called workup. It'll be a four-at-bat, seven-in-the-field intrasquad kinda deal," he said. Mike Dougherty of *The Miami Herald* groaned and popped a beer. Larry Barnes yawned and rubbed a dollop of zinc oxide on her sunburned nose. Thumma surveyed his defense, taking time to move Albaugh a step in, shade Brown to the left. When he had backed Magruder to the warning track, he turned and faced the plate.

For the next forty minutes the New Becton Hot Dogs played semiflawless ball. McKay kicked a grounder into a two-base error. Magruder lost a ball in the sun. But hitters hit, fielders caught, and Mouse even ran out a walk.

Horton dropped to his haunches and sang to the Giant through the bars of his mask, "Hum to me, babe, you the man, whaddya say, whaddya chuck, easy out, no batter here."

The words were right, but his voice had lost that old staccato auctioneer quality. If he expected to be heard in a major league park he'd need more volume and resonance, he thought.

"I got your bat right here, Horton," the Bear said, giving his privates a loving little tug.

We want a hit! We want a hit! The chant flowed down the right-field line. Suehowicz, perched on the railing in front of the WORL-TV camera, looked like Mitch Miller directing the chorus of Little Leaguers.

The Bear swung the bat in a rhythmic way, keeping time with the distant chant. The bat touched the Bear's massive shoulder, pendulumed forward, then rose and froze in midair. He looked down the barrel and took aim at the Giant's head. The target spit and tugged his black NY cap. Rymoff came up on his toes and spat back. The brown glob arched toward the mound, sputtered, and nestled in the green thickness between the Giant and home plate.

Horton checked his fielders. Mouse hugged the line in right. Billy clung to the first-base sack. The Hot Dogs were in position! Playing the big left-handed hitter to pull. Had good cop-bad cop actually worked?

The Giant stepped off the rubber and looked Odie Wilt back to second base. He paused long enough to read WHAT'S SO BIG ABOUT BIG LEAGUE BASEBALL? on Suehowicz's bedsheet flapping from the center-field fence, then turned and toed the rubber again. He rocked once and came over the top. The pitch broke hard, down and in, catching the black of the plate.

The Bear unscrewed a swing that cooled the catcher's sweat-soaked face. Horton winced as the ball slammed in the pocket of his mitt. The Giant could still bring it. Bunny had clocked him earlier in the week at seventy-three miles per hour, a solid five miles above the old man's age.

"Two strikes and a ball," Horton said, reminding Rymoff that he was down to his last strike.

"Fuck you, Horton," the Bear said, and easing the bat forward, he took aim on the Giant again.

Horton dropped his hand in front of his cup and flashed the signals rapid fire. Wilt backed off the bag, crouched, and squinted. The sun was giving him trouble, making it tough to see Horton's signs. Stealing women and signs were Wilt's favorite sports.

I've gotta have the change-up, Horton thought. The hard one set him up. He'd have to pick his moment carefully, catch Wilt looking the other way. Between second and third, just inches off the outfield fringe, McKay pawed the dirt like a Shetland pony. Once, then twice, it was the pickoff signal, the one they'd used in Little League. The Rabbit sprang suddenly to his left, holding his glove as a target behind Wilt's head. Thumma turned to the bag and scowled at Bun-Bun. The old man had forgotten the play. The Giant toed the rubber again and directed his attention to the plate.

Wilt stooped suddenly, snatched a handful of dirt, and flung it in the Rabbit's face. Horton's hand flew down. His fist slammed shut. The Giant nodded. Change-up! The dirt bomb had done the trick.

"Easy, rock, what say, big guy, fire to me, you the man," he chattered. Behind his babble Horton heard the Hot Dogs pick up his chant. First Kline at second base. "Hum chuck, hum fire!" he shouted. Then Albaugh at third. "Be the man, Elmer, be the man!"

Cripes, Horton thought, they sound just like a baseball team. And as the Dogs' captain listened with pride, Russ Hodges slid behind the microphone again and took over the play-by-play.

"How you doin' everybody? Two down, second base occupied, and Bear Rymoff digging in, aiming the lumber at the mound. Rymoff's down to his last swing, but with this big guy at the plate, anything can happen, so light up a Chesterfield, sit back, and enjoy yourselves. Where there's smoke, there's fire."

"McKay, the Rabbit, eases in behind the bag at second. Wilt, always a dangerous runner, takes two, now three steps. Thumma gives him the look and Wilt sidesteps back toward the bag. Ernie, I've gotta be frank about McKay, he's been a real disappointment to the Dogs. He appears to be trying hard enough, but he just doesn't seem to be getting to half the balls he should at short.

. Frankly, we can't figure out why Horton hasn't made some moves to correct that situation. Ernie, I'm afraid he's just not in very good shape.

"Heck, check me if I'm wrong, but I have him down for a horse collar in four trips today, so it's not like the little scudder won the shortstop job at the plate.

"Thumma goes into his windup and comes in with a letter-high fastball. The old grizzly swings and pulls it deep, deep, and foul! He's been knocking monkeys and coconuts out of those right-field palms all week.

"Folks, this could be the last out of the Dogs' training camp, so it's mighty fitting that the go-ahead run dancing out there on second base be number nineteen himself, Odie "the Enforcer" Wilt. And frankly, Ernie, it's a real kick to watch the old right-hander still flinging them like he can. Thumma's sixty-eight years of age, still has his health, and one heck of a competitor, too. He's bearing down right now on a middle-aged truck driver like it was the '37 Series again and Lou Gehrig at the plate.

"Rymoff is the fellow who has to come through if Wilt's gonna get them that go-ahead run. Here's the pitch, the big guy swings and . . . pops it up, a little can of corn out toward center field. McKay races back, here comes Brown tearing hard from center, and it's falling, falling . . . base hit!

"Wilt's off and running, rounding third now, he's gonna try and score. Brown scoops and fires. Oh, boy, Horton's diggin' in, settin' himself at home."

The field exploded into a mass of motion. Horton tossed his mask, set himself, and watched the white blur fly toward the plate. He could hear Wilt now, thundering down the third-base line. The ball hit the grass, skipped, and slammed in the pocket of his outstretched glove. He squeezed and felt stitches through leather.

Hodges again. "One hop, perfect throw, here comes Wilt, Horton turns, and . . ."

Horton felt the initial shock in a numbing way. For a millisecond he was a wide receiver enjoying his first crackback block. He heard his mouth suck in search of breath. Then his feet were lost and he flipped and turned in the air. At impact his ears slammed shut. His eyes watered, and when they cleared, he was looking up at a gigantic pink thumb.

"You're out!" the Giant screamed.

Then the mike belonged to Hodges again. Horton felt no pain. It was as though he weren't there at all. He heard the voice of the announcer and saw himself back in the little brownstone on 127th Street, nosed up to the Halo-Lite on his mom's Sylvania TV.

It sounded like a Wednesday nighter. Had Hodges called boxing? Yes, Dunphy and Gillette were the Garden and Fridays. Hodges called them for Pabst on Wednesdays from St. Nick's Arena.

"Horton's down, and from here at ringside it looks like it may be for the count. Oh, Wilt really got away with one that time, Art Donovan missed that one. Wilt slipped the shoulder into Horton's midsection, and that, my friends, was no legal knockdown.

"Two, three, four. It may be bye-bye, baby for Horton. No, he's up on one knee now, rubber-legged but staggering to his feet. Here we go again. Horton shakes his head, he's clearing the cobwebs. Now he's up on his toes, flicking that left jab into the face of a very surprised Odie Wilt.

"Wilt's a southpaw puncher, he's in front of us now, circling to his right. Oh, and it's a sharp left by Horton and a right and another right! Whoa, Wilt's down, I can't believe it! This is unbelievable! Horton's stunned the favorite with a flurry of sharp, well-thrown punches. Wilt's on the canvas. He's bleeding from the mouth, and from here it looks like the favorite might really be hurt.

"Folks, it's bedlam above us, news reporters, beer cups, hot dogs, mustard flying through the air, TV cameras storming through the ropes.

"Wilt's on his feet, wobbly, spitting blood, saying things we can't repeat. Horton on his toes again, moves forward, stalking the wounded champion. Wait a minute, Horton's sticking out his glove. I can't believe it. Horton wants to shake, call it all off.

"But oh, no, now Wilt's gone stark raving mad, filling the air with wild furious punches. Both men are down again, rolling across the canvas. Wilt's on top, kicking, clawing. Horton's taking some really brutal shots," Hodges said.

The mike went dead. Hodges was off the air. Horton found himself suspended, in the grip of the Giant, dangling above home plate. Through blood-streaked eyes he could see Wilt hanging in a similar position. The Bear held his catch in one powerful paw, flipping and kicking like a freshwater trout.

"Wimpy little fuck!" Wilt screamed through swelling lips.

"Cheap-shot, blindsiding asshole!" Horton countered, spitting a stream of red.

"Clrocksucker."

"Pligfucker."

The fight had left them with swollen lips and talking in tongues. The Giant tightened his grip. Horton felt a rush of pain.

"Okay, boys, that's all for today," Thumma said. "Now, if you'd be kind enough to clean your language up a tad, I think our TV friends are going to want some airable quotes to go with all that good action footage they just shot," he said.

Horton spat another glob of blood, wiped his eyes, and looked up into a pair of wide, wet eyes. Was Larry Barnes a fight fan? She had that glazy look, the one Janie got when an orgasm was on the way. Barnes glanced at her feet, then looked at Horton again. She shook her head, then turned and walked away. Horton felt the Giant at his back, pushing him toward the lights of a TV camera.

"Well, if you don't think these guys mean business, just take the tape you just shot, slo-mo it, freeze-frame it, run it back and forth a couple a dozen times. If you can find a slipped punch, old Elmer the Giant will get in front of these cameras again and eat his good-luck cap," he said, and gave the bent brim a couple of tugs.

Then Thumma threw his hand up as if to stop the cameras, and turned to Larry Barnes. She was composed now, smiling at the Giant.

"Now, Larry, hon, if you'll step forward, I'd like you to examine these two ugly faces. If I'm not mistaken, I believe you likened our series to professional wrestling in yesterday's column. Well, you won't find any blood capsules here. No sirree sir, the New Becton Hot Dogs are the McCoy, 100 percent for real," he said.

AN EMERGENCY TAPE FOR DOC MARKUM

OKAY, DOC, I KNOW THIS SOUNDS CRAZY, BUT what's a shrink expect from his prize patient? I'm Fed-Exing this session on the sixty-minute cassette because if I don't tell somebody my side of the story, the next headline I make will be about three picas high and buried on the obit page of *The Johnstonian Advertiser.*

I'm bumping along here in the *Hot Dog,* drinking beer, watching night fall on flatlands and a blue-black horizon crowded with fields of waving wheat. Indiana road signs are flipping by on I-65 announcing towns like Ogilville and Fickle, burgs I'll never see again. The weenie's inching north like a slug. We've been stopping in podunks, picking up our keys to the "cities," and parading up and down Main Street, U.S.A., with Little League teams. You've probably seen some of it on TV. Cripes, I had no idea there were so many *PM Magazines.*

But Elmer's got the tip of the weenie aimed right at Chicago now, and if we don't get slowed down tomorrow by more of the Suehowicz God Bless Little League Baseball parades, we should be checking in at the Regency Hyatt about 6:00 P.M.

So anyway, if you'd kind of stay by the phone tomorrow evening, I'd sure like to talk. What I need is your reaction to some of the stuff I'm going to hit you with in this tape.

The Dogs are a pretty diverse little group: doctor, truck driver, promoter, gambler, teacher, drug rehab, and a political bookworm intellectual. Bunny, our shortstop, has MS and is going to die, and sometimes I think I might beat him to it.

At least Elmer's doing all right; he's whistling "Annie Laurie" and is leaning on the weenie's gas pedal harder than he used to thumb the old meat market scales. The rest of the Dogs are asleep, curled up like frankfurters in warm, homemade buns.

I'm closing my eyes now but not to nap. Get your egg timer out. Session is about to begin. The only difference is that I'm talking into my new tape recorder, I've got Bud number seven in my hand, and I guess I'm getting semiripped. I've got you visualized like this: You're perched in your chair, picking lint off your herring-bone, gnawing your number two pencil, and cutting your eyes at the clock. Just kidding, Doc. You know how Janie used to complain about how mouthy the beer makes me get.

Now this isn't the Budweiser talking. I'm not trying to be a smart ass or anything, but I'm going to kick this session off with one of your lead lines for authenticity and to get me going good.

"Well, any special agenda today, Walker? Anything we should talk about? Maybe something that came up since the last time we met?"

"Anything come up? Yeah, Doc, me and this bunch of guys I played Little League with jumped in a hot-dog–shaped bus with a baldheaded old man and a couple days later we're the hottest news story since they lifted the Lindbergh baby. Yeah, I'd say a few things have come up. The Giant's multimillion-dollar company is riding on the outcome of a baseball series that was supposed to be fun and games. He's named me captain because I was their leader as a kid. And for the past week I've done everything but hang an E on Grove Stadium's scoreboard for the big guy's error in judgment.

The rest, of course, is minor stuff. I'm out of Valium, drinking like a pipe fitter, and passing out in public places. The other day my recorder and a cassette of notes disappeared from the locker room. Oh, yeah, this morning there was blood in my stool. Did I mention that I still can't hit a breaking pitch to save my ass?

Now that we've taken care of the incidentals, here's a little disclosure that I needed a few beers and the privacy of a tape recording to make. Since I've been a kid, whenever I get a little nervous or something, Russ Hodges, the old New York Giants' play-by-play man, starts babbling away, announcing my life in my ear. Doc, I can't make him stop. He's been driving me nuts all week.

How do I sound so far? Pretty stable, turning the corner, coming around? I get the feeling that none of your usual mood lifters apply in this case.

CLICK!

"I'm back; that click was me signing out for a beer. Everybody's still z-ing except me, and the Giant, of course. Remember the ex-Chicago Cub? Wilt, the one from that two-session $140 lecture you gave me about the evils of hero worship? Well, cheer up, he's not my idol anymore. We had this big fight, really showed our asses. That's right—you probably read about it or saw it on TV.

Oh, here's one, something I haven't admitted: I'm ass over spikes in lust with Larry Barnes, the woman that's been popping me with the morning paper and rubbing my nose in the ink.

Doc, you ought to see the woman. I know what you're saying: "There you go, Walker, thinking with your dick again!" And, of course, you're right. Take away the soft green eyes, the honey hair, the legs, and you've got the woman that Bear Rymoff, our Shakespearean scholar, dubbed "the unkindest cunt of all."

Here's another thing about Barnes that I hate to admit: The stuff she's been writing is shitty as hell. But what she's said about the team has been right down the heart of the plate. Did I say that? Cripes, I must be drunk. Of course, if she knew what I know about these guys, she'd be shocked that they were able to do things like stand and open their eyes and flies in the bright Florida sunshine.

Like I said, Barnes might think she's a real hotshot reporter, but Woodward and Bernstein she ain't. Here's the box score on the Dogs, the vital stats she missed last week:

DRUNK AND DISORDERLY   2
ASSAULT AND BATTERY   1
PARKING TICKETS   16
DAMAGE TO PUBLIC PROPERTY $765.39

Oh, yeah, and Kliny personally treated two cases of clap. This bit of info would make a nice little color box in *USA Today,* don't you think?

CLICK

I'm back again, had to hit the john and grab a cold one. Now, here's another pisser that's been driving me nuts: There's this guy Daniel Gross on the Giant's board of directors hanging around the team a lot. He appeared at yesterday's kiss-off press conference. He's as elusive as hell. Around a lot, but somehow I never manage to see him. Anyway, the guy is trying to take over the big guy's business, and I've got my suspicions about a few things. More later on this when we talk on the phone. I didn't say anything to the Giant because I didn't want to upset him, but I did mention it to Wilt yesterday when we were waiting to get into the batting cage.

Here's my ex-hero's response: Wilt says, fuck it, that I'm to stick to my job, which is to convince these losers that it's good to bend over every once in a while when they see a ground ball coming their way. Then he gives me one of his little shit-eating grins, says he didn't mean it and asks me please not to quote him. I'm not sure if I still know him. Elmer says that I never did, "Odie's O.K. Hen, he's always been like that."

Next subject: the writing. I remember seeing your eyebrows fly up when I told you I had this great idea for a book. Well, I haven't had any publishers jamming contracts in my pocket, but when I locked myself in the bathroom at the Ramada last week, I wasn't just jerking off.

When Bunny goes to sleep, I talk into the old tape recorder. I'm filling about a cassette a day with notes on this zoo, keeping a diary of the trip. Oh, yeah, and I'm saving the "Barnstorming" columns. I don't know if it will work, but I'm considering opening each chapter with one of her bullshit quotes. Here's one I've been playing around with; it's from the Friday, June 31, column: "The New Becton Hot Dogs are God's warning to middle-aged men. Boys, stick to the onion dip, your easy chairs, and TV sets, and never, never wear double knits!"

I'm holding that one, and when a whaletail like the Bear pulls a gamer glove play, I'll drop Barnes' little blurb above a description of Rymoff's acrobatics.

Doc, I don't know how all this is going to end! Me in a padded cell babbling color commentary for Hodges' play-by-play—a headline like OLD LITTLE LEAGUE CATCHER DROPS POP FLY—THEN DEAD! Who knows? maybe I'll be off somewhere growing toupees in my palm big enough to coif Howard Cosell. But however it shakes down—crazy, half dead, or blind from masturbation—Hooter Horton is going to write his book. This is one commitment I'm going to keep.

CLICK

Back again. Women! Remember that gum card-torching blonde? The one that use to accompany me to your office for those famous "Did too!" "Did not!" sessions? Well, she called last night, saw me on the tube, she said, and has been reading about us in this guy Larry Barnes' column! She's going to try to come up from OSU to Cleveland to see us play. Can you believe it, Janie Horton a Little League groupie? You know what a fan Janie is. Hell, you sat there with me and listened to all her horseshit theories about how my attraction to the bat and balls was some kind of sexual inferiority complex.

Now, more about this guy Larry Barnes. The lady Wilt screwed under the lights last Sunday night while a balcony of deviates looked on is old Hooter's latest fantasy. Be sure to ask me about the balcony scene when I call tomorrow night. Anyway, the woman crosses her legs during batting practice, and I swear, Doc, I think I'm going to go right through my cup.

Last night at the going-away party the N. B. Dogs set yet another example for America's Little Leaguers: They trashed a place called Riotellia's Grill. I went because Bunny seemed to be feeling better. We haven't been going out much at night, and everybody's been saying how we're nerds and probably queer. Fuck 'em; the Rabbit's exhausted, and I've been making the nightly recordings. Besides, here's something that even Bunny doesn't know: There's a playground with lights across from the motel, and the Giant and I have been sneaking over there and working with Billy on the knuckler a couple of hours every night.

Anyway, Bun-Bun was feeling pretty chipper, so we went. Wilt and I had that run-in at practice, a bang-bang play at the plate. So at the shitkick a couple of guys who hadn't been speaking all week came up and said, "nice job." Then about six beers into the evening, what do you think? Wilt walks up like nothing happened, sticks out his hand and apologizes. Elmer's right, he's full of Billy Martin. Of course, I shook and made up. Which wasn't that easy considering the fact that my jaw's all puffed up like Billy's marsh-mallow salesman.

I did tell you about Elmer's good cop-bad cop, didn't I?

Sorry, Doc, I know. The beer drinker's rambling a bit. That's one of the reasons I haven't been partying with the guys. I can't seem to drink and keep my mouth shut. Oh, here's another one. At the get-together the Giant and I are shooting the crap and up Barnes walks like we used to date in high school or something. Am I suddenly doing something right? I mean, the bitch has been destroying me in print for the past week, and there's this big wet smile, flashing eyes, and then she's wondering if I'd like to dance.

Pretty soon we're bumping around and I'm about to trip over my tongue when she leans over and warm-breaths my ear with the following bit of news: "We've got to let bygones be bygones, Hooter; the Giant's invited me to ride the *Hot Dog* to Chicago with you guys."

CATCHER RIPS WHEEL FROM DRIVER'S HANDS
TAKES 48-FOOT *HOT DOG* OFF CHICAGO BRIDGE

What's God up to here, Doc? Have I been sent back to Little League to die?

Oh, here's the answer to your next question: She's here. I woke her up when I popped my last beer. She's in the back with Jug now, conducting an interview for a series of what she's calling personal-ity pieces.

CLICK

Just had another mood shift. Had to pass Bun-Bun when I went to take a leak and pick up a beer. The Rabbit's going to die, Doc. Giant says this is his home-run trot. Jeez, I love that little fucker. You've heard me talk about the Rabbit, but never as a grown-up before. I was pissed at first but now I'm glad the Giant roomed us together. Last night will tell you what kind of guy McKay is.

I hear him kind of gurgling and giggling in his sleep. I listen a while and when I finally can't stand any more, I kinda kick his bed, trying to get him to roll over and cut the sound effects. The Rabbit sits straight up, looks at me, and says, "Damn, I thought I'd died and gone to heaven." Except it wasn't a cliché, not the way the Rabbit said it. I mean, you could tell right off that Bun-Bun really meant it. He had this peaceful look in his eyes and a strange, faraway stare.

"I was dreaming," he says, "kneeling in the on-deck circle at Wrigley. I look up and there's Bonnie, Danny, and Mike wearing white Hot Dog caps and smiling at me from their first-base boxes. The noise is so loud and constant that you can't hear anything, the infield chatter, the vendors, the guys in the bleachers, it's like it just all runs together. I know it doesn't make any sense, but it's so loud that it's almost like quiet. Anyway, I'm watching the Pintail infielders whip the ball around the horn, following Pazerelli's warm-up pitches, when all of a sudden the voice of God booms over the PA system."

Get ready, Doc. Guess what God said! "And now, leading off for the New Becton Hot Dogs, the shortstop, Darryl "Bun-Bun" McKay. McKay!"

Way to go, Bun-Bun! Need an opinion, Doc. If I bench him now, will it be against God's will?

Oh, one more thing. I'm getting a little beery, so I'll cut it short. Last night at the party, just hours before God spoke to Bun-Bun over the Wrigley PA, the Giant and I were talking, and the big guy hit on the very same subject.

"Hooter," he said, "forget my business interests, your book, throw out evening the score with McKeen and whatever it was that made the rest of these guys give up three weeks of their lives, crawl into the *Hot Dog* bus, and commence to show their tails to

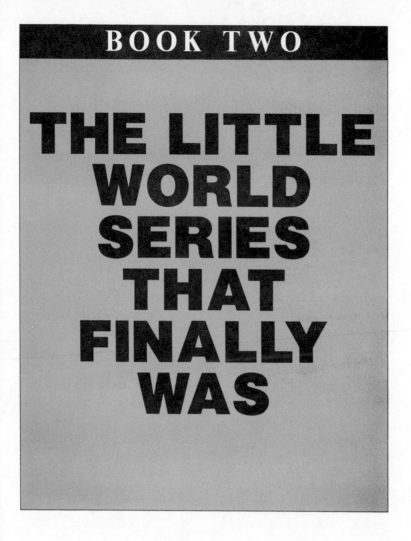

BOOK TWO

THE LITTLE WORLD SERIES THAT FINALLY WAS

• 1 •

THE WEENIE JERKED AND BUMPED ALONG WAVE-
land Avenue. A cab roared past the pinkish hood, the Giant
braked and swore. Horton tossed his lineup card on the dashboard
and joined his teammates in song.

"On State Street, that great street, I just wanna say . . . they do
things they don't do on Broadway. . . . You'll have the time, the
time of your life, I saw a man, he danced with his wife in Chicago,
Chicago . . ."

The light at the Seminary intersection flashed red, brakes
hissed, and the *Hot Dog*'s weight shifted left. A roar went up, and
players skirmished and fought for window seats. The signal turned
green. The Giant eased the bus over the crosswalk and pointed up
through the big bubble windshield.

"Wrigley Field!" he said.

A classic red sign was wrapped around the stadium front:

HOME OF THE CHICAGO CUBS
CUBS VS. CARDS TODAY 1:05

Red-and-white pennants topped a concrete facade trimmed in
pastel green. Blue-and-red Budweiser beach umbrellas shaded the
ballpark's sidewalk restaurant along Addison Street.

"Jeez, I must be uptight. I was looking up for stadium lights,"
Horton said, his face flushing with the admission.

A sea of pearl-gray uniforms filled the bus's rearview mirror. A
flock of Little Leaguers had the Dogs nosed up to the windows,
waving and shouting. Programs and autograph books pressed

against the glass. Street vendors hawked their Cub wares, hats and blue-and-white pennants bobbed with the moving crowd. Bunny reached down, took a baseball from the pool of churning hands, and scratched his name on the souvenir. As he dropped the ball into a grateful little palm, a huge yellow placard severed the Rabbit from the mobbing fans:

FUCK BIG LEAGUE BASEBALL

A potbellied crew cut in a yellow SCREW THE BIGS T-shirt waved the message in Bunny's face.

"I'm not so sure about this guy Suehowicz," the Giant said with a grunt.

A big Coors tanker turned left, slid in behind the left-field bleachers, and took its place in a noisy line of offloading vendors. Horton stared up at Wrigley's double decks and smiled. This is it! The Little Series That Finally Was. He felt surprisingly sound. He'd had several nice phone sessions with Markum. One long talk last night and another shorter "Good luck, you can do it" call about nine that morning. The good doctor would never believe what they were experiencing now. He watched the crowd tighten around the weenie. Bud-Man T-shirts, Cub pinstripes, more Little Leaguers, parents, and sign-carrying protesters than he'd ever imagined.

"It's so much bigger than I . . ." he managed, and pulling a fan's program into the bus, he signed his name. There, Hooter Horton, he'd done it—given his first autograph.

"Like the man said, you ain't seen nothin' yet," the Giant said with a laugh. " 'Member what I used to tell you boys, about the feeling, how it was when we'd be cutting through the parkin' lots at Ebbets and Yankee Stadium?"

The rear of the bus was madness, a collage of gray-and-orange uniforms, programs, and black baseball caps. The Bear popped a beer. Thumma turned and jerked his thumb. "Put her back where she came from," he said. The refrigerator opened and closed again. Horton watched the Dogs work the windows. They were signing, shaking, blessing the masses just like big league ballplayers now.

"You'll know what I'm talking about when we get in the lot. The crowds get so tight that the bus starts to shaking. It's a tingling feelin', somethin' you'll never forget," he said, and jamming his sweat-soaked head through the little side window, he grinned and waved the black Giants' cap.

"The Dogs are in town. Ain't nothin' wrong with baseball that a bunch of old Little Leaguers can't cure!" he shouted.

Horton focused on Larry Barnes. The columnist crossed her legs, giggled, and threw an ice cube at Kline. She gazed out the window and wrote a flurry of notes in her spiral book. He'd never understand Elmer. Love thy enemy, turn the other cheek, but you don't let a poison pen ride the team bus.

As the *Dog* nosed into the parking lot on Seminary Avenue, a familiar face squirted out of the knot of humanity. Suehowicz had the long hair back in a ponytail and wore a T-shirt displaying the group's FBLB (Fuck Big League Baseball) acronym. Joby's bull-horn blasted. Rails shook as the el clacked by. The rumble of the train subsided. Joby's horn blasted again. Thumma said with a shrug, "He's a noisy one, all right."

Today is payback day. Today is payback day. When the Little League game is over, please leave the ballpark. I repeat, please leave the park. This is our one chance to save the game from greed. Baseball belongs to the fans, it's up to us to step in and take it back!

The combo of middle-aged men in red FBLB T-shirts looked like a South Chicago pawnshop band. They snaked among the sidewalk tables, raised their dented brass horns in salute to the bus, and cranked up a tinny version of "Take Me Out to the Ball Game." The Giant blew the *Hot Dog*'s horn and tapped the brakes. The crowd parted, and the bus inched forward again, headed for Gate K and the third-base locker room.

"How 'bout a look-see at your lineup, Horton?" Barnes said. And dropping down on the step to the cab, she rolled over a clean page in the pad.

She looked up from the book again and gave Horton her toothpaste ad smile. They had spoken only twice since the bus left Florida, once briefly in the lobby of the hotel when she'd been researching a sidebar on the selling of the Doggie Dugouts, and again last night on the phone. Barnes wanted a quote from Bunny. Horton refused to wake him, saying that the Rabbit had been asleep for hours.

"The lineup? Well, you won't be starting. But don't get me wrong—it's really been great having you on the team and all," he said.

Barnes laughed. "Very good, Hoot, very good. Now let's go bottom line for a second. Are you starting McKay at short?"

Horton looked through the bubble. Signs of protest popped up like crocuses among the brightly colored shirts.

LITTLE LEAGUE IS WHERE IT'S AT
THE FANS STRIKE BACK
STEAL BASES, NOT $$$$

"I haven't written anything down yet. You representing *The Baltimore Sun* or Odie Wilt?" he said.

"Always *The Sun,* but here's what Odie said on the subject," she said, and flipping the pages of her book, she read the quote. " 'If McKay plays and we lose because of one of his screwups, it's going to be Horton's ass. I'm not going out there throwing my brains out, putting my reputation on the line, to watch some little sieve let the game go through his legs,' " she quoted. " 'The other ex-major leaguers in this thing will understand where I'm coming from. If Horton wants to keep us in this series, he better get some people behind me!' "

"Wilt said that? You hear that, Elmer?" Horton swallowed. The Giant nodded, licked his finger, and gave his cap a tug.

"Okay, Larry, how about 'No comment'?" Horton said.

"That's fine. I guess we'll know soon enough," she said. She yawned, patted Thumma on the cap, and walked away.

Horton felt a sense of falling. The stomach was flipping and turning again. "How 'bout it, Elmer? What do you think about Bunny?" He turned back to the window and stared down into the wall of people wrapped around the big brown bus.

"It's your call," the Giant said.

Horton misinterpreted the sensation. He took the queasiness as a full-fledged warning and touched the sack for reassurance. He belched, swallowed, and prayed, "Don't let the breathing bag see action today."

"Thar she blows, feel her?" the Giant said with a grin.

Horton offered a contorted smile, stared at the Gate K sign, and tried to concentrate.

"That's it, that's the shaking feeling. Can you feel her? The crowd's moving the bus! That's when they love you, Hooter, when they press in tight like this. It's just like afore the '37 Series. It's the big leagues; welcome aboard, boy. Millions of men out there that would give their right testicle for an experience like this," he said.

The bus shimmied and shook. The mirror framed a picture Horton would never forget. The New Becton Hot Dogs were as white-faced as their nauseous captain. Bear, Mouse, Blinker, all quiet as mimes, like choirboys sitting there in their gray double knits.

Horton's eyes roved the aisles. Albaugh worked the brim of his black cap, flipping it up, then down. Rymoff yawned and stretched. Then yawned again. Ballard and Brown had a high-five abort. All four hands groping, missing in mid air. Even Magruder was feeling the pressure. He pounded the door of the john, screaming at Billy, "Do it or get off the pot!"

The Giant looked over at Horton and winked. "A little pregame nerves never hurt a club. No, sir, just need to get that first pitch thrown, then we'll be all right!"

"Be back in a minute. Gotta take a leak," Horton said.

"That's what's so great about fantasies. There's so much unbelievable shit going on," Rymoff said and squirted into the locker room like a big wet watermelon seed. Horton slammed the door and stopped to pant. Things were happening too fast. He needed time to catch his breath. The wild reception from the fans and now this: a long, yellow room divided by benches full of half-naked

Chicago Cubs. Jody Davis leaned against the wall, taping a bat handle. A barechested black man sat on a stool, rubbing oil into the pocket of his glove. "Crapola, that was Shawon Dunston," Horton said.

"Okay, move along. This here's a locker room. It ain't the Chicago Zoo," the Giant said. The Hot Dogs waddled along, adjusting uniforms, sucking in stomachs, following the Giant like ugly ducklings. "No lockers or showering privileges, but they've reserved us the lounge room so's we can have us a pregame meeting," Thumma said.

In a cubicle off the main room, B.J. Myers lay naked to the waist, stretched out on a rubdown table. Horton slowed down long enough to catch a snatch of the pitcher's conversation, something about his horse farm, the cost of stud fees, and being cheaper to do it yourself. Ryne Sandberg looked up from a box of baseballs, put down his pen, and told the Giant that he wished him luck.

A roar went up over by the dugout steps. "Lock up your kids and small pets, Odie the fucking Enforcer is back!" a Cub coach shouted. Wilt fired a roll of tape at the gray-haired man. Bull Durham reached out with his claw-size glove and picked it off.

"A hundred bucks on the Ducks!" the coach shouted.

"You've got it!" Wilt said. "The fuckin' wind's blowin' in!"

"Hello, Cubbies, how's it goin'?" the Giant said, cutting through the players with typical self-assurance.

When Thumma stopped to pat another Cub rear end, Graham Evans of *The Chicago Tribune* tossed a question to a man hunched over in a whirlpool bath. "You know Elmer here and his Little Leaguers are trying to screw you guys with your fans. They've got this Suehowicz out there working the parking lots trying to get everybody to walk after this exhibition game of theirs."

The big blond-haired boy stepped out of the swirling silver tub and shook his locks like a golden retriever. "Evans, here's a quote for you. I don't give a flying fuck about a bunch of old farts and their horseshit promotion. Christ, that's all I've been seeing on TV since we went on strike."

"Will you watch the game?" Barnes threw him a follow-up question.

The naked player bent over and picked up a towel, then turned on Barnes and slowly dried his hair. "Larry, we missed you, hon. One of our favorite pecker checkers," he said with a laugh. "Yeah, I'll watch. I used to be a Cub fan when I was a kid. So it'll be like old times watching Wilt get his dick knocked in."

The Giant corraled the Dogs into the Cubs' TV lounge, slammed the door, cracked his knuckles, and spat into an empty trash can. The players went ghost-faced again, sat stiff-legged on soft brown couches and a long Formica-topped table. The uniformed legs swung like pendulums ticking down a clock. Thumma shoved a fresh chaw of Levi Garrett into his jaw and began to count.

"Rymoff, Kline, McKay, Albaugh, Ballard, Brown, Magruder, Johnson, Horton. Where the hen is Wilt?"

The door open and slammed. Nine ballplayers jumped.

"Selling your frigging Doggie Dugouts. Zingraff from Quick-chow wanted to rub against some Cubs and get his kid some autographs," Wilt said.

"Oh, good. That's just fine. Now it's time we all had a little talk." The Giant was pacing, cutting up and down in front of his tabled players.

"Well, here we are. The drinkin' and womanizin' is over, all in the past. Now we're gonna have us some fun of a different kind. The Little Series is here just like I promised, and boys, we've got one horrendous opportunity in front of us," he said. Thumma's eye scanned the uniforms, then stopped on a tall, thin man cleaning his brown horned-rim glasses with a sheet of Eyesavers paper.

"Baldy, would it be fair to say that the president of the U.S. is going to be watching us for the next week or so?"

Albaugh folded his glasses and nodded. "Talked to him yesterday. Said he's got a sizable bet with the Speaker of the House."

"Okay. There you have it. The president of this country is bettin' on us. Who'da believed it? That's real encouraging to hear," he said. "Now, I'm not a meetin' man, you all know that, but I'm gonna open things up for the next couple a minutes, so if you got anything on your minds, for cripes' sakes, let's hear it now."

A refrigerator hummed. Jug stepped back into an empty metal closet. The door made a screeching sound. The Giant's pocket watch ticked away under his gray double knits.

Mouse looked at Horton and dropped his eyes to the floor. "All this team needs is a little leadership," he said. Kline cleared his throat, Rymoff tossed a roll of tape into the trash can the Giant had used as a spittoon.

Kline slid off the table and walked to Horton. His eyes were calm; he looked reassuring, doctorish, Horton thought.

"Hoot, I won't speak for the rest of them, but I'll tell you what I think. I gave up three weeks of a very lucrative practice for this experience. I want to win, but I'll be perfectly honest. The Little Series was a great idea, the TV, newspapers, it's all been a kick, but next week, when we wrap it up in Yankee Stadium, there are still gonna be a shitload of folks in China who don't give a damn about the New Becton Hot Dogs, Doggie Dugouts, or whether you get a happy ending for your book."

Horton scuffed his spikes on a wire mesh mat.

"Doc, you saying you don't want me to be captain?" Horton asked.

Thumma spat, hit the can again, and made it ring.

"Nah, just let us have fun. If we win, we win," he said.

The Giant ambled over to Kline and put his arm around the doctor's shoulder. "Well said, Doc, well said," the Giant said. Then retracing his steps, he nodded to Horton and continued to talk.

"Doc's got a point. In fact, a lot's been said about why something as crazy as a Little World Series ever came about. Hen, I know that. Yep, I see Odie smilin', and it's true. I'm sellin' Dugouts, and like Doc says, Hooter here is writin' a book."

Wilt's eyes found Horton's. The lopsided smile creased his face, and Horton nodded. The Giant continued.

"Odie's got his reason for being here, too, wants to be a big-time promoter. Mouse, you got yours. All of us do. Now, as long as they ain't illegal or immoral, then what these reasons are, well, I couldn't care less. And yep, we're here for fun. But I'm gonna tell ya, when you step between those white lines today I wanta see the team I know you can be."

The Giant was on the move again, circling the room, stopping occasionally to spit in the tall green metal can.

"Some of ya's got a lot of talent. Some of you don't. But there ain't a man in this room that can't help us win a game or two.

"I know you, seen you do it too many times. Baldy, on hands, well, you're a might questionable, but you still got guts at third. I've seen you stay down on shots that woulda made Brooks Robinson flinch. Kline, well, you chose a nice profession, but you and I both know you coulda gone a long way in this game."

As the Giant clicked off his players one by one, eyes cleared, heads lifted, and Horton watched color come back to his teammates' faces.

"Now, Bunny, I'm saving you till last because, well, I shouldn't steal Hooter's thunder on this one, but your captain's paid you the ultimate compliment. Horton's got you inked into the leadoff spot and playin' short.

The refrigerator door caught the shock of Wilt's karate kick. Kline shook his head. Rymoff passed air. Ballard echoed the sentiments with one of his handmade farts.

"Now if there ain't any questions, let's scoot on out there and play the caliber of baseball that will make middle-aged male America sleep like babies tonight!"

Then the Giant suddenly dropped to one knee. "Now, how many of us remember the prayer, the one we used to do afore every game?" he said. The blue eyes rolled up and panned the table and couches. "Well, I'm ashamed of you boys, that's one I thought you'd never forget."

Heads dropped and caps doffed. One by one they joined the old man on the floor.

Dear Lord, Let the fastball move,
Let the bats be hot,
Let my Dogs play
With all that they've got.
                    Amen

Horton looked up and ducked. Wilt's glove nicked his ear and slapped into the yellow wall. A roar went up and the players shot through the door. "Let's get 'em!" Ballard shouted. "Nothing but heat, Lefty," Kline said and patted Wilt on the rump.

Wilt had to shout to be heard. "Listen, I meant what I said! You don't show me up. I'm talking about playin' McKay at short!" Wilt's teeth were clenched and he drove his forefinger into Horton's chest.

Horton stepped back into the Cub locker room, where Bunny waited. The Rabbit cocked his head, looked up, and wiped his nose. "Thanks, I won't let you down," he said and clacked off across the room. Rymoff reached out and patted the little man on the shoulder, then fell in step with Horton.

"He hear Wilt?" Horton asked.

"Yeah, the man's got a point. Hooter, get your head out of your ass. Bunny leading off and playing shortstop? We've got five thousand bucks a man riding on this thing, I mean, give us a fucking break!" Rymoff said.

At the steps to the dugout, Horton turned and looked back for the Giant. The locker room was a hot, noisy din, a mass of changing Cubs in white and royal blue, no gray uniforms in sight. Horton tucked his catcher's mitt under his arm and walked up the passageway.

• 2 •

WALKER HORTON LOOKED OVER BRICKS AND IVY into the sun-splashed, sign-waving, beer-swilling fans. Across Sheffield Avenue, high above a Suehowicz STRIKE-A-MANIACS banner, a Chicago rooftop measured Cub clouts with a hand-painted sign marked "495." Behind the neighborhood homes loomed the city skyline. Chicago big and loud—a 1980s version of the tool-making, wheat-stacking metropolis that Carl Sandburg had so aptly described.

Inside, the "friendly confines" cliché still applied. Wrigley Field—the perfect place to kick the Little Series off, Horton thought.

Horton short-hopped Albaugh's throw, turned, and tossed the ball up at Thumma's bat. The Giant stepped back and beat a high hopper into the hole between Rymoff and Kline.

"Get it worked out with Odie?" Thumma asked. Horton watched Kline cut in front of Rymoff and flip the ball to a vacant first-base sack.

"Looking good, Elmer, looking real good." McKeen whistled and shouted from the first-base dugout.

Bear lumbered off down the right-field line, dodging hoots and catcalls from a Pintail pepper game.

"Yeah, it's all worked out. If Bunny fucks up, Wilt's gonna take a hike," Horton said.

Rymoff's throw arched in toward the plate. Horton backhanded the ball and dropped it in the Giant's hand. Down the left-field line, the Hot Dogs' bullpen heated up. Wilt's throws slapped and popped in Billy Johnson's mitt.

"Same temper. Same kinda crap he used to pull in Little League. But Wilt ain't goin' anywhere," Thumma said, tapping a grounder toward McKay.

"But why shortstop?" he asked. Bun-Bun charged, beat a quick retreat, and snagged the ball at shoulder height.

"Right-handed hitters will be late on Odie? Right field would be a slap in the face? I don't know, I was up most of last night trying to come up with some sort of solution. I guess I just think it's right."

The Rabbit's throw rainbowed across the infield and settled gently in Rymoff's outstretched mitt. The Giant tipped his cap to the seats behind the third-base dugout. The guests from Quick-chow and Fastfood applauded politely. The bleachers had been jammed for almost an hour—bare chests and tank tops wearing the beer vendors out. Horton watched the flow into the reserved seating—Cub caps, pennants, and programs—the boxes behind home plate were filling up.

"Well, you're the boss," the Giant said. "I know you wanta do right by the Rabbit."

A bell rang in the Hot Dogs' dugout. The Giant whistled between his teeth and smacked a worm burner into the gap between short and third. Albaugh turned his head, threw out his glove, and spun in the hard-packed dirt like a ten-cent top. The brown-rimmed glasses flew in the air. Baldy staggered to one knee, wedged the ball from the webbing, and fired a strike to first.

"Thata baby, that's the way. All right, Bear, bring her in now, everybody in! We got us a ball game to play!" the Giant shouted.

Behind the Hot Dogs' third-base dugout a photo opportunity was underway. Commissioner Stonesifer loved good publicity more than he hated bad. Stony grinned and tossed the game ball in the air. Cameras clicked. He repeated the trick. Larry Barnes gave her cameraman the high sign. Horton tripped on a television cable and looked up into a familiar smile.

"Holy cow, Harry Caray!" he said.

The ruddy-faced announcer shoved a WGN microphone at Horton, turned him to the camera's red light.

"Folks, this is Hooter Horton, the captain of the New Becton Hot Dogs, the World's Oldest Little League team. Hoot, how 'bout tellin' the old ballplayers out there what it feels like to suit up and play in a park like Wrigley Field," Caray said.

Horton paused, rolled the toothpick across his teeth.

"Good," he said.

Caray nodded and pushed the mike in closer. This was it, the scene he'd envisioned, the one he'd dreamed about. Harry Caray would toss him a question, and he'd regale America.

"Good?" asked Caray. "That's it?"

"Very good." Horton felt the heart kick. "Now, if you'll excuse me, I better get going. Big game."

He'd choked before Stony even had a chance to throw out the first pitch.

Horton distanced himself from his players. He sat alone at the left-field end of the bench, rubbing neat's-foot oil into his glove and describing the pregame festivities into his tape recorder.

"I'm watching a media zoo!"

A wiener queen pulled the *Hot Dog* bus through the big green gate in left and treated the fans to one hand-waving, kiss-blowing loop around the park. Frankie, the Giant's all-meat answer to the San Diego Chicken, raced out of the Hot Dogs' dugout and did a hook slide into second base. A raffle ticket pulled by the midget frankfurter in the brown blintz suit sent a Peoria Little Leaguer and his dad to Cooperstown for a weekend in August.

For Horton the speeches, introductions, and giveaways ran together—Stonesifer, the mayor of Chicago, Elmer the Giant, major leaguers milling around the dugouts flashing looks of disgust. Then Monk Campbell, "National League umpire retired," was introduced. Campbell and his twin sons would work the series in all five parks.

"An old horseshitter from way back, but he's got a good eye, always liked left-handers." Thumma winked at Wilt and spat.

"AND NOW WILL THE HOLDER OF TICKET NUMBER 34591 PLEASE WALK OUT HERE AND PICK UP A GENUINE NEW BECTON HOT DOGS CAP AND TEN FREE DINNERS AT AN AMERICAN FUN FOOD DOGGIE DUGOUT RESTAURANT. KIDS, BE SURE TO LOOK FOR A DUGOUT IN YOUR NEIGHBORHOOD," the announcer droned.

The team looked drawn and haggard to Horton. Elmer's pregame had worn them out. The Bear pitched forward and dribbled tobacco juice on his freshly shined shoes. Odie and Mouse combed the stands with Thumma's binoculars, spotting for women. Ballard hand-massaged an off-key rendition of "Nola." Kline blew an accompaniment into an empty Pepsi bottle.

"AND NOW HERE ARE THE NEW BECTON HOT DOGS!" the PA boomed. The Hot Dogs yawned; groped for gloves, gum, and tobacco; then fell into the sunshine to a thunderous ovation. Horton paused on the top step of the dugout to check his pulse and take in the madness. Suehowicz had turned Wrigley into a funny farm: Thousands of them—men, women, children of all ages—wielded the signs against big league baseball.

A sheet hanging over the ivy in right:

FAN POWER FBLB

A Little Leaguer in a white pinstriped baseball suit held a cardboard poster lettered in red:

THEY'RE KILLING THE GOLDEN GOOSE
BIG LEAGUERS ARE LAYING AN EGG

"Go, Hoot!" the Giant said and slapped him on the rump.

Horton picked up his mask. "What'd the commissioner have to say about all this protest stuff?"

"Oh, Stony's real pissed, just real unhappy, but there ain't nothing we can do about it, is there? Now get your tail out there and catch me a game," the Giant said and pushed Horton off the step.

• 3 •

HORTON FLASHED WILT A HANDFUL OF FINGERS. One for fastball, two for curve. The thumb and forefinger rotated slowly back and forth. He dropped the big brown Rawlings fastback mitt off his knee, shielding the signals from the third-base coach's box and the eagle eye of Bracken McKeen. Horton flicked the fingers again. He wanted the slider.

The wind shifted. The huge Old Style and Budweiser balloon bottles anchored on the rooftops behind the left-field wall pulled at their tethers and lunged toward the center-field scoreboard. Horton heard a popping firecracker sound, one bang after another. Little Leaguers stomping Old Style cups! Then the wind changed and Wrigley went silent. Bats quit beating, Suehowicz's activists had gone dumb. Bleacherites stood, naked to the waist, beer cups held high. The reserves and box seats followed—Little League uniforms, short-sleeved shirts, sundresses, and blouses. The old ballpark rose to watch the game's first pitch.

Wilt glass-eyed the broad black uniform digging in at the plate, tightened his jaw, and clenched his teeth. The cowboy good looks had disappeared. Out past the pitcher loomed the hitter's backdrop, a section of green in straightaway center. Above the bank of empty seats the old scoreboard flashed, announcing the game's first hitter:

SKIPPER WEST, POUGHKEEPSIE PINTAILS, AVG. 000

Wilt's right leg kicked at the clouds and a tight, spinning slider shot out of the blue. The pitch dipped like a swallow, Horton slid left, the long white aluminum shaft flashed in the sun.

"Heerike hun!" Monk Campbell bellowed.

The bleachers exploded. The reserved seats echoed the cry. Two thousand Little League bats banged their approval. "Keerist," Campbell shouted to make himself heard, "this fucking guy still has an arm!"

A casual observation—typical icebreaker between umpire and catcher—but five innings later, when Campbell punched out Fritz Smith with a deafening "Heerike three!," the man's opening remark seemed almost clairvoyant. Twelve Pintails had fallen to the left-hander's slider, but the story of game one wasn't all Hot Dogs and Odie Wilt mustard. Biggie Ensor had served New Becton a smorgasbord of unhittable pitches—off-speed curveballs, knucklers, and drops.

Horton dropped down, scooped Wilt's half-speed warm-up out of the dirt, looked to the center-field scoreboard, and tried to recall the five fastest innings of his life. He counted the goose eggs rowed along the big kitchen green scoreboard and thanked God for New Becton's one lone run. A smile broke under his mask as he recalled the strategy that put the mark there.

In the bottom of the first Kline punched an Ensor two-out

fastball down the right-field line. The ball bounded foul, rolled to the wall, and died a noble death under a clump of Wrigley ivy. Triple! Then Horton made his move. Strategy that Barnes later would call bush. Horton knew better! He'd read the play the night before in *Billyball,* Billy Martin's book. Martin had bragged about how he'd conned Ted Williams with the play back when the Thumper was a fledgling manager with the old Washington Senators.

Bear Rymoff walked. Two out and Dogs on first and third. Horton leaned over from his first-base coaching box and whispered to Rymoff:

"Steal on the first pitch, then get your big ass caught in a rundown," he said.

The play worked to perfection, just as it had in *Billyball.* Bear broke for second. "Get that cocknocker!" McKeen screamed from the dugout, and while Rymoff lumbered back and forth, Kline slid home with the game's only run.

Just the beginning of another high-scoring Little League game, Wilt thought. But here they were, in the sixth and final inning, and Kline's run still up there all by itself. Horton felt the adrenaline surge. The Pintails were down to two lousy outs.

The game had been a blur for Horton, a parade of hard-breaking sliders, whiffing bats, and Campbell "Heerikes." There'd been Albaugh's errors, a pair of kicked ground balls that Odie erased with strikeouts; Jug's great running catch in right-center; and Bear's drive, the one that the wind knocked into West's glove out on the warning track.

In the bottom of the fourth, Horton flipped on his recorder and made another assessment: "I can't really describe this; it's relaxed excitement, I guess. The dugout is full of ass-slapping chatter. Nine ballplayers and one great old man trying to win a baseball game."

Behind the plate, things had even been better. Horton moved around, framing Wilt's pitches, setting up Pintail hitters with fastballs and sliders. No threat of hyperventilation. Not once had he touched the bag or thumbed his neck to check the pulse.

Playing quietly behind it all was the ambience of Wrigley Field, of course—green seats, ivy, balloon beer cans bopping back and forth on the Waveland rooftops, the big black-and-white Torco sign on the building in right, the jerks in the bleachers dropping their pants, vendors crying "Old Style" in that midwestern twang, and the odor of free Little Giants going down the gullets of some two thousand bat-banging Little League ballplayers. But the game's most lasting impression blasted from the park's old brick dugouts. Thumma and McKeen had been magpies since Campbell "Heeriked!" the first pitch.

"Be there, baby!" Thumma shouted, following his encouragements with long, shrill, ear-piercing whistles. The airwaves never went dead. When the whistles died, McKeen cut loose like an auctioneer with his New York mumbo jumbo. "Dat's da man, you and me, rock an' fire, thro da heat!" he shouted.

Horton pushed down one finger. The sixth inning was one-third gone. Fastball! He slid to his right. They'd start Boobs Barbin high and wide. Let him chase one out of the strike zone. He'd first-pitch hit both trips to the plate.

"Hall hun!" Campbell screamed. McKeen had the left fielder taking. Horton rubbed up the ball and lobbed it back to Wilt.

"We're better off at this distance." Sixty feet, six inches, the perfect measurement, he thought.

Barnes cocked back in the box seats behind third and chatted with Stonesifer. Horton could see the golden tan and the white teeth flashing through the bars of his mask. The dugouts buzzed and swarmed with color. Cubs in white pinstripes moved back and forth, ganging along the blue railing at third. Along first he could see the reds and grays of Herzog's Cardinals.

In a sense the New Becton Hot Dogs and Poughkeepsie Pintails had made history. They'd proven Larry Barnes a liar today. The crowd of rabble-rousing fan activists and freebie-seeking Little Leaguers had been treated to five innings of outstanding baseball. Cripes, even the big leaguers were enjoying the game.

Cub reliever Tom Davis leaned out of the dugout and underlined Horton's point.

"Hey, Odie, knock that big-assed guy down!" he shouted in a slow Texan drawl.

The fastball tailed away, grazed Horton's shinguard and rolled all the way to the brick backstop.

"Get in the game!" Wilt shouted. He was feeling the pressure. Horton called time out and trotted to the mound.

"You okay?" the catcher asked.

"Christ, you're asking me? You hold that last pitch and Campbell calls it a strike." Wilt turned his back and looked into the third-base dugout. The silver-maned Cub coach, the guy Wilt had flung the roll of tape at, stepped out on the grass, bowed, and doffed his Cub cap.

"Come on, Odie, two more outs and we'll own Chicago," Horton said.

"Two more outs and that old peckerhead in there owes me a hundred bucks," Wilt said, flicking his glove at the heckler. Then he snatched the ball from Horton and proceeded to throw three pitches up and out of the strike zone.

The walk to Barbin brought Wilt off the mound like a turpentined terrier. "Get in the fucking game, Campbell!" he shouted.

"No, Wilt, you get your ass back up on that hill or I'll run you! I ain't being paid to take no Little League shit!" Campbell shouted. Elmer and McKeen arrived at the plate seconds later, the Giant berating the umpire for his postage stamp strike zone, McKeen screaming, "Throw the sons a bitches out, Campbell, they're arguing balls and strikes!"

Horton blinked at the swing, threw the mask, and watched the ball climb above second base. Bunny waved, then backed away. Kline drifted back, turned, and watched Brown glide into short right-center. "Mine!" Brown shouted, and turning his glove, cradled the ball in a Willie Mays basket. Barbin scampered back to first ahead of his throw.

"Two away," Campbell's clone son intoned.

Game one of the Little World Series is just one out short of the bag, Horton thought.

Tiny Wyatt, the Ducks' Tweedledeeish right fielder, tapped his

Eason on the hard-rubber plate, expectorated something pink in the dirt, and pointed the bat at Wilt.

"Horton, do yourself a favor: Give me something to hit. I'll pop one outta here and we'll go drink a beer," he said.

Horton dropped one finger down and slid it up high near his cup to show Wilt location. Elmer's pregame scouting report was explicit on Wyatt.

"You can't take chances on big-assed guys like him. He gets his butt into one and the next thing you know, them kids'll be scrambling for it out on Waveland Avenue."

Tease him with the fastball away, then work him low. Slow runner; the situation had ground-ball out written all over it.

"Hall hun!" Campbell shouted.

Wilt checked Barbin back to first, then came with a low, hard slider. The ball shot off the bat, the worm burner snaked past Wilt's flailing glove. Horton tossed the mask. McKay dipped low and beat his little three-fingered mitt. An explosion of activity to the right of second base. A cloud of dust kicked up, Barbin loping like a deer toward the sack, Kline sliding gracefully to the bag, glove extended, ready to take the toss from short.

Force-out, we win, Horton thought. The ball hit a stone and kicked high in the air. The Rabbit grabbed his throat and went down like he'd been snared in a trap. Horton watched the ball roll free in the center-field grass.

Two errant throws later, Pintails were panting safely on first and third. Thirty-eight thousand fans booed as one. McKay hung his head and rubbed the large red blotch on his throat.

"High and away!"

"Low and inside!"

Six more pitches and the Pintail runners had company. Suddenly Wilt's slider was all over the place. "Frigging walk," Horton muttered. The bases were loaded, jammed with black Pintail ducks.

"Get outta here!" Wilt spat the words. Horton paused between the plate and the mound, took several steps forward, then had his say. "Just take your time. I'm thinking we should maybe set him up with a fastball or two, then come with that change-up you showed me back in West Palm. They haven't seen it all day."

"Change-up my ass," Wilt said. "McKay just fucked us out of a game-ending play."

The old silver fox was up again, waving his Cub hat, gripping his throat, screaming "Choke!" Wilt waved the long middle finger in at the bench. "Bases loaded, a play at any base!" Horton held up two fingers and jogged back to the plate.

"Ball Kubeked your shortstop, jumped up, and hit the little fucker right in the throat," Campbell said. "Hey, good ball game. I'm enjoying the hell out of this."

The Giant's whistle was shrill. He blew two short blasts, then doubled his fist at Wilt. Horton threw down his hand and repeated the manager's request. No wonder he loved the old man, they thought just alike. The Giant wanted the change-up. Horton flexed his hand and showed Wilt the fist again. The big left-hander broke off a lopsided grin and pushed back his cap. Then Horton saw his eyes go blank.

Horton was lost in the ocean again, waves breaking, battering his psyche. One out away from winning the game of his life. Time for another anxiety attack. The sweat flowed. His heart flipped into overdrive. He reached back for the sack and heard the voice. Russ Hodges was calling the action again.

"Well, hi again, everybody, it looks like the New Becton Hot Dogs are determined to make a great game better. Bottom of the sixth, the Pintails need one to tie, but they've got the bases loaded. A base hit would give them the ball game.

"Elmer the Giant is up on the top step of the dugout now, whistling to Wilt. The Pintails have got West, their big center fielder, up and the wind's blowing out. You can bet Wilt will be mighty careful with him.

"The left-hander steps off the mound, walks back, and picks up the resin bag. What a beautiful occasion in a great old ballyard! Frankly, I was a bit skeptical about this Little World Series thing, but the consensus up here in the booth and along press row today is that we might just be witnessing the finest Little League game ever played.

"Oh, there's been a miscue or two here and there, but by and large a beautifully pitched, well-played game, and boy, can that guy Brown go get them in center. He reminds us of a middle-aged Willie Mays out there."

A fastball shaved the Pintail batter. Campbell generously pronounced it a strike. Then West came up on his toes and flailed at a pitch he'd have needed a footstool to hit. The wiry old umpire "Heeriked," and the game was one strike out of the books.

"Ernie, Wilt seems to be having trouble out there. Maybe Horton should go settle him down a bit," Hodges said.

Horton gulped air, slipped his throwing hand inside his glove, and took a quick check on his pulse. Galloping horses. Cripes, no wonder, he thought. This was it. They had West set up for the change-up. Horton flashed four fingers, then closed the fist. Wilt nodded, pumped once, and came in with the pitch.

The bat flashed. The ball jumped skyward. Somewhere between the nod of his head and the ball's release, Wilt's change-up became a hanging slider. Wilt spun, bounced on his toes, Kline and Bun-Bun drifted and gave way to Brown. The center fielder turned his back to the infield and raced for the ivy. Horton threw his mask. Where was the ball? Was Jug decoying the runners? Not with two out!

"Son of a biscuit!" the Giant screamed, and tossed a handful of bats out of the dugout. The Cub coach leaned over the blue railing and fanned the ball with his cap.

"Go, you cocknocka!" McKeen shouted. The wind blew. Jug's cap fell off; he was on a collision course for the bricks and ivy.

"Brown goes back, back, back, way back and it's . . . bye-bye, baby! The Pintails win! The Pintails win! The Poughkeepsie Pintails have won the ball game on a towering Skipper West home run to right-center!"

Horton was shocked, numbed by the home-run clout. But the events that followed would take his state of confusion to a higher level. "Barnstorming" would describe Wilt's postgame chase of Bun-Bun McKay this way: "The losing pitcher would surely have killed the little shortstop had it not been for a brilliant tackle in the short grass along third by the eminent gynecologist Steven Kline."

Horton remembered the tackle fading into pushing and shoving. Cardinals and Cubs milling around, swearing at Wilt. He recalled seeing a number of Elmer's giveaway bats hit the field. Reporters and TV guys with cameras and cables backpedaled in front of him, holding up microphones, asking stupid questions. He'd tripped on a rake and dodged a little green John Deere tractor.

Then Elmer the Giant appeared and spoke to the press. "Hold it right here," Thumma said. "We'll be with you in a minute. I want a word with Horton."

He wedged his catcher behind home plate, pressed him against the screen into the Plexiglas TV window. Horton felt Elmer's breath. The old man was hot. Someone held a John 3:16 sign up and pushed it to the glass.

"You hear me whistle twice?" he said. He emphasized his point by poking an oversize finger just above the catcher's chest protector.

"Change-up, two whistles, change-up!" The Giant stuck his fingers between his lips and blew two shrill blasts in Horton's face.

"Jal Baile, *Chicago Tribune:* Elmer, I wonder if I might have a word—"

The Giant wheeled the big finger at the intruding reporter. "When I'm done here we'll talk to you all, but right now we're having us a private, off-the-record conversation. Now get those cameras and recorders outta my face."

Horton had never seen Thumma like this. "I called for a change-up!" he said. He had to shout to be heard.

"If I called for a change-up and you called for a change-up, then how come we just watched a friggin' hangin' slider sail outta the ballpark?" the Giant said.

"Talk to Wilt!"

Elmer lunged forward, pressing Horton tighter against the smooth Plexiglas. "I will," he said. "I sure as hell will," the Giant said.

"Sorry! Baile from the *Trib* again. I've gotta know what you think of—"

"Hey, Elmer, how 'bout a few words at home plate with those bozos comin' over the walls as a back drop." A blond-haired suit-and-tie stuck a microphone in the Giant's face.

"Horton, Jill Johnson, WGN, need to get your reaction to the walkout. Do you consider yourselves part of the protest against big league baseball?"

The reporters had them corraled, pressed against the backstop. "Give us some room to breathe," the Giant said. "Now what's all this about?"

A camera moved left. A reporter sidestepped a cable, and Horton was staring at the castle scene of *Robin Hood* run in reverse. They were scaling down the ivy walls by the hundreds. Fat, thin, tank-topped, barechested, they jumped, fell, and clawed at the ivy. A cadre of uniformed police raced across the outfield, stretching a long yellow rope.

"What the hen?" the Giant said.

"Protesters! Suehowicz is emptying the bleachers for the Cubs-Cards game. Says half the ballpark will follow him out," Baile said.

In left field, two policemen chased after a banner that said FUCK BIG LEAGUE BASEBALL.

In right, a bare rear end hung over the top ledge of the wall. Across his bare bun in Red Magic marker the following sign flashed the park.

NO MORE
STR   KES

"The 'I' in 'strikes' is the crack of his ass," a reporter said. Thumma nodded. "Oh," he said. Then, he shook his head and cleared his throat.

"Well, I'm disgusted with all this. It has nothing to do with the Little World Series, and I guess that's about all I can say." Thumma shot Horton a look of despair. Suehowicz had the bull-horn blasting now.

"Line up, let's get in line! No more confrontations! Fall in, everybody fall in!" he shouted.

"Elmer, Terry Nusbaum, *Detroit Free Press.* You don't think that you and your Little Series have been the catalyst of this thing?"

"I do not," the Giant tugged hard on his cap and reached for a wad to replenish his plug.

Horton saw the blond hair and felt himself cringe. "Elmer, the commissioner sure doesn't see it that way," Barnes said.

A TV camera turned and the *Baltimore Sun* reporter stepped forward. "Let me read the quote. Hell, the ink is still wet. 'If those degenerates walk out on the major league game today you can kiss Elmer's Giants, his Hot Dogs, and the Little World Series good-bye.' "

The Giant turned, spat at the ground, and half-whispered to Horton. The black brim of the cap was down. He was afraid to look up. "What are they doin' now?" he said. "Just sorta protestin' or somethin'?"

"No, Suehowicz's got 'em on the move for the big green door in the right-center-field wall," Horton said. A bugle played "Charge!" "Hell, they're marching. The bastard's Pied Pipering them out."

THE BRAKES HISSED. THUMMA MASHED THE BUTTON on the dashboard with his oversize mitt. Horton cringed. *Bink-be-bink-bink-bink-bink.* "Take Me Out to the Ball Game" blasted from the bus's rooftop PA.

How could the Giant motor around Chicago like the Good Humor man with the commissioner of major league baseball about to cancel his Little World Series?

"Eight to five he shit-cans the whole thing," Magruder said, poking his head between Horton and Thumma.

Horton looked through the glass into the mass of moving confu-

sion. Tourists and early-bird shoppers clotted Michigan Avenue.
A boy in a red and blue FRIDGE T-shirt yanked at his father and
pointed up at the big *Hot Dog* bus. Horns blew, a red-faced police-
man motioned to Thumma. The Giant hit the PA again. The cop
spun, aimed his whistle up at the windshield, and fired off three
short, shrill blasts.

"Keep your odds to yourself, Magruder. We've got reporters on
board," the Giant said. Mouse shrugged. "Just givin' you the
Vegas line," he said, and sulked down the aisle to his seat.

Horton folded his *USA Today* neatly and dropped the newspaper in the aisle.

"Here, I'll trade you," Kline said, and handed him a rumpled
Chicago Tribune. Horton flipped to the sports section.

"Barnstorming." He'd been saving his favorite writer for last.

FANS PULL BIG LEAGUE STRIKE AT OLD LITTLE LEAGUE GAME

That's what he hated about the Barneses of the world. Newspaper people, they were all alike. They'd bitch about gimmicks like
the Little Series, then sensationalize their stories with this kind of
crap.

The lead was typically snide.

"If Wrigley's ivy should turn brown and drop from the vine, it
will be with good reason. The beasts who scaled down the walls
of the friendly confines today are out to kill big league baseball."

Quotes near the head of the story pitted the Giant against the
commissioner and Suehowicz.

Horton speed-read the zingers.

Suehowicz: "We're just thankful for the Little Series. It's the
perfect opportunity for us. And unless management and the players sit down and talk with people who pay their salaries, we'll keep
lining the fans up and marching them out of their parks."

The commissioner's quote about Thumma kissing his wiener
deal and the Little World Series good-bye was followed by a line
from the Giant. Thumma's quote was clearly out of context, he
thought.

"We're just trying to play a thirty-year-old grudge match. I can see the commissioner's view and, of course, the fans have a point, too. . . ."

It made the Giant sound weak.

Horton's eyes flew down the page. Was this a gossip or a sports column? Had she even seen the LWS game?

He read farther. An entire half page was devoted to Odie Wilt's clubhouse tirade. "The warm yellow paint on the clubhouse walls curled and cracked from Odie Wilt's obscenities," she said.

"That's the worst I've heard since the day Lee Elia trashed the Cub fans back in '82," Lonnie Hamrick, a Cub clubhouse man, said.

Wilt's quote reddened his neck. He was playing the ex-major leaguer, trying to laugh off the home run, calling it a windblown batting practice pitch. Horton couldn't believe the trash that Barnes could get into print. *The Johnstonian Advertiser* would have his tail for submitting this kind of crap.

Wilt: "After all, we're here to entertain the fans. An ex-major leaguer doesn't try to show up a guy like West; he's a garage man, for C—— sake."

He looked into the rearview mirror. Wilt was cocked back in a recliner, chatting with Barnes. Garbage today! News tomorrow!

Horton's eyes drooped. He let his mind fog and drift. He remembered the balcony scene at the West Palm Ramada, Barnes and Wilt naked now. The comely reporter put down her notepad and crawled into Wilt's recliner. Long brown legs and apple-shaped buttocks covered the pitcher. The recliner rocked gently. She tossed her head. The golden hair swept the blades of her long, shapely back.

The brakes hissed. Horton rubbed his eyes, looked back at the newspaper, and skimmed another column. Barnes was cynical, sarcastic, a big-time bitch, but sacking up with a guy like Wilt? Hell, maybe it's likes that attract, he thought.

Wilt was throwing bad ink at Bun-Bun now. "A confused little accountant . . ." the story said. Horton checked the mirror again. The mirage had cleared. Barnes and Wilt were fully dressed, no longer tossing one off in the recliner. More paranoia, he guessed. But you don't play poke and giggle with a reporter who just drilled

you and your team in print. There was still something between
them. The balcony scene never failed to tighten his stomach.

Hodges' voice cracked and popped, then faded into the hum of
the bus gearing down. "Well frankly, Ernie, I'm not sure Horton
is being fair to his old pal Wilt. An ex-major leaguer puts himself
on the line for his buddies. Granted he's got a short fuse, but then
Horton knows that. To be honest, the business smacks a bit of
jealousy, don't you think?"

Wilt nudged Barnes. They both laughed. Even Hodges had
turned on him. Horton had all he could stand. Across the aisle,
the little lump tucked in the recliner tossed in his sleep. Bunny's
eyes fluttered, then fell. The shortstop hadn't spoken since the
grounder clothes-lined his throat. A guy's dying, and then Wilt
goes out and kills him in print.

Elmer's voice cracked when he spoke. "I'm really up for this
one, son," he said. "I can handle 'em, though, not gonna take any
crap, of course. Activists need to quit trashing the fields, no more
vulgarity in their signs, that kinda thing. Commissioner has to
realize that we got nothing to do with them. They're protesting the
majors, not Little Giants, Inc. Gross is gonna take advantage of
it all, of course. Just have to handle him later. First things first."

The catcher grunted and turned the newspaper pages. There:
C-16. About time! Barnes had finally gotten around to mentioning
the game.

". . . pitcher hangs gopher ball, team loses, pitcher throws glove,
pitcher chases shortstop whose error put the tying run on base,
second sacker makes game-saving tackle on pitcher, a pretty typical Little League game, I guess. But before we move on to the
really fun stuff, I guess I better slip on the old bib and eat a few
words (it will take some chewing) from yesterday's column. Old
players, tight uniforms, I was right on two counts. But (this is so
hard to say) I took a strike on the game. The old guys played
surprisingly well for their age."

Horton reddened, grinned, then read the paragraph out loud to
the Giant. Thumma smiled and mumbled something about Suehowicz and the commissioner.

Horton's eyes went back to the page.

"So much for sentiment. Now, if you're one of my Motown readers and happen to have tickets for game two, I wouldn't get too excited. I watched game one in the presence of the commissioner. Here's what I think: We've enjoyed the first one-game series in baseball history."

What a wiseass, Horton thought. He closed his eyes. The bus bumped forward, and he exhaled a pleasant thought. Barnes would have traded a month of bylines to have attended yesterday's postgame meeting back at the Regency-Hyatt.

The session was vintage Elmer—a real tail-kicking, name-taking, rip-fucking snorter. The Giant pranced around the hotel room dodging beer cans, tripping over ankles and feet. The Dogs slumped against the walls, covered the beds, and burrowed in the corners in the Hyatt's thick gray carpet. Bear and Billy were high, Odie livid, Bunny silent and Casper white. Thumma wore long, loose-fitting boxer shorts, the black cap, and nothing else. His head was a ripe red from the Wrigley sun.

Mouse Magruder flipped the TV dial full circle. The Little Series. Every channel. Good timing. Old Little Leaguers playing the American game. It made the perfect July Fourth story. Peter Jennings and Dan Rather closed with the piece. Tom Brokaw was on vacation. His substitute, a middle-aged woman in oversize black-rimmed glasses, ran a puff piece on a wounded American eagle.

"Screw NBC," Bear Rymoff said. "Turn on ESPN."

The Chicago stations aired almost identical footage.

They watched in silence as West mashed the slider over the ivy.

The Hot Dogs hissed and booed. Then Suehowicz's protesters piled over the wall and, as one anchor said, "assaulted major league baseball."

The stories closed with a bobbing camera chasing Kline chasing Wilt chasing Bun-Bun. Keystone Kops—it was classic video.

"You'd think someone would run a shot of your triple, Doc, or that runnin' one-hander that Jug pulled off," Thumma said and walked over to the wall and pulled the plug on the set. Then he popped a cud-size chaw of Levi Garrett between his molars and jaw and proceded to chew every ass within spitting distance.

"Horton, when a catcher wants a change-up and he's working with a cocky son of a biscuit like Mr. Wilt over there, the man marches his fanny out to the mound and makes it clear that if he doesn't see a slow one, he's going to personally kick a certain left-hander's butt."

The Giant spun. Albaugh lay back on the bed and Sight Savered his little half glasses.

"Baldy, I don't know how you and the president deal with the Russians, but when you're playin' third against a McKeen team, and a ball's hit up the middle, you don't think, you *know* that runner on first will be coming hell-bent for third.

"By the way, Jug, that was one fine throw."

Thumma pulled his loose white boxers up over his navel and turned on Wilt again.

"Now, when a mistake is made on the field, the worst thing a player can do is show up one of his teammates. Odie, I heard you tossing the word 'bush' around to the press after the game. I suspect that we'll be readin' about the target of your abuse in the morning paper. When you chunked that glove and then took off after Bunny, well, that was as bush as anything I've seen in my sixty-eight-year life.

"By the way, Doc, that was a real fine tackle you put on Odie. Your teammates and I are forever grateful."

And before the New Becton Hot Dogs escaped to the pleasures of State Street, the Giant accomplished the following: Wilt and Bunny shook hands, Albaugh retracted his request to leave the team, and every Dog in the room agreed to suck up his gut and play the game of his life in Detroit's Tiger Stadium. "It's a hitter's park," the Giant said. Then he kneeled and led them in prayer again.

When Horton opened his eyes, the Giant had the receiver dangling from his hand.

"Don't leave, boys, I want you to hear this," he said. "Yes, returning your call," he said. "Well, you can tell your editors that you talked to Elmer the Giant and that he said Mr. Gross is an employee of his. That's right, I'm the chief executive officer of Elmer's Little Giants. Elmer, that's me. And I'm telling you that there is no connection between the strike and the Little Series.

"Now, don't you think that would be kinda like biting the hand that feeds me? That's what I'm saying. If I were to encourage the kind of behavior you saw out there today, I'd be sabotaging the game I love and committing financial suicide."

Thumma slammed down the receiver, looked into the room of blank faces, and made one final point:

"Boys, the press will be crawlin' all over the place tomorrow, all of 'em tryin' to make somethin' out of this fans' walkout thing. Nothin' Gross would like better than to see the commissioner put a stop to our series. Well, that ain't gonna happen, not in my lifetime.

"Me, the commissioner, and Suehowicz are meetin' tomorrow at our franchise offices above the Doggie Dugout we're inaugura-tin'. While the cooks are preparin' the food for the grand openin', we'll be twenty-two stories up, ironin' out this protest misunder-standin'.

"So we're all gonna motor over there about 9:00 A.M. When I get things cleared up upstairs, I'll come down and we'll greet the fans. We'll hand out some hot dogs, pat some Little League tails, then head the *Dog* toward Detroit.

"Oh, you might want to say a special little prayer for the com-missioner and that fellow Suehowicz tonight. They're gonna be goin' toe to toe with Elmer the Giant first thing in the mornin'," he said.

Horton rocked gently in his seat. The Giant smiled. His nod was one of satisfaction. It was the first smooth stop the Giant had made on the entire trip. Bear held up his beer and saluted Thumma. "Not a drop," he said.

Heads on Michigan Avenue turned with the hiss of the brakes. Another mob scene. Reporters, cameras, Little League uniforms storming the doors of the *Hot Dog*.

"Givin' away ten TV's, two tickets, and an all-expenses-paid trip to this year's World Series. Nothing like a good raffle to bring them out," Thumma said.

Horton heard commotion behind him—vulgar language and running feet as the fourth estate scrambled to the street side of the vehicle.

"Anybody see the commissioner's limo?"

"Hey, there's Suehowicz's bus, very tasteful, major league stickers, sort of a decoupage."

"Holy crap, Elmer, that pink thing with the bread-colored awning, is that your Doggie Dugout?" Rymoff asked.

Horton looked over the craning necks and bobbing heads. The Dugout was buried under a twenty-six-story building. Camp, Horton thought. A long, green, glassed-in dugout with a brown, pinkish roll for a roof. Horton leaned forward and squinted. Little mustard-colored stools, a catsup-red counter stretching the length of an atrium glass window.

"Whaddya think?" the Giant said.

"I think you've got yourself a winner," Horton said, and glanced down at his Adidas shoes.

"Judas Priest, I hope so, boy!" he said and bumped the intercom button on the bus's dash.

"You press people are the guests of Elmer the Giant. While I'm up there working things out with Commissioner Stonesifer and Suehowicz"—he pointed at the top of the skyscraper—"I want you to continue to help yourselves to the refreshments. It's a mite early for the beer but suit yourselves." Thumma paused.

A cacophony of popping cans' tops.

"When we come out on the street, try to have your paraphernalia set up and ready to go. We want to answer your questions, but the commissioner has a plane to catch, and I've got a restaurant to open."

"What if Stony says no more Little Series?" Dan Hartzler shouted.

"Hasn't said that yet. Now make way for the Giant, I got me a coupla windmills to fight," Thumma said, and he stepped out into a swirl of cameras, notepads, and autograph books.

Horton counted the floors. Twenty-two. He spotted the gold-embossed lettering. ELMER'S LITTLE GIANTS, INC., spelled out on the window. The conference was on. The glass had steamed over. Horton perused a copy of *The New York Times,* searching for a mention of the LWS. He whispered a note into his tape recorder, then cut his eyes twenty-two stories up. The letters had grayed over. He checked his watch and stole another look. Things were heating up. The window was limestone, almost opaque in color.

"Stony and the Giant must be trying to talk some sense into the rebel," Horton assessed.

He closed his eyes and listened to the press's reaction.

Liz Nixon, *Boston Globe:* "I wish the old man luck."

Matt Hunter, New York *Daily News:* "Hey, Odie, how 'bout a coupla Miller Lites back here."

"Here's tomorrow morning's story, boys: The Series is history, Suehowicz is back on a Chicago barstool reminiscing about his strike, and Gross is running around the corporate offices at Elmer's Little Giants, changing the locks." The voice was Larry Barnes'.

"Who's got lucky number thirty-four in the pool? We're coming up on thirty-four minutes." Horton eyeballed the mirror. Magruder stood in the aisle, waving a fistful of dollars, counting the seconds down.

The air conditioner groaned. Horton smelled the familiar perfume and felt his temperature rise. Barnes leaned over his shoulder; her right breast touched his arm. He jumped and looked up into a pouty smile.

"Looks like they're fogged in up there! Elmer must really be kicking ass," she said.

Horton nodded, "I hope so," he said.

"You think he'll really try to get a court injunction to play this silly thing if Stony nixes it?" Barnes asked.

Those eyes, so damn green. Were they contacts? Horton missed the question. He felt his lips move, then heard himself talking: "Off the record, he's a tough old—"

The bus lurched. A sudden and terrible jolt. Barnes fell face forward and landed in Horton's lap. Behind them, reporters played leapfrog, pushing their way to the door. Horton looked into the eyes again and wished he were wearing his cup.

"What's so exciting? They drawing for the TV already?" he said.

"For Christ's sake, Horton, are you blind? The Giant's dangling Suehowicz out the freaking window!" she shouted.

The scene would take Horton a while to sort out. But what he stuttered into his recorder was close enough. "Elmer's got Suehowicz out the twenty-second-story window, shaking him like a rat!"

His first clear recollection was one of Stonesifer squirting out of the Dugout and into the mob of reporters.

"The Giant's got that little prick Suehowicz out the window!" he shouted. "Call the cops! No, wait a minute, where's that catcher? Where's Horton? We've gotta settle this thing ourselves!"

Horton's head bobbed like a back window toy terrier in a loosely sprung Chevy coupe. Above him, twenty-two stories up, was a real-life puppet show. What happened next was blurry at best. He recalled Stonesifer pushing him through the crowd and then disappearing, a lonely elevator ride, numbers climbing slow motion, and a frazzled thought that it would never work for the book. Too many elevator scenes; it would look like bad fiction. There was a blind race down a hallway, a wrong turn, and finally the gold-lettered door.

The action that followed was much clearer. He saw an open window, curtains blowing, just like in a B picture. The Windy City. He actually had that thought. He called gently to the Giant, so as not to startle the big fellow. He could see Joby upside down, gray-faced, frog-eyed, staring across Michigan Avenue into windows jampacked with wide-eyed secretaries and men with faces as white as their shirts. The Giant's forearms, knotted like ropes, wrapped the activist's waist. The ponytail swung in the wind. One false move and Michigan Avenue would need a haircut.

"Coach, it's me, Hooter," Horton said.

Thumma's eyes bored ahead, locked on the window pool of spectating secretaries. Suehowicz flutter-kicked and rolled his eyes.

"Bring him in, Coach," Horton said. Then he leaned out, looked down, and got a foul ball's view of a crowd that's expecting a souvenir. He steadied himself, looked back at Elmer, and spoke again.

"Coach, I've got the door locked. Get him in here right now, and I think we'll be okay. The commissioner doesn't want to call the cops. We'll resolve it right here, right, Suehowicz?" Horton said.

The bulging eyeballs rotated up and down. The dangling mop tossed back and forth. The protester was saying "Yes."

"I go nowhere until the commissioner agrees to let us finish the series," the Giant said. The demand came at Horton in a surprising fashion. Thumma had never spoken out of the side of his mouth in his life. His teeth were jammed tight together. The words made a grinding sound.

"Bullhorn," Suehowicz said. The words sounded funny upside down.

Horton saw the gray metal megaphone lying on a nearby desk. Cripes, doesn't that creep go anywhere without this thing? he thought.

Seconds later Horton was blaring the message down to the street. The answer was indiscernible at first. Horton heard muffled roars. Then the wind calmed for a second and the chant filtered up. "Stony says yes!" "Stony says yes!" was the call.

"Good call, Commissioner!" Thumma said under his breath.

The Giant nodded, the wind whipped. He staggered, then took an agile crossover step and, like a cat dropping a baby bird, deposited Suehowicz on a long brown desk. Elmer looked at Horton and grinned like a Chessie.

"Now, Mr. Suehowicz, nobody hates violence more than me, but there are two things that you and the commissioner need to know." The Giant hoisted the limp T-shirt up from the desk and put his arm around the protester in a loving way. "You don't settle disputes without some kinda compromise, and you don't try to sabotage Elmer the Giant's Little World Series."

The sun's haze gave the water a dull sepia look. The Giant punched the gas pedal. "Heck of a day," he said and motored the big bus across the bridge. Horton nodded, took a sip from his Natural Light, and pushed the button on the tape recorder. A patch of chill bumps sprouted up on his arm. A bumper crop. Days like this and high bridges scared the hell out of Horton.

"Chicago, July 5, Doggie Dugout Day, notes for the book. The franchise is off to a fantastic start, overflow crowds. The *Dog* is motoring through North Chicago leading a wild jalopy caravan of fan activists, people who appear to have missed Elmer's message. The way they're following us to Detroit, I'm afraid the Giant may have made Joby a martyr." Horton raised his voice, reached over, and adjusted the air conditioner. He stole a glance at Thumma. The Giant was staring in his wing mirror at the convoy of protesters. His pink forehead was wrinkled tight. The Giant pulled his red bandanna and gave the grooves a wipe.

"Thanks to Elmer Thumma, the series continues," he said. "At least Stonesifer backed off for a while." Then he clicked the off button and closed his eyes. What Horton couldn't record would be on his mind for a long, long time. When Suehowicz wobbled out of the Giant's twenty-second-floor Chicago office, Elmer fell face down on the desk. Horton had never seen a case of the shakes like that in his life. He shimmied a stapler and pen set off on the floor, then sweated halfway through the big green blotter.

They were quite a pair, the men who called the shots for the New Becton Hot Dogs. Elmer sweating and quaking. Horton sucking air from a wrinkled paper sack.

The bus braked for a toll booth. Horton looked at the Giant. Shadows played on the tired old face. The sky was graying now, the sun had disappeared.

"You need some rest. Hell, Rymoff's a truck driver, he can handle this thing, it'll be a piece of cake for the Bear," he said.

The big head nodded. "You'll take the team tomorrow night. When we get to Detroit I gotta fly back to Baltimore, keep Gross from trashing me, let my people at ELG see I'm all right," he said. He wiped his head. Sweat showered the dashboard.

Lord, get us to Detroit, gotta call my shrink. The big guy is losing it, Horton thought.

"DR. HAAKENSON TO EMERGENCY, CODE BLUE! DR. Haakenson to emergency, Code Blue!"

Horton shifted in his seat and looked down at the dog-eared *Field & Stream.* A siren wailed out on Clinton Street. Smoke shrouded the dimly lit room. The half-empty coffee cups, piles of open magazines, and spewing ashtrays summed up Horton's day perfectly.

Horrible ball game! Tragic ending! Bunny lying in a coma in Detroit Memorial Hospital—and all because of him. He stared at the magazine's cover, a man in hip waders. The arms were tense, the rod bent like a bow under the weight of the fish.

"Dr. Dornberg to surgery! Dr. Dornberg, surgery!" the PA blasted.

He'd begged to pinch-hit. "It might be my last chance to make a contribution," he'd said. "MS is funny. Strong today, dead tomorrow!" Somehow, standing there in the on-deck circle, the crowd, the game on the line, it all made sense. The Rabbit would confirm the conversation. If he ever came around.

But there'd be no more copping out for Hooter Horton. The buck stopped with him, all right. Bunny wouldn't be in critical condition and he wouldn't be staring at a waiting room magazine if it weren't for his own mistake. You don't put a nearsighted little guy with MS up against a wild-assed blind man like Pazerelli. It was his decision. He'd have to live with it. Even if Bun-Bun didn't.

Across the table of cigarette butts a kid in a Tiger hat tugged at his mother's arm. A grin of recognition swept across the boy's freckled face. Horton tossed the magazine on the table, rubbed his sweat-soaked hands on his pants, and looked the other way. Cripes! No wonder people had been eyeballing him all night. How often do you see a grown man in a hospital decked out in a Little League uniform?

The clock above the nurses' station jumped: 1:25 A.M. The kid was really bugging his mother now.

"Go ahead," she said. And before Horton could grab another magazine, the pug nose and freckles were staring him right in the face.

"You're Hooter Horton! One of those old Little Leaguers, right?" the boy said, pushing the blue Tiger cap back on his head.

Horton spun sideways. An Exit sign, steps, elevator, a manhole cover, he'd take any route of escape. Heads came up from magazines. A gnarled old man snorted and shook himself awake. A nurse with long brunette hair pushed a tray of medication down the hall. Horton's eyes followed her tight white uniform.

"Been watching you on TV," the kid said. "We were at the game tonight!"

Horton swallowed, nodded, then reached back and touched his paper sack.

"Mom, I told you it was him. See, it even looks like a Little League uniform," he said.

Horton hunched over, brought the magazine up chest high, covering the orange HOT DOGS lettered across his chest.

"You here with the little guy, the one Pazerelli creamed in the head?" the kid's voice was louder now. Horton guessed thirteen, maybe fourteen. Sounded like his hormones might have just kicked in.

"Keep it down a little, we're in a hospital," Horton said.

"It was 21–20. You guys were horrible. You stay for the big protest?"

Horton shook his head no. "Left in the ambulance with the injured player," he whispered. "Try to lower your voice."

"Well, you missed it. Those protest guys marched people out of the park again. There was a lot of pushing and shoving. My granddad got so upset we think maybe he had a heart attack!"

"That why you're here?" Horton asked. The boy's eyes became wet. He nodded yes. Then Horton flashed with sweat. Above the mound of ashtrays, two black, piercing eyes appeared. The mother ground out a cigarette and nodded. Horton felt like the guilty party in a Detroit police lineup.

His eyes fell to the page of blurry print. The image of Bunny's EKG was back again. Earlier, while doctors and nurses had milled around the emergency room probing and squeezing the little towhead, Horton had entertained himself by watching blips on an EKG screen. The lines hopped up and down above the Rabbit's bed.

It reminded him of the old electric Miller Beer sign, the one on his dorm room wall back in college. The blips, hills, and valleys looked like a time line now, a moving record, all the depressing lows and manic highs he'd suffered since Janie left—from the burning of the gum cards to the emergency room of Detroit Memorial Hospital. The machine that monitored the Rabbit's heart could have just as easily been documenting Walker Horton's life.

He sneaked a peek across the waiting room. The kid shook his head in a pitying way. Something to do with the play of the New Becton Hot Dogs, Horton assumed. He closed his eyes, saw the EKG screen again, and watched the blip dive for the bottom. The initial drop was Janie leaving. The line skyrocketed. Little League reunion and the announcement of the LWS, he thought. Now the line was falling fast. It deep-sixed again and then, except for a short upswing here and there, slow-crawled along the bottom. The year of the divorce, he thought.

The tiny upswings were the weekly visits to Markum. The final period was pure wildness: the ups and downs of the training camp and the onset of the Little Series. He could thank Barnes, Wilt, and now the Giant for that erratic reading.

"The doctor will see you now!" Horton jumped. A plastic cup of cold coffee and wet cigarettes splashed across the photo of the fisherman yanking in the bass.

A white-haired man approached and stuck out his hand. Short, dark tan. Sixty, maybe older. The grip was strong for a man his age. He wore a blue blazer and a navy and gold club tie. The white oxford shirt was starched, stiff at the neck.

"Ron Kemp. It's a pleasure, Mr. Horton," he said.

Horton looked at the nurse for reassurance. She smiled. "This is Mr. McKay's doctor. He's in the best of hands. Dr. Kemp's one of the city's foremost neurological surgeons," she said. Kemp reached out and patted the nurse's arm.

"Donna, it's almost two o'clock in the morning, let's cut the crap," he said.

"Just want to let you know that I've been following you guys ever since you started working out in Florida. I've got a box behind home plate at Tiger Stadium. Lousy game tonight, but you did a nice job of handling Kline. Games like that can be brutal when you're behind the plate. I used to do a little catching myself," he said.

Christ! Was the entire city of Detroit in the stands tonight? Had anybody in the Motor City missed the game? The warm rush took Horton by surprise. He reddened, grinned, then reached out and pumped the doctor's hand again.

"Well, it was a heck of a way to get a win, but at least we're going into Cleveland tied in the thing," he said. His face went icy wet. What a shitty thing to say.

"You didn't put the little guy up there to get hit by a pitch, I hope?" The voice had changed. The doctor's hand slowly pulled away.

"Oh, no! I never . . . He begged to bat. Ah, how is he? I mean, Bun-Bun's my best friend. He's going to be all right, isn't he? I mean—"

"He seems to be coming around. It's a very severe concussion.

It's still too early to make any accurate prognosis," he said. "We've learned some interesting things from him, however. He came around for a second or two and mumbled something about MS. We've talked to his wife, of course. She confirmed it. Were you aware that McKay has multiple sclerosis?"

Horton listed slightly to his left, found the wall, and steadied himself.

"Yes, me and Elmer. We're the only ones. He thinks he's going to die, Doc." Horton's voice caught when he said it. The large hand reached out and took him by the arm.

"That have anything to do with him going in to hit tonight?" the bushy white brows flickered above kind hazel eyes.

"Everything, Doc! Everything!"

"You're a good man, Horton. We'll keep your friend McKay here until he's well enough to go home. His wife will be here in the morning. Now you and your Hot Dogs get along to Cleveland and stick it to those Pintail guys. By the way, pitch that guy Ensor high and tight. That last ball he hit on Kline was six inches off the outside corner, got his arms extended."

Horton stuck out his hand. The doctor took it and smiled. The warmth and firmness were there again.

"Okay if I go by and see the little guy before I leave?"

"Sure, he's right down the hall. Fifth door on the left. Room 3445. His sister is going to sit with him tonight. She lives in Detroit. So that should be a comfort. She'll help get the family back and forth when they get in from Terre Haute tomorrow."

"Sister?" Horton shouted.

The eyebrows flew up like white shag window shades. "Yes, she came in right after they brought him into his room."

Horton backpedaled down the hall, talking manically as he walked.

"Sister, my ass! A blonde with nice boobs?"

The doctor nodded enthusiastically. "Yes, well endowed," he said. "A very pretty girl!"

The room was full of shadows. The only light flickered above the bed, a flashing blip on the EKG screen. The line fell. Horton nodded. Where the hell was she? The bed was jacked up high at the head. He spotted a pillow and followed the outline of a small, hilly protrusion. The Rabbit was under those covers. Horton blinked. A red digital readout flashed 103. Pulse. At least the little guy's heart was still tripping away.

"Over here," Barnes said and stepped out of the shadows, shaking her hair.

"What the hell are you doing here?"

"Waiting for the little fellow to come to. Looking for a quote or two from you. I just wanted your reaction to what everybody was saying in your locker room after the game."

"Well, you can file your fucking story because Bun is too sick to talk and I'm too smart to fall into another one of your—"

"Your teammates say that you stuck him in against Pazerelli because you were afraid to stand in against him yourself!" Barnes said.

She smiled and took a long drink from a bottle of Coke.

"Why don't you get your ass out of here? This guy's lying here in a coma and you're trying to get him to give you a quote. Really important story. When did the Little Series become something that merits this kind of attention from the great Larry Barnes?"

"Oh, since protesters started using the thing as a vehicle to rally rednecks against major league baseball, and since old guys started holding protesters out of twenty-second-story windows. How's that for starters? You should read the papers, Horton. You guys are news these days. You passed sports and camp last week," she said.

Barnes and Horton stood at the foot of the bed. The shadows covered her face. She wore a robin's egg blue boat neck blouse, white shorts, and sandals. Her hair was tied back and wet. Horton looked at the window. Raindrops dinged against the glass. The little lump shifted in the bed. The red meter flashed 108.

"Look, Horton, the score is tied 20–20. Pazerelli, a fucking wild man, has just loaded the bases by heaving ninety-mile-per-hour grenades all over the place. So we got the team captain coming to the plate. The writers are already wrapping up their play-by-plays.

"Hooter Horton, team captain, walks. Hot Dogs 21, Pintails 20. Tied series. Bring on the protesters so we can write the real story of the night. Then you walk out of the on-deck circle and screw things up royally by handing the bat to a little fellow who's so uncoordinated he can't even get out of the way of a simple ground ball!

"You're a reporter. Don't you think you might want to ask the guy who takes one in the head for his captain how he feels about playing for a guy like you?"

"The team thinks I set him up?"

Barnes shuffled through her spiral notebook. Then turned to catch the light spill from the doorway.

"Albaugh: 'No comment!' He's stopped talking to the press. Doesn't want to embarrass the president any more than he has!

"Magruder: 'If the Rabbit dies, I kick Horton's ass. Anybody doesn't believe that, I'll take all the action I can get and give them whatever odds they want.'

"Rymoff: 'If Elmer isn't off in Baltimore trying to keep Gross from screwing him out of his company, this doesn't happen. The Giant would never have put Bunny up there against a Pazerelli. I walked on four straight pitches. If any of those things had come even close, I'da been looking at a change of underwear.' "

"And Wilt?" Horton asked.

"Wilt: 'I rest my case. Ask Horton, he's the guy writing the book.' "

Horton looked blankly at Bunny's EKG. The blip plummeted again. Barnes' voice was fading, coming in and out. She continued to talk.

". . . and oh, yes, when you went along in the ambulance, Wilt called you the Steve Garvey of Little League baseball. But this is all I want to know. You put this guy up to hit. Okay, maybe you had your reasons, but now I'm sitting in this room—"

"Where you shouldn't even be," Horton injected.

"And I overhear two doctors talking about his condition and how everybody knows that it comes equipped with double vision. Is there something about McKay that we don't know?"

Horton iced up.

"Larry, you write what you want to. Use up all those quotes from guys like Wilt—"

"What's he got? Cancer? Cataracts? Come on, Horton, don't make me write this story without the facts!"

Barnes pushed past Horton, leaned over the bed, and pulled the covers back. The little protruding teeth were out, touching his lower lip. McKay exhaled in a wheezing way. His eyes batted.

"Larry Barnes, *Baltimore Sun*. McKay, do you have anything to say about the beanball incident?"

Horton spun, grabbed an arm and slung her halfway across the room. "Get your ass outta here!" he screamed.

"Cligger Night!" the voice was weak and muffled by the sheet.

Horton turned to the bed. "What?" he said.

The white lump rose, his lips parted. "Have a Cligger Night!"

"Sure, Bunny, you get some sleep now. We'll have a good night," Horton said. "I promise. Just relax and get . . ."

Behind Horton, Barnes leaned over McKay's bedside table, writing furiously.

". . . get outta here. . . ."

"Just a minute. I want you to read tomorrow's lead. It may be one of the best I've had in years."

McKay had turned sideways now. The pulse was 98. The EKG looked good. But what the hell did Horton know?

"Okay. Here we go," she said. "A loss to the Poughkeepsie Pintails tonight and the New Becton Hot Dogs find themselves standing at death's door. Then with the bases loaded and the tying run on third, Hooter Horton made a move that kept the Dogs alive and almost killed an old friend. Horton takes himself out of the lineup, sends up little Bunny McKay, who promptly takes a Pazerelli fastball to what doctors at Detroit Memorial described as the left temporal area.

"Dogs 21, Pintails 20. McKay, the game's hero, now lies in semiconscious state in Detroit Memorial Hospital with a game-winning RBI that he may not live to celebrate."

"You wouldn't print shit like that," Horton said.

Barnes walked across the room, then stood in the lighted doorway and laughed. "Horton, it's now 3:15 A.M. I've got an editor holding a phone line open for this story. If you don't want to wait for tomorrow's paper, you can follow my pretty little rear end down the hall," she said.

The slap of the sandals and squeaking sneakers filled the empty corridor with strange little echoes. "Don't print that crap. I'm telling you right now, do not print that shit."

Barnes looked ahead. Horton tailgated the tight white shorts.

"Give me the story on McKay."

"There is no story."

"What's he got?"

"A concussion!"

"What else?"

"Nothing!"

"Bullshit!" Barnes screamed as they passed through the waiting room of sleeping people.

The kid in the Tiger cap leaped to his feet. The old man snorted. Two nurses "shushed" and shook their heads.

"You write that crap and you'll regret it." Horton's voice cracked. He'd seen the bank of phones earlier in the evening. They were right around the corner.

The sandals slapped. The sneakers squeaked. Barnes yanked the receiver off the hook and speed-dialed her credit card number.

"Joe, yes, I do, yes. I know what a nitpicker I am, urine samples from all my sources, want everything to be just right," she said, and waved her middle finger at Horton. "Yes, here's the lead. Little Series, graph one. Here goes. A loss to the Poughkeepsie Pintails tonight leaves the New Becton Hot Dogs scratching and whining outside death's door—"

"Don't print that death shit!" Horton grabbed the receiver and jerked the cord. The black earpiece flew down the hallway, bounced along the tile floor, and slid to a stop in front of the nurses' desk.

"He's dying!" Horton's words were choked.

Barnes couldn't find her voice at first. "He's got a severe concussion," she managed, easing another receiver off another hook.

"MS. He's got MS. You don't print this! And you don't tell anybody on the team." Horton softened the threat with a sob. "If I didn't bat him tonight, he said he'd die a failure . . ."

"McKay's dying?"

"Six months, maybe less."

Barnes and Horton walked down the hallway. The squeak, slap, squeak were slower and more distant than before. Horton's head was down. Barnes' eyes were glazed. A nurse waited under an Exit sign, tapping her foot in a rhythmic way. One hand was planted firmly on her hip, in the other a black phone cord swung from the broken receiver.

REDS, BLUES, AND GREENS RAINBOWED UP FROM lake-size puddles. Barnes stepped over a gushing sidewalk gutter. Walker Horton plowed through the water like a harbor tug. He looked into the deluge and shook his head. Water ran from the beak of his Hot Dog cap. Not a cab in sight. Barnes crossed without looking at the corner of Macomb and Randolph. Horton stayed with her stride for stride. A wave from a passing truck rooster-tailed across the couple's path. "Son of a bitch," Barnes swore. "Don't walk so close to the curb," Horton said.

"I'll walk where the hell I please," she said.

"Don't write the story on Bunny!" he said.

"You know how reporters are, Horton. I've never been happier in my life. I just had one great big scoop fall right in my lap!"

They slugged along Beaubein Street bent like deck sailors fighting a nor'easter, Barnes in the lead, Horton pacing along in her wake. The rain stung his face. Large, warm, pellet-size drops. He hated reporters. When he got back to North Carolina, *The Johnstonian Advertiser* could get themselves a new boy. He'd write the book, then go back to teaching—anything but newspaper work.

"Why don't you call it in then? Christ, nobody's holding you back!" he said.

"A maniac ripped the phone out of my hand. I've blown my deadline now."

A cab cut through a curbside river. Horton spun and swore at the driver. The glare of the streetlights was blinding. He rubbed his temples gingerly. His head was a grenade. Barnes was working furiously, trying to pull the pin.

"Do me a favor: Before you spread this across America, slip over to the hospital and tell McKay's kids. They'll be in from Terre Haute tomorrow. They deserve to hear it from you first, don't you think?"

An air horn blasted. A produce truck ground gears, then pulled around a long black limo. Up ahead, at the corner of Randolph and Michigan avenues, reflections from an amber traffic light glowed in the shiny black street. Horton didn't need Barnes to find the Dearborn Hotel. They were back in civilization now. He'd grab himself a cab and split.

"Hey, if you're pushing guilt, you're wasting your time," she said.

The conversation stopped with the rain. The flapping sandals and squish of wet sneakers filled the damp night with a strange, soggy cadence.

"You ever have anything shitty written about you in the paper?" Horton said.

"I saw *Absence of Malice* three times. Does that count?" She stopped under a streetlight and looked back over her shoulder.

"Are you threatening me, Horton? What are you going to do, give me a bad shake in the book? Tell everybody what a sarcastic bitch I am?"

"Don't write about Bunny having MS!" he said.

"And if I do?"

Horton moved under the light. Below him a vague gray reflection stared up from a mammoth puddle. He could see the outline of his rain-soaked cap; the orange HOT DOGS looked like rust in the murky puddle.

"Half the team was on the balcony watching you ball Wilt!"

The sandals slapped twice. She'd started to walk. "What?" A horn blew. The night turned quiet.

"What did you say?" she said.

"Just wondering if you knew. That morning I ran into you coming down the back steps of the Ramada. You'd just been the main attraction of the late, late show. Magruder, Rymoff, and Kline were out on the balcony. I happened to be down by the pool, saw the whole thing!"

Down Michigan Avenue, back toward Detroit Memorial, a siren wailed weakly in the night. Car horns made trumpeting sounds. Shadowy vehicles passed. More water splashed at their feet. The rain picked up again. Horton watched the drops ricochet off his shoes and splatter softly in the puddle.

Barnes' laugh was high, a keening sound that blended with the approaching siren. Horton spotted the red lights swirling in the distance.

"You thought I . . ." she pushed back the wet blond hair and looked up into the fluorescent streetlights. Her face contorted for a second; then she was laughing wildly, convulsed, out of control.

Horton cringed.

"You thought it was me with Wilt when the guys were out on the balcony?" The laughter was more controlled. "Hooter, Hooter, right church but wrong pew. You got the right john but the wrong whore!"

Horton sat on the curb. A river raged across his shoetops. The strings kicked up the froth like white-water rapids.

"You are such a pitiful little asshole," she said, looking down at the soaked gray uniform. He pushed his head between his knees. A bottle cap caught in the race bobbed off into the darkness.

"Who, then?" he said.

"Who knows? I got a tip from the bell captain earlier that evening. Your precious Little Leaguers had been doing a brisk business with the guy's stable of hookers all week. On that particular night"—she laughed again—"Magruder and Rymoff had ordered a girl for Odie. She was supposed to show up at the room no matter what time he got in."

"I saw him get out of the cab with somebody, but—"

"That was Odie; he got in earlier than the rest of them and got tired of waiting. So—"

"He went out and picked somebody up," he said.

"No, he called the front desk and they gave him directions to the girl's house," she said.

"The one Bear had booked? And he went all the way out there and brought her back?"

"Sure, that was the deal. Rymoff and Mouse weren't going to pay the bill unless they got to watch!"

"You're kidding! You mean Odie was in on the thing?"

"You must really be close to your players. Hell, that was the running joke for the next two or three practices. When the balcony boys couldn't see, Bear tapped on the glass. Wilt spun her around until she was facing the window. How's that for sick?"

"What the hell were you doing up there at six in the morning, then?"

Horton looked into Barnes' eyes, then took on his own reflection in a pavement puddle. The laughter was gone from her voice. The sentences were cool, each word clearly enunciated.

"Following up on the lead, deep background. One of the assumptions I'd made was that if given the opportunity, you and your Little League jerks would act just like major leaguers." She shouted to be heard above the hiss and splash of the traffic.

"But not to write it?"

"I'm going to go real slow. Try to read my lips. I'd been writing from gut instinct. The assumption I was making when I was blasting you with those sarcastic columns was that the series was no more than a promo for a hot dog franchise and that the players, you and your asshole buddies, weren't ex-Little Leaguers chasing the boyhood dream but a bunch of middle-aged crazies trying to see how much they could get before their wives wised up and called a halt to the thing."

Barnes stopped to catch her breath. Her hair had fallen over one eye. She continued talking, never bothering to push it back.

"When I found out that a gynecologist had joined the boys on the balcony to watch Wilt that was all I needed. You put yourselves in the public domain, then acted like world-class dorks. The balcony scene not only eased my conscience, it also said, 'Larry, go get 'em, you've been right on the money.' Horton, I'll write anything, anything that I think has anything to do with this story."

He found the rump of his pants. Too late; the sack was soaking wet. "I guess I owe you an—"

"Apology!" she finished his sentence.

"You guess you owe me an apology? Fucking-a-tweetie you owe me an apology, but you don't even know for what. Thinking that was me in the room was a pretty natural assumption. I flirt around a lot with Wilt. You see the guys on the balcony. Hey, I can live with that."

Horton dropped his head again and studied his face in waves of the swirling puddle.

"I come tripping down the steps about sunup. Two and two make four. But thinking that I'd call in a lead like the one I read you back in the hospital room—that was pretty insulting. *The Baltimore Sun* doesn't print that kind of crap, and I'd don't write it!"

Horton's head flew up. He tried to speak.

"Show me one case when I've been tasteless about something that wasn't begging for it! And don't say your Little Series. A midget hot dog called Frankie? Pregame magic acts with guys pulling baseballs out of women's blouses, guys in the bleachers yanking down each other's pants? Give me a fucking break!"

"You're not going to write about Bun-Bun?"

"Are you slow? Is all this rain giving you swimmer's ear? No, Horton! No, I'm not."

"Then why did you—"

"Go to the phone? I didn't say I wasn't a shit, I said I didn't write it. I'm trying to cover this World Federation of Baseball

Series of yours like a real honest-to-God reporter. To do that well I've got to know where the good guys and the bad guys are."

"And—"

"Well, you are a slow one. Good, but slow as a slug," she said.

Horton felt the sleepless night circle his stomach. A sharp pain in his knee reminded him of the 21–20 game. He raised up slowly and shook his rain-soaked head. The cap tumbled forward, making a splatting sound as it hit the wet cement.

"When a guy plays a guy like McKay and has the balls to take the heat you have, well . . ."

"Then you feel better about the series? You're saying maybe we aren't what you thought we . . . ?"

Horton was confused.

She pulled him toward her. The Shalimar was weak, watered down by the night.

"Slow, Horton. Nice, but dumb. Just the way I like 'em. I may only say this once, so listen up: I'm sorry about McKay. I think you're a hell of a guy, and the rest of them, well, we'll just have to see, won't we?

"The truth is that I thought you were playing Bun-Bun for all the wrong reasons. Something to do with the book, to piss off Wilt. Maybe because you wanted someone in the lineup with a weaker bat than yours. Hell, I couldn't figure it out."

A gust of rain cut across Horton's face. He looked up Michigan Avenue. Black peaks and rough edges of high buildings broke the skyline, separating the city from the morning light. The streetlights blinked, then dimmed. He could see the outline of her near-perfect nose. Full lips, an easy target, he thought. Barnes' kiss was sudden and warm against his cheek.

"What the hell was that all about?" he said.

"Apology. Some people know how to give them. Some don't," she said.

"The last time you did that I woke up as the laughingstock of America, the centerpiece of a rather tasteless sports column," he said.

"Okay, I guess I was a degree or two out of line there. But the

World's Oldest Little League team! The *Hot Dog* bus! I didn't believe that a forty-year-old man could be that sincere about anything, let alone playing Little League baseball."

The green eyes had darkened. Everything—the hair, the blouse, the shorts—was warm and wet. Her lips parted into a perfect pout. She tipped her chin. The curious puppy look! Horton felt the kisses move across his check. It was so sudden and tender. He couldn't respond. She pecked a raindrop from his chin. He turned his head. Her tongue pushed past his lips.

The siren ended the moment. A hook and ladder chased by. A cadre of smaller trucks splashed along in its wake. He looked at Barnes and smiled. A tailgating chief's car threw more water on their embrace. They held the kiss and listened to the siren fade into the night.

"Where's the fire?" she asked.

"Figure it out. You're the smart one," Horton said.

There would be a day when details of the game, the beanball incident, and the frantic night would seem like some old brown picture, a look into an ancient scrapbook. Familiar faces, but names, times, and locations lost forever. But the wet gray sky, the old park bench, and the daybreak conversation, those were something else again. CAPITOL PARK, DETROIT CITY. THE BEST NIGHT OF MY LIFE. Horton wrote it with a stick in the soft brown mud right there in front of the park bench.

The rain quit. The sky cleared. The little bench felt downright comfortable. Somewhere between the embrace and the park, Horton found his second wind. He didn't know Detroit. But he took her by the hand and walked right to the spot. And by the time the morning traffic began to move along Griswold Street, Larry Barnes had heard things about Walker Horton that would make Dr. Benjamin Markum blush.

He laughed softly at one of his admissions. She lay her head on his shoulder and rubbed the wet hair against his neck.

"One little kiss and the Hot Dogs' captain tells all. Larry, you are one hell of a fine little reporter," she said.

"Print it, I don't care. Hell, it'll take you a week to sort it out," he said with a laugh.

"I don't know. Horton, you're dealing with a photographic memory here!"

The morning grays grew lighter. City sounds were cranking up. Birds chirped, trucks backfired. Another stack of newspapers hit the street. Horton looked up and smiled at the soggy thunk. Traffic backed up on Griswold Street. A whistle blew. The cops were up.

"You think I haven't been making notes. I've heard enough tonight to give your family tree a pretty decent shake," he said, laughing again.

"So you spent the first forty years of your life idolizing Wilt," she said, opening an imaginary notebook.

"You got your foul mouth from your grandmother," he countered. "That's my favorite."

"Ah, you've spent the last year pining for a woman who, excuse me"—she laughed—"set fire to your gum cards and ran off with a guy who charms snakes."

"The way I see it, you hate your father for naming you Larry," he said. "Now you're playing payback."

"Did I say that?" she said.

Horton kissed her ear. "Deny it!"

"Your mom's really in a mental institution?"

Horton pulled away.

"Sorry. I wasn't trying to be funny. I thought—"

"Forget it. I'm . . ."

She stood and shook her hair. "Look, I don't know what the kissing and groping back there under the streetlight was all about—the rain, the moment—I'm too tired to even try to figure all that out. But let's don't let this slip away. A girl on the road—who knows?

"By the way, would you like a reporter's opinion?" she added. Horton cocked his head. She continued before he could speak.

"You really need to deal with your mother's situation. Go see her. You say she won't know you. It doesn't matter. For God's sake, do it for you. Every once in a while it's okay to do something for yourself, you know!"

Horton shook his head. Barnes was making sense again. Markum had said it a hundred times: "She's just a sick woman. Go see her, *talk* to her. It's not your fault your father died and you didn't put your mother in an institution. Confront the situation and you'll relieve a lot of this unnecessary guilt."

"And while I'm still on my stump, here's something else," Barnes said. "You still love this Janie girl. I can tell; this kind of thing is one of my specialties. You say she's coming to the game in Cleveland, right?"

"She called, left a note at the hotel in Chicago. Said she wanted two tickets," Horton said.

"Well, my guess is it isn't to see a Little League game. The lady's tired of playing with snakes and probably is slithering back," she said. "She'll roll in with some fat little girlfriend and tell you how much she's missed you. You're going to have to make a decision. And whatever it is, don't let tonight's little fun-run influence you one way or another." Barnes stood and stretched the blue blouse across her chest. "But for Christ's sake, Horton, be tough. Don't roll over and play dead. You do and she'll be torching your gum cards again."

The wet pine cone felt good in his hand. He cocked his arm and fired. The brown clump floated and fell into the path of a speeding delivery truck.

"Yeah, I don't know what I'll do. I guess we'll have to see. By the way, where do we go from here?" he said.

"Us? How about Cleveland?" She laughed. "Hell, somewhere, nowhere. Never press a sleepy woman." She yawned again and gave him a loving punch. "The beginnings of a pretty decent friendship? I don't know," she said.

He stretched, pulled at the brim of his cap, and took her by the hand. "We've got five hours before Elmer opens another Doggie Dugout. You want to grab a motel, maybe catch a nap before we—"

"After being up all night? Wouldn't want to see an old fellow like you be anything less than his best."

She walked off toward Washington Street.

Horton followed. "I love the wet look," he said. "Smart and wet."

"Now, take a guy like Wilt. There's a guy who knows his way around women," she said. "He'd wait, bide his time until he knew he was at his best, I'll bet. Then, whammo! Horton, we've got to wise you up!"

•7•

WALKER HORTON RUBBED HIS HANDS. SHOOK HIS fingers to chase the sting. He slumped down on the bench and sat on his palms. The pins and needles persisted. The game's final out was still very much with him. He'd hit a dart down the first-base line, raced toward the action, watched Graham dive and throw his oversize glove at the ball and then arrived at the bag to hear Campbell shriek, "Herout!"

Horton rolled off his hands and gave them another shake. Television cameras paraded by. A radio man shoved a recorder in Wilt's unshaven face. They came down the dugout steps stride for stride, pitcher and reporter. Wilt's glove slapped against the dugout wall. "Fuck it, screw this circus," he said. Magruder threw a bat on the gravel flooring. Rymoff belched and kicked the water cooler.

Municipal Stadium rumbled above them. Suehowicz was on the move, leading them out. Horton flexed his fingers, saw his line drive again, and tried to shake the thought. Thousands of fans this time, bunny-hopping through the first-base boxes, waving banners and holding signs. Suehowicz! What a hardheaded little prick. Didn't the guy know when to quit?

"Ten men left on base in a six-inning ball game. We got us some clutch-fucking hitters, no question about it," Wilt said.

Grant Dole of the *Cleveland Plain Dealer* puffed on a short-stemmed pipe, listened to Wilt, nodding as he wrote. Dole exhaled. A gray cloud floated along the bench and settled down over the Hot Dogs' captain.

"Looked like you got into that last ball pretty good, Hooter. What'd he throw you?" the reporter asked.

"Fastball, away. It's as well as I've hit one in the series," Horton said and rubbed his hands again.

Wilt grabbed Dole by the arm. "Hey, I'll tell you what I think! When you're a .200 hitter, you don't swing on a three-and-one count!"

The Giant stepped between Wilt and Dole.

"Graham made a real decent catch. It was a bang-bang play. If he's a split second off, that ball's past first, in the right-field corner, and it's us instead of McKeen with the one-game lead."

Wilt jabbed his chin at the reporter again.

"What we got now is no friggin' pitching. If you're talking Boston, we've got about as much chance as a tea bag in a canoeful of pissed-off Indians. You can quote me on that one, Dole," he said.

The left-hander walked away, muttering under his breath. "Who's shitting who? We've blown both games when we had pitching. And we're going to win the next two? My ass!" he said. He pushed past two white-uniformed Cleveland players and ducked into the dugout runway. "Fuck it!" The glove cracked like a rifle against the runway wall. Dole released more blue smoke, smiled, and jotted another line in the pad.

The Giant surrounded the reporter with long, circling steps. "Don't let Wilt kid you. Just a little perturbed losing a one-run game. Pitchers tend to be a little melodramatic," he said. "The boy's a competitor . . . one of his strengths. We're still in this thing. We've got a few surprises waiting for McKeen. Ain't gonna be no Boston Tea Party—no, sir, we've got more breaths in us than McKeen might think. I got me a pitcher that . . . ."

Horton perused the stands behind home plate. Six innings of

quick, over-the-shoulder glances had brought on a crink in his neck. He tipped back his cap and rubbed the soreness. Typical Janie, he thought. Leave a note saying you need two tickets, then don't show up. She must have done it a dozen times back when they were seeing the shrink.

Horton scanned the Indians' comp area. Blue box seats and good-looking women—blondes, brunettes, ladies with small children. Players' wives. Janie's T-shirt, shorts, and fat-girl sidekick should be easy enough to spot.

Cleats scraped against the cement steps. Joe Carter, the Indians' left fielder, looked up from a rubdown he was giving his bat. Horton took a cone cup and pushed the button on the water cooler. No Janie; he might as well give up. The Giant was over by the bat rack entertaining Barnes and Dole. Horton leaned back on the bench and listened.

"Now, all this is off-the-record. But Larry, you wrote such a beautiful piece about Bun-Bun that I think I owe you an explanation of where I was that night. While Pazerelli's sticking a heater in the little fellow's ear, I'm back in 'Balmore' doing battle with my board, a group that's been acting like they been in basic training with Attila the Hun," he said.

"Yep, they was all upset about me holdin' Suehowicz out the window. I lost my temper with the fellow, and I'll admit that airing him out there in front of all those people wasn't exactly the best thing for a corporate head like myself to do. Sort of went out on a ledge on that one, I guess." He laughed and cracked his walnut-size knuckles.

He waved the black cap toward the upper deck in right, screwed up his face, and spit a line of tobacco into the grass.

"Look at him out there leading that snake dance, trying to get more fans to leave. Don't look like that flying lesson I gave him did a hen of a lot of good."

Horton watched the conga line spiral along the rim of the stadium. Below the protest, grass sparkled under banks of bright, white lights. Horton smiled and remembered Ebbets Field. Night games, he thought. He glanced at Barnes. She winked him away.

Two thousand people in tonight's walkout, maybe more. Even bigger than Chicago and Detroit. Had Elmer's advice to the commissioner been sound?

"Let the series continue. You don't have an option. The protest will eventually run its course," Thumma had reasoned. "Cancel the series and every newspaper in the country will be down on the major leagues. The LWS is selling more than hot dogs. The media can't let it end now. Newspapers, TV, and radio, everybody's riding along. Just relax and let the ole' *Hot Dog* bus go as far as she can."

A bat cracked. Horton watched the ball shoot out of the cage. He followed its flight until it disappeared in the lights. Cory Snyder raced to his left, spun, and made a behind-the-back catch. The Giant's big hands clapped like Ping-Pong paddles. He continued his monologue.

"So anyways, that's where I was the night Hooter over here pulled off that 21–20 squeaker in Detroit. Hoot, I told you that was a hitter's ballpark," he said, and spat politely into the cone-shaped cup.

Barnes laughed. Horton looked down at his feet and chewed his lip. Vintage Elmer. Dole tilted his spectacles and entered another short, jerky burst in the book.

"Well, I pulled her out. Marched right out from behind the podium, got down among them, and looked 'em right between the eyes. Said we would win the series. Told them the franchises would skyrocket and our stock would ride in the nose cone, go right along to the friggin' moon.

"Even suggested that when these rabble-rousers run their course that I'd like to sponsor a number of good well-behaved fans, take 'em to the All-Star game ever' year, let 'em sit down and talk out their problems with the commissioner and player reps. Don't print it, but that's what I'll do when this thing's over."

The Giant zigzagged his pace, cutting the gray of the Hot Dogs from the white-uniformed Cleveland Indians. He tugged the black cap, spat on the dugout floor. The reporters wrote, sucked cigarettes. The big guy had mended nicely. Elmer the Giant was back.

"Then Gross weasels up out of his seat and asks how the hell I expect to recoup all the damage we've done already, all the negative publicity this Larry Barnes and her friends are spreading from coast to coast." The Giant looked at the blonde and clicked off an exaggerated wink. Then he turned to Horton and fired a round of tobacco juice at the catcher's feet.

"I told 'em that the Doggie Dugouts were opening to record crowds and that personally I appreciated all the newspaper and TV coverage. Thought it was a little rough at first but getting better. Showed 'em that nice piece you wrote on Bunny, Larry, held it right up for all of 'em to see. Oh, yeah, told 'em about my plans for a series of ads featuring the Hot Dogs, kinda like the Miller Lite concept. That's a winner, boy." He pointed to Horton and winked. "We win this series, ever' one of these boys has got a shot at being the next Uecker or Madden.

"Then I made it clear that if they wanted to page through a bunch of old New York papers that they'd learn somethin' about me. I'm a man with a history of comin' from behind. I'd fall back a few runs in a game. That's when I'd get my dander up. Wasn't nearly as effective with a lead. But you get me in a jam and I was damn near unbeatable. Look it up, I said, my record speaks for itself!"

A bell rang behind Thumma's head. The ground crew pushed the big silver cage off toward the right-field corner. Hoses and rakes attacked the infield. A wooden frame dropped over home plate. Horton watched the lime go down.

"So what's the deal? You got your company locked up tight again?" Barnes asked. She tipped the oval pink sunglasses back on her head, pushing them down to hold the long golden hair in place.

"No, I didn't say that. I got me a little reprieve. They voted real close on the thing. Final decision? Well, we win the Little Series, they meet again," he said.

"We still gotta win or you're out?" Horton said.

"Ain't quite that good. We win and they'll reconsider. But right now the majority of 'em are still packing my bags. I told them how much I appreciated their vote of confidence. Said it would mean a lot to you boys and, of course, to Sammy and my wife, Marie, if they were still alive."

Horton gulped.

"Walker! Walker! Up here!"

Horton looked over the dugout roof.

"Walker?"

"Over here, Hooter!"

Oh, cripes, Janie! The woman was upside down. Flat on her stomach, peeking backward into the Indians' dugout.

"Walker. Too big a celebrity to speak?"

Cold sweat. Hot flashes and ice chills.

"Hey, I thought you weren't going to show. Be right up," he said, taking the dugout steps by twos and threes.

Upside down, right side up. Janie Horton didn't look like herself. She'd done the old caterpillar-butterfly trick. Barnes had warned him.

"She'll be looking her best, you can bet your tail on that," she'd said.

Horton leaned across the blue rail into the boxes and shook her soft pink hand. A great start! A kiss, a hug. Anything but a handshake! Horton acting stupid. Janie was back, working her magic again.

"Cripes, you've changed! I guess I was looking for a different woman," he said. Milk complexion. Silver-blond hair. The pixie cut hung over one eye.

"What the hell is it?" he said, fighting the urge to sneak-check his pulse. Janie blinked. The same soft eyes, robin's egg blue.

"Maybe it's the dress. I left my walking boots and T-shirt back at OSU. Big city, seeing an ex-husband turned sudden celebrity." Her laugh confused Horton. Janie could be sarcastic when she wanted to.

What the hell was it—anxiety, panic, a case of the hots? Horton wasn't handling this well at all. Larry had her pegged. The woman had come to Cleveland to mend some fences.

"I looked for you in the stands the whole ball game. Left two tickets. Where's your friend?" he asked.

She laughed. Nice teeth. Not dazzlers like Larry's, but even and white. He'd forgotten how good she could look. A year of anger can cloud your perspective.

Horton turned to the field and wiped his brow. I almost said, "Where's the fat girl?" he thought; no wonder the woman lit up my gum cards.

Whitney Houston's "How Will I Know?" blared over the PA system. Four rotund umpires strolled in from second base. Pat Corrales charged out of the dugout, brushed past Horton, and trotted out toward home plate.

"Ah, did you come by yourself?" he said.

"Oh, we drove in late this morning. Had an exam to give, so we didn't get to the ballpark until your little game was almost over. Sorry!" she said.

"Oh, I thought you were coming to see us play," he said. Janie read disappointment in Horton's voice like musicians read notes.

"Oh, well, I thought we might go out to dinner. I want you two to meet, get to know each other," she said.

"Sure, I guess we could get a bite to eat. We've got some catching up to do. Let me check with some of my buddies; I'm not exactly a native of . . ." His voice fell off. He was scouring the crowd. Where the hell was her friend? He wasn't going to make a commitment until he'd seen the woman. Line a guy like Kline or Wilt up with a dog and there'd be one more thing to rag him about.

He glanced up into the stands again. The sidekick was probably at the snack bar. Horton closed his eyes and tried not to guess her weight.

"You want me to get a date for your friend? Don't believe everything you've been reading in the papers and seeing on TV. A lotta good guys on our team," he said.

Janie laughed. A bit too sincerely for Horton's taste.

"Actually, I haven't been following you all that closely. We've been team-teaching in summer school, busy with a new grant proposal. And Walker, my friend really isn't interested in other men," she said with a laugh.

No voice clues this time. Words wouldn't come. He flashed hot again. Then grinned like Wahoo, the Indians' bucktoothed mascot, and looked up once more into the crowd.

"Oh, fine," he said. "Sure. Love to meet him, sure we can get a bite to eat, I guess, but I . . ."

Janie waved up into a mass of moving T-shirts and dark blue Indian caps. The protest was over. Suehowicz and rabble were gone. People were pouring into the stadium now.

A man in wire-rimmed glasses wearing a BANKERS DO IT WITH INTEREST T-shirt stood up and tapped Janie on the shoulder.

"Hon, how long is this powwow gonna drag on?" he said.

Janie dropped down in the aisle like a catcher.

"Sorry, hon," she said, over her shoulder. "Just give us another second."

"Horton, your Little Leaguers suck," the man added and laughed in a way that made Horton know he meant it.

Horton was watching a tall, athletic man dance down the steps. He had Wilt's body. Black hair, broad shoulders. Almost no waist at all. Where was the fat, balding scientist he'd had his heart set on? Why couldn't he have been the jerk in the banker's T-shirt?

Janie's eyes widened. A familiar look, the one she used to get just before and after sex.

"What do you think?" she said.

The man pumped Horton's hand.

"Dr. Beckner, good to see you, Walker. Friends call me Doc! I thought the three of us might go out and hoist a few. I know a great rib place over in Lakewood, a real laid back little spot, old warehouse, right on the water."

Horton's mind spun like a game show wheel. The categories on Janie's Ph.D. were blurred, tough to read. The grip tightened. Was the man shaking hands or Indian wrestling? Horton smiled and focused on the wheel's categories. Handsome! Big-mouth! Asshole! Take your pick.

Horton looked at Janie. Her smile was up a notch, somewhere between smirk and gloat.

"So you'll join us!" he said.

"Sorry, the boy already has plans." The answer came from below Horton's elbow. The big pink sunglasses popped out of the dugout. Horton took a deep breath. The blond hair swirled. Barnes threw her arm around his shoulder and gave him a hug. Sunglasses. Pink halter top. Cream shorts. Florida tan. Thank you, God, he thought. What a decent thing to do!

"Mine," she said. "Team meeting last night. Opening Doggie Dugouts today, bus ride from Detroit the night before. Nobody gets him tonight. I've got dibs," she said. "Now let's go, baby, you've got that TV thing with NBC, and then we're out of here."

Horton was caught in the crossfire. Janie and Beckner machine-gunned looks of disbelief.

"You look awfully familiar. You didn't by any chance go to Ohio State?" Beckner said. His voice took on a purring quality.

"Dartmouth. Class of '78," Barnes said.

Janie dropped her lip.

Beckner spoke again.

"Really, we'd love to have you two join us. It's on Clifton Avenue, a place called The Feed Store. I've got a table for eleven o'clock. I figured if we left by the seventh inning we'd make it in plenty of time!"

"Oh, I don't know. Whaddya say, hon?" Barnes slipped her arm around Horton's waist.

"Yeah, sure. I'll grab a shower, take care of that thing with NBC. Oh, I'm sorry—Larry Barnes . . . Janie Horton, my ex-wife," Horton said and turned Wahoo red again.

The crowd roared. Spikes clacked up the dugout steps.

The man in the banker T-shirt leaned around Janie, took a sip of beer, and directed his comment at Horton.

"Hey, pal, if the dating game's over now, we'd kinda like to watch some baseball. Okay?"

•8•

THE STEAM FOGGED WALKER HORTON'S CONTACT
lenses. He blinked and rubbed his eyes.

Television! Lights cascaded off the tile flooring. Clouds of steam
rolled over long blue benches. The Indians' locker room looked
like the set for Michael Jackson's *Thriller.* Horton smelled wet
clothes and liniment. A tall, thin man studying a clipboard adjusted his headset and pointed at the brightly lit lockers. A huddle
of T-shirts and blue jeans rolled a thick rubber power cord across
Horton's shoetops.

"Five minutes and we're rollin' tape. Let's hump it!" The man
yanked the earphones off and shouted into the confusion—men
stretched cables, opened light stands, positioned cameras, and
adjusted dials on portable monitors.

Three stools placed in front of a long row of dark blue lockers.
The set, he thought. Before the game a PR type had given Horton
a sketchy explanation of what to expect. A big deal, from the
sound of it. Bob Costas, Marv Albert, and Tony Kubek were going
to be part of the show. NBC was going all out.

"The network is in town to do tomorrow's Indian-Yankee
game. It's simple: Since most of the talent is here, we decided to
do a special on the Little Series."

They'd interview the commissioner in New York, Suehowicz
raising hell outside the ballpark, Dogs and Pintails in their locker
rooms, get some repartee going, and see what happened. If it
worked they'd edit and run it on their new *Later* show along with
a Thumma interview.

"If it really cooks we'll edit a longer version, send it out on the feed, and try to convince affiliates to sponsor game five as the lead into next Saturday's *Game of the Week.*"

Bob Costas beamed up from all six monitors. Costas laughed and nodded off-camera. The screens flashed again and Tony Kubek appeared against the wall in the visitors' locker room. Kubek draped his arm around Bracken McKeen. Ensor and Pazerelli's stools sandwiched the old redhead. Two big, fat bookends, Horton thought.

A parking lot scene came up on the screens. The camera moved in tight on Suehowicz. The scraggly salt-and-pepper beard and broken front teeth looked especially ugly under the TV lights.

"That little peckerwood!" The Giant leaped to his feet. The stool spun sideways. "He's wearing one of my Doggie Dugout T-shirts. We got no connection with him or his freakin' protest. Next time I'll drop him," he said. "I swear it, I get my hands on him again, and he's a spot on some pavement."

Wilt stood and shook hands with a man in a navy blue NBC blazer. Marv Albert, one of Hooter's favorites.

"Coach!" "Horton!" Albert smiled and shook hands as he walked down the line. The hair looked much darker than it did on TV. His smile was ironic, more like a grin, Horton thought.

"This is Odie Wilt, ex-Chicago Cub," the director said.

"Oh, I know Odie. Remember, I'm a fight announcer. Hell of a chase you gave that little shortstop after the game in Chicago, Wilt!" Albert said with a laugh.

Wilt looked at Thumma. Horton saw the jaw tighten. "Who the hell did you ever play for?"

Horton watched the screens light up. "We're rolling tape!" the director shouted and pointed to Albert. The announcer's voice dropped an octave; he smiled, stepped into camera range, and said, "Baseball, a boring game? Well, not lately. And still 100 percent American, my friends. Where else could 683 men play a boys' game for six-figure salaries, walk off the job, and come back a week later to find that a bunch of middle-aged Little Leaguers and a forty-eight-foot hot dog have taken—no, stolen—their fans, their press, heck, the entire world of baseball away?"

The director's hand flew up. "Cutting to B-roll!" he shouted.

"That's a keeper; we're on in sixty seconds," he talked softly into the little chin mike.

Horton watched with interest as the feature played on the screens. There they were dipping and bending, sweating in the Florida sun; then the big *Hot Dog* was motoring along a highway, great overhead stuff shot from a helicopter; game highlights, runs, hits, and errors, Wrigley, Detroit, even a few shots from tonight's game. They watched Albaugh kick a ground ball, saw Horton's line drive and Graham's game-winning catch. The piece closed with the city shots, tall buildings, and the bus hissing to a stop in front of the Chicago Doggie Dugout.

The headsets flashed another sign at Albert.

Costas came up on screen three. His voice sounded clear, almost like he was right out there in the fogbound locker room.

"Well, Marv, you're right. It's a story that's captured the imagination of all baseball fans—Little Leaguers, parents, grandparents, kids of all ages—and, of course, the question America is asking is this: Is this thing just some kind of publicity stunt? Some excellent examples come to mind. Professional wrestling, the House of David, Bingo Long's All-Stars? Take your pick," Costas said. "Tonight we'll be asking some hard-hitting questions to the guys who've been making the LWS news."

Albert introduced the Hot Dogs. Horton and Wilt turned on their stools, smiled, and nodded at the camera.

"Bob, we'll be back with these boys later. Elmer the Giant and Odie Wilt are never at a loss for words and, of course, we'll want to ask Horton about Bunny McKay and why he pinch-hit him against a wild man like Pazerelli back in game two. And Tony, can you hear me? We'll see if that bad-hop ground ball in game one brought back any memories for you."

"We're cutting to Tony now," the floor manager said.

"Bob, I'm here in the visitors' locker room in Cleveland with Bracken McKeen, manager of the Poughkeepsie Pintails. Alongside the old Yankee right-hander are some other names that big-league baseball fans are sure to remember, Biggie Ensor and

Danny Pazerelli. Paz is the fireballer Marv just mentioned, the man who almost separated Bunny McKay from the world of the living several nights ago."

Screen three flashed white, then pink. Costas came up on his anchor set again.

"We'll be showing you both sides of the series, a best-three-out-of-five affair that stands, as of tonight's 6–5 Pintail win, Poughkeepsie 2 and New Becton 1. And we'll also deal with the controversy that has been shrouding the games in recent days. Of course, we're referring to the fans' protest of the professional players' walkout.

"But before we get to the turmoil that seems to be following the big *Hot Dog* bus these days, let's see how the commissioner of baseball is enjoying the Little World Series That Should Have Been. How about it, Commissioner? Thumbs up or down? You approved this thing. How do you see it now?"

Screen five went solid blue in color. The commissioner materialized out of a swirling red-and-white major league logo. He looked stately sitting there in his gray suit and red tie. The blue shirt matched the backdrop. A gold-framed picture of a man with snow-white hair sat on the left of his desk.

"Judge Landis," the Giant said, elbowing Horton's rib cage.

The floor man pointed to the microphone and shushed the Giant.

"We'll also be talking to Joby Suehowicz, the man who has led a group who call themselves the FBLB. Please don't write in and ask us what that stands for," Costas said with a laugh.

Horton watched Suehowicz come up on screen two. A bull's-eye close-up of the unshaven face and dirty hair.

"Don't show that little shit," the Giant said. The director's hand flew at Thumma. The series was taking its toll on the Giant. He had never cussed before. Horton didn't count "dodcast it," "son of a biscuit," "Judas Priest," or any of his other toy swear words.

Costas spoke. There was an edge of authority to his voice.

"Commissioner, when you approved this series of quote exhibition games, did you ever think it would evolve into anything like this, the national media event we have on our hands right now?"

The commissioner tugged at the lapels of his dark gray suit, hedged on the series question, then directed his remarks to Joby Suehowicz.

Screen three lit up. Stonesifer's face was a brilliant red.

"Mr. Suehowicz and I spoke for the last time in Chicago, just before Elmer saw fit to hold him out the window. The owners and players can work out their differences without the help of a bunch of—excuse me, Bobby—vulgar drunks. These people claim to represent the average American fan. Well, I don't think the average fan is someone who comes to a big league ballpark to wave dirty messages around, get drunk, and pull down his pants!"

Costas laughed. The Giant's elbows flapped like a big white turkey. Wilt's guffaw cut through the foggy room.

"Well, Commissioner, I don't know, maybe we'd better let Joby Suehowicz respond to that one," Costas said.

The camera had a three-quarter shot of Suehowicz. Behind him a sea of signs turned and spun.

"How about it, Joby, your thoughts," Costas said.

"Well, my response to the commissioner is that I don't think he's ever seen a game in the finest seat in all of big league baseball, the bleachers at Wrigley. We drink, pull down our pants, and have one hell of a good time out there. Even throw the ball back when some candy ass like Dale Murphy hits one at us. . . ."

"Okay, Joby, let's get back to the Little Series. How do you see it? Why the attachment of your protest to the Hot Dogs, and what are you trying to accomplish?" Costas sounded like Mike Wallace spotting a twitch or a sweaty lip.

"Bob, I see it as a great opportunity."

The camera did a slow pullaway. Behind Suehowicz colorful signs and swaying T-shirts milled and waved. A trumpet blew. The crowd screamed, "Charge!"

"Excuse me, Joby, we're having a little trouble hearing, you'll have to speak up," Costas said.

"Bob, what I was saying is that we want to let baseball know that the game can be played and played well by other than spoiled millionaire major leaguers. So when the Little Series games are over, if you'll point your cameras toward the stands, you'll see a bunch of working stiffs, guys taking a hike. Guys like me and this crowd behind me here, the people who fork over their money day in and day out to watch big league baseball. We're walking out on the big leagues just like they did on us a couple a weeks ago and, of course, like they did back in '82."

"Okay, Joby, sounds like you guys mean business. Now let's—"

"One more thing, Bob. My friends and I have one last message for the commissioner."

The camera dollied back. Suehowicz disappeared into the swirl of signage.

"What's the big leagues, boys? BULLSHIT . . . BULLSHIT . . . BULLSHIT—"

"Cut! Cut! Cut!"

Suehowicz and crowd attacked the camera with their signs like sword-wielding pirates.

"An aggressive little group," Albert said.

"Ten minutes. Let's break for ten and go at it from the Hot Dog-Pintails angle," the floor manager turned to Albert and said. "Is this fucking thing for real? Are we going to try to sell affiliates on guys with their pants down waving fuck signs at the camera?"

A red light flashed. Horton blinked. "Let's get this frigging thing shot. I'm missing Cleveland," Wilt said.

Costas came up on all six screens.

"How about it, Marv? You've got 'em there in the locker room. What's on the minds of the New Becton Hot Dogs? They must be a little unsettled, knowing that they have to take the next two ball games to win this Series?"

The camera panned past the stools and froze on Albert. He took one foot off a bench, waved his arm to the perched players, and strolled their way.

"Yes, Bobby, we've been talking here, and the Hot Dogs are

seething. Odie Wilt put it in rather graphic terms, and yes, you can say that there is no love lost between these two ball clubs."

The director waved. A picture of McKeen, Ensor, and Pazerelli appeared on one of the the little screens.

"How about it, Tony?" Costas said.

"Same story here, Bobby. In fact, I don't know if we can hold the old Yankee fireballer back. McKeen says he's got a message for Elmer. Right, Bracken?"

"Well, Tony, what I'm saying is that we're taking it easy on these guys. Trying not to get anybody hurt. But it ain't because Thumma's about to have his company snatched away from him. We ain't tanking. What we're doing is trying to take them out of their misery with as little pain as possible."

Horton wasn't sure his hearing was right. The Giant was making growling, guttural sounds. He watched the big guy crawl off the stool, drop to one knee, press his nose to one of the monitors, and start to talk.

"Bracken, when the New Becton Hot Dogs win game five, I'm going to jack your little red ass up so high you're gonna have to unbutton your shirt to shit," he said. The Giant was down on his hands and knees now, babbling at the thousands of matrix dots that made up the red face of Bracken McKeen.

The director held up his hand. "Mr. Thumma, is there a chance that we might finish this show?" Then he spoke into the microphone to the men in the truck. "Guys, I'm not trying to be cute, I really mean it. Is this a fucking cartoon we're shooting, or what?"

Wilt affected a nasty grin and made the comment away from Elmer, out of one side of his mouth.

"Horton, we need to talk. And whether you believe it or not, I'm thinking of the team on this one. The big guy is drifting foul. A little puff of wind and he's out of play—senile, crackers! One little gust and he's gone, outta here, bouncing around in the funny farm's bleachers!"

•9•

WALKER HORTON HAD THE TOOTHPICK MOVING, playing along his caps, tickling the old ivories.

"Why would anyone go out to eat with two people who just screwed up his life?" he said.

"Because you want to see what they've got going. That's not so unusual. Dogs sniff. Humans do dinner!" Barnes said.

The blue Avis rental beat along the Cleveland street. Horton pinballed off the dashboard, hit the seat back, and bounced against the door. Barnes whipped the wheel like an overnight trucker and talked baby talk to her reluctant date.

"Looks like we've got an unhappy camper," she said.

"Let's just pack it in," he said. "I got a lot of work to do. I gotta talk to Elmer about Billy's knuckler. He's our only hope for Fenway."

Outside, horns blew and traffic hissed. Horton craned his neck and looked up at a tall, smoke-gray building. Bright lights glared off the glass skyscraper.

"Here's an off-the-record: Wilt's right, Elmer's losing it. The old man needs me. I never thought I'd see the day, but he does. I can't be screwing around with Janie and her egomaniac all night. The Giant's trying to do too much at once, opening the Dugouts, staying ahead of Gross. Hell, he probably hasn't thought about the knuckler in days."

"You like the scientist?" Barnes said, changing gears.

"Did you?" he asked.

She tapped the brakes. A rust-colored 280ZX pulled even with the hood. A blond tennis type revved his engine and stuck out his tongue. She slipped the car into neutral, gunned her motor, and watched him jump through the light.

"Mr. Wizard? He seemed harmless enough to me. A bit pompous, but not as academics go. At least the guy doesn't dress like a Kmart mannequin," she said. "Not a bad bod, either."

"I hate those tweedy, pipe-smoking fuckers," Horton said.

"It's tenure," Barnes said with a laugh. "Does wonders for the confidence."

"What'd you think of Janie?"

Barnes turned the wheel. The tires banged the curb and slalomed through a field of crater-size chuckholes.

"I don't know."

"What's that supposed to mean?" Horton swayed in his seat belt and grabbed the door handle.

"Just that. I don't know. She's cute. And certainly intelligent. But I'm not going to make any judgments on someone I've talked to for a grand total of five minutes," she said.

Juices stirred in Horton's stomach. He hadn't eaten since late that morning.

"This place have normal food?" he asked.

"The Feed Store? If you want something that used to be alive. Steaks, ribs, chicken, this is the place," she said and swung into a parking space large enough for three midsize rental cars.

The lot was packed. Fluorescent lights lit the field of car roofs in a bluish-white. In the distance Horton could see the outline of a huge old brick building.

The Feed Store's interior confirmed Horton's opinion.

"Nice little laid back place my ass," he said.

But if you overlooked the stacks of Purina Chow bags and oaty smell, the place had its merits. Piano music, waitresses in short-short denim overalls. Charcoal smoke mingled with "eau de oats." Horton took a deep breath. He liked the combination.

"Beckner? Yes, right this way," the hostess said.

They'd done a respectable job with the renovation. Dark wood partitions, hanging plants, a country and western combo wailing away on an old wooden stage. For a warehouse the place approaches intimate, Horton thought.

"Your friends are quite the couple. Thought we might have to get a bucket of cold water to break them up a while ago. What are they, honeymooners?" The hostess tightened the red bandanna around her neck and walked them through a series of small, dark rooms. They passed wooden stall-like booths lit by hanging lanterns. Barnes' mauve blouse and baby blue shorts flexed as she walked. Horton watched heads come up from drinks and dinners.

"Don't It Make Your Brown Eyes Blue" played on a tacked piano. Horton looked over a long brick wall topped with ivy plants. Cowboy hats doing the two-step. The bar was hopping. A cowgirl swung through double wooden doors balancing a silver tray on her fingertips. "Watch out, podner," she said. Horton smiled. Barnes took him by the hand.

Detroit seemed distant, a long, long time ago. Strolling along a dirty, rainswept street, watching morning against the jagged skyline. Standing there in the gutter's raging river, kissing someone he thought he hated. It seemed so unreal. Her touch felt soft and warm. He could smell the Shalimar. Larry Barnes, he thought.

"Hey, mood change. I've decided to go ahead and enjoy myself," he said.

"Promise?"

"You got it," he said.

The hostess stopped. "Over there. The lovebirds in the corner cage," she said. Beckner swung a feed bag of flowers to one side and kissed Janie on the lips.

Horton's stomach flipped. Barnes gave his hand a squeeze.

"Promise?" she said.

"They've been carrying on like that for about an hour," the hostess said. "Do me a favor: Mention something to them about eating. I'd like to turn that table over at least once more tonight."

The predinner conversation was predictable. Janie and Larry complimented each other's clothes. Beckner and Horton made noises about how glad they were to get to know each other. Janie hated Larry's looks, which pleased Horton immensely. Beckner small-talked, gulped Manhattans, and asked rhetorical questions.

"I want to hear all about this book or diary. Whatever it is. Janie mentioned that you were writing something," he said.

"Oh, it's nothing, just something to help pass the time of day.

Tell me about Ohio State. Do you raise your own snakes and rats?"
Horton said.

He wouldn't drink tonight. Horton surprised himself with the
idea. A stroke of genius, he thought.

"Walker can't write, make love, or mow the lawn without
downing a six-pack first!" Janie's first words. Session one with the
shrink. Horton would never forget them.

Well, tonight the ex would be real disappointed, because he
wouldn't drink a beer if Beckner held him down and Janie poured.

A waitress and busboy arrived in tandem, more bandannas and
overalls. Beckner ordered another Manhattan. The moment of
truth had arrived for Horton.

"What are you having? Or do you want to take a look at the
wine and beer list first?" Beckner asked.

Horton waved him off, turned and spoke to the waitress. "I'll
pass. But I would like a pitcher of martinis, squeaky-dry, for my
friend here," he said. "Keep them coming as long as she's sitting
up and appears to be making sense."

Beckner touched the waitress on the arm. "Don't be silly. The
beer's on me—"

Horton cut him off.

"I'll pass. It's my night in the barrel, designated driver," he
said.

"You're not drinking?" Janie said. She pushed the peak of hair
out of her eyes and gave her head a toss. Disappointment. Hooter,
one. Janie, zip.

"Nah, I've been dry ever since we started this series thing.
Training. Can't say as I miss it, either," he lied.

Now all he had to do was go cold turkey, refrain from shaking,
keep his hands off the paper sack.

Beckner and Janie were still teacher and student. At least that
was Horton's impression. While Beckner droned away about the
Western rattler, Horton watched her face.

"Christ, why doesn't she take notes?" he wondered.

Horton counted Beckner's empty glasses. Five Manhattans.
The prof looked over his shoulder and ordered another.

Barnes freshened her own martini. Everyone but Horton was nodding and smiling, sucking up to Beckner shooting the bull about frogs and snakes.

"Larry, it's the African clawed frog, I've found chemicals in the mucus in the frog's skin that helps the animal defend itself, gives snakes lockjaw. The jaw actually catches midbite. I've been working with them in the lab all summer. Damndest thing you ever saw," he said. "We think the work will lead to major breakthroughs in the understanding of human nervous disorders. Horton, you seem to have a little tic in your neck. You could be a beneficiary of the work. You never know how these things will turn out."

"I think Tom means 'we.' I wrote the grant," Janie said, flashing a look at Barnes. "We're interested in finding out what the chemicals are and what goes on in the snake's brain that would cause the jaw to freeze like that. The analysis shows the mucus is made up of peptides and indoleamines. These, of course, are chemicals that are commonly linked to human nervous disorders."

Barnes smiled and nodded. "Very interesting," she said. "You know, I worked as an intern for *Discover* for a summer. I toyed with science writing as a career idea. Now look at me, covering Little Leaguers," she said with a laugh.

Horton took another sip of tea. He felt his neck. He hadn't noticed any nervous tic. Why would Larry encourage a dork like Beckner?

Horton felt a hand brush against his leg. Barnes playing kneesie, he guessed. But Larry's was waving at the Ph.D., describing a boa constricter she'd seen in *National Geographic*. Janie? No, she was two-handing her daiquiri, trying to break eye contact between Beckner and Barnes.

Beckner made reference to a snake's eating habits. Larry's tongue darted out. "Like that?" she said.

Beckner laughed. "Exactly. You've got it down pat," he said.

Janie's face went white. She pushed the hair out of her face, then did it again.

Beckner excused himself. "Little boys' room," he said.

"Make that two," Barnes said and followed him out.

"Alone at last," Horton said.

Janie teethed on the handle of a pewter spoon. Horton felt like a cat full of bad canaries. Things weren't working out quite like he'd hoped. If Larry and Janie weren't groping around under the table, then it had to be Beckner. The bastard was looking for Larry, he thought.

Janie pushed her hair again. Horton nodded. The busboy stopped. "Can I get you anything?" he asked.

"I'll have that beer now," he said. "How about you, another? What is that green thing, anyway?"

"Daiquiri. Well, you set a world's record for staying on the wagon. What was it, twenty-five minutes?" she said.

"You love him?" he asked.

The waitress pushed a pitcher in front of Horton. Janie turned her daiquiri up and pursed her lips. "I'll have another one," she slurred. It had been years since he'd heard her lisp. Probably since college. She was always perfect, never high. Always in control, calling the shots.

"He's up for department head. A brilliant scientist. Alice Burman, the Ag. and Life dean's wife, says that he's a shoo-in for the National Academy of Science. Dr. Burman talked to some of the review committee last month at a seminar in Los Angeles."

"Do you?" Horton asked the question again.

She took the long-stemmed glass from the waitress and drank.

"Are you even aware of the kind of prestige I'm talking about? We have a faculty of three thousand plus at OSU. Do you know how many of them are members of the Academy? Two. That's the kind of a figure a Little League ballplayer should be able to comprehend. Two for three thousand. What kind of a batting average is that?"

Horton stood, then sat back down. A busboy cleared Beckner's empty glasses. Where the hell are they? he thought.

"Mrs. Jane Department Head. Mrs. Jane F. Academy of Science. Nice ring to it. Sounds like love, all right," he said. Horton hit the beer and forced a frosty smile over his glass mug.

Janie's nose twitched. "You look like Bun-Bun," he said, giving the needle a twist.

"Screwing the woman responsible for making you America's laughingstock must give you a certain sense of pride," she said.

Horton picked up the pitcher and poured.

"Well, it's give-and-take, this celebrity national spotlight game," he said. He was losing ground. Larry and Beckner had reversed his night.

Janie screwed up her mouth. A line from a Willie Nelson song came to mind. She's a whiter shade of pale, Horton thought.

"What are you popping these days? Valium? Demerol? Walker Horton, Mr. Laid Back. Big-deal McNeal, screwing blond bimbos. How does she like sleeping with a paper sack under the pillow?"

The sting hit liver high, under the rib cage, inches below his heart. He'd done so well to be wavering now. His mouth had dried. He turned his head and looked back through the restaurant where Barnes and Beckner had disappeared. His mouth was ahead of his brain again.

"Janie, level with me on something, will you?"

She drank more daiquiri. He gulped the beer.

"What?" she said.

"Was that you trying to rub my leg a while ago?"

"What!" she laughed. "What!?"

"Well, we have a problem, then." He checked his watch. "I don't know how long it should take a national columnist and an academy scientist to pee, but twenty minutes is fucking ridiculous!"

•10•

"THE GUY'S A POSTER BOY FOR DATE RAPE!" HORTON said.

The Dodge swerved and hit a crater. Horton banged against the dash. A stabbing pain cut his kidneys. Cleveland: the pothole capital of America.

"Nice piece of driving. You haven't missed one yet," he said.

They clipped north along Route 90. Horton glanced at the driver. Mad as hell, he thought. He rubbed his back. Then touched a sore spot on his bicep where a foul tip had left its mark. Lake Erie sparkled behind Barnes' silhouette. He looked away. Blues and grays, a misty summer sky. The "city of potholes" looked like a postcard tonight.

"How the hell do you think I felt? The man who stole my wife starts feeling up my leg, gets up and leaves, my date follows him, and a half an hour later I find them playing footsie in the bar, sharing a drink! And with one fucking straw! Christ! Talk about rubbing a guy's nose in it."

"I went to make a phone call," she said.

"Nice booth. Music, drinks, guys giving rubdowns. Ma Bell's really getting her shit together," Horton said.

"I thought ballplayers were bad, but Horton, you lead the Fucked-up League. I mean, you really bring new dimensions to neurosis," she said.

"The guy's an asshole!" Horton said. His voice was lower, less contrite. "Where the hell are we going? Stauffer's Inn is back there. Don't you want to hit those washboard streets again, give my kidneys another workout?"

"And you figured he might be trying to—excuse the term—'snake you' again?" she said.

Horton watched the bump of distant taillights, traffic wending out into the night. The road followed the lake though the city, twisted for several miles, then stretched out long and flat for as far as the moon would let him see. Tall, leafy trees filled the median. Subtle dips and gentle sways. Horton looked back toward the driver. The lake had disappeared. The engine surged. He leaned over and flipped on the radio. Donna Summer sang "Hot Stuff" for the next few miles.

"Where are you headed? I've really gotta get back, need to talk to Elmer tonight. It's almost two o'clock," he said. The green digital clock on the dash flipped: 1:56 A.M.

He felt the Leatherette upholstery crinkle under his weight, leaned forward, and squinted at a green road sign. Chagrin Falls 8 or 18. It was too dark to see.

"I was coming down on Janie pretty hard. Being an asshole, baiting her about Beckner, when all of a sudden it hit me: The bastard is out there trying to screw my date!"

"Which, of course, he was!" she said.

"He was?"

"Sure. When I got out of the phone booth, he was waiting. We had a drink at the bar."

"His idea!" Horton said with satisfaction.

"No, mine," she said.

"Yours?"

"Horton, do you know why more puppies aren't put to sleep? Because after they've peed all over the carpet, they're so damn lovable," she said. "I don't know what you are in dog years, but puppy no longer applies. Grow up!"

Horton gave her a quizzical look.

"Quit fouling the rug," she said. "Do I look that desperate to get laid? Did it ever occur to you that I might have had that drink for you and Janie? You two may never be Mr. and Mrs. again, but it sure as hell wasn't going to hurt to let her see just what an asshole the boy scientist is."

Horton opened his mouth. The yawn surprised him.

"You look like the snake in Beckner's story," she said. "It's this wild mucus I omit. Makes the jaws lock, renders them harmless. Couldn't bite if you wanted to."

Horton pushed the window button. The night had cooled. He took a deep breath. Not a trace of the city. The air smelled clear and fresh. He followed up with another breath. Mint! Must be near a creek. What an asshole I am, he thought. Barnes tuned the radio. "Doin' it for my baby! Doin' it, doin' it, doin' it for my baby!" Huey Lewis sang.

"Horton, didn't I hear you and Wilt bragging about what great horsemen you used to be?"

She braked and nosed the Dodge down a narrow macadam road. Clouds covered the moon. No road signs. It was still too dark to read.

"Elmer always had horses and ponies. We did okay, I guess. Why?"

Snatches of moonlight played on the bluish fields. "Pretty country," he said. White board fence skirted the road. Cloud shadows slipped across a distant hill. The light appeared for a second. Horton saw a herd of groggy horses, heads down, frozen in their sleep.

"What the hell's the deal here?"

"I just felt like riding. How 'bout you?" she said.

"Horses?" he said.

White bricks flashed by. Brakes screeched, they swerved and went into a semispin. Barnes jammed the car in reverse and manufactured a 180-degree turn. Gravel flew. She used all of the road and both shoulders. "You'd think I'd never been here before," she said with a laugh.

A dim light shone in the white brick gatehouse. Horton saw a leather hat, an old man staggering to his feet.

"That you, Larry?"

"Hey, Donnie! Wake you?" she said, laughing.

"Place is all set. Mr. Coe will bring the horses around about sunup. Thanks for the call. Always good to see you." He tipped his cap and slumped out of sight.

"What the hell's going on?"

"Chelsey Farms, friends of mine," Barnes said.

"At two-fifteen in the morning? I've gotta—"

"Guest quarters are all ours. I think you'll find them comfortable. If I can whistle Betty in we'll sneak us a ride tonight," she said.

Had life snuck up on Horton again?

"Don't worry, you'll be back to open Elmer's Cleveland weenie emporium in plenty of time tomorrow," she said.

"We're staying in guest quarters?" Horton said. His voice had crept up an octave, a bit like a whinny, he thought.

Barnes laughed again. Horton tried but failed.

White fencing serpentined the narrow drive. Long beige barns trimmed in scarlet scattered the rolling landscape. Two rooms? Single beds? Visions of accommodations danced in his head.

"You know everybody?" he said.

"Chelsey's an old friend of my dad's. They survived World War II and George Patton together. When I'm in Cleveland, I come out here and stay, ride the horses. Old, old friends. Great people. They're in Europe for the summer. I've got my own key!" she said.

"Thoroughbreds?"

"Trotters, one of the biggest farms in the country. The biggest next to Hanover Shoe. I'll show you Chelsey's Girl tomorrow, Little Brown Jug winner a couple of years ago," she said.

The car eased up to a wooden hitching post. Barnes turned off the ignition and opened the door. Night sounds flooded the car. He could hear Larry in the shadows fidgeting with keys.

"Over here," she said.

"Where?"

"I'm trying to open the door," she said. A light flashed. Horton blinked. A minimansion materialized.

"Holy crap!"

"Like it?" she said.

"Holy keerap!" he said.

Horton took a silent tour. Barnes preceded him, flipping on lights. Chandeliers; oriental rugs; deep-pile carpets; hardwood floors; big, soft comfort sofas and chairs. The kind of furniture you'd see ribboned off on a Williamsburg tour. Rich, wood-framed oil paintings of beautiful horseflesh—chestnuts, bays, blacks, and sorrels—covered the walls. Horton stopped and admired a watercolor of a jockey in Chelsey's red and beige silks. Barnes touched another switch. "The kitchen," she said. A huge range with a copper hood. A big butcher block table as the room's centerpiece. The walls displayed more horsey art.

"Three foals of Chelsey's Princess. They were killed in a barn fire back in the late seventies," Barnes said. She reached in the refrigerator, pulled out a bottle of champagne. Horton admired the paintings. The bottle popped and fizzed.

"Unbelievable," he said.

"There's more," she said, taking a long pull on the bottle. Horton took a more realistic drink. The refrigerator door slammed, and another bottle popped.

"Here, one for each of us," she said.

The hallway was carpeted in racing red pile. Barnes kicked off her sandals. Horton short-hopped them off of the spongy red rug. She opened a door and turned on the light. Horton laughed out loud.

"Unbelievable!" he said. "And this is the guesthouse?"

Deep red curtains and matching carpet. The rest of the room was done in beige—sofas, chairs, the silk canopy on the big four-poster bed. Horton saw his reflection in a mirrored wall behind a mahogany bar. He counted the bottles. Chevas Regal, Vat 69, Old Grand Dad, Smirnoff's—everything imaginable.

"Saving the best for last," she said and turned out the lights. Horton heard a squeaking sound and watched the curtains crawl open. It was his Aunt Maude's old stereopticon with a life-size view. White fencing, two gigantic horses nuzzling noses, a giant willow tree, all bathed in soft, yellow moonlight. "Like the scenery?" Barnes touched his arm and turned up her bottle. They walked to the window and kissed.

The big roan mare lifted her head, shook her mane, and whinnied at the couple.

Horton jumped. "How close are they?" he said.

"Right outside. They'll be our roommates. I like to sleep with the screen open." Horton lifted his bottle and drank.

"Come on, let's go see them," she said and took him by the hand. She opened the screen. Another cork popped.

"Plenty in the fridge. Here's an extra one for the road," she said.

Horton kicked off his shoes on the stone patio and padded out through the cool, wet grass. Long, stately heads came up. A big, thick-chested bay snorted, looked at Barnes, and made more horsey noises.

"An old friend," she said.

"Here, take this apple. There's a bowlful in the bedroom," she said.

Horton cupped it in his hand and walked toward the white

board fence. "Lay it flat in your palm. That's Betty. We're going to be up on her in a minute, so you'd better make friends," Barnes said. Horton's look was lost in the dark. "Tonight?"

Barnes put one foot on the rail fence and threw herself up. She whistled softly. Four shorts and a long. The big bay trotted over, nuzzled against her blue shorts. Horton offered the apple and watched Barnes slip up on the big horse's back.

"Here, baby, here's a second helping," she said. The horse crunched at the fruit.

"Get up behind me!" she said.

Barnes turned the animal with a touch of her heel.

"She's was a stable horse for Chels Bells, one of the trotters killed in the fire. Ever since then I've kinda been her love interest," Barnes said. The horse walked easily down through the meadow. The breeze blew. Horton bounced. Barnes shivered. He slipped his arms around her waist. In the distance, cloud shadows moved, uncovering long, thin necks, stately silhouettes, dozens of horses. Betty snorted. A friend back by the guesthouse whinnied an answer. "Easy, baby," Barnes said. She stroked the horse's mane. Horton leaned forward and kissed the nape of her neck.

"Pass it on," he said.

They ambled down the hill, watching the moon play on the hill.

"Help me unbutton," she said, lifting her arms. The horse slowed its gait.

"What?"

"It's a tradition. Betty and I always ride bareback at night," she said.

Horton felt the pins and needles back in his hands and eased the blouse over her head.

•11•

IT WASN'T WALKER HORTON'S SHOWER FANTASY
after all. A warm, pulsating Jacuzzi, lovers laughing, talking
softly, Barnes sliding a big cake of perfumed soap along the soreness in his lower back. The water jetted. Barnes laughed, tossed
her hair, and kissed him gently on the neck.

Streisand's "Wintergreen" played on the bedroom stereo.

"A great nude. I should have brought my brushes," Horton
said, rubbing his head against her breasts. "More champagne?" He
lifted a tall, green bottle from the wet tile floor and floated it in
the swirling tub.

They'd taken forever to settle down from the ride—raced to the
tub like naughty, naked children, leaving clothes strewn across a
mile of meadow, then giggling their way through two bottles of
champagne, they floated the bottles in the soapy water, shook
them up, and sprayed each other.

"A circus act we weren't," Horton said. The water rose and
splashed the white tile floor.

Barnes turned to face him. Her eyes were a deep jade now.
Horton saw that wonderful distant look. She held a finger to her
lips. "Shhh," she said and kissed a soap puff from his cheek.

"We didn't really fail. Creative foreplay," she said.

"Horseplay," Horton said.

Barnes closed her eyes and inhaled the perfumed soap. Her
breasts rose and fell with the kick of the water. She stretched her
legs and pulled him to her.

"I think I'm madly in like." She said it softly, above the hiss of
the surge and spray. He pushed off the back of the deep, round tub,
felt the warmth of her breasts slide across his chest. The water

swirled, her legs were around him now, pulling him forward. Horton closed his eyes and was gone, lost in the ecstasy of Larry Barnes.

Walker Horton tossed and turned on wet silk sheets. A bat cracked. The crowd roared. The dream had them playing in Shea.

"Two outs, bottom of the sixth. Odie Wilt and the New Becton Hot Dogs are on the verge of one of the greatest comebacks in the history of grown-up Little League baseball." The voice was Hodges'. Horton rolled, pulled the sheets, and exposed Barnes' nakedness in the predawn moonlight. A horse whinnied in the distance. Thousands of crickets answered in chorus. Barnes smiled and nuzzled his neck.

Horton jerked and jumped like a sleeping dog chases rabbits. He was in netherland, somewhere between sleep and reality. In the dream, horses and mounted police ringed the playing field. The men in blue were ready to ride, prepared to protect the grounds from Suehowicz's degenerates.

"Come, Odie, fire it, baby!" Horton said. "You the man, be there, baby!" The crickets of Chelsey Farms played behind the dream, crowing for the sun like tiny roosters.

Horton saw Shea's big Budweiser scoreboard. Hot Dogs 1, Pintails 0. He checked his players: Kliny, Albaugh, Ballard, Jug, Mouse, Bear, Wilt.

Bunny looked weird to Horton. He was thick through the chest, like one of those Nautilus creations. His face was tanned and handsome. Downright healthy-looking, Horton thought. He watched the Rabbit come up on his toes, pound his glove, and slide gracefully toward the runner at second base. The dream flashed. A different view now. Some kind of commotion. He heard a racket behind the outfield fence. The men on horseback, New York's finest, had changed their mounts. Horton pitched in the bed, and death gripped his pillow. The policemen were saddled up on huge, bug-faced crickets, the kind on the top of the Terminix cars.

"Wilt rocks and fires, Ensor swings, and oh, my! This one could be way back! Way back and it's—"

"Aaagh!" Horton screamed. He threw the pillow up like a shield.

His eyes searched the dark room. Where was he? Horton was in another world.

"Quite a little dreamer!" Barnes said.

"Huh?" He ignored her nakedness. His eyes were fixed on the screened double doors. The chirp of cricket sounds filled the room.

"Cligger Night!" he said. "That's what Bunny was trying to tell us. Don't you see? Clicker Night! Pazerelli!"

Barnes pulled at the sheet, making a pup tent over their heads.

"We'll talk about it in the morning. Now, I believe you promised me something. Then we'll see about this business of Clicker Night."

"The Rabbit was trying to tell us. I—"

"One rabbit at a time," Barnes said.

He felt himself sliding toward her warmth. He caressed her breasts. A reflex action. First one and then the other. She stroked his head downward, encouraging his lovemaking to stray.

"Lower," she said.

Horton kissed the softness below her navel.

"Clicker Night! It could win us the Little Series! The Rabbit's a genius!" he said.

"The Rabbit's a what?" Barnes moved down to help him.

Their voices were muffled, distorted by the satin tent.

•12•

IF THE PHONE RANG, WALKER HORTON DIDN'T hear it. Daylight splashed his pillow. He blinked it away and drifted back to sleep. He heard a dull buzzing sound. It played on the fringe of his consciousness, faded in and out. He opened one eye. Barnes was naked, sitting Indian style on the edge of the bed, shouting obscenities into the phone.

"Why in the hell can't someone on the city desk, for Christ's sake, ask a simple question like, 'And who shall I say called?'?"

He closed his eyes again and recalled the night, scene by scene: the horse ride, the Jacuzzi, the fireman's carry to the canopy bed. Horton reached out and cupped her breast. She batted him away and swore at the phone.

"Fucking-a-tweetie we tell time here in Cleveland! It's six thirty-five, just like Baltimore! I don't give a damn if he is in bed! In about two minutes his phone is going to be ringing off the hook!"

The receiver slammed. The phone's plastic cradle shook from the jolt. Outside, horses snorted and pawed at the grass. Barnes wrapped the beige sheet around her chest and pounded numbers into the Touch-tone phone.

"How long have they been standing there?"

"Tethered to the patio when I woke up," Horton said. "Must have brought them in while we were asleep."

Barnes nodded, pushed back the long blond hair, and began tying it in place with a red elastic band. Horton snorted and made another move for her breasts. She rolled his hands clockwise in slow, deliberate circles. "Here, dial 1-800," she said. Horton closed his eyes. He could feel her now responding to his touch. He made the horse sound again deep in his throat.

"You better cut it out; those two are liable to bust right through the doors," she said. The horses tossed their heads, snorted, and sniffed the morning air.

"It's like having several thousand pounds of Peeping Toms watching you," Horton said.

She covered her ear and talked into the receiver. Horton pulled the sheet away and began to work his tongue along her neck.

"Hello, Billy? Yes, I know it's six-thirty, but . . ."

He ran off a string of little kisses, starting with her neck, finishing under the tan line just below her breasts. She pushed him away.

"I'll do my mounting out back," he said, and stopping by the bar, he grabbed four ripe apples from the big silver bowl.

Larry swore again. Some kind of editorial fight, he guessed. He held the apples flat in his palms and offered them up above the railing. Long white teeth chomped at shiny metal bits, a flurry of lips, gums, and gnashing teeth.

Barnes was louder now, impossible to ignore.

"I get a message on my answering service telling me to follow up on a lead like that! No sources, no phone numbers, and you want a 'hard-hitting, solid piece of investigative reporting' by three this afternoon?

"For two weeks I tell America that this is the quintessential piece of puffery, Wrestle Mania in baseball suits, the Harlem Globetrotters playing the Washington Generals," she said.

She was quoting her newspaper columns. Horton was interested now.

"And on the strength of one lousy phone call you want me to write about some kind of fix . . ."

The bay chomped down on the core of her apple. Horton missed the end of the sentence.

"A friend of mine?" she said. "Well, why the hell didn't you say so? From Florida? Does he own a restaurant? Lanny said that? Well, that's a lot different. No, I'm not promising anything. I, yes, I will. Thanks, Billy, sorry about the early wake-up. I'll check it out. No! Right now? Well, I'm going to see a man about a horse."

Walker Horton called the Doggie Dugouts architectural genius. Barnes stirred at her coffee with a plastic spoon and begged to differ.

"If you're ten years old and get off eating curled up in a booth that looks like a hot dog roll, I guess 'genius' would be an apt description," she said.

The Dugouts were another reflection of the taste of Elmer Tiner Thumma—cushioned, bread-colored booths; a long, meat-red counter curved up at the ends like a thirty-foot Formica-topped hot dog. The big water cooler dispensers full of orange and grape drinks, plastic tableware shaped like baseball bats—Elmer the Giant, no question about it.

Construction veiled the tiny booth. Hammers rang, paint brushes squished and slapped at the thirsty wall. A bearded man in a yellow hard hat leaned between Barnes and Horton and yanked a handful of wires out of metal wall box.

"Elmer! Your electrician don't get these covered, you don't open today. I told him twice about it this week already."

The Giant's bellow was distant. "He'll have her by two o'clock. Keep your drawers on. Besides, those wires ain't hot!"

Under a counter or in the walk-in freezer, Horton thought. He rubbed his temples. "Boy, do I feel like crapola today. Need some sleep or something, starting to feel real jittery, not looking forward to telling the Giant, I can tell you that," he said.

A colorful placard waved at the window. Horton shook his head. A maze of signs and posters milled along the shopping center promenade.

STRIKE THREE ON MAJOR LEAGUE BASEBALL
LITTLE LEAGUERS AGAINST BIG LEAGUE MONEY GRUBBERS
HOT DOGS DON'T DIG WHAT BIG LEAGUERS DO TO US
BUT GETTING SCREWED SURE AS HELL AIN'T NEW TO US!

"Why do they have to attach themselves to us?" Horton said.

"Wouldn't you?" Barnes said. "You're just the vehicle they need. That's the protest game—whatever it takes to get the message out."

Horton tapped the plastic-bat-handled spoon on the restaurant counter and read the menu again.

ELMER'S LITTLE GIANTS—OUR COOKS TEACH OLD DOGS NEW
TRICKS

He checked his watch. The little weenie-roll booth was killing his back. They'd been waiting for over an hour now, fighting off wisecracks from his teammates, sucking up the sickening smell of steaming hot dogs.

Magruder dropped another handful of quarters in the pay phone.

"Hang it up, Mouse!" he said under his breath.

Horton needed to call Markum. He'd beg, crawl through the receiver—whatever it took to get a Valium prescription phoned in before the bus pulled out of Cleveland.

The Giant was brewing coffee now. The steam had a rich A&P fresh-ground smell.

"If he doesn't stop soon, I'm going to go over there and tackle him," Barnes said.

Thumma ducked through the swinging kitchen doors.

"Now you see him, now you don't," she said.

A stainless steel window framed the Giant. The coffee fog from the silver containers rolled across the restaurant. Thumma was decked out in a white kitchen cap and matching T-shirt. He wore a long, mustard-colored apron tied loosely around his waist.

They watched him throw racks of mugs and glasses into a big metal dishwashing machine. His biceps bulged. Water rolled down his big pink forehead. Barnes checked her wrist. They'd been waiting for an hour and ten minutes now. The Giant couldn't sit still: one interruption after another—the phone, employees, equipment problems. Horton was beginning to wonder if the conversation would ever happen.

"Grand openings—they drive me nuts!" the Giant shouted. "I'll give you a few minutes when I can; you're just going to have to be patient."

Kline ducked into the Dugout and called out to Elmer for coffee.

"Elmer, don't let those protest jerks in here," Kline said. "They think we like them! That one guy said they've got a couple of buses ready to follow us to Boston."

Elmer's reply was indiscernible. Horton stood and looked into the kitchen to see where the mumble had originated. Huge feet hung from under some kind of pressurized cooking contraption.

Albaugh straggled in with his nose buried in a copy of *The Times* of London and whistling the overture to *Carousel.*

Nobody spoke. They all looked hung over. Wilt and Rymoff sauntered past. They ignored Horton's nod.

The heavy glass door clicked shut again. The purple bags below Billy Johnson's eyes looked like mail sacks waiting for a local train. Wilt might be right about the man's drug habits, but he'd perfected the knuckleball. He just needed a little more polish.

"Throw it for strikes in Fenway and them Pintail Ducks can forget the Green Monster," the Giant had said. "You can't hit the ball, you ain't gonna hit no fences."

Horton checked his watch. In fifty-five minutes the Giant would be in front of the restaurant, heaving free wieners into crowds of hungry Little Leaguers.

Thumma crawled up a ladder and hoisted a box through an attic trapdoor.

"He'll quit in a minute. He's just nervous. Works like a madman, always has, used to be that way back in the meat market when he was running some kind of a sale or something," Horton said.

"Wait till he hears this one," Barnes said. "I think we're going to see nervous with a capital 'N.' "

Magruder looked up from the pay phone and deposited another handful of quarters.

Barnes nodded at Mouse. "A good suspect," she said. "Calling bookies. I've heard him myself."

"Well, you haven't convinced me on this. We've got a few assholes, and Mouse is one of them, but I'm going to need more evidence than a conversation between Lanny and some Mafia type," he said.

The Giant was in the kitchen now, giving a hairnet-paper cap lecture to his cooks and counter staff.

"Hey, Elmer, make sure they wash up after peeing! You handle a coupla thousand hot dogs a day, pretty soon you're thinking, what the hell, one more won't matter!" Rymoff shouted.

"Play the cards, Bear," Wilt said.

"Gin!" Rymoff said. "How do you like that shit?"

Wilt shuffled the deck and tipped his cowboy hat at Barnes.

"Hey, Larry, ran into a reporter from the *Plain Dealer* last night. Said he heard you've been screwing my catcher. Any truth to that?"

Horton saw red in the black Formica top.

"Odie, he meant in the print sense," she said. "It's a newspaper term. It means we're really writing awful things about someone. Kind of screwing them. I'm sure that's what he meant."

The Giant slid into the booth. Barnes inched toward the wall.

"Hoot, Odie's been fuming about you staying out all night," Thumma said. "He says you and Larry being seen together don't look good for the team."

Horton tapped the plastic spoon on the tabletop. It wasn't like Thumma to worry about what anybody thought, let alone Wilt.

Barnes wheeled in her seat, "Hey, Odie, I was lying. Call your friend at the *Plain Dealer.* Tell him last night at 3:00 A.M. Horton and I were out practicing screwing on horseback. When this fucking Little League series is over, we're going to run off and join a circus," she said.

The flush was back in the Giant's cheeks. "I'll never get used to women sportswriters. And talkin' trash like that. Larry, honey, what would your momma think?" he said. "You listen to that Suehowicz talk and you'd know how it sounds."

Sometimes the Giant was like a ventriloquist act. Horton couldn't tell where all the air came from. He was off and running, telling Larry about the projected crowd for the Cleveland opening.

"Gross will crap a brick when he sees today's receipts. We've got Little Leaguers busing in from as far away as Toledo," he said. "Hoot, I want you guys to work with the kids out in the parking lot. Do whatever it takes to make 'em happy. You'll have plenty of time to rest tonight and tomorrow. It's a long ride to Massachusetts."

He poured black coffee into a saucer, swirled it around, and drained the steaming black liquid into the heavy glass cup. "Hot!" he leaned down and slurped from the cup. "Real hot," he said.

Barnes cleared her throat and looked at Horton. The Giant continued to talk.

"Hey! Am I crazy? Forgot to tell you. Bunny called last night!"

Horton's pulse accelerated. "He okay?"

"Who, the Rabbit? You can't keep that little scudder down. Plans to meet us in New York. Can't play, of course, but he'll be in the dugout just for good luck, he said!"

Horton felt his mood lift.

"Elmer, you won't believe this one. Bunny said something back in Detroit that might just be the key to beating Pazerelli. Just as he was passing out he sits up—"

This time it *was* Barnes' hand on the knee of Walker Horton.

"Look, let's do Bunny later," she interrupted. "I've got a deadline. Elmer, there's something we need to tell you."

"Shoot!" the Giant said.

"We think the Little Series might be fixed."

Thumma took a long, slow sip of coffee and rose slowly from the plastic seat.

"Look, I've got a few last-minute things to do. We open in twenty minutes. You'll have to excuse me," he said.

He loomed above them like a cloudful of rain. Then he smiled, stretched, and cracked his knuckles behind his head.

"Boy, oh, boy, that's good java. Put hair on your chest," he said.

To Horton the reaction wasn't surprising. In fact, it was typical Elmer. The Giant refused to acknowledge his son's death until he saw the name on the Vietnam monument. That was just last March. Sammy had been dead since '68.

ANOTHER EMERGENCY TAPE FOR DR. MARKUM

"DOC, HERE'S THE TAPE I PROMISED. THANKS FOR listening to my story about Janie and the professor via the phone. I'm pissed about you nixing my Valium request, but as long as Elmer stocks beer on the bus, I guess I'll survive this thing. The sun's up, beating down on a bypass around Worcester, Massachusetts. But inside, the bus is full of gloom. We're about forty miles from Beantown, the Bear's behind the wheel, and I'm drinking my liquid Valium and talking to you on the tape recorder. Behind me are eight guys scratching little plastic McKnives around on their styrofoam plates. If it were real silverware, they'd be cutting each other's throats.

Elmer flew out of Cleveland. He's in New York trying to finalize a deal with NBC. If God and Stonesifer let this thing get that far, look for me on TV Saturday from Yankee Stadium.

I mentioned my good fortune on the phone, the night with the horses and Larry Barnes. Well, it's been an uphill ride ever since. Larry got this call from one of her editors—get ready for this, now they're saying that our games have been fixed. I didn't take it seriously at first, but the more I think about it, the more it all makes sense. When Larry tried to talk fix to the Giant he put the blinders on, refused to listen. I'm caught in the middle. I don't want to think the worst, but like I said, I've been driving most of the night recalling called third strikes and kicked ground balls.

Anyhow, Elmer flies off to New York, Larry wings away to chase down her sources, and I'm left with a twenty-six-hour bus ride to try to decide how to ask the New Becton Hot Dogs the following question: "Which one of you pricks is on the take?"

Well, about an hour ago, Bear solved my problem. He whipped the *Hot Dog* through McDonald's window, and while he's ordering a slew of McBreakfasts, I scoot over to a shopping center and get me a morning paper.

While the Dogs pick away at their eggs and bacon, I read them "Barnstorming's" accusation. Larry's column says that the fix may have been on from the very beginning, cites the takeover of ELG, Inc.; gambling; and point shaving as all possible motives. Her sources say two, maybe as many as three Hot Dogs have been tanking. You've probably read it by now. Then she ends it with a simple "more to follow." No names, no sources divulged, just enough conjecture to get a busload of hung over ballplayers crawling all over each other's butts.

Here's Kline's quote. He called Barnes "an irresponsible leech. One minute we're Wrestle Mania, a circus, a bunch of old phonies, the next we're something akin to Watergate. Give me a fucking break," he said.

Then Baldy stands and makes a semiconfession. "I want this thing over. I won't deny that. Back in Cleveland wouldn't have been too soon for me."

Wilt comes flying out from under his hat and accuses Baldy of kicking all those ground balls on purpose.

Baldy denies it, then pisses everybody off real good by saying his association with the New Becton Hot Dogs is an embarrassment to the president of the United States. Christ, it's not like we haven't heard that before!

Jug gave a real tearjerker about his two little girls and how they're planning to come to New York with their momma to see their old man play in Yankee Stadium on Saturday. Then he walks over to Magruder and says, "Mouse, nobody better let me catch them tanking in Boston." Then he goes and pulls Billy's earplug and repeats himself, "Nobody, Billy."

Billy yanks off his headset and tries to calm Mouse down.

"Go easy, my man," he says. "He just used my name in the same sentence with yours, and you don't see me getting all bent out of shape!"

Quite a team, huh, Doc?

Ballard admitted to blowing his series check before he got to Cleveland. He's into his teammates for another six hundred.

"My wife will be on a nut hunt when I get back to Albuquerque without that five thousand. But I'd never tank on the Giant! Wouldn't catch me screwing the big guy for love nor money," he said.

Wilt was the grand finale. After Bear stood up in the driver's seat and threatened to kick two asses or nine, however many there are in on a fix, Odie flips into his Dr. Jekyll mode.

"Here's what I think," he says real calm and cool. "I think we've still got a shot at the five thousand dollars.

"And no offense to Billy, it's the knuckler I'm worried about. It's like trying to train fleas or something. There's no controlling them. And if we're gonna win, somebody's gotta throw strikes."

Then the man who claimed he couldn't pitch back-to-back games offers the guys an alternative: "If you want to win in Boston, give me the fucking ball," he says. And before I can think, Bear grabs the mike and brings it to a vote. "Okay, who wants to see Odie crank it up in Fenway?" Bear says. This, of course, is like saying, "Anybody need a beer while I'm up?"

Seven hands for Wilt. Johnson looked kinda funny—real pissed like. Then he just settled back. Never did participate in the vote. He had the Walkman turned up. Just sorta ignored the whole thing.

I don't know how the Giant will take all this, I mean learning that his Eliza Doolittle knuckleball ace got himself yanked en route, somewhere between Worcester and Beantown, I think. Hell, you gotta win two games to get a shot at game five. I voted with Elmer, of course. But I mean, in a way I can see Wilt's point.

Anyway, I'll Fed Ex this one from the hotel. Give you a call when we hit New York. I've got some suspicions about the fix and some questions about Elmer to boot. Doc, it's like I said before, I think the big guy is losing it. One anxiety bag to a team . . .

Right?

BLUE SKY, DARK GREEN TREES, A CATCHER'S BACK-ground if Walker Horton ever saw one. He sat back and counted the stitches. The pitch ducked into a cloud, then dove out of the sky like a World War I biplane. A direct hit. The ball caught Horton flush on the shin.

The Giant stepped back from Horton's Frisbee home plate and watched the catcher's one-legged dance.

"Hurts, don't it? That bone's a tender animal. Real sensitive," he said. He turned and called to Johnson.

"Good one, Billy!"

The pitcher filled out the old gray sweat suit in an unathletic way.

"Sort of looks like a black Pillsbury Dough Boy, don't he?" Elmer said. "He ain't gonna intimidate them with his body. 'Course, neither did Eddie Lopat, Stu Miller, or any of them other junk and knuckleball fellers."

The Giant spat in the grass and waved the bat menacingly over the round rubber plate.

"No rotation on that last one at all. Wilt can hold all the polls he wants, but he ain't pitchin' tomorrow. We need him for New York. Johnson gets the nod for Fenway," Thumma said. " 'Course, Wilt's right, Billy's gotta throw the thing for strikes. And you're gonna have to help him, make sure you mix 'em up. Set them up with fastballs and hooks off the plate. But when we get ahead in the count, I don't wanta see anything that ain't flutterin'!"

A nice setting for the final knuckleball session. Sixty feet, six inches of lush green lakeside grass rolled out like a wedding carpet between the squat little pitcher and Horton's Frisbee home plate. A liver-shaped pond canopied by ancient oaks and elms. Typical Boston, Horton thought. Ducks drifted in the cool gray shade, orange feet flying skyward as they bobbed for food. A relaxing warm-up for a rowdy park like Fenway. If Billy could handle the crowds, he'd dust the Pintails real good.

"Throw strikes," Horton muttered under his breath. "Just throw strikes."

Another knuckler soared out of the sun, skydiving the Frisbee from the brilliant glare. Horton crabbed left, trapping the ball in the huge leather webbing.

"How's the satchel working?" the Giant asked.

"Good; needs more neat's-foot oil," Horton said. "You sure this thing is legal?"

"Paul Richards had a monster glove. Made it special for Triandos to catch Hoyt Wilhelm. Called it Big Bertha. I call this one The Satchel. All it needs is a handle. You could pack a week's worth a clothes in the thing." He laughed softly, and spat on the Frisbee again.

Billy had a jerky, half windup, no leg kick at all. He faced the plate and fired. Horton moved in the soft grass and picked off another floater. Thumma nodded approvingly. Hot sun, low humidity, a beautiful New England day.

"You think Barnes is on to something?" Horton said.

The Giant fell back from an inside pitch, spun, and watched it strafe the plate. A wild quacking and hissing filtered up from the pond. Horton watched pink drain from the old man's face.

"Had my say on that in Cleveland! Ain't nobody tankin' on Elmer the Giant. Raised you boys from kids. We been together too long for somethin' like that to happen. Must really need to sell some papers to print a story like that," he said.

Billy turned the ball over slowly in his glove. The Giant

scrunched up his face, then nodded approvingly. The ducks squalled on the water, fighting over the last of some bread crumbs. A boy fishing from the bridge played a lure along the pond's glassy surface. The Giant took the bat back over his head and pantomimed a long, graceful cast.

"Hope that boy's more patient than you and Odie were when you was kids. If you guys didn't get a bite right off, you'd be racin' around throwin' rocks in the water. Remember that time I snagged Wilt's cap with my jitterbug? Snared it right off his head," he said. The reminiscing agreed with Thumma. His cheeks were pink again.

Horton waved two fingers behind the oversize mitt. Billy herked and jerked. Thumma's eyes followed the pitch into Horton's mitt.

"Nickel curve. An old man like me can hit a ball when it hangs there on a string. Judas Priest, I'da clocked that one clean across the duck pond," he said. "His hook ain't worth as much as a nickel. Fastballs away and plenty of knucklers salted in." Thumma tipped back the black cap and furrowed his big, high forehead at Billy.

"Yep, we'll save Odie for the Big Apple. The network requested Wilt and Ensor. They want two ex-major leaguers goin' in the grand finale. It'll be a big day if we make it. We just gotta. It's gonna have to be," he said.

Sunshine cut through the overhead foliage, splashing Horton's face with a mixture of shade and hot, white light. The Giant's blue eyes sparkled. "Coupla more, nothin' but floaters now," he called.

Elmer hadn't mentioned Clicker Night. It wasn't like him. The man lived for a good promotion.

"Like my idea for the giveaway?" Horton asked.

"Got some flak from the accountants back in Baltimore. I'd promised to hold down expenses the rest of the way. They weren't real happy to see a bill for a thousand bucks for some kinda little tin hot dogs," he said. He squirted a brown stream at the shoreline. A frog splashed the pond.

"It'll be the best thousand bucks you ever spent," he said.

"I'm glad to hear it. That's the old confidence, boy. Hen, maybe you're catching what I'm losing. That would be nice," he said.

Thumma looked up and waved his long, thick-fingered hand, motioning to Johnson for another pitch.

"Where the hen did he go?" he asked, pointing the bat at the vacant lump of dirt that had served as a mound.

"I guess he was finished. He's a strange one." Horton came slowly up out of his crouch. The shinbone ached, and he bent over and gave it a rub. "Just listens to the radio all day. Real quiet. Bear calls him Harpo."

The Giant hooked the wrist strap of his old three-fingered fielder's glove with the knob of his bat.

"Left-handers and knuckleballers. Two of a kind," he said with a laugh. "Heck, let's you and me have a little catch. See if I can't beat a pocket into that new satchel you're wearin'," he said.

The ducks waddled out of the water to the sound of popping gloves. They fell into a line, pecking at the grass and offering occasional looks of disinterest at the pondside action.

Horton loved to catch the Giant. The old man still had it. Only the motion had changed. It wasn't the windmill action he'd seen in Elmer's old movie reels. The left leg barely cleared the ground now. You had to look hard to see daylight under his shoe. But the ball still moved, he could throw the hook for strikes, and his sinker fell half a foot at the plate.

A warm bath of security washed over Horton. He'd been worried about the Giant. The Little Series had taken one nasty turn after another. It was good to see him relax. Thumma turned sideways, brought the long arms to his waist in a series of jerks, glanced over his shoulder, and held an imaginary runner on first.

"What'd you throw DiMaggio in '37?" Horton called to Thumma.

"Joe? Nothin' he didn't hit. Most of 'um extra bases in that Series, if my memory serves me correct," the Giant shouted. Then he cleared his upper lip and spat.

He mopped his brow and tugged at the cap. The big guy was really enjoying himself.

Horton felt the breeze from DiMaggio's swing. Joe had yanked a high, inside fastball foul out over the pond, deep into the Stadium's left-field seats.

"Thumma got away with one. A long, long strike on the Yankee Clipper," Horton called the play.

Sunshine, a cool summer breeze cutting off the duck pond, Thumma throwing like a man half his age. He took a deep breath. Gardenias and freshly cut grass. DiMaggio watched a fastball cut the rounded corner of the yellow oval.

"Steerike two!" Horton shouted.

A day for fantasies. Maybe the Giants will finally win one, put it all together, shut the Yankees down at last.

A car door slammed. The mallards beat the water again. Horton turned and saw a green sedan rocking at the curb.

Thumma slammed the ball hard in the old three-fingered glove. His arms went up above his head. Another door slammed. A silver-gray limo. The Giant came set at his waist, glanced over his shoulder, and gave the intruders a threatening look.

"Larry!" Horton said under his breath. Larry Barnes and a tall, gray-haired man had replaced Horton's imaginary Yankee runners. So much for the pitch-and-catch fantasy. Barnes grinned and tossed Horton a kiss. It felt like Billy had cut a couple of knucklers loose in his jock.

Barnes was pink today. A rose blouse, matching heart-shaped sunglasses, and powder blue culottes. She waved to Thumma in a rather businesslike way and walked back to greet the suit-and-tie from the silver limo. The Giant dropped his head and trudged down the long stretch of grass.

"That was good," he said, throwing his arm around his catcher's shoulders. "Pitch-and-catch is about as much fun as a man can have with his son, I guess."

"You still got it. Coulda used a sponge," Horton said. Thumma rubbed up the ball and looked out over the water. Horton eyed Barnes. She was bending over now, digging around in the sedan's backseat.

"Recognize the man with Larry?" the Giant whispered.

Horton shrugged.

"Well, it's Gross. What I want to know is what the hen's she doin' draggin' him out here. I don't appreciate this one little bit."

"That's Gross?" Horton said. The man had Barnes by the elbow now, leading her toward Horton and the Frisbee.

Elmer stone-stared the pond, refusing to look up.

Gross was much taller than Horton remembered, almost Elmer's height. Was this the man the Giant had called a little weasel, a miserly midget? Silver hair flashed in the sun. He gave it a brush, then turned to Barnes and smiled. Perfect teeth; dark glasses; gray, checked slacks. He wore a blue blazer and a yellow silk tie knotted tightly at the neck. Gross had sharp, ageless features; he could have been anywhere from fifty to sixty-five. Horton couldn't guess.

"This is Gross?" Horton whispered. Thumma nodded.

"This isn't the guy I saw in Wrigley Field. I thought you said he was the little guy, the one in the black Banlon shirt?"

"The guy in the black shirt was Murray Weddle, one of our nickel-squeezers. A comptroller," Thumma said, clarifying the remark.

Gross strolled up behind Thumma and stuck out his hand. "Elmer," he said. The Giant gave him his backside, kept his eyes on the water. Gross nodded to Horton. Hooter appraised the tie. Neiman-Marcus, 100 percent silk.

"Elmer, we came to talk," he said, aiming the conversation at the back of the Giant's battered black cap.

Horton shot Barnes a look. She circled the group, swung her blue culottes around the bench, and came at Thumma from the water. "Elmer, Mr. Gross wants to talk. He flew in from Baltimore to see you. Don't you think it would be a good idea to hash this thing out, get the conjecture cleared up?"

"Conjecture? What conjecture?"

Horton caught half a breath. Thank God! The big guy had spoken. Gross folded the dark green aviator glasses and slipped them in the breast pocket of the navy blue blazer.

"Elmer, the conjecture seems to be in Larry's mind. After all these years it looks like we finally have somethin' in common." Gross dropped the "g" in "something." Horton hated "Balmore" accents.

"And what the hen would that be?" Thumma said to the water. The ducks were in a wedge now, swimming off toward the opposite shore.

"Your ball games are an embarrassment to our company," Gross said.

"Sounds kinda familiar," Thumma said.

"But they aren't fixed!" Gross said. His voice was smooth and even. A vote of confidence if it had been anyone else.

"Can't tell you how much that means to me." Thumma chased his words with a rifle shot of tobacco.

"Elmer, I'm not going to take much more of it. It started in Florida, all this business about me trying to pull some big takeover coup. Now here we are again. Larry here seems determined to drag my name into more articles, quoting unnamed sources, linking me with that bunch of rabble-rousers who have been following your games, attaching my name to this imagined bribery of players."

Gross tired of talking to the back of the cap, turned slowly to the bench, and made his points to Barnes.

"Frankly, Larry, my sources link you and Horton these days. Sound suspicious to an investigative reporter? A little conflict of interest, perhaps? Maybe someone creating a 'fix' story to save a guy's grandfatherly old friend!"

Gross turned his chiseled nose to the sun and said it again.

"To suggest that I'd pay money to fix something as ridiculous as this Little World Series, something that's destined to self-destruct all on its own—well, that's the ultimate insult. I happen to be a respected man in Baltimore's financial circles. Hell, I'm a guest on *Wall Street Week* next Friday night." He dropped his head. The nose pointed down at the tips of his black patent leather shoes. "This crap keeps up, Rukeyser will laugh me off the show!"

The Giant turned slowly, arms folded, biceps bulging. The Mr. Clean look. His first step was sudden. What catchers call a crow hop, the little jump that powers a peg to second base. Gross reeled and caught himself. Barnes leaned back on the park bench, crossed her legs, and opened her notebook. Thumma dropped his head. The bald spot was bull's-eye red on top.

"Larry, I don't like you dragging this man in here unannounced. But it looks like you've locked us into it." He glared at Horton. The white eyebrows flew up. Blood rushed to his nose.

"Walker, I hope you didn't know these people were coming!"

Horton's head shook a quick denial.

"Okay, then, Larry—"

Gross cut the Giant off. "Hold it, Elmer, I want to—"

"Gross, I'll get to you in a minute. Larry, before anything else is gonna be said, I want to know what makes you think someone's fixin' my series."

Horton and Gross nodded. A minibike motored by.

"Elmer, if the information had come from anyone but Lanny Celebreze, I would have laughed the whole thing off. In fact, I did at first." She turned to Gross. "Your 'reporter sells out to lover' logic is a little weak, I'm afraid. Mr. Gross, what you're forgetting is that I'm read in 145 papers every day of the week. I intend to have the same audience reading "Barnstorming" long after this Little World Series and your hot dog tong war has been put to bed.

"I've been calling this thing a sham for weeks. How do you think it makes me look trying to convince my readers that we now have a legitimate sporting contest on our hands, one so competitive that it could actually be fixed by its players?"

"So?" Gross rolled his hand like a TV director. "Get it out. What's this great revelation? What would make a newspaper like the *Sun* associate the word 'fix' with a bunch of bums showing their tails at the expense of a company"—he hitched as if to catch his breath—"a company that I single-handedly put back on its feet?"

The Giant threw up his arms and walked to the pond. Barnes' voice rose. "Elmer!" she said. Thumma stopped just short of the water. Two frogs jumped, one after another.

"Elmer, if there's anybody wired any tighter to the street than Celebreze, then I wish you'd name him," she said.

"Who the hen's Celebreze?" Thumma said.

Gross flushed. "I know him. Owns a seafood restaurant in West Palm Beach."

"The guy with the camera?" the Giant asked. "The funny little fellow that took our picture?"

Gross spoke again. "He knows a lot of people. Sort of the Tommy LaSorda of restaurateurs. Celebreze said I'm buying Elmer's players?"

"No," Barnes said. "But a gambler, Hooter, it was the guy who Lanny said wanted to reserve the Hideaway the night I interviewed you. Anyway, Lanny's known him for years, he and his West Palm squeeze frequent the place as often as two or three times a week. So he sees those photos of Elmer, Wilt, and Horton on the wall, laughs, and tells Lanny that game five is academic. It's gonna end in Boston!"

Barnes continued. She outlined the story—from the gambler in the restaurant to Celebreze's tip to Barnes' recording machine at *The Baltimore Sun.* The sports desk laughed it all off. "Then Eddie Aldridge, a guy who writes racing for us, covers Bowie, Pimlico, and the lotto, got wind of it," she said.

"Aldridge traced the betting patterns on the ball games and found a dramatic upswing in interest following the game in Wrigley Field.

"The bookies took light money on game one. It was camp. They kept the distribution even, of course, accepted bets as a service to their regular customers. It was making news, people were having fun with the thing. Who the hell could get hurt? Then in Detroit, some big money went down. In Cleveland it doubled. More than a million wagered on a exhibition game."

Gross hunched his shoulders. Thumma put two blue eyes on Barnes' smiling face.

"You tell me," she said. "Point shaving? Cutting runs? That's what Aldridge thought. But now Eddie's confused. He's a man who's been around gambling all his life. Has more contacts than Jimmy the Greek. He bets, writes about it—hell, it's his life. Pretty soon he starts getting calls at the paper, sources saying there'll be a closeout in Boston.

"Eddie holds firm. 'It just doesn't make sense,' he says. 'If somebody's making money shaving runs, then a full-fledged dive would kill the golden goose.' "

Gross shined a black pump on the left leg of gray, checkered slacks. Thumma pushed a brown wad so deep in his cheek that a couple of the big fingers disappeared.

Barnes slid over. Gross took a seat. He straightened his pants cuffs, adjusted his tie, and defended himself by chronicling the history of Elmer's Little Giants, Inc.

"A gambler sees a picture of a guy on a restaurant wall, makes a comment. A reporter gets wind of it and puts your name in the newspaper. Suddenly the man who saved Elmer's Little Giant's, Inc., is a no-good, bribing, son of a bitch."

The Giant's head spun to the bench. The white bushy eyebrows flew to full mast.

"Well, I may be the latter, but I've fixed no games," Gross said. "Can't you see how insulting this is? These Hot Dog jerks are inept. The bastards are going to self-destruct. I'll tell you the story I'd like to see." His voice was even, the delivery like glass. Suddenly no accent at all. "The story I'd like to see is one that will never get printed. It's about a man who made money in the sixties in spite of himself, a man who practically trashed a business by taking fliers on scatterbrained schemes like Dog Catcher trucks, little food wagons that were supposed to sell wieners to construction workers."

Gross laughed. "Elmer, they had a mutt with a mitt on the side of the van, didn't they? That one cost us somewhere in the neighborhood of half a million. Then there was Squeeza-Dog, a frankfurter pâté for cocktail crackers; Baby Bunts; and now Doggie Dugouts. Help me, Elmer; there have been so many of them I've had trouble keeping up."

The Giant edged toward the water. Horton stood up. For a second it looked like the big guy might jump.

"I came to this company in 1974. Oh, yes, I forgot, something called Frank-Sickles, a frozen hot-dog-flavored ice product, had just gone down the dumper. Thumma needed cash. I saw potential in the company. He brought me in. I felt that with good management, ELG had a chance. It still does. But the food business is a different game today. You can't put your stockholders' money into every idea that comes down the shoot. Cute sold in the sixties. Hell, everything sold in the sixties," he said.

Horton hated it. Gross had stated his case well. Barnes put down her pencil.

"Well, what do you say, Elmer?" she said.

The Giant walked up from the water. He was bent at the waist, wrinkled in the face.

"Well, now, mine's gonna be off the record." His voice was soft but assured. "Yes, I took him in. Needed some cash flow, he had good recommendations. Found out later that I was the one taken in. He's been skimming for years, taking money under the table. I been turnin' my head, but no more. I've enjoyed about as much partnership as I can stand with Mr. Gross." Thumma looked right through him. It was as though Gross weren't there.

"Larry, the man screws more people in the name of business in a month than your average hooker does in a lifetime."

The air eased out of Gross's nostrils. It was a hissing sound like the ducks made on their swim to the bread crumbs.

The Giant looked down at the tasseled tops of Gross's black shoes.

"Now, Larry, you didn't come here to hear about the hot dog industry. First off, on this fix you've conjured up. It takes two to tango. Nobody on the New Becton Hot Dogs is shavin' runs or fixin' games. Now, the boys are wilder than I imagined. Frankly, I'da thought they'd be a bit more mature than they are, considering I gave them thirty years to get their hormones adjusted. But tank a game on Elmer the Giant? No way. Of course, I know what you're thinking. I lose this Series, the board votes Gross in as chairman of ELG, Inc."

Thumma's forehead straightened, smoothed out. The wrinkles were gone. He'd had a revelation. "I guess if you actually had a fix that this despicable son of a biscuit would be your logical choice," he said.

Gross stood. The pants legs fell to the tasseled shoes in a perfect press.

"Elmer, I thought you'd have a little more sympathy for a man accused of throwing a baseball series. I guess your memory's a little short. When we were up in Chicago, McKeen and I got to reminiscing. I'd forgotten. He reminded me that the only hope the Giants had against the greatest team in baseball history was this fireballing right-hander; you were the Giants only prayer."

"It was 2–1; 2–0; and 4–0." Gross read Thumma his losing scores.

Horton couldn't see the Giant's eyes. He was walking away, back toward the pond again.

"Larry, if you want a good story, I'd drop by the morgue at the *Sun*. Take a few minutes, research that World Series. You'll find that a lot of loyal Giants fans, a bunch of decent, hardworking people went down on that one.

"Get the Liar out of here!" the Giant boomed. Frogs leaped, ducks flew. The boy on the bridge jerked his lure out of the water. "Get him out!"

Heads went down. Grass rustled. A car door slammed. The motor ground, whirred, then started. Horton felt Barnes' arm slip across his neck. "Hooter, I'm sorry. I know the Yankees were unbeatable in '37. I just wanted him to believe the LWS was fixed. I'd never embarrass him like that to get a story. I didn't know that was coming. I . . ."

Thumma was hunched over the water again, jabbing his big canvas shoes into a bank of soft, gray clay.

"Say something to him," she said.

"Me?"

"You're the—"

"Only one he respects?" Horton said.

The bent back; the little black cap; the flat, bunless backside. Somehow the Giant had shrunk.

Horton plodded out through the mud, turned Thumma by his shoulders, and looked him straight in the face.

"Elmer, I'm going to Baltimore. I'll need the key to your office, need the master key and any alarm codes that will get me around in the place on the sly."

Thumma pulled a long, leather billfold out of the baggy brown pants. "Hooter, that was the worst thing a man's ever said to me. Liar accused me of taking a bribe, didn't he?"

The Giant turned to Horton and handed him the key. His eyes were on the pond again, watching the ducks. The wind moved the mallards along in the water and picked up their speed.

"Code's 1007002," he said. "Punch it in on the digital board before you enter any door. Hallways included."

"Anything else I need to know?"

"Just the dogs. Three night watchmen. They leave the building at ten forty-five ever' night. They go get the dogs, bring 'em in, and patrol the place. Run free up and down the halls all night long."

"You think he's fixin' it, don't ya?" Thumma said.

"Don't know!"

Thumma's voice was weak. He hadn't looked at Horton yet.

"Be out of there by eleven; that's when they cut the Dobermans loose!"

Horton started up the hill.

"Hooter, tell Larry to give my office a good goin'-over, too. I don't want her thinkin' that I'd—"

"Elmer, the Yankees were a lock in '37 and everybody knows it!

The ball was hidden in the palm of the Giant's oversize hand. He wheeled suddenly from Horton and fired at the water. The baseball skip-stoned the surface. Feathers flew from a sitting duck.

•14•

WALKER HORTON WAS BROWN-BAGGING IT AGAIN, sitting in the front seat of the car, sucking air from a sack. Barnes worked her fingers into his neck, deep-rubbing the muscles, trying to help him relax.

"Keep breathing, keep the rhythm up. Everything's okay," she said.

He lowered his head and continued to count. One-two, one-two; the bag billowed and sank in the darkened car. Outside, the Baltimore night made summer sounds. Crickets and frogs. Barnes had pulled the car between two vehicles along a greenway lake. Horton could see steamy windows. A horn blew. Kids making out.

"I Just Called to Say I Love You" played on a car radio. The music was distant and soft. A nice contrast to gunfire and snarling Doberman pinschers. Barnes worked the muscles along the nape of his neck. She stroked his head. Damp curls fell under the back of his baseball cap. Horton wanted to laugh or cry; either emotion would do.

The "strip" search of Elmer's Little Giants' corporate offices had been a near-disaster. The events of the night fast-forwarded through his head like a videotape.

"It was like a bad TV show, wasn't it?" Barnes said. Horton nodded. She slipped her hand under his dark green polo shirt. He was soaked. She unfolded a hankie and mopped his forehead. Then dropped her hand and slow-rubbed his back. Horton continued breathing into the sack.

It should have been an open-and-shut deal, a simple turnkey operation. Doors unlocked. They punched in the codes, and alarms cut off. A cursory search of Elmer's office brought no surprises. The room looked like the back of a truck at a paper drive. A big wooden desk smothered in brochures, letters, contracts, and agreements. Promotional points of sale carpeted the floor, big cardboard cutouts of hot dogs and rolls. The only orderly spot in the room was a small area on the edge of a white marble mantel, where three pictures stood in row. Horton had to look twice to be sure it was Sammy. Sambo lay back against a tree with a rifle slung over his shoulder, drinking some unidentifiable beer. Vietnam, May 4, 1968 was all the caption said. There was a snapshot of Marie framed in gold and, of course, an eight-by-ten glossy of the '54 Hot Dogs, the one Odie's old man took at St. Michael's Church the day Elmer broke out his new movie camera.

Records and notes on the Little World Series were strewn over his desk. Barnes speed-read them. Agreements with the league, contracts with hotels, a note from the law firm of Harkenhorn and Harkenhorn making McKeen's obligation to play official.

Gross's office was an easy find. They crept down a long, win-dowed hallway and made a right turn. The Giant had given them good directions. When they closed Elmer's door, Horton looked at his watch: It was 10:50 P.M. on the digital dot. Yellow lights from the parking lot played on the hall carpet. Dobermans barked in their waiting pens. At precisely 10:53 P.M. Barnes punched the code to cut Gross's alarm. Seven minutes to link Gross to the fix. At 11:00 P.M. the hallways of Elmer's Little Giants would be running with snarling Doberman pinschers.

Not since Jekyll and Hyde had there been a pair like Thumma and Gross. The offices told the story. Thumma's digs were *Sanford and Son*; Gross's looked like a posh set on a *Dallas* TV production.

Deep blue-piled carpet, wainscoting, dark window trim, and steel-gray curtains. A mammoth oil painting of Gross over a rich brown mahogany desk. The lamps in the parking lot streaked the royal blue carpet with threads of bright yellow-gold. Shadows from the window cast on the big oil portrait.

"Gross looks like a Jewish George Bush," Barnes whispered.

They worked the room with penlights, zeroing the thin, laser-like beams on neatly stacked papers and bound leather manu-scripts. Desk drawers, closet doors, the wraparound credenzas, everything locked. The shopping tear through a Boston Kmart for gloves, the race to Logan International, the fight at the Avis desk all seemed ridiculous. They'd killed themselves just to flash a couple of penlights around a tidy executive's office.

Barnes surprised Horton by revealing a screwdriver. She wedged it under the lock, and the desk drawer popped open. At 10:58 P.M. Horton had had enough. Then, just as he made his move for the door, all hell broke loose. Bedlam followed. Everything in one wild, ear-shattering wave. Barnes didn't budge. She screwdrivered locks and dug through drawers like a seasoned second-story man. The ruckus from out on the lot terrified Horton. Hundreds of pounds of snarling dogs pulling trigger-happy Rent-A-Cops. Red lights flashed in the hallway. Horton helped her shuffle the papers and begged to leave. She yanked open another drawer, speed-read a document. Horton beat a path from the desk to the window and back to the desk again. The dogs were closing in on the building, raging wildly. Then suddenly everything went silent. They were in the building. Barnes threw paper like parade confetti. Meat contracts, a deal on sausage casings, architects' renderings for a new addition to a packing plant in Dover, Delaware. The alarms cut loose again.

He might be safely locked in the front seat of a car now, but the picture remained vivid, the sounds life-threatening. Horton sweated into his paper bag, his thoughts returning to the great escape.

"I'm getting out of here!" he'd shouted, and grabbing Barnes by the shoulders, began pulling her toward the door. The dogs were on the steps, then slipping and sliding along the terrazzo floor of the hall.

Barnes snuffed her flashlight. They ran hand-in-hand down the hall. Then as they reached the corner, just steps from the landing, Horton remembered seeing the recorder. He pushed Barnes off the landing and screamed orders down the black stairwell:

"Get the car! Meet you at the dumpster we passed on the way in!"

The recorder was a little Olympus S911. Why hadn't he put it all together? He had to have it. This was a long shot he had to take.

The rest was truly movie stuff. He remembered snatching the recorder from the bottom desk drawer, hearing the hall door pop, and the howling Dobermans. They'd picked up their scent. He cracked the doorway, heard a watchman shout, "In here!" More howling and great gnashing of teeth.

The pack thundered into Elmer's office, keening and yapping. A big black-and-brown broke its leash. Horton edged out into the yellow light. A voice screamed "Freeze!" Gunshots. A bullet ricocheted past his head.

The memory blackened. He leaned back in the car seat and deep-breathed again. He had to maintain the rhythm.

"I slammed the door on the lead dog's nose. A blood-chilling sound," he said, wheezing. "If you hadn't been there with the car . . ."

Barnes dug her hands deep into his back and kissed his neck again.

"Why all the bravado? What was the point?" Barnes continued the massage. She slid her hands down his spine. "Bravado" struck Horton as an odd choice of words. You didn't see the hero panting into a bag at the end of a Bond movie or a *Magnum P.I.*

"All that just for a recorder?" she said.

Horton felt his lungs relax for a second.

"I think it's mine," he said, taking another toke on the sack.

"Your recorder?"

"The one I lost in Florida!"

"Your recorder in Gross's office!" Barnes was scrabbling madly, frisking Horton's pants.

He hiked up and pushed at the front pocket of his jeans. The black plastic lump fell into Barnes' outstretched fingers.

"Is it? Is this the one?" her voice was throaty, full of excitement.

Inside the car the night was black on black. Horton dropped his head and shrugged. Something about breathing, it tends to make everything else stand on line.

"Can't tell. Too dark," he said, panting. "Here, let me have it." He held the bag one-handed and pushed the rewind button. The tape hissed, clicked, and he hit another button.

"This is Hooter Horton, tape number nine, notes for the novel, June 27, West Palm Beach, Florida. I think this guy Gross is out to screw up the Little Series. I wouldn't put anything past him. The Giant agrees. If we win this thing, Elmer stays in control. If we lose and embarrass ourselves, Gross takes the reins of a multimillion-dollar company right out of the Giant's hands. It's as simple as that. And to make matters worse, things have really been going down the dumper since Elmer put this good cop-bad cop crap into play. . . ."

Barnes threw her arms around Horton. He dropped the bag. They held each other in a celebratory hug. He laughed. She cried. The tape ran on. She kissed him full on the lips. Breathing never entered his mind.

". . . shows me just how good we can be—not great, maybe, we've got our weaknesses here and there—but good enough to win three games.

"Hell, I've said it before and I'll say it again: The problem is attitude. They've been acting like a bunch of assholes all week."

They made out like kids. The windows steamed up. Horton's voice played in the background.

"Your tape recorder stolen from a locker room in West Palm Beach. It might not hold up in a court of law, but it's probable cause," Barnes said. "I think we just made our case for the fix."

"Let's go to Boston!" Horton said.

Barnes turned the key. The engine responded. "It's almost 1:00 A.M. We'll drop by my apartment. You've gotta get your rest. Big game tomorrow. Plenty of morning flights."

WALKER HORTON LEANED AGAINST THE WATER cooler in the first base dugout and drank from a paper cup. Wilt yanked the newspaper out of his hip pocket and read to Mike Dougherty of *The Boston Globe*.

"The guy's on some kind of an egotistical fantasy, pretending he's a writer, a baseball manager. Now he and Barnes are private detectives. Cybill Shepherd and Bruce Willis. It's the fucking *Moonlighting* show!"

Wilt had the fantasy part right. Horton looked off toward right-center field into the bleachers, where Ted Williams had deposited hundreds of dingers. Fenway's old green walls were blanketed under a chowder-gray sky tonight. Behind the Green Monster in left, the Citgo sign loomed above Boston's Kenmore Square. Horton blinked his eyes. The smog blurred the light's blues and reds. In right a Jimmy Fund sign touted the Thumper's favorite charity.

Thumma clacked by, scraping his cleats in a slipperlike shuffle. The Giant sauntered up the dugout steps and rested there, arms folded across his knee, watching Ichabod Nelson take his warm-up tosses.

"Looks like a poor man's Kent Tekulve," he said. "We can hit him. Just have to keep the front foot in, no bailing out."

The Giant spat, turned to Horton, and lowered his voice. "Looks like you may have hit pay dirt last night. Does that woman write everything she sees and hears?"

If divorce was hard on Horton's intestines, the Little Series had been worse. His stomach felt like it had been blown up with a bicycle pump. There was pressure everywhere he looked—the series, the book, the inheritance, the affair or whatever it was with Larry. And it all might end right here in Fenway. Horton had two strategic managerial moves to make. He had to eliminate Pazerelli once and for all, then ID the rotten dogs in Elmer's Little League package, uncover the players Gross had been paying to tank. The thought of the blind man's fastball brought goose bumps up on Horton's neck.

"Lord, let Clicker Night work," he said under his breath.

Bats rang, gloves popped. Fenway was warming to the Giant's occasion. The early birds were down on the box seat railing, passing pens and scorecards to the old Little League players. A pack of kids in Sox caps scrambled under a row of box seats for a loose foul ball. A woman shouted good-naturedly into the Hot Dog dugout.

"Hey, Thumma! Can't beat these old buzzards, ya bettah hang it up!"

The Giant snorted. "Talk funny as hell, don't they?" he said and trudged off toward the far end of the bench, where Johnson and Brown were pitching pennies. "Billy, how about stretchin' a little. I don't want you to throw none. We wanta catch 'em by surprise with the knuckler."

A bell rang. The black-suited Pintails loped off to the third-base dugout. The portable batting cage collapsed like a deck of cards. Men in coveralls horse-raced a canvas drag around the infield dirt. Horton moved up a step to where Elmer had stood and watched Fenway fill with people. The parade was endless—women wearing stretch tank tops; men in golf shirts, business suits, club ties, shirts open at the neck. A Little League team marched down an aisle, waving the Giant's mustard-colored coupons for the Grand Opening of a Doggie Dugout over in Brookline.

The bleachers in right were quite a contrast. Horton could see Suehowicz and his FBLB jumping like beans on a hot tin plate. Signs milled and turned in the haze. The same old stuff.

SCREW THE BIGS! TIGHTEN SALARIES!

Long, off-key bugle runs trumpeted into the night. Staccato blasts followed by reveille and "Charge!" The horn blasts were weak and distant. According to a piece in *USA Today,* Suehowicz had another exit-early parade scheduled following the Little League game. He was asking the fans to follow him out to an antibig-league rally and fireworks display behind the Green Monster, in Kenmore Square.

Horton looked for guilt on his teammates' faces and thought about the fix. Why had they worked so hard to teach a guy doing drugs the knuckler? Maybe Wilt *should* get the start tonight.

The Dogs were bunched in groups of twos and threes laughing, stretching, freshening tobacco, spitting seeds, going through their normal pregame routines.

"The only way I could tell it was in was the change in temperature," Magruder said. Kline and Wilt rocked with laughter. Baldy looked up from his *Washington Post.* Bear and Blinker had their heads together, planning an assault on Boston's bars and B-girls, Horton suspected. Johnson had distanced himself from the rest.

He sat outside the dugout and watched a groundskeeper climb a metal ladder and fishnet balls out of the screen above the Green Monster. Billy wore the Walkman. His shoe slapped the dugout step; a rap song, Horton guessed—they weren't the Little League buddies he'd planned to write about. *The Kids of Spring.* His first working title sounded laughable now. The one-for-all-and-all-for-one theme was out, so much had happened in the past several weeks.

Horton closed his eyes and saw Barnes' Baltimore apartment—white leather, white shag, and glasstop tables. The musky odor of Shalimar. She typed her story into a computer keyboard. He pecked away at her clothing. When "-30-" finally flashed up on the screen, Barnes was down to her black lace panties. She plugged the modem into the receiver, dialed the newspaper, then opened floor-length curtains to a spectacular view of Harbor Place. She shivered, said, "Sorry, no horses this time," and led him off to the warmth of her bed.

On the morning flight to Boston, Horton reread the words Larry had clicked into her computer:

BARNSTORMING
By Larry Barnes

WANTED! WANTED! WANTED!

Information leading to a mysterious note and package found on the desk of *Sun* reporter "Fast Eddie" Aldridge.

A recorder mysteriously appeared last night in the IN box of our resident racing tout. Expecting a threat on his life for his Pimlico picks from the day before, Aldridge wisely punched the appropriate buttons. A great sigh of relief—followed by a series of uncontrollable yawns. The voice on the recorder wasn't some wrong-done two-dollar bettor at all. What Aldridge heard was Hooter Horton, the ancient Little League catcher whose antics have been filling this column for the past couple of weeks. According to Aldridge, Horton was droning notes for the book he's planning to write, railing away how bad things were going for the New Becton Hot Dogs in their Florida training camp. He's got problems with a knuckleballer he suspects is hooked on cocaine, and a general attitude problem which appears to be rampant.

Oh, one more thing: The tape begins with Horton discussing the rift between Elmer Thumma, CEO of Elmer's Little Giants, and Daniel Gross, the company's comptroller.

Big deal, Larry, you say. Where's the stuff you promised us about the fix? Well, Aldridge, ever the reporter, was kind enough to read me the note attached to his new recorder. It seems that the generous depositor discovered the little Olympus S911 in the desk drawer of, are you getting ahead of me? Danny Gross! Gross, you'll recall, is the second-in-command at ELG, the man who's got Thumma on a sharp-pointed stick, grilling him slowly over a hot pit of ELG stockholders. It's all about this Little Series thing.

Now let's get down to the investigative reporting. I checked with Horton. He confirmed that the recorder was stolen from the locker room when the team was training in West Palm Beach. "Balmore" readers who had their Bear Cat scanners on last night may have already heard this next piece of news: There was a break-in at Elmer's Little Giants, Inc., around 11:00 P.M. last night.

So on the eve of what could be the final game of the LWS, Horton fears a link between Gross and members of the New Becton team. What's it all mean? Not sure yet. Gross, Elmer the Giant, McKeen, Wilt, Johnson, everybody from Vermont to Maryland had their phone off the hook last night. But watch this spot. Maybe game four will flush the culprits out.

-30-

The bat made a dinging sound. The crowd roared apprecia-tively. Horton turned his attention back to the field. Billy had fallen back on his heels and mishit a pitch to right. As the smog lifted into the lights, Horton watched the ball drift out into the clear, black New England night. Tiny Wyatt, the Ducks' top-heavy right fielder, slid to a stop and blocked the ball with the softness of his upper body.

Horton checked the left-field scoreboard:

PINTAILS 0 0 1 0 0
HOT DOGS 0 0 0 0

Billy's knuckler had been unbelievable. Three walks and a one-run error in the third, then nothing but butterflies and moths for the Pintail Ducks, unhittable pitches. And now the single to right.

How the hell can you suspect a guy of fixing a game when he's playing like that?

Horton pushed the toothpick to the side of his mouth and cut loose a long, birdlike whistle. Where the hell is Pazerelli? Bring in the blind man, he thought.

Fucking Pazerelli, he thought. The bastard doesn't even have to throw strikes. The Dogs would swing at anything close. A simple case of self-defense. The sound of the Pazerelli fastball ripping Bunny's helmet isn't something a hitter forgets. No, they had to get Nelson out of there and finish Pazerelli off once and for all. That's what Clicker Night was all about!

Rymoff tucked a chaw into his jampacked cheek, tossed away two bats, and strode to the plate.

"Come on, Bear, be there, baby, what say, you the man!" Horton shouted. The Dogs climbed out on the apron of the dugout and echoed Horton's encouragements.

"One down, don't take any chances!" The Giant paced the lines off the third-base box. He shouted, whistled, and followed his advice with a flurry of semaphore signals. Stonesifer leaped from his box seat and bellowed into a rolled-up program. The network suits and ties whistled and stomped. A Hot Dog win meant game five, Yankee Stadium, and national TV.

Nelson came sidearm with a fastball up and in. Bear backed off and tapped his spikes. "Hall hun!" Campbell shouted. "Hang tough, Bear!" Kline screamed. "Cockshot, your pitch!" Wilt hollered. Horton bowed and wiped his forehead on the long orange sleeves.

Boink! The metal sounded in the heavy night. West, the Ducks' center fielder, turned, numbers to the diamond, and raced toward the bullpen. Horton felt the adrenaline kicking again. The Bear had hit a climber to right-center, a "Teddy Ball Game," a shot Red Sox fans could identify with. The ball skipped once and banged against the bullpen wall. "Williamsburg!" The Giant threw up his hands to stop him at second. Too late—Bear was steamrolling past second, digging for third. Rymoff made a gooney bird landing, feet and legs skidding along in front of an oversize tail. As a dust storm swirled under Bear's backside at third, Billy touched home with the tying run.

"Haafe!" Campbell intoned.

Rymoff doffed his cap and did a curtsy. McKeen waved his cap at the bullpen. Horton felt his heart kicking around and touched the bag more for luck than anything else.

Thumma ambled over and called to his bench. "They're gettin' him up, boys. Suck up your guts!" he said.

"Bring the big bastard on," Horton said under his breath. "Clicker Night. Bunny's revenge!"

Magruder hopped up and down on the bench, squeaking obscenities at Ichabod Nelson.

"Friggin' pumpkin'-fucker. Hey, Ichy, no wonder you love Halloween!"

Wilt reached up and took a note from an usher. Two brunettes stuck their heads into the dugout. The DoubleMint twins! They'd been following the bus since the team left Detroit. Wilt waved and sauntered up the steps. Magruder screamed, "Fuckstick!" at Nelson, paused, then wandered over to the water cooler and pulled himself a drink.

Clicker Night would have to take care of itself. It was time to set the trap for a Mouse.

"Hey, Mouse. See you for a minute?" Horton ducked back into the doorway to the clubhouse tunnel. Magruder pulled at the water, slurped, then belched. "Screw you. We gotta rally goin', I'm not gonna miss—"

"Christ!" Mouse squeaked. Horton banged him hard on the toe with the butt of a bat. "Get your ass in here!" The catcher yanked him by the front of his oversize uniform shirt. The actions clearly surprised both men.

"Horton, you're a crazy son of a bitch, you know that? You were fucked up as a kid and haven't changed a—"

"The Pintails win and every one of us loses five hundred thousand bucks, maybe more," Horton said. Magruder rubbed his toe, struck a match, and held it to the end of his cigarette. Horton closed the dugout door. The tunnel blackened. "Horton, you're a fucking loon. You and that old man, both of you crazier than shithouse rats," he said. The tip of the cigarette glowed orange in the dark.

"Mouse, we're in the Giant's will. A fact: We are in the big guy's will!" Magruder inhaled hard, right down to his sore little toes. The cigarette flared. Horton watched the Mouse turn white. Out on the field the PA blasted: "Pazerelli for Nelson! Now pitching for the Poughkeepsie Pintails, number 37, Danny Pazerelli!" the message boomed in the night.

"We're in the what?" he coughed. "You tellin' me Thumma's dying?"

"No, but when he does, everything—Elmer's Little Giants, the mansion, the horses, all of it—goes to the New Becton Hot Dogs!"

"We're the heirs?"

"Yup. Thought you'd want to know. You've always been one of the big guy's favorites," Horton said.

"You're shitting me. He's willing us—"

"Whatever Gross doesn't fuck him out of," Horton said. He kicked the door open. Fenway's lights flooded the runway. Horton walked into the dugout, leaving Mouse behind to suck on his cigarette.

PA: "Your attention, please. Elmer the Giant Thumma, owner of Elmer's Little Giants, Inc., has designated this Hot Dog Clicker Night. So, kids, look for Frankie, the company mascot—he'll be distributing some special rally souvenirs. Elmer says the clickers are guaranteed to get the Hot Dogs going." Thumma tipped the old black cap. The crowd thanked him with light applause.

Rymoff lay on the bench, panting like a sunbaked old grizzly.

"You scored?" Horton asked.

"It's 2–1 us! Where the fuck were you?" Bear said. "Wild pitch. Now they're bringing the blind man in!"

Horton leaned into Bear. He could feel his stubbly beard, smell the trucker's garlicky breath. He whispered without moving his lips. "Keep Magruder busy. Don't let him talk to any of the other players." Rymoff rubbed his mustache. More garlic. Horton turned his head in defense.

"What's the deal? Is it the fix?" Rymoff said.

Horton shrugged. "Trying to find out. Just keep him from talking. Do that baby thing where you grab him by the uniform and lead him around with you if you have to."

If Mouse warned his accomplices, Horton's scam was dead. No, if he was going to nail the fixers, Magruder had to see the men tanking, sweat it out watching his inheritance swirl down the drain.

Ensor clicked the honing device behind home plate. Pazerelli cocked his head in a directional way and aimed a scorching fast ball toward the noisemaker.

"Hey, Mouse, c'mere a minute! Something I wanta show you!" Rymoff shouted. Magruder was set up behind Wilt now, trying to edge his way into the conversation with the Detroit brunettes.

He scurried down the dugout steps. "What's up, Bear?"

"Gotcha!" Rymoff shouted and yanked him on his lap. "How's my little Mousie?" Magruder struggled. Rymoff pulled off the rodent's cap and ruffled his hair. "Just wanted some company. See big ol' Bear slide into third?" he said.

Horton checked Brown for an update. He'd lost a few plays in the tunnel. Kline had walked on a wild pitch and Rymoff had scored. It was just like the Bear had said.

"Pazerelli's throwing darts. Everything's been in and around the plate during the warm-ups," Brown said. "You hear that racket? It sounds like Ensor's indicating direction, using that metal noisemaker again."

Horton went to the rack, pulled his thirty-four-inch Eason, and walked out into the magic of Fenway Park. He knelt in the on-deck circle and touched his back pocket.

Brown dropped down beside him. "Relax, my man! Just get your bat on the ball," he said. Relax? Horton thought about Mouse and the fix, then surprised himself with a smile. When Clicker Night kicked in, he'd be sixty feet, six inches away from a blind, fastballing maniac.

"Ain't no big thing. Just be cool," Brown said.

"Hlay hall!" Campbell spun his narrow rear toward the mound

and gave the plate a dust. Elmer tipped his cap and nodded. They had Mouse where they wanted him. Now where the hell was Frankie? Pazerelli stared in at Ensor and cocked his head again. Ballard inched back in the box and looked to the Giant for help. The click was crisp. The sound of a summer cricket. "Clicket, clicket." Pazerelli rubbed the black stubble and pushed the dark smoke glasses back on his nose. "Clicket, clicket." Ensor signaled him again. The beard nodded, the leg kicked, and a fastball sailed under a rusty gate swing.

"Heerike hun!" Campbell bellowed. "Nice swing, Mary!" Magruder shouted from the Bear's big lap. Horton searched the stands. No Frankie! The midget had his orders. The souvenirs were to be in the hands of the kids when Pazerelli took the mound. He'd made that specific. Ensor clicked twice. Ballard swung defensively. Campbell "Heriked!" again. Sweat cascaded down Horton's arms, ran to his knuckles, and flooded his palms. He looked at the bench and touched the bag again. Rymoff bounced the Mouse up and down on his lap.

"Be a hitter, Blinker," the Giant pleaded, flashing Ballard the sign to take. The initial wave was confusing to Horton, not quite what he'd expected. A roar went up from the FBLB in right. Behind it came a screeking sound, chalk on blackboard, Horton thought. Frankie was hysterical; hyenic giggles flowed in from right field. Suehowicz's boys had the baby-size blintz in the air, tossing him like a beach ball, batting him back and forth through the crowd. Horton saw little brown feet fly up. A handful of clickers showered down on the crowd.

Christ, how dumb can you be? He'd told him ten times to start the handout behind home plate.

Pazerelli breezed a third strike past Ballard. "What'd he throw you?" Horton asked. Ballard stopped. His eyes blinked like blacklight strobes. "Didn't see them. You know, with this condition my eyes are closed half the time," he said.

Another roar went up in the night. The human wiener had escaped from his captors. He raced freely down the aisles now, throwing the souvenirs like a mad paper boy. Kline stood on first base watching the stands, shaking his head in amazement. Horton called time out and ambled down to the Giant's box.

"Stallin'?" the Giant said with a grin.

"Give him time to get them passed around," Horton said. "Bear's helping us out, making sure Mouse can't run his mouth."

"I see him over there. Looks like the Bear is babying him a bit," Thumma said.

"Hlay hall!" Campbell had the mask off and was walking down the third-base line.

Ensor duck walked behind the plate. Campbell leaned over, got in tight, and pulled the metal bars in line. As Horton burrowed his spikes in the dirt, he heard the clicker go off in Ensor's crotch. Pazerelli did the head tilt. Ensor pressed the noisemaker again. Then Fenway Park erupted in one big, wonderful summer symphony. Clicks cascaded down from the stands. Kids pushed their magic twangers. Up from the crowd came the froggie sounds— bleachers, reserves, boxes—all erupting at once. Fenway was Walden Pond South. Thoreau would have approved, Horton thought.

Ensor countered with a click or two. Pazerelli shrugged and heaved a fastball high on the screen. The hard face suddenly went soft. Pazerelli looked hurt, confused, Horton thought. The sound was deafening, louder, more annoying than Horton had imagined. Frankie was wound up now, racing wildly through the right-field seats, tossing the metal gadgets into more eager, outstretched hands.

"Horton, what the fuck gives?" Ensor said.

"Clicker Night!"

"Hlay hall!" the umpire said.

The wild Duck's first pitch caromed off a backstop pipe, bounced once, kicked sideways, and sent McKeen flying from his little milking stool. Kline cruised into second, made the turn then eased back to the bag.

"Keep him loose!" the Giant shouted. The clickers came at the blind pitcher from every corner of the park. Pazerelli spat at his glove and missed, kicked at the rubber, missed again, then spun and cussed the froglike chorus. Horton bit his lip to keep from laughing.

A wave of cricket sounds flowed from behind home plate. Pazerelli tilted his head again, toed the rubber cockeyed, kicked, and threw. The ball grazed the green railing in front of Stonesifer's box. Kline took third standing up.

"Time out!" The long brown collie nose was behind Horton now, pecking away at the bars of Campbell's mask.

"Make 'em shut those little dickheads up. They're interfering with my pitcher, using a foreign substance to keep him from concentrating."

The Giant lumbered down the line. "Since you mentioned it, McKeen, how about your catcher's musical cup? The one with the built-in rhythm section. You've been beatin' out signals like a freakin' tom-tom on that thing, screwin' my hitters up!"

"Hlay hall!" Campbell shouted.

And while McKeen divvied up obscenities between Campbell and Thumma, Pazerelli shocked the Clicker Night crowd with one final bit of wildness.

The blind man stopped midmotion and staggered off the mound. "Time out!" Ensor screamed. And watched his pitcher grope his way to center field, flashing the middle finger of his pitching hand up at the stands. Pazerelli screamed at the cricketing crowd, challenged them into the ring. Barnes had a point: The LWS and Wrestle-Mania had their share of similarities, all right.

The protest flew by at a dizzying pace. Campbell ejected Pazerelli, McKeen protested the game, Stonesifer ruled against it, then Campbell came up on his toes and screamed "Hlayy hall!" in a voice that finalized the fracas.

The Pintails' new reliever tipped off the next pitch with a flip of his wrist. Curveball! How Little League could a series get? Horton watched the slow roundhouse arch toward the plate, held the front foot in, and banged the ball sharply to right. Three to one! Horton thought. But when the Dogs' catcher made the turn at first he saw Kline face down in the dirt crab crawling back to the third base sack.

"Tripped!" The Ducks' first baseman said. Horton watched his would-be RBI dust himself off and reluctantly added the name Kline to his suspect list.

DOGS   2
DUCKS 1

While Baldy Albaugh flailed away at Little League curveballs, Horton caught his breath. The press box was an ant farm in action. Hands flying over typewriter keys. Barnes' blond hair flashed briefly, then disappeared.

"Heerike two!" Campbell bellowed.

Horton looked over the left-field scoreboard, past the Citgo sign, and said a silent prayer of thanks for Clicker Night.

At least Bun-Bun had made his contribution. Pazerelli was history—psyched for the series. Now let's see who the hell's been tanking, he thought.

•16•

WALKER HORTON'S BUST-THE-FIX SCHEME WAS LOG-ical but loaded with assumptions. Assumption one: Magruder would know all guilty parties. Assumption two: If the "We're in the will!" bait worked, Mouse would go Judas and kiss every fixer in sight.

Horton dove and slapped the knuckler with his megasatchel glove. "Hall hore!" Campbell said. "Not one friggin' decent pitch to hit," Biggie Ensor swore and took first base.

"Dogs two, Ducks one, men on first and second, two out, and Ichy Nelson, a big, lantern-jawed right-handed hitter, coming up. Nelson's back playing third base now. If you're scoring at home," Hodges' voice was louder than usual, up a notch to be

heard above the belligerent crowd. "Johnson's gone bad so suddenly. We're not going to make any judgments, but when fix
accusations are being tossed at a team like they have the Hot
Dogs, you've got to wonder . . ."

Early that morning, while the Delta jet circled Logan International Airport, Barnes and Horton traded suspect lists. Mouse
Magruder stood alone at the top of both rankings. The rest were
a coin toss. Like throwing darts blindfolded, Horton said.

They were both still speculating at the baggage pickup. Barnes
suggested a bet. Then neither could decide on a name. "I feel like
Inspector Clouseau, 'I suspect everyone and I suspect no one,' "
she said.

Horton tugged at his cup and watched Nelson prance to the
plate like a greyhound entering the gate. He pointed the bat above
the Green Monster's screen and drew a bead on the Citgo sign. The
Giant asked for time and shuffled slowly toward the mound. Horton made the trip in a trot.

"Billy, you feelin' okay?" the Giant asked. He had the black cap
off, beating it against his leg. Johnson's eyes tilted up like big
brown almonds, then rolled forward and took aim on his shoes. He
sniffed several times and wiped his nose.

"Better get me outta here. I've lost it," he said. Johnson's voice
rasped. Horton lunged for the pitcher. Thumma's forearm held
him back. Drugs! A gavel banged. A jail cell slammed in Horton's
head. Guilty as charged. Kline's trip was legit. The cokehead's the
fixer! And Elmer's pulling him before I can prove it!

"Wilt!" Thumma shouted.

What kind of a bastard would throw a Little League game?
Horton swore under his breath. And how could Thumma let
Johnson go out and play second base? Why hadn't Mouse turned
on him? Had Horton misjudged Magruder? Maybe the Mouse
wasn't buying the story about the Giant's will. Was Mouse the
one? He might be just crazy enough to think he could fix it himself.
He should have told him the big guy was dying, had less than a
week to live.

Thumma handed the ball to the left-hander, slapped it in his glove in a personal way. "I want sliders, nothing but. You got an umpire who's dying to get out of this madhouse"—the Giant looked in at Ichy Nelson, watched the long arms stretch and tap the bat on the plate—"and a man with a strike zone the size of the John Hancock Building. Now let's see three right down the ole' poop shoot," he said.

Horton's attempt at eye contact failed. Wilt looked him off—behind the screen, into the stands, anywhere but into the eyes of Hooter Horton. Wilt's first pitch was a shocker. It blasted Horton, tipped him back on his heels. "Heeerike hun!" Wilt snatched the return throw, looked Ensor back to first, turned on Barbin at second, came set, and buzzed another breaker under Nelson's elbows. "Hall hun!" Campbell said. Pitches three and four were a matched set, fastballs away. Nelson refused to chase. Horton walked out and confronted Wilt. "I asked for a slider!"

"Oh, didn't they break?" Wilt snatched the ball from the pillow-size mitt. The next pitch boomeranged low. Nelson exhaled hard and trotted off to load the bases. Horton looked out toward second base at Billy and saw his thoughts as a newspaper headline again:

COKEHEAD AND GAMBLER SUSPECTED IN LITTLE LEAGUE FIX.

Horton tried to shake the notion and glanced back out at the mound. Knowing Odie, he'd run the count to three and two, then dazzle Graham with a breaking ball across the knees. The man had a flare for the dramatic.

Mouse appeared more active now. He uncrossed his legs and fashioned a little pirouette. But it wasn't just Mouse. The whole team was on its toes. Kline shouted nonsense in from short, a lot of "hum its" and "be dares." Rymoff's old brown glove pen-dulumed between his legs like an elephant trunk. The hulking first baseman swayed, right foot to left and back again. Thumma had the Red Sox up on the dugout fringe whistling, shouting, begging for strikes. The air was Horton's problem now. He needed more breath than Fenway afforded.

"Bases loaded, Donnie Graham, ex-Indian, facing Wilt, the

former Cub," Russ Hodges faded in for a second. Horton did a press box check. Heads were down, hands on the move. Where's Larry? No blond hair in sight.

"Hlay hall!" Campbell said.

"Come, Odie, be the man, what say, what chuck!" Horton touched the back pocket, then threw three fingers down. Wilt toed the rubber, nodded, kicked the leg, and windmilled forward. The slider broke down and in to the right-handed hitter. Graham swung and beat the ball foul in the dirt. Fenway went mad—clickers and crowd—a deafening combination.

"You the man, now whaddya say!" Horton went back to his crotch, fingers flying, ran through the numbers, and landed on three again.

"Yo, baby, yo!" Bear called. "Come, Odie, be there, baby," Albaugh chimed in from third. Horton saw the smirk, the line of a smile. Wilt pumped and threw. Slider again. Graham laid off.

Horton started to pay him a visit, then stopped and returned to his haunches. He asked for the slider. "Hall two!" the pitch was wild low, down in the dirt. "Odie, come to me," Horton shook the ball and fired it back to the mound. The paper sack! Mouse Magruder! Larry Barnes!

Wilt vs. Graham!

That was all that mattered now. Wilt kicked and flew off the mound, a runaway mowing machine. The pitch sailed high. Horton dove under Graham's ferocious swing.

"Keerist, don't help him out!" McKeen's voice made a high, keening sound over the clicks and shouts of the crowd. "Hoo and hoo!" Campbell said.

Horton pounded black dust from his mitt and looked out toward the wall in left. The line score was accurate, but Fenway's scoreboard had missed the story. It was a 2–1 game, two out, a two-and-two count on the hitter. Deuces wild! But one good swing from Donnie Graham and Horton's life could be rolling around in Kenmore Square. That was the catcher's thought as Wilt toed the rubber. He came set, broke off a cockeyed grin, and followed it up with a major league slider.

Campbell hesitated. "Hall three!" he said it softly, under his breath. Horton spun on the umpire, climbed the bars of his mask.

"Bullshit!" he screamed, shaking the ball in the old angular face. "Right on the black!" Horton lied.

"Hime hout!" Campbell threw his right arm in the air and directed his comment between the gaps in Horton's mask.

Christ, he's running me, tossing me out of the game! Horton thought.

"What the fuck's he want now?" Campbell's voice was soft, almost gentle. Horton heard feet scurrying along the infield grass. Magruder cut left, short of the plate, circled around the on-deck ring, and disappeared into the first-base dugout.

The crowd became an outdoor rhythm section, clickers backed up by the stomp of frantic feet. Wilt kicked the resin bag toward Kline at short. "Right fielder musta busted his jock leaning in trying to help me call that last pitch," Campbell said.

Horton buzzed inside. Speculation brought rivers of sweat. Now what? Magruder was a mystery man. Wilt turned and stared off at the left-field scoreboard. Suddenly uniforms parted in the first-base dugout. Elmer and Magruder chin to chin. One face white, the other red. Then Mouse squirted up the steps and trotted back to his position in right, stopped, made an exaggerated zip of his fly and tipped his hat to the fans. The crowd reached back for a little extra, a higher level, a wild, beating, clicking crescendo.

Wilt . . . ! Horton stopped in midthought.

"Now, what the fuckola!" Campbell said.

Thumma was making a move, head down, a hand jammed in each back pocket as he ambled slowly toward the mound. Horton watched him cross the line. His neck was changing colors, the pace was unusually slow.

The exchange was almost undetectable. All Horton caught were a few subtle moves. The Giant's hand slapping the ball out of Wilt's glove. Odie's chin jutting then falling, pressing against his chest. From the stands or press box they'd have needed binoculars to see it. The Giant simply put a big vise grip on the pitcher's shoulder and led him off the mound in what appeared to be a loving, fatherly way.

"Kline!" the Giant's voice tremored. Campbell wheeled and looked up at the press box.

"Kline for Wilt. Christ, Thumma, make up your mind," he said. "Looks like an injury. You boys are going to have to finish it one player short."

Horton took Kline's first warm-up toss.

"What's the deal on Wilt? A blister?" Campbell asked.

Horton couldn't find the air he needed. It wasn't Billy. The Mouse had just kissed Odie Wilt.

"Yeah, a blister," he managed and touched his bag. A blister, a recent sore spot in Walker Horton's life. Odie Wilt! The bastard had tanked on the Giant.

Watching Kline's room service warm-ups tried Graham's patience. And when Campbell said, "Hlay hall!" Graham lashed at the first white object he saw, undercut the pitch, and sent it rocketing into the night above home plate. Horton whipped off the mask and watched the oval climb into the lights.

Graham threw the bat. Horton circled once, turning his back on the diamond. "I've got it," he said and tapped the glove.

Campbell ran for the third-base dugout. Horton clung to his mask, stared up into the lights, searched the sky for the ball and tried not to think about Odie Wilt. The crowd went quiet and watched the catcher drift toward the Hot Dogs' dugout. Horton followed its flight. The series was coming down now, heading his way. He moved through the on-deck circle, and as he edged closer to the stands prayed that he'd judge the ball better than he had Johnson and Wilt.

"Horton circling under the ball, tapping the glove," Hodges again.

Voices from the first-base dugout. A gang of spikes scraped and clawed the cement, players scattering, running for cover. Horton glanced to the dugout. Odie Wilt, arms outstretched—the left-hander was there to catch him. The grin. Too late. "Odie!" Horton was lunging now, falling, out of control. The ball caught the heel of his mitt.

"I've got you!" Wilt said. Horton's hand stabbed at the ball, then his chin caught the edge of the water cooler, and he was catapulting off the bench, and into the wooden wall. Wilt had backed off, let him fall! In the daze he sensed people under him, over him. He felt big, strong hands, sorting through the bodies; now they were probing his glove.

"He's got it!" the Giant shouted.

"Her hout!" Campbell echoed the call.

For a time Horton lay in a heap, rubbing his bloody chin. He was buried alive, under a pile of well-wishing humanity. During the confusion, in the midst of his grogginess, Wilt leaned in and gave him a message.

"After the Red Sox game. Meet me out by the Green Monster. Something we need to get straight," he said.

HORTON SHOULDERED THE DOOR, STEPPED INTO darkness, and groped like a sleepwalker along the dugout wall. Cinders crunched under his Nikes. He reached out, felt for the cool metal seat back, and eased down on the Red Sox bench.

Fenway after dark. A good place to assess the situation. Clicker Night. Game-winning catch, then six stitches in the chin followed by a refreshing postgame round of dodge with reporters about the fix. Voices echoed in the night.

"Horton, you sure pulled Johnson all of a sudden like. You know something we don't?"

"Hooter! Ken Robertson of *The Springfield Gazette.* Thumma says Wilt got yanked because of a blister. I just took a look for myself. The only thing I can see are a couple of pop top cuts!"

The probe was relentless. Barnes, Lew Nixon of *The New York Post, Sports Illustrated*'s Peter Gammons. Bright lights, big guns, tough questions fired from the gut. And just when the press appeared to be cooling down, in walked the commissioner to cancel the Giant's Little World Series.

Horton replayed the scene there in the dark. A wooden door slapped into a metal medicine chest, a reporter shouted "Stonesifer!" and the press stampeded.

"Commissioner! Commissioner! Your reaction to . . ." Lights and cameras zeroed in on baseball's eminence. Notebooks and microphones waved in the apple-red face.

"Commissioner! Billy Reid, WBZ. What's your reaction to tonight's game? Did we see a fix, or what?"

The gray suit hung on Stonesifer like loose elephant skin. His glasses steamed. Thumma reached in his hip pocket and passed the blue railroad handkerchief up through the crowd. The commissioner shined his wire-rimmed spectacles, touched the rag to his head, and read a prepared statement into the confusion.

"I am appalled at information I received tonight concerning several New Becton players and their alleged attempt to fix the Little Series."

"Who?" "Can you name 'em?" "Commissioner, for Christ's sake, give us a hint. Pitcher? Catcher? Don't just let us hang on this thing, we've got stories to write!"

The chubby hand saluted the lights. "Boys, it's in the hands of the authorities. There will be a press conference in my offices in New York on Saturday morning at 10:00 A.M. But from the evidence that I have now—"

"Is it true NBC has already canceled their coverage for Saturday?" a TV reporter shouted.

Stonesifer cut his eyes through the lights, found the Giant, and offered up a look of regret. "Elmer, from the evidence the network and I received tonight, I'd have to say that you and the boys just played the final game of your Little World Series!"

"Final game!" Hard words for Horton to shake. He inhaled deeply and took in what smelled like a breath of salt air. Horton gazed above the shadowy flags, followed the hazy gray outline of Fenway's upper deck, and entertained thoughts of revenge. Light towers loomed over the park like monstrous black fly swatters. If one were to fall, it could squash an insect like Wilt. Wilt, still hard to believe. The moon made a brief appearance. The infield tarp shimmered white, like ocean water. A gate banged out by the Green Monster. Horton jumped, felt for his anxiety bag, then touched the puffy place where the Red Sox trainer had sewn six neat little stitches.

He hadn't lied to Larry Barnes. One last interview after the Sox/Mariners game and that was it. What he'd failed to mention was that it would be with Odie Wilt. Meeting at the Green Monster was crazy, typical Odie. But Horton was ready. Whatever it took to get the message across. Game five or no game five, Wilt was history, off the team. And the sooner he knew it, the better the New Becton Hot Dogs would be.

A tough night for the press. Stony had artfully dodged every question. Where did Mouse Magruder disappear to after the game? The locker was empty. Had he packed it in, left for good? If Wilt didn't have a blister, then why was he yanked so suddenly? What had the Giant said to him during that stroll to the dugout? Did he accuse him of the fix when he pulled him? To guess would be fruitless, a waste of time. Wilt and Thumma, two poker players who defied all reason and logic.

Horton took a whiff of the dugout air—popcorn, cigarette smoke, sunflower seeds and fresh tobacco. How do you figure a guy like Wilt? he wondered. He's yanked from the game, lets his catcher take a six-stitch fall, then sits calmly in front of his locker swilling beer, like he just won the Cy Young. And Thumma? Typical Giant, totally off the wall. He catches a guy he loves like a son trying to screw him out of millions of dollars and acts like a man who just won the Maryland lotto.

When the commissioner blows in and makes noises about canceling the series, Wilt shakes his head, tools over to the cooler, and pops another beer. The Giant breaks into a grin, slaps Ballard on the tail, and tells a *Globe* reporter to "remember that the key to Stony's statement is that 'all the evidence ain't in!' "

Hell, the commissioner's rear end hadn't cleared the doorway and Thumma was telling Dave Anderson of the *Times* how much fun it was going to be playing McKeen in Yankee Stadium.

"We'll be more together than ever. Adversity can do that to a team!" he said. The old man's eyes were a sky blue. Horton had looked right into the azure puddles. The Giant believed everything he'd said.

Above Fenway's Green Monster wall, fireworks lit the summer sky. Reds and greens, big displays boomed and sprayed in the urban haze. Suehowicz's FBLB rally. He'd led them out again; thousands had congoed away from the big league game to join the protest in Kenmore Square. Another salvo rocketed upward. Boom! Boom! Boom! Yellows and greens backlit the left-field wall. White archs crisscrossing in front of the Citgo sign. Inside, Fenway was alley black. Not an ideal place to meet a man like Wilt. Horton perused the outfield, looking for movement, a shadow, anything stirring. Horton heard a loud, grating squeak. A gull? A distant clicket from the left-field seats. A remnant from Clicker Night, snapping back to life, no doubt.

Horton skirted the infield tarp then groped his way along the lower boxes like a man on a lifeline. Step by step, one hand in front of another. Rockets fired in the distance. The warning track gravel crunched like glass under his smooth-soled shoes. He bent low and stared out into the darkness where men such as Williams, Jensen, and Piersall had roamed. The squeak flew out of the dark. A loud, irritating sound.

"Odie?" He stopped, cupped his hands, calling out into the night. Behind the right-field bullpen a yellow bug light cast a dim, orangish glow. Horton pushed down the left-field line, his eyes adjusting but still seeing shadows. Large protrusions, railings, and walls served as ghostly guides. When he got to the wall he'd feel for the ladder that the groundskeeper with the fishnet had climbed. He'd wait there in the dark. Hell, Wilt probably wouldn't even show. Maybe the Giant had given him his walking papers. That's why Wilt had been drinking so hard.

"Odie?" Horton groped along the scoreboard, running his fingers over the holes where the Hot Dogs' runs had hung. Suehowicz launched another salvo. It climbed above the wall and flashed the sky a milky white. The thick wall muted the pyrotechnic thunder. He called to Wilt again, stopped by the ladder, and took a long, deep breath.

Screek! Screek! Screek! Horton swore and grabbed his chest. Fucking gulls, Boston's on the water, he thought.

Screeking sounds came out of the dark again. Horton detected a rhythm to the noise this time. Some kind of vehicle rolling along out there in the blackness.

"Horton? That you?"

Wilt! Nothing but ebony sky. He bent and stared toward the direction of the pitcher's voice. "Over here," Horton said. "By the ladder."

The screeking had quieted now. Wilt talked over the noise. His voice sounded slurred to Horton.

"Horton, you saw what Mouse did tonight. Packed it in before I could get my hands on him. The little fucker was on the take, tried to bullshit Elmer, convince the big guy it was me!" The park was as quiet as death.

Horton brushed his sore chin and saw Wilt's arms again, reaching up, welcoming him in.

"Hooter, you still there?" Wilt said.

Horton called up the nasty grin.

"I'm here!"

"You believe me, don't ya? There's no way I'd tank on you and Elmer. Hell, we got 'em where we want 'em now. Commissioner will change his tune. Me against Ensor in Yankee Stadium. NBC, national TV, we can win the Giant his company back."

The wheels squeaked again. Horton bent low and squinted into the dark. Nothing but shadows, black on black.

"Odie, it's over!" he said. "I haven't figured out how, but if we play, we'll be doing it without you. You can bet your ass on that!"

The missile grazed a rung of the metal ladder and crashed against the base of the wall with a loud, scary thud. Horton went face down in the cinders like he'd been shot by a gun.

"Stay loose, cocksucker!" Wilt screamed out in the dark. Horton heard feet racing, the squeak of the rusty wheels. Wilt was moving. Running through the grass. The clouds winked for a millisecond, a camera flash of light from the moon. Horton could see the cowboy hat slung back on his head. Wilt had batting practice balls, a grocery cartful, pushing them into battle position.

Bang! Another shot smashed into the padded wall.

"Christ, Odie don't—" Horton spoke without thinking. A ball crashed at his feet, skipped, and busted into his shin. The voice had given Wilt direction. A ball rang the metal railing like a carnival bell. Horton held his leg and crab-crawled along the warning track. Another ball beat into the fence. He curled and knotted like a pretzel, jammed his head between his knees for protection.

"You and fucking Elmer. Daddy and son. Things don't fucking change. Looks like it's going to end the way it always was. Me on the outside, looking in." Wilt's voice was scary. Different, deranged.

"Speakin' of lookin' in, how 'bout lookin' this one in!" The ball caromed off the cushioned wall inches from Horton's head. High eighties, maybe ninety. Killer pitches. Fired at point-blank range. The night went quiet again. A beer can popped out by the grocery cart. Wilt laughed the laugh. Horton crept along the wall and shouted over his shoulder, trying to throw his voice.

"You trying to kill—"

"Hooter the Buddy Fucker. I thought I was supposed to be your hero."

"You were. It should have been Kline, Bun-Bun, anybody but you!" Horton scrunched lower. "Is this 'the Enforcer,' the Great Chicago Cub? Pinning a guy to the wall in the dark?" A ball banged high on the fence several feet to his left. Then Wilt soft-tossed one in behind it like a live grenade. "Change-up." He laughed the crazy laugh.

"That time Janie and I drove all the way to Chicago to see you play. You know what I remember best about that trip?"

"I shut out the fucking Dodgers three to zip!"

"No; my hero forgot to leave the tickets he'd promised. I had to scalp two outside the park."

"How's that Barnes pussy? Writers must go for pencil dicks," Wilt said. The balls hit like machine-gun fire, tattooing a line above Horton's head. He went face forward on the ground again.

"You know what Elmer thinks?" Horton said. He lay prone, talking sideways through the outfield grass.

"Fuck Elmer. When Gross is through with him, he'll probably give me the old man's office. How do you like that shit?" he said. A ball banked into his lower back. Horton yelped and rolled in the gravel.

"Elmer says Bun-Bun was the best!"

He cringed, covered his head, and waited. Nothing. The comment quieted Wilt and his grocery cart. A split second later Horton was shrieking again, clutching his side in pain. Another bullet had found its mark. The ball short-hopped Horton in the ribs.

"Best at what?" Wilt's tone took on a subtle change.

Horton lay face down in the grass, sucked a deep breath, and quoted the Giant.

"Wilt could play but never had the head. Of course, Bear had all that power, but pound for pound the best that ever came out of New Becton was Bunny McKay! And that goes for basketball, too!"

"Bullshit!" Wilt spat the words. The cart banged. Another fast-ball crashed the fence.

Wilt was closing in. He could hear him breathing. The barrage was sudden; balls sprayed the wall like a pitching machine run amok. Mortar fire from ten feet, maybe less. High, low, ninety-mile-per-hour fastballs beat dents into the monster wall. Close now, the breath was heavy, erratic. Horton wanted to run but lacked the guts. Broken ribs, he thought; two, three, maybe more.

"Elmer's wimp. You could use some balls, Horton. Here, hang this one between your legs . . ."

"Ooof!" A rush of steam, an exploding boiler, wind escaping from a hot-air balloon.

"Oh, Christ," Wilt said with a moan. Then Horton heard the thud, the soft, heavy sound a body makes when it lands in freshly watered grass.

"You okay, pal?"

"Elmer?" Horton said. The pain streaked, took an electrical lap around his ribs. He sucked hard, fighting for another breath. The shadow hulked above him. Big, rounded shoulders supported an oversize head.

"Coach, is that you?" Horton asked, wincing.

"Naw, McMichael, Sox security. It's okay. I decked him. Son of a bitch stole a cart of our batting practice balls," he said. "Gonna have to write you up, too. Nobody's allowed in the park after a game. Christ, you protest fanatics don't know when to quit!"

THE GIANT FEATHERED THE *HOT DOG* PAST A YEL-low cab, tapped the brakes, and mashed down on the bus's musical horn: *"bink-be-bink-bink-bink-bink!"*

"Dodcasted horsecart," he said, wedging the weenie between a produce truck and a wagon pulled by an animal wearing a large straw hat. As Thumma wheeled the team through the Bronx traffic, Horton fought the urge to pop another pain pill.

Doc Kline made the diagnosis at about 2:00 A.M. in the lobby of the Boston Marriott: busted chin, two cracked ribs, and multiple bruises. Kline listened to the story while punching and probing away at Horton's broken body.

"Stayed late to do an interview. Got myself rolled just outside the park. Blindsided, never saw what hit me."

No sense in advertising the truth. Elmer's Little Series had enjoyed all the bad ink it could use.

Thumma pulled around a delivery truck. "We used to call Route 1 Boston Road," he said. Horton held his ribs and stared out at the unfamiliar city. Sun beat through the big bubble window. The Bronx on a ninety-degree day, great medicine for a man suffering from acute depression. The iron-barred stores, broken plate glass, and boarded windows tilted and shook with each brake and jackrabbit start. Horton read the city's menu: CUT RATE LIQUORS, COIN OP LAUNDRY, DOLLAR STORE, CREDIT NO MONEY DOWN—the signs flashed behind waves of concrete heat.

"You mind dropping me off around 135th Street when we cross the river? I promised Larry I'd show her my old stomping grounds, walk her up to Coogan's Bluff. She wants to do some kind of a feature story on me coming back to New York. Cripes, that's the last thing I need right now," he said. Pain shot across his chest. He lifted his arm and adjusted Kline's corset wrap.

The Giant aimed and spat into a paper cup. "Probably oughta do it if you can. We're in sorry shape with the commissioner. All that bad press about the fix didn't help." He looked at the morning newspapers stacked at Horton's feet. "Need a miracle, somethin' like the Mets pulled back in '69 or when Thomson kissed Branca in '51 . . ." The Giant's voice cracked, and the sentence died a natural death. When they pulled out of the Marriott that morning, Thumma had tried to whistle. He'd even tried a chorus or two of "Dear Old Girl" but had to give it up. And his spirits had plummeted by the mile. No way for the Giant to hide emotion. The man was a human thermometer.

The New Becton Hot Dogs mirrored their leader. Horton could see it in the rearview glass. Heads down, glassy-eyed, whispering about the fix, the whereabouts of Magruder and Wilt. This wasn't the team Bear had trumpeted to the Boston writers moments before the Stonesifer speech.

"We'll take Manhattan, just like the fuckin' Muppets did back in '84!" he'd said.

The Giant was right. It would take a Metsian miracle to get the commissioner and the network suits and ties to budge. A fifth game meant another arena for Suehowicz and would refire the story about the fix. A tanked series surrounded by rabble-rousers and played by carousers—too risky for baseball, too shaky a product for a network to sell its affiliates. The Hot Dogs were trouble. A proven commodity in that respect.

"We got seven players now that Wilt and Magruder are gone. You got anything up your size 38 sleeves?" Horton said. The Giant pumped the brakes, horned a cab, and glanced up at the mirror. He held the gaze until he'd nosed into the brushes of a street sweeper. Brakes hissed. The *Hot Dog* skidded to a jerky stop. The Giant could wish in the mirror all day. McKay, Magruder, and Wilt were gone. The New Becton Hot Dogs were a seven-man baseball team with a basket case for a catcher.

Horton checked the mirror again. Barnes had the sunglasses down—hiding out, he suspected. Still miffed because he'd failed to call her room last night. At breakfast, when Horton told her he'd been mugged, she'd threatened to hit him with her grapefruit.

"Oh, you didn't think I'd care? Afraid I might write it?" Horton couldn't remember the reaction verbatim. The grapefruit cocked back in her hand was too distracting.

"Bobbi Roop," the Giant said.

"Who?"

"Bobbi Roop." Thumma did a bubble gum blush. "A woman who I . . . who worked with me as a girl Friday for a number of years."

"Bobbi Roop is your secretary?" Horton was confused.

"No, used to be. We had a little problem. Hell, Hooter, it's been more than a decade ago." The wrinkled brow was a poinsettia color.

"I had to give her a kind of lateral transfer. She heads up the company's steno pool now."

"And . . ."

"Anyways, out of the clear blue she calls my room last night in Boston. She's been following the series on TV and reading Barnes' column. Let me know up front that she owed me nothing. But thought she might have a piece of correspondence I might like to see. Something she's been saving—found it in the Xerox machine at ELG, Inc."

Horton reached under his seat and pulled out his catcher's mitt.

Pain rocketed a 360 around his ribs. The back of his left hand was covered in purple, a splotch the size of the Answer Grape. "She's got something on Gross?"

"Don't know; she's faxing it to the Sheraton," he said. "We'll have to see." The color weakened, Elmer's forehead was back to pink.

"Thar she blows! Yankee Stadium!" The Giant slapped the wheel. Horton leaned forward and looked up through the bubble. Big and brown, triple-decked with high, windowed archways. Above the roof, blue and white pennants whipped in the wind. Horton hadn't seen the stadium in more than thirty years.

"Ruth may a' built her, but I laid a few bricks there over the years." The Giant's eyes were distant. Only once, '37, Horton thought. The big guy would never let it go. Losing three to a man like McKeen. A hell of a lot more painful than a few cracked ribs, he thought.

The ride down Eighth Avenue was a rolling testimony to the Giant's bus. New York stopped to look. Cabs honked, kids waved, a mounted cop galloped up and gave the rounded hood of the weenie a pat.

Barnes stood in the doorway, looking into the quagmire of noisy traffic. The Giant braked for a light at Eighth and 118th Street.

"This close enough?"

"Fine," Horton said. He tucked his arm against his Red Sox T-shirt, assumed a Napoleonic stance, and limped out behind the reporter.

They walked north against the crowd. Horton moved his hands and arms, adjusted his shoulders. The pain was constant but he hobbled along, staying with Barnes step for step.

"Hey, who's leading this tour? You or me?" he said. A black man carting a crate of fish bumped Horton and spun him sideways. Chunks of ice scattered on the steamy sidewalk.

"Sat up until four-thirty waiting for you. I rang your room a hundred times," she said.

"Didn't get in until after two. Doc gave me something to sleep. I didn't hear it ring. I was hurting too bad to come to your room!"

Two blocks of silence. Bad neighborhood. Not the kingdom he remembered. Where was the little park at 124th and Eighth? The place he and Izzy played.

"Look familiar?" Barnes broke the silence.

"Not really. We lived in a brownstone at 127th and Seventh, one street over. But I don't remember it looking like this. We had trees, little corner groceries, a mix of people, Italian, black, some oriental, but it wasn't rundown and dirty. Hell, nobody was rich, but I never felt poor, nothing like this," he said.

Across 127th a vendor hawked ices from behind a white metal cart. "That's more like it," Horton said, and cradling his rib cage, cut into the city traffic.

"Two cherries!" he said.

They sat on the marble steps of an old bank building. FIRST KNICKERBOCKER, according to the brass nameplate. Barnes pulled her tape recorder and pad out of her purse and said, "So, Horton, what brings a guy like you back to Harlem?"

"There's this reporter who needs a story. Promised me sex," he said.

She clicked off the recorder and dropped it back in the big white bag.

"Hooter, what happened to you last night?"

An air horn blasted. A chorus of motorists turned their wrath on a stalled Stroh's truck. Horton felt his anxiety sack and looked down at the cone of bright red ice.

"Love is never having to say 'off-the-record,' " she said with a laugh. Her kiss felt cold against his cheek.

"Now what's the deal? Okay, here's the way I read it by some suspicious absences. Mouse and Wilt were on the take. Elmer nailed them, and they double-teamed you after the game?"

"Close enough," he said.

Walking through the 130s, Horton re-created the entire story, from the setup of Mouse to Wilt's Fenway rifle range.

They sidestepped an unloading transit bus at the corner of 134th. Barnes draped her arm around his waist and kissed his cheek again. "You're forgiven for not calling. Where's the bastard now?" she said.

"Don't know. The security guy said he was going to have us both arrested. Let me go when he saw how busted up I was."

"Freeze, muthafucka." Horton's Nikes screeched to a stop. A gang of teenagers raced by, waving pellet pistols at a pack of smaller kids.

"Nice neighborhood," Barnes said.

Horton smiled apologetically. "Cripes, there's Weisberger's Books. I wonder if the old man's still alive?" Volumes piled high in the storefront window, everything from comics to how-to books.

"Closed Thursday." Horton read the orange Day-Glo sign out loud.

"Siegfried. That was his name. He'd let us stand in there and read all day long if we wanted to. Mom bought me my first *Baseball Encyclopedia*. It was buried under a bunch of cookbooks on the bargain table."

Through the 140s Horton regaled Barnes with Manhattan reminiscences. Stickball games against kids from the 140s were some of the best. "Good players. They had a three-sewer guy up here. A kid named Robin something witz." He told her his mother's stories about her New York childhood, the Cotton Club, and how she'd snuck out at night in the summers to watch the Cadillacs, Lincolns, and limos roll in and drop off the rich and famous. "She saw Al Jolson and Jimmy Durante get out of a cab together one night. Jimmy was in *Jumbo* at the time. Lena Horne. Billie Holliday. Cab Calloway. Duke Ellington. You name them, Mom saw them. She was a great storyteller before she got sick," he said.

"Maybe that's where you got it," Barnes said.

Barnes had him by the hand now. The sound of a jackhammer drowned their conversation. The air drill stopped. A man in a hard hat looked up from a hole in the street and whistled between his teeth. "Over here, make my day!" he shouted up at Barnes. She smiled and looked off at the burned-out city. High-rise brick buildings abused by graffiti and breakage.

"Getting a little rough. All projects now, I guess. Used to be some kind of city. Come down Eighth about five o'clock following an afternoon at the Polo Grounds and the smells would drive you crazy. Spaghetti, cabbage, chow mein. The neighborhood was a smorgasbord."

"You're making the Army brat jealous. You know that, don't you?"

"Naw, just different, that's all. Heck, you saw Japan, Germany, and how many states?"

"Twenty-one. But I never stayed long enough to smell the cooking," she said.

"Well, I talk like I was here forever, but they shipped me to New Becton when I was nine. Except for that one visit to my mother in the hospital, this is as much as I've seen of New York City in thirty years," he said.

Project people milled about in the street. Horton felt out of bounds in his own neighborhood. A guy limping along in a Red Sox T-shirt and Bermudas, a ravishing blonde on his arm. Two bull's-eyes. The perfect targets, Horton thought. Barnes stepped over a man curled up in an overcoat.

"Sleeping it off," Horton said.

"When are you going to visit your mother?"

Horton pointed to a sign, 155th Street, and filled the recorder with trivia about the Polo Grounds.

"Cripes, did you know that a guy named Matty Schwab and his family lived in an apartment under Section 3 of the left-field stands? The apartment is how Stoneham lured Matty away from the Dodgers. Izzy and I used to holler at the guy from the bleachers, begging to be adopted. His kids had one hell of a backyard," he said.

"Center field backed up to Eighth and the Harlem River. Third was West 159th and the IRT rail yards. Home plate, the Harlem River Speedway, Coogan's Bluff, and the IRT elevated tracks. When we had the cash to ride, we'd run down the ramp from the train, buy a nickel scorecard, and get nosed up against the gate. First ones in had the best shot at bleacher seats. Izzy and I were hell on wheels. One Saturday in '51 or '52 we were first in line, got in real early, and caught Mays coming down the third-base line. He signed my 'Say Hey' gum card. One of the ones Janie burned. How do you forgive something like that?"

Horton's pace had quickened. It was as though he'd walked right through the pain. Barnes had her tape recorder out now, documenting the reminiscences. "Everybody talks about the memorials in Yankee Stadium. But we had a memorial in center to Eddie Grant, a genuine Giant war hero who was killed in action in the Argonne Forest on October 5, 1918. Jeez, I hadn't thought about that in years," he said.

As they approached 159th, Horton's voice quietened. Barnes shifted the recorder to her left hand and held it closer. "Coogan's Bluff. The old horseshoe. So ugly it was pretty. Screw Three Rivers, Riverfront, and all those domes. I hate toy grass.

"Stoneham took a square of the sod with him to San Francisco, dug it right out of center field." Horton stopped and looked up at the red brick apartment buildings. "Well, here we are, Polo Grounds Towers. That must be Willie Mays Field. A bunch of macadam and basketball backboards. There's supposed to be some kind of a marker."

Kids shucked and jived on the hot asphalt. Horton watched a jump shot swish through a metal chain net. He turned and looked back toward the buildings. "They tore it down in '64. Used the same wrecking ball that O'Malley took to Ebbets Field," he said. "Now I know why the Giant didn't want to come along. Couldn't have stood it!"

They sat on a bench and watched basketballs beat the rusty rims. Two white spots glistening in the summer sun. Barnes listened to more Giant trivia, then turned the conversation again. "Game five or no, you've had one hell of a series," she said.

"Right!" he said.

"Taken one of the more cynical of America's sporting press, showed her a lot of good stuff," she said.

Horton laughed a sarcastic laugh.

"Wisdom, compassion, guts, and some really top-notch sex," she said. "Do I need to go on?"

"Sure, but what have I done lately? How's the wizard of New Becton going to talk the commissioner into letting the Hot Dog seven take the field on Saturday?"

All six baskets were busy now. Five-on-five games. Shiny black torsos banging away in ninety-degree heat. A bounce pass resulted in a thundering, rim-shaking dunk. Behind them a bottle fell from a balcony and exploded on the street.

"I don't know," she said. "But I'm not going to count you out. You and that old man are an amazing pair. I'm not sure, but I think I may be in love with you both."

The cab eked along Eighth Avenue. They cuddled in the back-seat, defied the heat. Horton elbowed his ribs for support and gawked and gaped at the city he loved so much.

"Realistically you've got until tomorrow morning. If that Xerox copy doesn't prove anything, then I'll be honest, I don't see the commissioner backing down. He's like a flag in the wind when it comes to controversy. The only reason he didn't cancel it after Elmer held Suehowicz out the window was because the network saw a chance to sell game five," Barnes said.

"Well, I almost pulled it off," Horton said. "A hell of a finish. A team with seven players, a tied series with no rubber match— that's a book without an ending no matter how you cut it!"

The cabbie laid on his horn and slid through a yellow light. "Youse guys are lucky youse din't get rolled up there in the 150s. Rough neighborhood!" Horton could see his eyes in the mirror. Thick dark brows flickered in the late-afternoon sun.

"You movie people, or what?" he said. "The bote of youse look familiar." Barnes flashed the teeth. Horton slipped his hand out of the mirror's view and ran his fingers up under her blouse.

"Wait a minute. Don't tell me. You'd dat Little Series guy. The catcher playin' for Elmer the Giant." He leaned back and laughed. Ashes and cigar smoke snowed down on his fares. "I seen the Giant pitch many a ball game. Hell of a thrower. You tell him that one of his fans is still alive. Tell him Bennie Wharton said hello. McKeen was a good one, too, but I never liked him or the Yankees that much!"

Horton coughed an acknowledgment. "I'll tell him," he said. "We said the Sheraton Towers, didn't we?"

The flat cap tipped. "Got ya. Sheraton Towers. Fifty-second and Seventh. This is Second Avenue now. Pretty, ain't it. Won't find many hacks that enjoy the city like I do. Yanks and Dodgers always were out-of-towners. The New York Giants was the only team in this city."

"Agreed," Horton said.

"What's the commissioner gettin' all riled up on this Little Series thing of yours? Looks like just a bunch of old guys tryin' to have a few laughs. Nothin' wrong with that. 'Course, this guy Larry Barnes says in this morning's paper that it looks like Wilt and the little ferret-faced guy you got in right have taken a hike. They on the take, or what? Barnes ain't one of my favorites—he's either gotta be snide or leavin' ya up in the air!"

Horton tickled Barnes in the small of her back. The glasses were down. "Nice view," she said to stave off a laugh.

"Here, let me whip you down Park Avenue, oughta get you one of those hansom cabs, this heat lets up it's gonna be a pretty night for a ride in a park," he said.

In the street the "movie and TV" New York flashed by. Granite and smoked-glass skyscrapers higher than Horton could see. Women in stylish summer dresses with low-cut jogging shoes, high-heeled pumps under their arms. Men in Wall Street attire. Bums sleeping in storefronts, racks of clothes flying by trying to make the garment district before the clock struck five. A woman in boots and miniskirt looked at Horton and sucked her thumb suggestively. A Manhattan rush hour. If you don't see it here, you're not looking, Horton thought. The cabbie horned his way back onto Madison Avenue into the swirling cacophony of moving humanity. More bumper-to-bumper traffic.

"How is the Giant faring?" Barnes wouldn't have had to lower her voice. New York's horn section was up.

"He's trying to put up a good front, but I think he's scared. If Gross pulls this thing off, he might be going home to nothing. The Doggie Dugouts are still company-owned. Elmer's signed for all six of them. Gross takes over, jockeys the figures, and the Giant ends up with a garageful of water coolers, long pink counters, and funny little stools."

The cabbie whipped the wheel. "Sheraton Towers," he said. A stand of colorful flags fronted the huge glass building. "Hey, there's that damn *Hot Dog* bus parked right out in front. We try to do that we'd get our butts towed," the cabbie said.

Horton crawled out and limped up to the driver.

"Twelve-fifteen," he said, peeling off a five-dollar bill and making change for Horton's twenty.

The motor started. Horton put his arm around Barnes and walked her off toward the towering glass building.

"Hey, Horton!" the cabbie shouted over the motor. " 'Mear for a second." Horton looked at Barnes, shrugged, and walked back to the cab.

Barnes watched the encounter at the cab window with interest. Suddenly Horton was animated, talking with his hands. The cabbie's flat cap bobbed up and down. Horton's head shook no, then yes. Then he reached into his pocket, pulled out a wad of bills, and threw them in the window. The bubbling fountain drowned the cabbie's salutation. Barnes watched him grin and spin the hack into the race of traffic.

"What was that all about? Another tip?"

"Yeah, he had one for me," Horton said and kissed her squarely on the lips. "It's about game five. I think we're going to play it!"

•19•

NEW YORK SPARKLED UP AT WALKER HORTON. A starry sky turned upside down. Larry Barnes on his arm, a lull in the storm. Could life finally be turning around?

"Umpire State Building! Good meetin' place." The Giant walked between them and dropped a quarter in the binocular machine.

A warm breeze whipped at the bridge of the observation deck. Horton felt the sway. Fried grease from the promenade's food stands gave the night a carnival air. Horton wiped a bead of sweat from the end of his nose. Larry Barnes shook the gold hair and strolled off down the deck, distancing herself from the conversation. A hectic evening for Horton. Clandestine phone calls to the commissioner, NBC, and Bracken McKeen. A skirmish with Barnes. He'd laid down the law: No notes, no recorder, everything off the record. And now for the fun. Watch the Giant go bonkers. All he had to do was give the big guy the ball.

Horton looked down on the city's hot spots. Broadway and Times Square glowed, electric prisms, long tubes of fluorescent white. A million windows, little TV sets each with a story, offices, restaurants, people working, eating, you could see them moving around.

"Didn't you used to come downtown in your Giant uniform?" he said.

Thumma's smile was tired, slow, and deliberate. It wasn't the old Thumma ear to ear. He nodded and pushed a pinch of snuff under his upper lip.

"Heh! You got a good memory on my stories. Only did that once. Bill Terry'd-a sent us back to Class C if he'd-a caught us that night. Mancuso and me did it in '37 on a bet. That was the year I was 21–9. You can pull that kinda crap when you're hummin' along like that.

"Caught us a cab and rode all the way down here. Looked out over the city just like we're doing tonight. You shoulda seen the ticket taker when we stepped off that elevator wearing the uniform of the New York Giants. We had us some times," he said.

Horton dropped a quarter and spun the binoculars toward the Bronx. "Yankee Stadium," he said. "Clear enough night, but too many lights. Everything's blurry and white. Good weather for tomorrow's game."

The Giant slipped a coin in his viewfinder and rotated the glasses, following Horton's direction.

"You feelin' okay? Busted ribs are painful as hen; I had me a couple once myself," Thumma said. He kept his eyes glued to the glasses. "Yep, she's a pretty city, all right!"

Horton patted Thumma's right arm. "I'm fine. How about you? You hangin' in there with all this crapola we been puttin' you through?"

Silence. Thumma's binocs turned left to right. He was up in the 150s now, looking for Coogan's Bluff. Behind them an elevator opened and closed. The deck's night man coughed and flicked a cigarette in the path of his mop.

"Lowerin' whale shit. Now that you asked," Thumma said. "Gross, McKeen, the press, that beggar Suehowicz. I wanted you boys to have a time, kick off the Dugouts, help build your own inheritance. I screwed the pup on this one, Hooter. I knew it was risky, but I never thought it would end like this!"

Horton jammed his hand deep in the pocket of khaki pants and felt for the baseball. Why did the Giant always answer rhetorical questions? He gestured as if to answer. His rib cage burned. The Giant cut him off.

"Magruder, yes," Thumma said. "But I never thought Wilt!"

"Me neither. I guess we're all at fault in a way. We've been saying. 'Oh well, that's just Odie' since he was a kid."

Toy horns honked on Fifth Avenue. The traffic moved in slow motion behind tiny flashlight beams. Horton's skin goosed up. Odie had to be forgotten, he had to lift the Giant's spirits now. The series hung in the balance.

"We can quit bullin' around, Hooter. I know the bastard got you after the game," Thumma said. "Called me from jail. Some cock 'n' bull story. Hell, I got dressed, went down, and bailed him out. Boston cop gave me the straight poop on the way out the door."

"Seen him since?" he asked.

"Wilt?" Thumma asked. The black cap shook no.

Horton gripped the baseball. He felt the stitches, tumbled the ball over and over in his throwing hand. He needed a break in the Giant's mood. Any little upswing would do.

"Nope. He and Magruder are gone. Both of 'em mean as hell to Bunny, now that I think about it. I guess I shouldn't-a overlooked that like I did," he said.

Bunny! McKay would be in tomorrow. Horton had lost track of time.

"You used to say the Rabbit was our good luck charm. Rub his left foot before every game." Horton lifted his voice over the traffic. "Wait until the Rabbit comes in tomorrow. The luck of the Hot Dogs will change!"

The Giant dropped his head. "Hooter, it's over. Like the sign says, NO GAME TODAY. You know it and I know it. So we might just as well—"

Horton yanked the ball out of his pocket and jammed it in Thumma's shovel-size hand. Then he pounced at the Giant, attacked him like Yogi jumped Larsen following the perfect game. "I can't stand it anymore! I've been about to bust a gut to tell you!" he shouted.

"Elmer, the Little World Series, it lives! You and McKeen are pitching tomorrow. It's the matchup of the century. The Giant against the Redhead. Yankees vs. Giants. The '37 Series all over again. New York will love it. Hell, New York deserves it! Christ, NBC is nuts about it. Even the commissioner says it sounds like a hell of an idea."

It wasn't the Giant's retreat. It was the slow-motion way he pulled at the brim of his cap. Horton missed the clue. He was staring up at the eyes, wondering why they weren't blue.

Thumma gazed at the ball, fondled the horsehide like it was some fragile egg about to hatch or break. Then he dropped it gently back in his catcher's hand. Horton stared at the ball, turned it over, and read the commissioner's name. The Giant pinched open a little plastic purse and dropped another quarter in the binocular machine. The glasses turned slowly on the metal turret. The backside of the wrinkled old neck opened and closed like a cheap accordion. Horton looked down at New York and listened to Thumma's quarter tick.

The Giant spoke. "Good idea, but I pitched them games already. Did it in '37. Let history be history, Hooter. Pretty much like they say, our deeds tend to repeat themselves!"

Horton felt himself drifting, backpedaling from the ledge and the wire mesh safety screen. Had one of America's premier promoters, the father of the *Hot Dog* bus and the Little World Series, just squelched a scheme that would save his interest in a multimillion-dollar company? Was he backing down from that prick McKeen?

"Are you saying 'no'?"

Thumma kept his eyes glued to the rubber cups. He spun the silver focus knob and tilted the glass slowly toward the sky.

"Because if you are, you're saying 'no' to a lot of people. Back in Florida, when I told Barnes we'd be chasing our dream, I wasn't shitting, you know. You said it, and I believed it. Now when you get a shot at yours, you give me a history lesson and stare off at the stars!"

Thumma talked into the wind. His voice drifted over the ledge and blended with the swish of traffic a hundred stories below.

"I never said—"

"What, that you'd like another shot at McKeen? Hell, you said it sittin' there on the freezer in the meat market a hundred times.

" 'I never got another shot at him. Different leagues. The war. Boys, I'd give up this business for another go at Bracken McKeen.' Well, you got half your wish, because tomorrow when the commissioner calls the series, Gross will be walking off with Elmer's Little Giants, Inc.!"

Horton was livid, circling the Giant and his telescope.

"I been busting my ass for this? 'Hooter, it's up to you,' you said, 'you're the only one that can do it, the only one they respect.' So I go out and act like a prick for two weeks, get a ton of bad ink, pass out in public, kiss ass, get machine-gunned by baseballs, whatever it takes to get the job done. And do you know why?"

Thumma hunched the big, bony shoulders. "I reckon it's—"

"Because I believed there'd be something at the end. A night like tonight. Riding down here I thought, this is it. This will be the payback for all he's done for me. I was going to meet you at your favorite spot in New York and make your dream come true!

"Fuck Wilt, Magruder, and Gross. Hell, screw me! How about Bunny, Kline, Baldy, Doc, Bear, Jug, Billy? Don't they mean anything to you? Oh, yeah, and Bennie Wharton!"

"Who the hen's Wharton?" the Giant managed.

"Just a New York cabbie. An old fan of Elmer the Giant's. The guy who came up with the best fucking idea since the *Hot Dog* bus and the Little World Series," he said.

The wind suddenly felt cold to Horton. He'd been sweating again. He turned his back to the ledge. Shadows played on the Giant's face. Red and wet. His big chins appeared to be twitching.

Horton felt himself weaken. "Cripes, Elmer! I'm sorry. I wouldn't of, but I—"

"I know you thought I'd be bustin' a gut to pitch," Thumma said.

The light made a subtle move. The Giant was stable now. He steadied the chins, aimed them right at Horton.

"Well, there's a lot you do know and a lot you don't," he said. "While you were on the phone with the commissioner and NBC I was . . ." he looked down the promenade. Barnes tossed her hair, turned, and walked the other way. "Are we gonna see this conversation in tomorrow's paper?" he said.

"No, everything is off-the-record. We have an understanding on this one," Horton said.

Thumma did a tobacco trade. The snuff hit the deck, and he jammed a fistful of Levi Garrett into his cheek.

"While you were on the phone with NBC," he continued, "I was trying to work out a compromise. Half the members of my board of directors musta called the room."

"You get that Xerox letter? I hope you read them that!"

"Yep, it came today," Thumma said.

"Great! Screw Gross. Stick it to him!" Horton said.

"It's on ELG, Inc., stationery. Written to Wilt and from Gross.

A payoff, all right. It talks in a roundabout way about how bright Wilt's future looks at ELG, Inc., and how Gross will talk him up to the board, tell them all the "good" things he's done. He promised him a job to take a dive. 'Course none of that's spelled out in writing."

"Well, it says it, anyway. Take it to the board. Fry Gross's ass," Horton said.

"I showed it to Baldy earlier this evening. 'Circumstantial evidence,' he said; courtwise it don't add up to much at all. It really says nothing at all. Board members I talked to backed up Baldy's opinion. They weren't impressed worth a toot. Hell, they've made up their minds—ever one of 'em wants me gone. I'd put the phone down, another one would call. All of 'em saying compromise or else!"

Larry Barnes had disappeared. He looked south toward the end of the deck, when he'd seen her last. A sailor slipped his arms around a girl in a bright red parka. He dropped the white cap on her head, turned her toward the Statue of Liberty, and kissed the back of her neck. A sister and brother raced up to the neighboring telescope and hand-fought to deposit the first quarter. Below them New York blinked at the night. Red, blue, and green surrounded by white. Horton focused on an office building. A woman in a white blouse and burgundy skirt bent and dipped, filing papers in a metal cabinet.

"What compromise?" Horton asked.

Thumma fired a shot of tobacco though the metal mesh screen.

"I take enough cash to pay off all the players. Everybody, winners and losers, will be paid in full. Then I stay on as a consultant for the rest of the year."

"And after that?"

"I retire to my farm like an old stud horse without no pecker," he said.

Horton circled the Giant, stopped, and looked above them at the Empire State's tower. Lights played on the building's Art Deco design. Gross had the Giant up there under those gaudy archways, shaking him, holding him aloft where the gorilla waved Fay Wray.

"Elmer, pitch for us tomorrow. NBC's a big ticket. More than enough money to pay us all off!"

"Nope. Money for the game goes to ELG, Inc. Baldy looked into that one tonight. I signed it, but the contract with the network is in the company's name. After Monday's vote Gross'll be callin' the shots. One way or another. That's what all those phone calls were about."

"Unless you . . ." Horton let the sentence glide to a stop.

Thumma's spit dribbled, slipped off his chin, and splashed at Horton's feet.

Horton changed his tactics. "How about McKeen? I told him this game was in the bag. You know what he'll say to the press when he finds out that you . . ." Horton said.

"If he agreed to pitch against me, you paid him. There's no way he puts thirty years on the line for free. Not an old whore like Bracken McKeen!"

"He'll be at the press conference tomorrow telling the world that you—"

"Hooter, I appreciate what you're tryin' to do, but . . ." Thumma dropped another quarter into the machine and turned the glasses a notch to the north, then backed it off in an easterly direction. Horton lined up behind the Giant and looked across the orange button that topped off his cap. The yellow glow's the Bronx. Yankee Stadium, he thought.

Thumma wheeled away from the machine. Horton backpedaled half a step.

"Screw Gross and McKeen and the horses they rode in on. The Little Series is off!" Thumma said.

Horton walked down the promenade by himself. It was best to leave the old man with his thoughts. Barnes stepped out of the shadows and took his arm. "What the hell was that all about?" she said.

"Don't miss tomorrow's press conference. That's all I can say! Hell, that's all I want to say!" he said.

Horton mumbled under his breath.

"What?" Barnes said.

"When you go to give your startin' pitcher the ball, stare him right between the eyes. If he looks like he don't want the baseball, you better run from the bastard as fast as you can," he said.

"What?" Barnes said.

"One of Elmer's first rules of baseball. Used to tell us that when we were kids," Horton said.

THERE WAS SOMETHING ABOUT THE STAGE. THE long, low riser reminded Walker Horton of the platform Mayor Ricks used for his press conferences back in Rocky Mount. Same stage, slightly more prestigious address, he thought.

But Horton wouldn't be easily impressed today. All the 99 Park Avenues and plush office suites in the world couldn't make up for the news they were about to hear.

Horton leaned back in his chair and watched a familiar scene unfold. Lights hit the risers from a dozen directions. Blue jeans and T-shirts jockeyed cameras and tripods. Larry Barnes smiled, tipping back in her seat.

"Nice turnout," she said. The chair pitched forward, and she caught herself on Horton's arm. Onstage, above the rows of folding chairs, a podium was under siege.

NBC, ABC, CBS, ESPN. All the networks were there.

In a matter of minutes Stonesifer would walk out, call off game five, and the death of the Little Series would be national news.

The New Becton Hot Dogs sat picketed like a fence along the row of metal chairs. Larry Barnes, Horton, Kline, Johnson, Rymoff, Ballard, Albaugh, and Brown. A ravishing blonde and seven broken-down men in Little League uniforms. Horton studied the jowly faces. Sad-looking pups, the back of a dog catcher's truck, he thought. Kline looked like a bad night on the town. Deep blue circles under blood-red eyes. Sharp ruts from cheek to ears. He'd taken the Wilt thing harder than the rest. Doctors hate to be wrong, Horton guessed. Kline checked his wristwatch. He'd already booked an afternoon flight to the Coast.

Billy sat in the prayer position, fiddling with the dial on the Walkman. Jug and Ballard looked like family at an old friend's funeral. The men's eyes were pink and washy. Blinker squeaked out taps with his hands. Brown stared at the empty podium like an open casket. Baldy twisted his right leg over his left and turned a page of *The New York Times*. The president's attorney was one who had reason to celebrate. It was over. Never again would a mishandled ground ball embarrass the Republican Party.

Bear shoved a chaw in his cheek and flicked a middle finger at a group of Pintail players. McKeen looked up from an interview and arched a stream of Red Man toward the Hot Dogs. Pazerelli tipped the black glasses and asked Graham what he'd missed. The broken-toothed grin made Horton cringe.

"Where's Elmer and Bunny? They should have been here by now," Barnes said.

"Hell, there's the commissioner," Rymoff said. Bear hefted out of his chair, threw the foot with three toes on the stage, and jump-started the press pencils with a leading quote. "Stony, we gonna play this thing or not? Let's do it or get off the pot."

Of all the bad scenes that had played in Horton's life—New York disappearing through the back window of his uncle's old Mercury, going limp on the skinniest Thornton sister, Janie's gum card fire, Bunny's death look into that bathroom mirror, the snarling Dobermans and the run for his life, Wilt pinning him to Fenway's wall—this scene could be the worst of all. Hell, the compromise was the logical thing to do. But the big guy backing down? Anything less than the final duel in the sun with McKeen and the Giant was copping out.

Behind him the room swirled with what the Giant called "vidiots." Fifteen TV cameras, a dozen tripods and more notebooks and pencils than you'd find in a good college bookstore. Horton felt

vibrations from the hallway protesters in the legs of his metal
chair. Suehowicz's chants, yelps from the security officers shook
the walls. They blended together in a jungle beat.

"Feeding time at the Bronx Zoo," Barnes said.

Horton searched through the smoke for a convenient exit. It
hurt him to breathe. He slipped his hand behind his back. More
pain sawed through his ribs—Barnes' smile reassured him somehow. He nodded and touched the anxiety bag. Where were Elmer
and Bunny? Why did the old man have to live life out on a limb?

A microphone whined. Horton took Larry's hand. Barnes had
it together as usual. Gray knit blouse, yellow skirt, almost no
makeup at all, Horton's favorite look.

Stonesifer's head glowed like a hundred-watt bulb under the
camera's lights. "White balance!" someone shouted and two T-
shirts stormed the stage.

"Hey, ABC, how about cutting that spot. Stony looks like he's
caught in a fucking prison break."

"The commissioner don't look half bad. He cleans up real nice,"
Rymoff said.

Dark blue suit, blue shirt, red tie. No whites, stripes, or patterns. The man knew how to dress for TV.

Horton looked at his watch. Five after ten. Still no Thumma or
Bun-Bun. Last scene, he thought. The big guy finally makes the
catcher go nuts.

The commissioner smiled. Cameras whirred.

"As the commissioner of major league baseball I consider this
opportunity . . ."

Fanning the rear of the stage were three metal folding chairs.

"I thought Stonesifer was the only one allowed to talk at one
of these things," Horton whispered to Barnes.

"That's what they told us," she said.

While the commissioner droned on about the worth of baseball
to American society and made references to the "disgusting scene
going on in the hallway," Horton inventoried the room. Still no
Giant. A door banged. Another camera entered.

"And now in fairness to the company that sponsored what

today's *New York Times* called 'a good idea that went bad,' I'd like to present Mr. Daniel Gross, the acting president of Elmer's Little Giants."

The room erupted.

"Stony?" "Commissioner?" "Mr. Commissioner?"

Questions on questions. A tripod tipped, a camera crashed to the floor. The commissioner clung to the podium like a treed baby kitten.

Rymoff pulled his six-foot-four-inch carcass out of the chair, turned to the bank of cameras, and offered his assessment.

"Is Gross calling the shots? You can pack up your shit and go home. The Little Series is over. File your fucking stories," he said.

Kline twisted Horton's head like he was delivering a baby. "Did you know this?" he said. "Christ, thanks for the tip. I could have caught an earlier flight!"

The commissioner held up two round white fists. "In fairness to Mr. Gross I've agreed to let him explain the situation. Elmer's Little Giants has had a long, rich history of working with major league baseball. They've been selling wieners in our parks since the late 1950s. I think when Dan is finished speaking, you'll have had most of your questions answered."

This wasn't the deal Elmer explained. "No fanfare, just a quiet changing of the guard," the Giant had said. "Gross in, me out." Nothing as immediate as this.

"What's the story here?" Barnes leaned over his shoulder and whispered the question. The Shalimar had taken on a smoky scent.

"They're screwing the Giant. He cut a deal so he could pay us all off. But it was supposed to be hush-hush. Gross takes over the company, Elmer stays on as a consultant, then retires in—"

"Where is he now? Really!" she said.

"Airport to get Bunny! Like the commissioner said!"

The blue silk suitcoat tapped at the mike.

"Please! When Mr. Gross makes his statement I think you'll appreciate our position!"

Gross was smooth. Just the right guy to give a man like the Giant the hook. Compliment, then dig. Sunshine, rain. Positives followed by negatives. He had the act down pat. Gross the under-standing. Gross the patient. Elmer the recalcitrant. Not a bad person. Just a bit too eccentric to survive in today's marketplace. A good CEO had to think of his stockholders; the customers come first. If allowed to continue with his wild ideas and harebrained schemes, the Giant would kill ELG, Inc.

"So we've come to what we think is the perfect compromise. The board of directors has agreed that, with consent of the com-missioner and apologies to NBC, the Little World Series will not continue!"

The room exploded again.

"No game five?" "Are you the final word?" "Commissioner! Commissioner! I thought that this would be your call!" Tripods shifted. Flashes popped and burned. The doorways jammed as reporters raced for phones. The bass beat pounded the walls. Hor-ton saw the ponytail wedge past security. Suehowicz broke down the aisle, wielding a red FUCK THE BIGS banner at the TV cameras. He sidestepped a cop, slalomed through the tripods, took a billy club to the ankles, and skidded to a stop at Horton's feet. Two enthusiastic blue uniforms thumped a tune on the protester's back. Horton held his ribs and tried not to look.

Anxiety had been a faithful friend to Hooter Horton. No reason for the affliction to let him down now. He swallowed. Bacon and eggs! Breakfast, he thought, hot cakes and syrup coming right up! The officers panted at his feet and applied some kind of pressure hold on Suehowicz's neck, just below the ponytail, it appeared.

"Oh, that did it." Barnes craned her neck to see. "Joby's his-tory. He just kicked the fat cop between the legs!" Horton crawled up on his chair in search of a better angle. A flashbulb burst in his face.

"Horton, what's your reaction?" "Hooter, where's the Giant?" "Horton, are you going to sit there and let—"

Stonesifer banged his fists into the battery of microphones. Hor-ton half swallowed and slunk back in his chair.

"Order! We will have order or I'll call it off right now. We will let Mr. Gross finish his statement," the commissioner said.

The newly announced CEO of ELG, Inc., brushed back the silver hair and pulled hard on a tumbler of ice water. The voice was candy. His eyes cut back to his audience.

A wink. A nod. A look of concern.

"You should know that the compromise was Mr. Thumma's idea. Elmer was up against it. He somehow managed to lose two of his best players following the Boston game."

Bullshit, Horton thought. He would keep count, a running tabulation of Gross's lies.

"Personality problems. We have no evidence that there was ever a fix."

Numbers two and three, Horton thought.

"Of course, you'd have to ask Elmer why Odie Wilt, an ex-major league pitcher, was yanked in Boston just as the game went on the line. Certainly Wilt wasn't involved in a fix. The man was like a son to Thumma, you folks have been writing that for weeks. In fact, it's my inclination that Wilt will have a future with ELG. He's an excellent promoter, the kind of young man who could serve this company well."

Horton looked at Barnes. She shook her head. He'd need all of his fingers and toes to keep track of a liar like Gross.

"I hope you and the fans see this thing for what it is. No evidence of a fix. Two players just up and quit. And because of what would appear to be a managerial problem, the Hot Dogs are a seven-man team. Nine wasn't really enough, was it, Bracken?"

The Pintails laughed and spat as a team. The tobacco sounded like a drummer's snare as it pinged into their wax paper cups.

"So I think that we'd all have to agree that seven against nine would be out of the question!

"Now, Elmer's position with our company is another matter entirely. But if he'd shown up today, I'm sure that he'd say that retirement is something he's been looking forward to for a long, long time.

Horton turned to Rymoff. "The man's a pathological liar. He's in double figures already," he said.

Rymoff scrubbed his red mustache with the back of his hand.

"In about a New York minute I'm gonna jack up his pathological ass and—"

The door opened briefly. A reporter squirted in. Horton tried to catch the protesters' chant: "Bring him back. Bring him back. . . ."

"Suehowicz is gone. They've got him on inciting a riot and a couple of counts of assault," a reporter whispered to Barnes.

Gross took a statuesque pose. Eyes riveted into the camera nest, smiling, weaving the concerned look into his act.

"We think that the Little World Series was a fun idea. It's not the way I'd choose to bring attention to one of America's premier food companies, but that's neither here nor there.

"Since Thumma's not here to speak for himself, I'll tell you this much about the agreement we struck. The old man's been treated fairly. He's going to stay on at ELG, Inc., as a consultant and then retire next year with full company benefits. To his Little League team"—Gross looked down at the uniformed players—"well, I wish you the best. Since you can't field a full team, you'll get the losers' share. Three thousand dollars for an all-expenses-paid vacation is nothing to scoff at.

"McKeen, your folks will take home our congratulations"— Horton watched the Redhead bob to attention—"and five thousand dollars a man, of course. Although some of you may be disappointed now"—he looked down at Horton in a condescending way—"I'm sure that when you think back on these past two weeks, you'll understand our reasoning. This little circus cost the company in excess of a million dollars! Probably four times that in negative publicity."

Gross thanked the commissioner, the players of both teams, and turned to take his metal seat. As he touched down on the folding chair, he looked up into something akin to World War III.

The press jumped on the Dogs like back porch fleas. Lights flooded Horton's face. A series of popping flashes. He dropped his head and blinked at the blindness. The questions came out of the light in fragments.

"Where's the Giant?" "In bad health?" "Sell you out?" "Thinking of himself?" "Been acting strange?" "Wilt and Gross! What's the deal here?"

The PA system blared. Earsplitting feedback from the podium microphones. Horton covered his head.

"Block for me, Bear," Barnes said. "I've gotta get up there to Gross."

"Please hold your questions! I repeat, please hold your questions! If we don't have order, this conference is over!" Stonesifer shouted. The noise leveled out. Horton batted a radio mike away from his face.

"Any idea why he'd make a deal? Didn't you think he'd somehow manage to pull the thing off? You're the captain. Gross and Wilt! Why haven't you stepped in?"

The commissioner smiled politely.

"That was Mr. Gross. Now, one of the empty chairs behind me belongs to Elmer Thumma. Unfortunately, Elmer isn't with us today. He went to the airport to pick up Bun-Bun McKay, the little fellow who got beaned in Detroit. That's all we know. So he's a no-show. Right, Horton?"

Horton shrugged. He could feel Barnes next to him, smell the perfume. She touched his cheek. Suddenly the Shalimar was strangely unsettling.

"So we're going to let Bracken McKeen say a few words, then we'll turn it back to what better be a polite and orderly Q and A session. Those security gentlemen back there, the boys with the big wooden sticks, are the men who were forced to take a little batting practice on Mr. Suehowicz," he said.

Was this it? Was this how Horton would end his book? Gross and McKeen nosing up to the press, trashing the New Becton Hot Dogs in front of network cameras? Cops playing hall hockey with degenerate protesters? McKeen spat in a tall McDonald's cup and wedged it behind the podium microphones. He pushed back the old-time baseball cap. The Redhead's eyes sparkled under the lights. They were burying Elmer the Giant today. He cleared his throat and began shoveling dirt.

"Mr. Gross"—he turned toward the chairs—"we thank you for

throwing Elmer the financial rope. There'd-a been some mighty sore folks in black uniforms if we'd been stiffed on this thing!

"And Commissioner, I'd like to thank you for bearing with this extravaganza for as long as you did. I think that Clicker Night business in Boston was unfortunate as hell but typical Thumma, really no great surprise"—he spat in the cup and aimed the collie nose at Horton—"using a foreign substance, a goldarned noise-maker against a handicapped, ain't no way to win a ball game.

"I lost my protest on the game. But I'll tell you one thing, and you can take this one to the bank: There was no fix in this series. All you gotta do is look at that wall of men back there. Then feast your eyes on the folding chairs down here in front. Here we got a bunch of misfits, bodies that do obscene things to a double-knit uniform."

Rymoff rose. Horton and Kline pulled him back.

"Those broad shoulders along the back are athletes. Well, hell, what am I tellin' you folks for? You saw 'em play. And that, my friends, is why Odie Wilt walked off the mound the other night. Elmer cited sick as the reason for yanking him with the game on the line. Well, I can't disagree. Sick of Thumma's Clicker Night crap, his *Hot Dog* bus, and all that other promotional hype."

The commissioner cleared his throat. Gross took another drink. Horton swallowed, sampling the breakfast again.

"And there's one more thing that you Hot Dogs should know. If you want to blame somebody for game number five going down the dumper, don't hang it on these two guys up here," he said, hitchhiking a thumb at Gross and Stonesifer. "If Thumma had any guts, we'd be playin' tomorrow!"

The room went quiet. Like a pregame prayer. Cameras whirred, a tripod creaked. The rear door opened and slammed. Horton heard a loud, slapping sound. Someone was applauding McKeen.

"Nice job, Bracken!"

Elmer the Giant!

Wildness again. Cameras spun. Lights played on the big pink face, danced at his feet, and led him through the congestion. The orange button on the black cap bobbed along above the mob.

"Where's Bunny?" Barnes questioned.

Horton shrugged and dropped his head.

Thumma pounced on the riser. Gross and McKeen fell back in their chairs. Then he was lost in the swarm. A thousand questions. They were all over the Giant.

"Order or it's over!" Stonesifer warned. The microphone screeched again. "Or it is over! Don't make me clear this room!"

"Elmer, Bob Ziegler, UPI. McKeen says you could have made it happen! True or false, and if so, why not?"

The commissioner smacked the butt of his hand on the mikes again. The questions softened in tone.

"Ladies and gentlemen, Elmer the Giant," he said.

Wet blue eyes fell on the New Becton Hot Dogs.

"My apologies, boys. That old wiener bus of ours got caught in Big Apple traffic!

He stepped back, tipped his cap to Gross. "Dan," he said, "Commissioner, Bracken, and distinguished baseball fans."

Barnes' photographer flashed at the old man at the podium, then popped shot after shot at the New Becton Hot Dogs. Horton struck a thoughtful pose. Captain listens to manager's excuse would be a good cutline, he supposed.

"So where was I? Good question," he said. "Boys, these mikes okay? Can you print and radio folks hear me there in the back?"

Feet shifted, equipment slid on the hardwood floor.

"Well, when Mr. McKeen delivered his eloquent speech, I was right outside the door. Protesters raising cain, but I heard every word of it. I'll deal with that piece of malarkey later.

"Gross's diatribe I read in that same hallway, looked over a reporter's shoulder while he was phoning his story in. Now, Commissioner, I don't know what your decision is on the Little Series, but I can tell you this much: Daniel Gross spoke for Elmer's Little Giants today without an iota of authority."

Gross's chair tipped toward the podium. The Giant turned and bunched the banana fingers deep in his concave chest.

"No authority. Elmer's. E-L-M-E-R-'S Little Giants," he said. "Not Dan's Little Giants, or Bracken's Little Giants. I'm the man.

Now, I'm going to make this as brief as I can. No sense in takin' any more away from baseball than we already have."

He dug into his back pocket, pulled out the black recorder and a white sheet of paper. "Exhibits A and B," he said. The audience sat and listened to what the Giant called a "lost and found" story about how a stolen recorder with "unpleasant comments about Wilt and Gross" wound up in the desk drawer of "the man who just lied to you about who's running the show at Elmer's Little Giants."

When the tape had been rerun to the satisfaction of all, he held a Xerox letter aloft, spun slowly, then brought it to a stop in the face of Daniel Gross.

"It's a letter from Mr. Gross here to Odie Wilt, encouraging him about his future with Elmer's Little Giants, Inc. Now, you all know that I loved Odie like a son. But never once did I mention to him anything about signing on with my company. Oh, there was a time before we kicked this thing off that I thought he might make a fine employee. He was creative and in many ways smart, but the boy had him some character flaws that. . . .

"Well, Odie and Mouse Magruder are no longer with the team. Sick! Personality conflict! Bad attitudes! All of the above I suspect."

"Fix!" Rymoff shouted.

"Fix!" said Ballard.

Brown, Johnson, Kline, and Horton. Nods of agreement fell like dominoes along the row.

"Well, there you have it," Thumma said. "The New Becton Hot Dogs think they had a couple of teammates go south on them. I never thought I'd come to say it, but I'm inclined to agree."

"Prove it!" Gross shouted above the Dogs' canting.

"Never happened!" McKeen said. "Commissioner, he's doin' this to demean my team."

Horton sucked smoke in his search for fresh air.

"I've got the story," he said, rising slowly. "Commissioner, it was fixed. Elmer, tell them about the will. If you don't, I'll do it myself."

Thumma appeared reluctant at first, but soon warmed to his task. He talked slowly, made his point to the cameras. It was a heart-wringing story of an old man fighting for control of his company, a business he wanted desperately to leave to his beloved Little League team. Then he stepped down off the stage and yanked Horton's baseball jersey up over his head.

"Might as well show them this, Hooter. Boys on the team don't even know the real story here. Wilt!" Thumma said. "Hooter booted Wilt off the team so he beat him with baseballs. Threw 'em at him at point-blank range in the darkness of Fenway after the game. Could have killed him. Horton didn't press charges. Before I knew what happened, I suckered up and bailed Wilt out. It's all a matter of police record. You can call Boston P.D.!"

The Giant strutted to McKeen and pinged his cup with a shot of Levi Garrett. Where's Bunny? Horton thought. He tucked in his shirttails and slid back in the chair.

The Giant continued to talk. "Now, I wanta tell you folks a little story, then I think we ought to clear the room because when I'm finished, the commissioner and these NBC boys in the white-collar-and-cuff shirts and eight-hundred-dollar suits"—he gestured to three men grouped midway back in the crowd—"are going to have themselves a decision to make!"

Gross had a good act. But the Giant played in a higher league. He stepped off the stage again, walked down the line, and patted each Dog on the head. "Baldy, Blinker, Jug, Billy, Doc, Bear, and Hooter," he said. "But no Wilt, Magruder, and Bun-Bun. That's a shame," he said. Then he dropped his head, tugged at the cap, and opened his heart to America.

"Slightly over a year ago I promised these boys a chance at a major league dream. We were goin' to re-create history, settle a score that never got settled, while samplin' what it's like to play in places like Wrigley, Fenway, and Yankee Stadium.

"Well, to answer my question. Two of 'em—Wilt and Magruder—didn't want a part of the dream, and when it came right down to it, neither, I guess, did Elmer the Giant. The rest of 'em wanted it, the men you see sitting here with their faces down past

their knees. But the one that wants it most of all ain't with us
today."

Horton felt numb. Arms, chest, the side of his face. Larry's gaze
was there. No use in looking. Words would have never come. Say
it! Go on and say it! Bunny McKay is dead!

"To tell this story right I gotta go back a ways." The Giant
strolled to the rear of the riser and spat in McKeen's cup. "Thank
ya, Bracken," he said. Bunny would have company soon. The
Giant wouldn't quit until he'd killed Horton, too.

"I never said this publicly, but the best player I ever coached
wasn't you, Bear; you, Doc; Horton, or even Wilt. No, if this old
butcher were to put them on the scales and weigh them pound for
pound, the best was Bunny McKay. Oh, how he could go get 'em.
Small diamond, of course, but made the play in the hole as well
as any major leaguer I ever seen.

"Now, McKay's been in the hospital. But he was due in on
Delta's Flight 338 this morning. Little fellow was lookin' forward
to joining the team for this last big wingding in New York. And
while I'm sittin' in the airport lounge waitin', I'm thinkin' not
about the Rabbit's health or the Little Series but about some horses
I'm plannin' to breed."

Rymoff muffled a belch. Kline checked his watch. Albaugh's
half glasses drifted back to the newspaper. "Herk," Horton said
and laid the bag on his lap.

The press belonged to the Giant.

"Well, the plane come in and I'm standin' there watchin' the
faces like people do. Thinkin' things like, do I hug him, shake
hands? Hen, you never know how to act."

"Herk." Horton made the strange noise in his throat again.
Bear threw him a quizzical look. "Herk." He did it again. Something new from the world of anxiety. Funny noises in public, he
thought.

"Of course, the Rabbit's face wasn't among the ones at the
deboarding gate. He's back in the hospital, I think, taken a turn
for the worse. And that's when I sit down and have myself the little
talk I'm about to share. Here's McKay, who frankly ain't been in

good health but a guy who wanted to play so bad he walked up and faced a blind man with the arm of one of them Uzi submachine guns.

"Took a pitch in the head for the team. Won us that game in Detroit. Then practically on death's bed musters up enough strength to suggest a piece of genius like Clicker Night. Now what I was thinkin' at first is, maybe it's good that he didn't make it, because a gamer like Bunny couldn't-a stood what I had planned to say here today."

Gross stood and stretched. The commissioner shrugged at a shadow off-camera. "Elmer, make your point," he said.

"You see, in a long-winded way what I'm trying to tell my players; you, commissioner; hen, all of you, is that last night Hooter Horton handed me a dream and I, Elmer the Giant, opted to compromise, turned on the boys I love, walked right out on them."

"Hrrumph," Stonesifer said. "Elmer, could you possibly wrap this thing up?"

The Giant spat on the stage.

"Gettin' there, Stony," he said and dug deep into the khaki pocket. "Commissioner, Hooter handed me a baseball last night, and now I'm passin' it along to you. Folks, what Hooter suggested was a way to salvage game five, one that I'm sure would be equitable to all involved. If the commissioner and our friends from NBC are in favor and McKeen ain't as old and fat as he looks, then America is in for one whale of a hardball game come Saturday afternoon. Because, Bracken, I, Elmer the Giant Thumma, am gonna take the mound and put baseball history and that '37 Series of yours where the sun rarely ever shines!"

A war zone! Strobes flashed. Horton felt light inside, caught in a runaway wave. Reporters, photographers stampeded. One of those 3-D movies racing his way. The back door cracked the wall, making a gunshot sound. The protesters were loose. Long sign sticks pushed forward like battering rams. Cameramen and dissidents fought hand to hand. Barnes backed into Horton; the mob turned them, pushed them together. Pressure from all sides. Horton was in her arms. "Hold it!" a cameraman shouted. Lights flashed. They kissed for the press, held it under the flash of the bulbs.

"I love it," she said. "Hell of a story. The Little World Series! You and the old man. Geniuses with balls," she said and kissed him again.

Horton wrestled for the bag, desperate for air. The room spun in long, crazy circles—cameras flashed by, a ghostly Gross, a macabre grin on the commissioner's face, suddenly the Giant was reeling, colorless, game ball white. Horton was seeing life in a fun house mirror again.

"The Giant," he said. "He's going down!"

His lunge was late. The podium crashed. Microphones flew, and the PA made an ear-damaging whistle. The big guy was face down, breathing like a horse into the tangled cords and pile of mikes.

More craziness. Microphones jammed in his face, baseball questions, Kline down on one knee checking the Giant's vital signs.

Thumma looked like some kind of larger-than-life corpse stretched out on the stage. He rolled his eyes and blinked at his attendants. Barnes applied a cool, damp handkerchief to his oversize forehead. Kline held his wrist. McKeen and Gross looked down in a doubtful way.

"Just nervous exhaustion. No heart attack here," Kline said.

The Giant smiled and kicked the baby blues up a candle watt or two.

"I'm all right. Just didn't sleep last night. Got awful excited wrestling with this thing," he said.

"Elmer, I hate to ask this question, but where the hell's McKay?" Barnes said.

"Go ahead, we can take it." Horton bit his lip.

"Oh, I never finished? Bunny? Fogged in at Baltimore-Washington International. Coming in on a later flight. Be here this afternoon," he said.

Thumma lay his head back down on the wooden stage.

"Seeing a lot of red above me. That you, Bracken?" he said.

McKeen made a guttural sound, something deep in the bowels of his system.

"Lean down here if you would." Thumma's voice was a whispery rasp.

McKeen's face oranged up as he kneeled.

The Giant boomed up at the cameras. The commissioner and the NBC people looked up from their conversation.

"That fifteen thousand bucks I promised you for organizing the Pintails. What say we go double or nothing, put it all on tomorrow's game?"

Horton listened to the whir of the cameras. A dozen TV crews zeroed in on the two old New York pitchers and recorded the historic shake on the bet.

That's how we differ, Horton thought. I pass out in bus johns and elevators. The big guy picks his spot, passes out on national TV, and takes that prick McKeen down with him.

WALKER HORTON WATCHED THE FIRST PITCH OF the last game of the Little Series settle into the blue swirl of Yankee Stadium's right-field seats. He heard a high, whining hiss and explosion as the noise stormed down the lines. Horton yanked off his mask and pointed at Elmer Thumma with the flat of his hand, making a knifelike motion across the letters of the Hot Dog uniform.

"Wheelhouse!" he shouted.

The Giant nodded, spat, and kicked the rubber. The seats behind the 310 sign looked like a human sinkhole to Horton. Rear ends and elbows, an upside-down fight for the game's first souvenir.

An unfortunate beginning for the last game of the series. The Pintail dugout up and screaming, Gross behind home plate waving a towel, whipping the board of directors up. Matt Zingraff and Jeff

Milks from Quickchow and Funfood looking on, the two men who could pull Elmer's franchising scheme out of the fire.

Horton saw the big Seiko clock in right-center field and heard the ticking again. He'd been listening to an internal clock since he'd set foot in the Bronx. A good one to tell Markum about, he thought. It was a ticktock, tick-ticking pendulum sound clapping around in his head. He closed his eyes and let his mind drift above the clock and the cheers. He saw the stadium in miniature now, a tiny green grass diamond surrounded by matrix dot people, baseball seen through the eyes of a Goodyear blimp captain. His thoughts floated west, crossed the river to Manhattan. A much warmer place than the Bronx, Horton thought.

And as Biggie Ensor completed his home-run trot, Horton mentally slipped himself under the Sheraton's freshly starched sheets. He sensed the warmth of Larry Barnes at his side, smelled the Shalimar, and heard last night's pillow talk.

"Tomorrow will be a piece of cake. Anticlimactic after a day like today," she'd said.

"A walk in the sunshine, baby, a stroll in the park," he'd countered. "Bunny to bring us luck. The Giant on the mound. We can beat them eight against nine. I'm just going to relax, go out there, and enjoy the game."

"Wilt, Magruder, Suehowicz are gone. No problems. All the nuts are in the jar," Barnes said.

They'd made love on the words, then slept with the same reckless abandon.

As Ensor touched third, Horton began to see events that he and Barnes had been unable to imagine. They came to him like electronic newspaper headlines, flashed in his face like the marquee on *The New York Times*' building:

GEORGE PUTS CLOCK ON OLD LITTLE LEAGUE GAME

When the teams arrived at the stadium to play game five, the Yankee owner was ready, waiting to make yet another unprecedented baseball move. Baseball would have a timer. "They've got ninety minutes," Steinbrenner said. "Hell, I've fired and hired managers in a damn sight less time."

The ticktocks had been beating around in Horton's brain ever since. The Dogs had an hour and a half to beat McKeen, a mere ninety minutes to win the old man's company back.

Horton saw the headlines in colorful bursts of white light. One shocker after another chronicled the game day—from Steinbrenner's clock to Ensor's first-inning home-run trot.

RABBIT INSISTS ON PLAYING. HORTON HAS DOUBTS: BUNNY, ASSET OR LIABILITY?

FANS STRIP *HOT DOG* BUS. EIGHT HUBCAPS GO AT BRONX FAST-FOOD GRAND OPENING.

CATCHER'S EX ARRIVES—SPLIT WITH PH.D. SUSPECTED

GIANT DENIES CONNECTION WITH FBLB
PROPOSES ANNUAL MEETING BETWEEN
NEW FAN ALLIANCE (NFA) AND COMMISSIONER
AT MAJOR LEAGUE'S ALL-STAR GAME. ELG, INC.,
WILL PICK UP THE TAB, GIANT SAYS.

FBLB STREAKERS PULL STADIUM AIR STRIKE
NAKED PARACHUTISTS INTERRUPT NATIONAL
ANTHEM WAVE "FREE THE FBLB ONE" SIGNS

DIRECTORS OF ELG, INC., TO DECIDE FATE OF
OLD HOT DOG: WILT JOINS GROSS AND BOARD,
EX-DOG SITS ON HANGING JURY BEHIND HOME
PLATE

Horton kicked dirt and watched the headlines fade into the explosive home-plate celebration. McKeen pogoed through the crowd, dodging airborne caps and batting gloves. He pointed and jeered at a red-faced Thumma. The Giant turned his back on the party and looked off at the Marlboro sign, then fixed his eyes on the clock in deep right-center. Horton followed his gaze. Twelve thirty-two. At this rate Steinbrenner's curfew wouldn't be much of a factor.

Horton felt a bit of uneasiness stir in his stomach, something foul climbing up toward the esophagus. The Little Series anticlimactic! He and Barnes must have been thinking with their libidos last night.

"Hlay hall!" Campbell shouted.

And for the next four innings the New Becton Hot Dogs and Poughkeepsie Pintails did just that. Thumma was masterful, McKeen brilliant. The rhythm of Thumma's pitches settled his catcher, softened the ticks and tocks of his subconscious clock. McKeen threw junk at the Dogs—big half-moon curveballs, knucklers, and slip pitches. Four innings, five hits. Three for the Dogs, two for the Ducks.

And as Horton slipped on his shinguards to catch inning five, he looked up at the big black scoreboard—three zeros and one run stacked neatly behind the name of each team. Dead even! Kline's double had chased Johnson home to knot it up. Two innings to play. His eyes strayed to the clock again: 1:22 P.M. In thirty-eight minutes Steinbrenner would throw in the towel. The clock began ticking again.

He looked at the jury perched behind home plate. Elmer's board of directors were tough birds to read. Horton saw frowns, yawns, a grimace or two. They'd have to be blind not to see it. The two old pitchers had been spectacular—taken the crowd back more than fifty years. It was a great day for the media. A great day for baseball, in fact. How could they overlook a spectacle like this? Wilt stood and waved his cap. Gross circled the towel above his silver head. A tie would win those two bastards a company, the Giant was right about that.

One thirty, the Seiko said. One more out and the Hot Dogs would be out of the inning. Nelson did a wobbly-legged dance off second base. His fly-ball double past Bunny had opened the inning.

McKeen was up on the steps now, giving the Giant the business. "You're SOL when Nelson starts taking you long!" he shouted. Thumma had fire in his eyes. He straddled the rubber and launched a series of spits toward Albaugh. Donnie Graham flexed the stevedore shoulders and beat the bat on the plate. Horton could hear chatter from all his players, seven distinct voices above the fifty-six thousand.

He flashed a finger, then slid to his left. The big digital clock flipped up a new number. The Giant fired one final salvo from his overstuffed cheek and kicked the half kick. Quiet engulfed Yankee Stadium. The eye of a hurricane, Horton thought. Moments to tuck away for the book. He could hear conversation from up in the press box, beer hitting a glass. Behind home plate, a long silver microphone hummed in the background. They'd forgotten to cut the thing off after testing it for Robert Merrill's pre-game national anthem.

The clock ticked again.

"Fastball!" Wilt screamed through the net. The ball came in low and dipped away from the hitter. Graham's knees bent like an oversize golfer's. The metal shaft whooshed at the dirt. "Clunch!" is the sound that Horton heard. He yanked the mask, crow-hopped to his right, and watched Ballard track the ball's flight. It climbed like a jet, up through the stadium, deck by deck. The left fielder turned his back to the infield. The Giant's head dropped like he'd been guillotined. Blinker threw up his glove. The difficult catch looked almost routine.

"Fuckin' guys are playin' today. Hell of a nice grab!" Campbell said. "Hustle in! Only got about twenty-eight minutes to get in another inning and a half!" Horton shot him an over-the-shoulder look. The umpire followed him into the dugout.

"Hey, catch! Steinbrenner's not shitting about the curfew! I got my orders from Stony on this one. If it's a tie, it's a tie. If the losing team don't get its last at-bat in the sixth, then nobody wins. All predetermined. So I don't want any bull crap at the end. The LWS is history at two o'clock sharp! Just an exhibition. That's what George said!"

The Dogs huddled at the end of the first-base dugout. Half watched the curveballing old redhead, half had their eyes trained on the clock in right-center.

Horton tossed the weighted warm-up bat, strode to the plate, stopped, and stole another look at the big Seiko clock. The minute hand jumped. One thirty-four. A run and three outs and only twenty-six minutes to get them.

"Hlay hall!" Campbell shouted.

Horton looked into the stands from the edge of the dugout and saw Wilt waving the cowboy hat at the mound. "Stall the bastards, Bracken! A tie's as good as a win!" Wilt shouted.

"You hear that?" Horton asked. The Giant nodded, walked back into the dugout, and spat.

At one thirty-nine Campbell bellowed, "Hall hree!" At one-forty he "Heeriked!" Horton out.

"Easy, Hoot, just a ball game, don't lose your lunch," Graham said through the bars of his mask. Horton had cost his team twice—precious time plus an out.

Elmer pranced in the third-base coach's box, screaming at Campbell, jockeying McKeen. "The carrottop's dickin' around, Monk, goin' for the tie! Make that clock-watchin' cocknocker throw strikes! He's makin' a mockery of the game!" he said.

At exactly 1:40 P.M. the Giant's verbiage bore fruit. McKeen tried to slip a fastball by Rymoff's bottle-barreled Adirondack. The smash jumped out of the park, hit the facade in right, and bounded halfway back to second base.

Pandemonium. Hands slapping, and humping and jumping around home plate.

Hot Dogs 2, Pintails 1.

The Giant whistled and stomped, then went into a signaling seizure in his third-base box. Billy and Jug followed instructions and swung and missed six times in world record time.

Horton happened to be studying the Giant's face when the color change occurred. The bright red cheeks that had spit venom at McKeen suddenly looked like the gills of a sickly fish. Thumma had gone limp-eyed and weak.

"We got three outs to get yet. They got eleven minutes to stall, one of them catch-22's," Thumma stuttered. He dropped his head, picked up his glove, and did a funny, Chaplinesque walk out toward the mound.

Horton stayed with him step for step, climbed the hill, put his hands on the bony old shoulders, and started to talk.

"Barnstorming's" account would say it best. Barnes claimed

she saw a light go on. "It was like Horton plugged the big guy in. Suddenly his whole body turned on. You could see it from any seat in the house," she said. "With the clock ticking away, Horton got right in his ear. Then the big guy bolted off the mound and didn't stop until he had his nose on the screen and was looking his board of directors right in the face."

Horton saw it pretty much the same way. The Giant snatched his advice, jogged in to the screen, grabbed Merrill's anthem microphone, clicked a button, and started to talk.

"One two, one two," the big voice bounced across the stadium and echoed back again.

Horton yanked off the mask, smiled up at the sunlit sky, and wondered if Gehrig might be looking down.

At exactly one forty-nine Elmer the Giant Thumma held up his huge right hand and asked the Bronx to be quiet.

"Is ever' body havin' a good time today?" Fifty-six thousand rose to their feet, a few at first, then the entire house. The Giant got himself a foot-stomping, standing ovation. "Not too bad pitchers for old fellers, are we?"

Another shock wave. A ten on the Richter scale. "Well, if you fans will bear with me, I'd like to take a second or two to address somethin' that's a bit of a personal nature. I need to have a word or two with the folks who made this Little Series possible, the board of directors of Elmer's Little Giants. They're the folks sittin' right here behind the screen. Stand up, boys, and take a bow!" Relentless applause forced twelve angry men to their feet.

"Now, one thing about this series we'll all agree on: There ain't been no secrets. Mr. Wilt and I had a fallin' out in Boston. I see that Mr. Gross has taken him under his wing. That's mighty charitable of you, Dan. He'll be some sort of vice president, I reckon, if the vote goes against me on runnin' the company." A quiet stadium now. A subway train clacked by behind the right-field stands.

"Look, companies get raided ever' day and old horses like me go out to pasture, nothin' new there. But that's not what this speech is about. I'm a purist, I guess, but to my mind there's no way on God's green earth that a game of baseball should ever be ended by the tick of a clock."

Wild cheers. Thumma pounded the microphone for quiet and cut an eye toward Steinbrenner's sky box.

"So here's what I'm suggesting: Forget the clock. Bracken McKeen picks his two best hitters to face me—Ensor and Graham, I would guess. And just to sweeten the pot, since Gross and Odie have such a stake in the outcome, Wilt steps out here and takes his licks at the man he's tryin' to depose.

"That way we'd end this thing with three ex-major leaguers at the plate tryin' to retire an old man. And, o' course, the old feller tryin' to retire the three of them, so to speak. Be a fittin' way to go out, don't you think? If any one of them should get on base, that's the game. I walk away, no consulting at ELG, no retirement, a clean break, nothing but the uniform on my back and this here old flannel cap. How 'bout it, Dan, Odie, Bracken? Any takers? How 'bout you fans? Like to see somethin' as attractive as that?"

Horton covered his ears, looked up at the TV booth, and watched the blue NBC blazers backslap. Along press row heads bobbed, people were jumping up and down, hands flew at the typewriters, rewriting leads.

The Giant reached for the sky. "Just a second: Just another word or two with the boys from ELG. Now, if we get these buggers out, then, of course, you vote on my tenure same as you'd planned. There's some real fair people among you, so whatever you decide will be right, I'm sure."

Gross and Wilt were in the aisle now. Horton saw hand movement and great animation.

"Oh, now, if Messrs. Wilt, Gross, and McKeen aren't up to my proposition, then I'd be mighty obliged if you'd just put the few minutes back on the clock and we'll proceed as directed." Thumma tilted the mike's long metal pole back and looked up at the sky box again.

Astonishment flew around the horn—Albaugh, Johnson, Kline and Rymoff—each face lit up in its own special way. He looked at Bunny, a little white lump in the right-field grass. The Rabbit's hand went up and waved Horton a thanks. He turned back to the infield in time to see Thumma's answer rushing toward the mound under a mop of disheveled red hair. McKeen brandished a score-card over his head.

"Thumma, you ain't cutting me out of the picture. Four ex-major leaguers! That's the deal. Graham, Ensor, Wilt, and if you don't mind, since it's my game and my fifteen thousand bucks to win or lose, I'll just stand in and have a whack at you, too."

The Giant had stunned his board like slaughterhouse cattle. They stood in a quiet daze and listened to the thundering ovation. A head jerked. Wilt was moving now. The left-hander flipped his cowboy hat in the air, tossed his suitcoat at Gross, and Fonsberry flopped over the blue metal railing. The Giant smiled and turned his attention to the box above third, then gazed up into the sun-splashed sky.

"George, it's up to you and God," he said under his breath. "Now, why don't you two fellers just sit back and enjoy it? Let me and the boys settle this thing once and for all!"

FIFTY-SIX THOUSAND HEADS TURNED TO THE RED tie and blue blazer in the Yankee sky box. Walker Horton heard a cup pop deep in the right-field seats, the clank of another subway train, and the chant of a few straggling protesters wafted in from the left-field bleachers.

At 1:56 P.M. Barnes leaned out of the press box and blew Horton a kiss. The sun-splashed hair turned a strawberry color. He gave the catcher's mitt a gentle wave, touched his bag, and wondered if he might be in love.

The blocky blue jacket twisted suddenly. Steinbrenner uncoiled like a discus thrower. An oval blue object shot out of the sky box, drifted down over the third-base seats, dipped, and feathered off toward home plate.

"A friggin' Frisbee," Rymoff said and slapped his glove.

Horton watched the blue sphere kite in the wind. It dipped downward, sailed, then settled in the grass just short of the Giant's size thirteen kangaroo shoes.

"It's a Yankee cap." Thumma waved it high above his head for all to see. Steinbrenner had blessed the Giant's proposal—thrown his hat in the ring so to speak.

The Hot Dogs met on the mound. McKeen and the Pintails convened in the privacy of the third-base dugout. Black uniforms circled the Ducks' latest acquisition. The Hot Dogs stared at the huddle in amazement. Wilt was hunched down, pulling on the black uniform of the opposition. He cackled and threw his shirt, socks, and shoes in the air.

Thumma's eyes bore down at the white pitcher's slab. Horton looked at his teammates and saw something he liked. They were fidgety, nodding, snapping wads, maniacally chewing their cuds.

"Hell of a speech, Elmer," Kline said and jammed a handful of fresh Double Bubble to the bulge in his cheek.

"The talk was Horton's idea. Credit goes to your catcher. Good thinkin', Hoot, worked out real nice," he said. Then Thumma tugged at the black cap and delivered the final pep talk of the Little World Series.

"We got us just four outs to get. Ain't nothin' we haven't done before," Thumma said. Then he did something Horton had never seen him do before: The big man's face went kaleidoscope—white, pink, red, all patterns and splotches.

"No offense to you, Billy, but I want Bunny in at second for this. He's got the hands, a natural infielder. That's my decision!" Horton looked at the bird shoulders and smiled. Good for you, Elmer, he thought. Behind third, a pocket of FBLB protesters made one last stand against stadium security. A blond woman stood in the crowd and waved a big white poster. For a second he thought it was Janie and found himself lip-reading the big blurry letters.

COME BACK, HOOTER—WE'LL PUT SOMETHING ELSE IN THE OVEN

He yanked out his bag, folded it double, and jammed it back in his pocket. Janie wanting to have his baby—nerves again, imagination run amok. Thumma droned on. His words had an up-and-down quality, soft sentences, then loud ones followed by whispers.

"Infielders, knock everything down, that's a must, and come up throwin'. Bear will catch anything close. Outfielders, I want you divin' out there, whatever it takes to make a catch. If a ball's hit in front of you, find a cutoff man or make a throw, but for the Lord's sake, somehow get it to first.

"Now, I'm not gonna go into a lot of Knute Rockne crap, just gonna tell you boys what a manager I had in the Sally League used to say on the day of a getaway game: "Boys, we ain't gonna be in town tomorrow, so let's get us some tail today!"

Campbell and Stonesifer stood at the microphone behind home plate. The commissioner looked solemn. The umpire grinned and held the microphone like a nightclub singer. Horton heard the PA click, then the h's echoing off the stadium steel.

"Hleading Hoff for the Phintails, hnumber 37, Bracken McKeen. HaMcKeen," Campbell said. The old redhead pin-wheeled bats in the on-deck circle, doffed his antique cap, and fashioned a little bow.

"Hitting hsecond, the Hpintail catcher, Hdonnie Hgraham!" more applause. "And in the hnumber hthree spot, the recently acquired Hodie Hwilt." The boos started deep in the stands and bounced off the back of the upper deck. Horton couldn't pinpoint the direction. The racket raced through the stadium section by section, up and down the lines, and burst in a magnificent angry crescendo over Gross and the ELG, Inc., board of directors.

"Hand finally, hbatting hfourth, the Poughkeepsie cleanup hitter, Hbiggie Hensor! The umpire paused and waited for silence.

"Hif hany of these men hreach base, the game is hover!"

If Campbell's "Hlay hall!" echoed, it never bounced back. The screams were for blood, a Carolina cockfight crowd magnified by thousands.

Horton felt Campbell's balloon protector pressure his back, heard him grunting, smelled coffee on the old man's breath. McKeen stepped in on the left side of the plate, ground his spikes in the dirt, and tapped his metal bat on the hard rubber plate. The Giant smiled in an unnatural way. A kind of goofy, Clarabell Clown, upturned look. He's losing it, Horton thought, and beating his mitt, he walked out in front of the plate and shook his fist at the Giant.

"Hlay hall!"

The Hot Dogs chorused. "Hum and fire!" "Whaddya say, whaddya say!" "Rock 'n' fire, Rock 'n' fire!"

Bear, Bun, Kline, and Albaugh all up on their toes. Gloves and butts dropping as though they'd been choreographed. Ballard, Brown, and Johnson bent low, gloves on knees. The Giant's first pitch sailed over Horton's glove and smacked into the screen.

"Hall hun!" Campbell intoned. McKeen did his digging half a step back. Pain played Horton's ribs like a xylophone. He touched his bag. A familiar voice scratched around in his head.

"Hi again, everybody! Well, the Giant certainly got everybody's attention with that one. A wild pitch right into the faces of the folks who will decide his fate.

"But frankly, that may be academic. If Thumma gets the four tough outs he has to face, sports history will have been made here today."

Horton's stomach felt like a washing machine. Everything moving, spinning inside. He saw Yankee uniforms bunching up on the dugout step. Lou Piniella and Don Mattingly eyeballed Thumma and nodded knowingly. No one was laughing at the LWS now. Reggie Jackson stepped out of the California dugout and swung an armful of bats. The biggest hot dog of all, Horton thought.

The Giant changed colors again. Pink, red, white, something that approached a robin's egg blue. McKeen's face looked like a leathery old glove, lined and cracked. The brown knuckles whitened as he death-gripped the bat. A great confrontation. A fifty-year rivalry separated by sixty feet, six inches.

"Hum fire!" Horton shouted. A cut fastball rode in on the redhead's gnarled fists. McKeen threw his right leg toward first, swung weakly, topped the ball, and slung the bat at the ground.

"McKeen swings and hits a climber down the third-base line. Tough play for Albaugh. Wait a minute, here comes Kline. The shortstop backhands the ball, wheels, and throws low to first. Rymoff stretches, scoops, and . . ."

"Her hout!" the blond Campbell twin barked.

"Ohhh, a bang-bang play! And that, my friends, could have been the ball game. McKeen almost legged that one out. The old redhead darn near won his own ball game."

Horton rubbed the paper bag. The Hot Dogs sang. One down and three to go, he thought.

The crowd began a rhythmic clap. "Dun, dun, dun, dun—dum, dum, dum, dum"—the organ played the hitters' song. He recalled Wilt's "book" on Donnie Graham. "Just like the one we had on Frank Howard. Throw the fucker curveballs for strikes." Fastballs and pinpoint accuracy had been Thumma's secret. "Dance with the one that brung ya," Horton recalled the Giant's words. They'd spotted breaking balls and had been helped by anxious Pintail hitters. Three Pintails had fanned on "outshoots" low in the dirt. Horton stole another look at the press box. A flash of white shirts, Costas and Kubek in their blue NBC blazers. No red tank top in sight. Gotta get Barnes out of my head, he thought.

"Hlay hall!" Campbell said.

Horton dropped one finger between his legs. "Hum fire, you da man, hum and fire!" A fastball beat in the dirt. Horton spun, short-hopped the ball, and shook it at the Giant.

"Ernie, the Giant looks a bit peaked out there. He's always thrived on pressure-cooker situations, but I'm afraid he may have pushed himself a step too far this time.

"Graham, big right-handed hitter, digging in. The black suit and old-type cap. He cuts an impressive-looking figure, no doubt about that."

"Hum and fire, hum chuck, you and me!"

"Thumma toes the rubber, staggers back, and—wait a minute—the Giant is asking for another time-out! He doesn't look good. There goes Horton out to the mound. Boy, that kid's really been through the mill for the past two weeks, now what's . . ."

Horton saw milk and blood in Thumma's eyes—several colors freewheeling in circles.

"I ain't got it!" the Giant said.

Kline ran in from short. Horton waved him away.

"It's gonna be another '37. I shouldn't-a shot off my mouth, always been my biggest enemy. We coulda got them in eleven minutes. Bottom of their lineup was due up!"

"McKeen would of stalled." Horton slapped his glove, climbed the mound, and looked the Giant right in the teeth. "Fastball away! Fastball in! Curveball away! Now let's cut the bullshit and get this guy!"

The wind from the swing stung Horton's face, turned him half-way around in his crouch.

"Heeee rikeee hreee! Campbell screamed. More stadium thunder. He squeezed the foul-tip third strike in the web of his glove, raced back at the mound, and shook the ball in the big man's face.

"Great movement. It hopped. Now let's make this one look bad"—he raised his voice over the chorus of boos and hiked a thumb back toward Wilt. The Giant added a clump of brown to his jaw.

"I still ain't feelin' so hot. All the screamin' and everythin'. First time I ever remember hearin' a crowd."

The infield coasted in for a visit. Albaugh tapped a tune on his cup. Kline looked at the Giant like a diagnosis might be in order. Bunny did the nose twitch. The Bear rubbed his unshaven stubble and watched the ebony-suited Wilt dig in at the plate.

"Cocksucker's right on top of the dish," Rymoff said.

"Watch the bunt!" Horton excused the team with his eyes and raced back to the plate.

"Hey, Campbell, next time you eat in Boston, try the ribs." Wilt turned to the catcher and grinned. "Horton, how are the ribs? Good in Boston, aren't they?"

Horton chewed on his tongue and flipped down one finger.

"What's the deal on the Giant? When you go out there again, tell him I said he looks like a shit salesman with a mouthful of samples. He choking or what?"

Horton flashed the finger again and slid to his right. The Giant went white-faced, kicked the leg skyward and came in with a fastball that sent Wilt spinning in the dirt.

Yankee Stadium erupted. The organ played "Catch a Falling Star."

"Don't crowd me, son!" Thumma shouted. He slap-caught Horton's throw and got off a long, high, arching stream of tobacco that hit just inches from where Wilt sat.

"Odie, he said he's afraid he might kill someone!"

"Bullshit!" Wilt took his stance a good half step back.

"Ump, does the name Ray Chapman mean anything to you?" Horton asked.

"Cleveland infielder. Killed by a fastball, 1920," Campbell said.

"That's the guy. Last night the Giant kept saying that name. Said he once knocked a guy senseless down in the Sally League. We were in his room. Me, Bear, and Kline. That's where he said it. Told us he was afraid he might slip up, put someone away. Just like Chapman and that minor league guy he dropped!"

Wilt waved weakly at a fastball. "Heerike hun!" Campbell shouted. Horton saw the red blouse behind the third-base dugout. Barnes and several TV cameras had worked their way downstairs. They were perched there for the grand finale.

"Elmer said he came up with this Little Series thing for the two of us. You and me. Knew we'd never grow up if he didn't force us to do it. In another couple of years the company would have been ours to run."

"Heerike two!"

"Bullshit, Monk! Where the fuck was it?" Wilt came up on his toes, screamed above the crowd.

"Quit runnin' your mouth and you'd know!" Campbell said.

Horton glanced over his shoulder and saw Barnes sidestep Reggie. She nodded and grinned. Jackson's lips were flying—interviewing himself, Horton guessed. More gray Angel uniforms, a dugout jammed with stone-faced men watching the action. A nice compliment, Horton thought.

"We'd always been like sons, even more so after Sammy died. Came up with the idea for the reunion and Little World Series because he knew we'd been floating, not really facing up to life. Thought this might be the chance to prove ourselves. Me running the club, you selling the franchises. Odie, it was all one of the Giant's master plans."

Wilt tilted the bat back on his shoulder. "Monk, tell him to shut the fuck up!"

"Last night he got going on about you and the fix. That's when he started going white in the face. Look at him now. You ever seen Elmer that color before? He picked up a water glass still in the wrapper, turned, and threw it into a frigging wall mirror. Glass all over me, Bear, and Bunny. 'That's what I'm afraid I might do to Wilt tomorrow.' Then he stood there and looked like he didn't know us. Glass in his eyebrows, all over the cap. First time I ever saw Bear scared in my life."

Elmer Thumma took an unnaturally long breath of air and fired a dart at Odie Wilt. Hodges called it a perfect drag bunt. Wilt running scared, dodging an inside fastball, the way Horton saw it. The Giant sprang to his left and dove flat out; the ball skidded under his outstretched glove. Horton raced along behind Wilt. Rymoff slid in behind the Giant's carcass and plucked the ball out of the short green grass, wheeled, and flipped it to an empty bag at first. Horton saw a flash of white. Rabbit feet chasing along through the dirt. Three objects hit the bag at once—two crashed and went flying, arms, legs, and spiked shoes pinwheeling into right.

Bunny screeched, rolled, and grabbed his spiked shoe. Over and over he went, snowballing along in the grass. Horton brushed by Wilt, watched McKay make one final flip, then reached up and held the third out aloft like a five-cent scoop of vanilla.

"Feeble fucking little queer," Wilt screamed and dove at the Rabbit.

"Her hout!" a Campbell twin shouted.

"Touch him and you're dead meat," Rymoff said and kicked dirt on Wilt with the three-toed foot.

Horton saw Wilt's mouth go slack, watched his eyes drop. Bear was breathing a garlic fire in the cowboy's face now. Then Rymoff dipped down, scooped up the Rabbit, and one-handed him up to the crowd. Earthquake! The crowd's off the scale on this one, Horton thought.

"Big fuckin' deal!" Wilt spat at the little white feet.

"Not to you. But the big one for me. The play of my life." McKay wheezed, tipped his cap to the crowd, and limped back to where the grass met the dirt.

Ensor strutted to the plate, a heavyweight champion entering the ring. In the Ducks' dugout Graham aimed Pazerelli toward the action and shouted in his ear, "Five thousand bucks riding on three fuckin' swings!" Horton read his lips.

"Ensor, big left-handed–hitting first baseman, steps in. Calls time out and adjusts that shinguard he wears on his right leg. The crowd's going crazy. I don't know about you folks, but I'm going to light up a Chesterfield; this is a moment that ranks up there with Thomson and Branca. Hundreds of working press, national TV. Folks, Ensor gets into one it'll be heard round the world, you can take it from Russ on that."

The Giant asked for time out.

Horton jogged out. There were no surprises when you were catching Elmer the Giant. Thumma looked up into the wildness and complimented the swing of a Yankee security officer. "Caught him right across the back. That's got to be about the last of the protesters. Stony's done a nice job of cleanin' them up!

"I get the reins back at ELG, I'm going to take care of the good fans, do that All-Star game thing—let fan reps talk face to face with Stony and the player reps. Both sides air things out."

Horton looked nervously at Ensor and mentioned a teasing approach. "There's no way a guy like Biggie's gonna take a walk. Let's be cautious, set him up with breaking stuff away, no sense in taking any chances. We're too close to payday!"

"Boy, Bunny made him a play. Fine little athlete, a good baseball player." Thumma wiped a tear with the back of his glove.

"Curveballs until we fall behind. If that happens, we'll talk again! Now let's go!"

"Hooter, turn around, enjoy the moment. Look at Larry, how pretty she is. Hair all shiny and yellow like a field of New Becton hay. Now, on the other hand, there's Gross. Kinda fun watchin' him sweatin' away in there. Let's you and me just relax until Monk makes us quit."

Horton checked the eyes. Clear and blue in the summer sun.

"Curveballs!" Horton slammed the ball in the big black glove and walked off the mound.

Horton shook dirt from his glove and watched a breaking ball skip past, to the backstop. Hodges again. "Two balls and no strikes. Thumma's digging himself a hole with these hooks. It's a classic matchup, fastball pitcher against fastball hitter. Ernie, I don't know why they don't go strength against strength."

Horton tried to return to the mound but the Giant waved him away.

The Dogs chirped in tenors, hum babed away in high falsetto voices.

Two fingers down. Horton asked for one more curveball. The Giant shook him off with a wave of his glove. He set the jaw, tugged the cap, and kicked. That's what Horton loved about baseball. Nice and easy, a game in a rocking chair, then bang! Everything going in a hundred directions at once. The big leg fired up at the sun. Horton felt the swing fly by his mask, heard the crowd go berserk. A moon shot above home plate. Horton drifted west toward Manhattan, took two steps east, then sidled back to the Bronx.

"Back to the infield," he said to himself and, patting the glove, drifted along toward the third-base dugout. "Watch the bats!" Wilt screamed. "Easy, easy," Albaugh said, trailing along, shouting encouragement. He led with his throwing hand, groped blindly for the box seat railing. Beer flew in the air. A woman shrieked in his face. The ball smacked into a seat back half a glove's length from his reach.

"An inch and I'd-a had it. That was the game," Horton said, panting.

"He catches that pitch a little higher and it's in the right-field seats. That's baseball. Hlay hall!" Campbell said.

Ensor spat, adjusted the special shinguard that protected his front foot, then dug back in at the plate. The shinguard, the big number 23 across the broad back, both struck Horton as odd. Déjà vu? An omen of some kind?

"Three-and-two count, it's come down to one pitch, one swing," Hodges said. "Ensor, the big left-handed first baseman, aiming the metal bat right at the orange NY on the old Giant cap. Thumma sets, spit-fires a stream of tobacco juice, kicks, and fires . . ."

CRUNCH!

Horton froze. Fifty-six thousand Popsicles joined him. The stadium iced in the ninety-degree heat.

The impact knocked Hodges off the air. It was as though the crowd wasn't there. Horton watched the Giant spin, saw the bald head catch the afternoon sun. Bear, Bunny, Kliny, Baldy, Ballard, and Billy, one pivot after another. Gloves dropped, hats hit the dirt as the New Becton Hot Dogs team-watched the footrace in center field. Jug was off with the crunch. Horton tossed his mask and watched Brown's number 24 get smaller and smaller. The ball climbed, a jet streak of white in the blue summer sky aimed at the stadium's distant center-field fence.

"Brown going back, back, way back . . ." Hodges came and went.

Horton dug in his pocket, felt the bag in his hand. Jug's cap flew off. The ebony arms reached for the sky. Horton's fingers tore at the sack, ripped the paper to shreds.

The crowd thundered.

"He caught it!" Campbell shouted. "He caught the freakin' ball!"

Horton looked at the smiling pink face of Elmer the Giant, saw the big man wheel, watched him toss the antique cap in the air. Players stormed the mound—Hot Dogs, Yankees, and Angels. Black uniforms slumping and slinking away. Bunny rode Rymoff like a rodeo cowboy. Jug raced crazy eights in center. Ballard tackled Billy. Albaugh jumped Kline. Kids again—a winning Little League team! The redhead lay back on the bench, running his hands through the disheveled hair. McKeen's ruddy face looked distant and hurt. That's baseball. It *is* more than the money! Horton thought.

The catcher spun to the screen. A group of Little Leaguers stomped a circle on the stadium steps. They were doing a hat dance on Wilt's Stetson. Matt Zingraff from Quickchow leaned over the railing and gave Elmer the high sign. Cripes, he's buying the Dugouts, Horton thought. Fans poured around Elmer's board of directors, hoisted the old men up on their shoulders. Gross fought to get free. Up he went, gray hair, legs and arms flailing. Then they balanced him there, held him on high for all to see. Elmer's trophy, Horton thought, pass the bastard out here to the Giant!

Somehow the ball made its way back to Elmer. The old man shook it at Horton, plunked it in the pocket of the mitt, and gave his catcher's glove a loving squeeze.

"Nice game, Horton! What was the key?" Barnes said laughing through tears. She hugged him, waving her recorder in his laughing face.

He flung the brown bag confetti in the air and watched the little pieces of paper fall to the infield grass. He had Barnes in his arms, tasted the warm tears, deep-breathed the Shalimar, took it in with deep breaths.

"Nineteen fifty-four!" he whispered. "We just saw the same catch. It's the one Willie made on Wertz. Here's your quote: 'Hooter Horton's back; life just did a three-sixty!' "

EPILOGUE

Walker Horton sat barechested at the kitchen table, banging away at the old Smith-Corona. The smell of Solarcaine filled his apartment. Larry Barnes rubbed the white balm into his sunburned shoulders. Charred gum cards looked up at him from the plastic tablecloth.

"It's been fun," Barnes said. "Gotta go. It's a three thirty-five flight. Raleigh's what, an hour away?"

Horton nodded and held up his hand. The rub cooled his back. He bent over the keyboard and typed *The Comeback Kids* on a blank sheet of paper, read with satisfaction, and popped a fresh toothpick between his teeth.

"Stay," he said. "I'll write. You edit!"

Her long, tanned arms draped around his neck. He felt the soft hair on his sunburned shoulders.

"Orioles in Cleveland this week. Ballplayers to chase, deadlines to meet. Send me the chapters Federal Express. I'll put the Barnes blue pencil to work—we'll see how well you take directions out of bed."

The phone rang. Barnes pulled away. He held her arm and hugged her backhanded until the ringing stopped. "Janie," he said. He paused, listened, then began pecking away at the keyboard again.

"At least answer her calls," she said. "I thought you two had a good conversation after the game. That you parted friends," Barnes said.

"We did, but I asked her not to call," he said.

"And?"

"I gave her my itinerary. Told her we were going to visit my mother, then go off to the beach for a week. And then I was going home to Rocky Mount to write my book!" he said.

"How's this sound? The bus bounced along Maryland's route . . ."

Barnes leaned over his shoulder. He ripped the paper from the carriage, balled it up, and pegged it across the room.

"Wait just a second—*I'm* taking you to Raleigh," he said.

"Can't. I'm returning the rental car. We've been through all that."

Horton felt the heat on his shoulders. She nuzzled his neck, working good-bye kisses around to his ear.

"I thought we were finished with that!"

"We are! Literature and sex spared by a plane schedule. Write your old book." She laughed and walked a coffee cup back to the kitchen.

Horton stared at the paper. The phone rang again. Horton counted six rings, then went back to his page.

"I told her I didn't want to talk until this book was finished. Told her that I learned more about myself in the past three weeks than I did in forty years of life, ten years of marriage, and a year of analysis. I need to get this LWS thing down on paper."

"Hooter, last tip: If it's going to be good, you've got to be honest. So don't misplace the credit. You won the old man his company back!" Barnes picked up her suitcase and walked to the door.

"*We!*" Horton said. "You beat Gross and Wilt with the fix story. The Dogs and I cleaned up McKeen."

Horton hunched over the keyboard and typed another flurry of words. He leaned against the cool, plastic-backed chair, read, then added another burst to the paragraph. The door clicked behind him. The tap of his keys covered Barnes' exit.

"Just listen to this before you go!" he said.

"The stub of the wet toothpick rolled along Walker Horton's freshly capped teeth. He rocked the big captain's chair, curled his tongue, flicked the wooden pick again, and grinned. Hooter was riding shotgun, sitting in the bus's catbird seat."

The kitchen phone rang. Horton didn't hear it. He had the toothpick flying and the Smith-Corona clacking again.